BOOKS BY JEFFREY POSTON

ACTION/ADVENTURE THRILLERS

American Terrorist: Where is the Girl?
Contagion: American Terrorist 2
Escalate! American Terrorist 3
American Terrorist Trilogy

The Joshua Experiment (Call Sign: Raven Book 1)
The End of Everything (Call Sign: Raven Book 2)
The Queen (Call Sign: Raven Book 3)

JASON PEARES HISTORICAL WESTERNS

Courage (Book 1)
Legacy of an Outlaw (Book 2)
Warriors (Book 3)
Manhunter (Book 4)

JEFFREY POSTON

CONTAGION

AMERICAN TERRORIST 2

Contagion (American Terrorist 2)
Copyright © 2014 by Jeffrey Poston, Lomas & Turner Press

For more about this author please visit http://www.JeffreyPostonBooks.com

All characters and events in this book, other than those clearly in the public domain, are fictitious and any resemblance to real persons, living or dead, is purely coincidental.

All rights reserved. No part of this publication may be reproduced, distributed, or transmitted in any form or by any means, including photocopying, recording, or other electronic or mechanical methods, without the prior written permission of the publisher, except in the case of brief quotations embodied in critical reviews and certain other noncommercial uses permitted by copyright law. For permission requests, write to the publisher, addressed "Attention: Permissions Coordinator," at the address below.

Lomas & Turner Press
www.JeffreyPostonBooks.com

Ordering Information:
Quantity sales. Special discounts are available on quantity purchases by corporations, associations, and others. Orders by U.S. trade bookstores and wholesalers. For details, contact the publisher at the address above.

Editing by The Pro Book Editor
Cover art and design by Deanna Dionne
Interior design by IAPS.rocks

eBook ISBN: 978-0-9916194-5-0
paperback ISBN: 978-0-9863328-1-4

     1. Main category—Fiction>Thrillers
     2. Other category—Fiction>Political, Espionage, Terrorism

First Edition

"If you gaze long enough into an abyss, the
abyss will gaze back into you."

–Friedrich Nietzsche

CHAPTER 1

ALBUQUERQUE, NM

FBI SPECIAL AGENT LENORE CUMMINGS awoke with a gasp. She lay perfectly still on her back as she tried to process what had snatched her away from the nightmare. Her nerves were wired, and her body trembled. She hugged her blanket under her chin and took a deep breath, held it for a few seconds, then blew it out slowly.

She hated this part of herself for feeling so vulnerable and afraid. A highly trained federal agent, she could go hand-to-hand with any man on the planet and win against all but the best elite soldiers. She'd been trained to endure the harshest environments on earth and survive, and she was a rated expert at nearly a dozen different weapons. Yet, none of that training could conquer the fear that had nearly paralyzed her for almost a week since her ordeal.

"Recovery is going to be a long, hard road," they said. "There will be good days and bad," they said. "You have to get back in the mix," they said.

She'd dealt with many victims over the years, so she already knew that. But still, the shrinks reinforcing it had made it real to her on a personal level.

They said you couldn't return to your old life after being victimized. They said even professionals need treatment after an event such as what she'd suffered through. Professionals were not immune to post-traumatic stress disorder. That's why she'd been put on administrative leave pending evaluation.

The mental torment was crippling her, so she could only wonder what her daughter was feeling. Lisette had been victimized by the same man—the man that she so desperately wanted to kill; the man that now totally dominated her mind, every minute of every day. He entered her dreams every night and tortured her again and again. It was the same nightmare every night, the same tears every time she awoke from that nightmare because she wasn't strong enough to push him out of her mind.

He was Carl Johnson, the man known to the entire world as the *American Terrorist*. Lenore let out the cry of anguish she'd been holding inside and rolled onto her right side. How Johnson managed to make her wake up lying on her back after every nightmare was a mystery to her.

The exterior streetlights played through the branches of trees swaying in the wind in her front yard, causing obscene shadows to move along her walls. Too often, those shadows looked like a dark outline of Carl Johnson. A few nights ago, she'd hung blackout drapes to keep the man out of her room and out of her dreams. She hated herself for hanging those too, but the shadows scared her the most.

Even with her eyes closed, she could see Johnson's face as clear as day, hovering over her. He had her tied to the gurney on her back, with her hands restrained over her head and her legs spread. She'd been helpless and vulnerable, and she was just as powerless in her recurring nightmares a week later. He had leered at her, his brown eyes totally devoid of all emotion except hatred, drinking up her nakedness. And he had touched her. He still touched her. Every night. In the nightmares.

He hadn't raped her, though he could have. He didn't need to. His purpose hadn't been sexual assault. He only wanted to break her will, to make her betray her fellow government agents. And betray them she had, but not because of what Johnson did to her. It was what he threatened to do to her daughter that instantly destroyed her ability to resist or fight.

Lisette had been similarly tied to another gurney next to hers, and Lenore had absolutely zero doubt that the man would kill her daughter in retribution. He held Cummings directly responsible for his son's murder, and there was nothing she could say that would change that belief. In truth, Lenore knew she *was* directly responsible for Mark Johnson's death. She hated that she felt deserving of her fate.

The terrorist had told her in explicit detail what he was going to do to the eleven-year-old girl before he killed her. She'd seen in his eyes his wish that she would not cooperate. That's how much the man wanted to kill her child as payback. He even said he was going to let Lenore live so she'd feel what he felt—the loss of a child—for the rest of her life.

So she broke. She cried, begged, and pleaded. She told the man everything he wanted to know. It was the only way to save her daughter.

That was why she hated herself. Because he broke her. Because she couldn't protect her child. Because she allowed the man to repeatedly violate her mind night after night.

She opened her eyes and examined the only source of light in the dark room. The dim face of the digital clock read a little after one in the morning. Usually, she awoke around four—too early to get up, yet too late to go back to sleep. Now she wondered what had awakened her earlier than normal. She remembered hearing some kind of sound.

A primordial sense of awareness that might have been hard-wired into the human DNA tingled down her spine and informed her she was not alone in her room. She smelled *man-scent*—a musky odor born of sweat and bad breath. The impossible thought that Carl Johnson would come after her a second time and actually be bold enough to sneak into her house froze her for half a second.

Then, she realized a second fact.

Someone is moving upstairs!

The slight creaking of the wood floor wasn't the result of the quick patter of a preteen girl walking down the hall to the bathroom or coming down the stairs to climb into mom's bed. The motion was slow and deliberate. Heavy. A man was moving upstairs, trying not to make any noise. Lenore knew her old house intimately, and she could tell the man was creeping, not quite stealthily, from the top of the stairs toward her daughter's room. She heard another creak from above. Someone else was moving up there, in her mother's room across the hall from Lisette's room.

Lenore threw her blanket off and reached for her service weapon on the nightstand beside the digital clock. She had barely wrapped her fingers around the square pistol grip when she froze at a metallic *click* that resounded through the utter silence of her bedroom.

"I wouldn't do that, Agent." Not miss, not ma'am, but *agent*. The man in her room knew exactly who she was. He knew what her capabilities were.

The voice was deep, almost baritone, but it was not the voice she remembered from her nightmares or from her torturous ordeal last week. It was not Carl Johnson.

For a fraction of a second, Lenore wondered if she could roll off the far side of the bed and simply fire quick shots at the invader. She realized the metallic sound was the man disengaging his safety. He was ready and would shoot first. Even if she managed to shoot at the same instant, her mattress would be no kind of barrier to his bullets, especially if he was armed, as she suspected, with an automatic assault rifle. Even if she killed the man in her room, she'd never get upstairs fast enough to save her daughter.

"Okay," she said.

"Now, turn on your bedside lamp and keep your hands where I can see them."

Lenore knew instantly that the intruder could see in the dark. He had to be wearing some kind of night vision device. No other way he could know she'd been reaching for her weapon or that there was a lamp on a nightstand beside the bed.

She did as she was told, and light flared into the room. The appearance of the man surprised her. He was a big guy, well over six feet tall, and was decked out from head to toe in full tactical gear. He dropped his left hand from his head, and she knew he had just lifted a night vision monocular from his right eye.

The man's black face—or maybe it was a white face hidden behind black camouflage paint—matched the darkness of his tactical gear, and he wore clear acrylic combat goggles. The goggles were the bubble wrap-around kind that allowed clear peripheral vision while protecting from hot shell casings or splinters flying around during a firefight, or pepper spray in the hands of a panicked civilian.

The man wore a black combat helmet and black body armor and held a wicked-looking MP5. It wasn't the civilian semiautomatic knockoff fancied by hunters or militiamen or mercenaries employed by third-world dictatorships. This man's weapon was the real deal. It was the easy-to-use, easy-to-maintain, highly reliable and extremely accurate nine-millimeter machine pistol model 5, from the translation of the name given to the weapon by the German company that manufactured it. It was military-grade weaponry, like the rest of his gear, unavailable on the civilian market. He was a US soldier or a private contractor funded and equipped by the US military.

The man took two steps to his left, keeping the business end of his assault rifle pointed at her midsection. "Now we wait," he said.

She didn't have to wait long, for the apparition that tormented her every night suddenly stepped into the doorway.

Lenore gasped. The terrorist had finally come back for her, but she couldn't imagine why. He'd already won. He broke her, and her superiors knew it from her after-action report.

The FBI shrink said she needed time off to recover, but she knew the truth was that she was being evaluated to see if she was still psychologically and emotionally fit for duty. After all, she'd been captured and tortured. That wasn't something most law enforcement officers could ever fully recover from.

Now here he was, standing in her bedroom doorway.

"You!" Lenore looked from Carl Johnson to the armed intruder and back again. "Please, leave my daughter out of this."

The armed intruder chuckled. "Like I'm going to fall for that trick?"

Carl Johnson, who had approached the doorway out of view from the armed man, said, "You should have."

Lenore sat on her bed, stunned as her torturer raised a silenced pistol and shot the man in the neck just below his armored Kevlar helmet. The bullet passed through the man's spine and thumped into the wall with very minimal blood splatter. The commando collapsed where he'd stood.

Carl disappeared, and Lenore heard him pounding up the stairs as she leaped from her bed and grabbed the dead man's MP5. The safety was already off, so she ran into the hallway, holding the automatic weapon with her right hand and the lower part of her cotton nightgown with her left.

What the hell is happening?

The terrorist who had kidnapped her and nearly tortured her child—the man she had sworn to kill if she ever saw him again—was in her house and had just saved her life.

Lenore heard a scuffle come from her daughter's room, along with a confused shout and another muffled gunshot. Though the shot was suppressed, the sound echoed through the quiet house like a loud clap. She stopped at the foot of the stairs and gazed upward as Johnson emerged at the top of the stairs with her daughter, Lisette, trailing in his grasp.

Lenore brought up her weapon and aimed at the terrorist as the thought entered her mind that maybe he hadn't saved her at all. Maybe he just needed to eliminate the *other* intruders first. Maybe the men were TER agents, elite operators from the classified Terror Event Response agency. Maybe they were here for him. Maybe she was just bait.

Still, if any of that was true, then Carl Johnson should have killed Lenore. He knew better than anyone not to leave her alive in a situation where she could arm herself.

She was just about to shout at Johnson to release Lisette when she saw a shadow move from the darkened doorway of her mother's room. She screamed as the shadow raised an assault rifle and aimed, not at her and not at Johnson, but *at her daughter*.

A fraction of a second later, directly behind her, the front door exploded off its hinges, and Lenore was knocked off her feet by the blast. Her weapon slid across the hall's wood floor. Through a foggy haze, Lenore saw more shadowy figures enter the doorway. They were all clad in black combat gear, just like the first intruder. One aimed a sleek P90 at her and fired at point-blank range.

But he missed.

CHAPTER 2

1000 EST, THURSDAY – TWO DAYS PREVIOUS
WASHINGTON, DC

Aᴜɢᴜsᴛ Sᴘᴏᴋᴇ ᴏᴘᴇɴᴇᴅ ʜɪs ᴇʏᴇs with the first chime of his cell phone. It took him nearly a second to remember where he was. He lay on his back, and the woman, Cynthia Manford, lay half beside him and half on top of him. She purred but did not wake up as he reached out his right hand for the glowing faceplate of the cell on the bedside table.

His mental clock told him it was midmorning, but the room where he slept was dark. He recalled his new girlfriend's obsession with blackout curtains in the bedroom. She was absolutely the most beautiful woman Spoke had ever dated. She was stunning with her tall and slender, yet curvy, physique. She had dark brown skin, worked out every day, and ate excessively healthy. She had a perfect face to match her perfect body, yet she considered herself ugly.

That, Spoke thought, *is the true reason for the blackout curtains. Maybe she has a scar or a disfigurement and doesn't want anyone to see it. Women. Never satisfied with themselves.*

He brought the cell up to his face and saw the familiar number. He flipped the phone open and whispered, "One minute."

He snapped the cell closed. He knew the caller would not talk on an unsecured phone line. The call was merely a notification that Spoke was needed.

He slid from under the woman and the sheets, then felt on the bedside table for his pocket pouch. He found the tiny cloth pouch and palmed it, pausing a moment to orient himself in the darkness. Then he remembered where the bathroom was and went there. He closed the door behind him and opened the pouch, sliding out a single item. It was a tiny earpiece designed for secure satellite communications.

Spoke turned on the faucet to provide a background noise shield against eavesdroppers—one never knew who was listening in his line of work—and fitted the device into his left ear. He activated the comm channel with a light press of his index finger. The device had no dialer, as it only connected to a single channel owned by one man.

"Rainman," came the instant reply. "Are you secure?"

Spoke said, "I am."

"Good. The operation is a go. The girl has just been delivered from Mexico. We will now move to the second phase. I would advise you to call in sick for a few days. On your next assignments, touch nothing and no one. Always wear gloves. Understood?"

"Affirmative."

"You are to proceed with total operational security."

In other words, kill anyone who can be linked to me.

Spoke glanced at the bathroom door, dimly lit by a nightlight. Operational security included sterilizing his new girlfriend. He knew Rainman didn't waste words or time with the obvious, so he waited patiently for the other shoe to drop.

"But we have a problem," Rainman said.

Of course you do. That's why you called me. "Specify," he said.

"There is a man, an intern for the president's chief of staff, who has uncovered some evidence."

Evidence. For August Spoke, that word carried many connotations, all of them bad. Evidence meant Rainman's plan had potentially been discovered. Evidence meant someone had to die. Evidence meant Spoke had to kill again. Eventually, the killing would evolve into a pattern that would itself yield more evidence, which then fed into more killing.

"Who and where is he?"

"The intern's name is Marcus Aurelio," Rainman said. "His location is unknown."

Spoke considered the response. "If he has disappeared, then he understands the significance of his evidence. He'll be in hiding, and there are precious few places a person like him can hide. He'll be wanting to reach out to someone, but he won't know who to trust." Spoke paused for a moment, thinking. "He'll need to reach someone of rank and status, someone in the government with real power. An underling won't be able to act on his information, so I'll put the most likely power players who are not aligned with you under surveillance. He might even reach out to you."

"Find him, Agent Spoke. If that information gets out, we're sunk before our operation begins."

"I can deal with the intern. But just so you know, if he has already passed the information, there may be little I can do."

"Find out where he has been and who he has talked to."

"Very well. I'll have my assets ping his passport, driver's license, credit cards, and bank accounts. This is DC, and it's expensive here, so he'll need several days' cash to live on until he meets whoever to deliver his evidence."

"There are a million hotels in DC."

It was not a statement, even though it was stated as such. Spoke knew his controller was really asking how he hoped to find a needle in the proverbial haystack.

"Every hotel, except maybe the fleabags, requires a credit card to register. If he's paying cash, they'll require his passport or some form of picture ID. If he checks into any reputable hotel, I'll find him. If he rents a car or gets on a bus or a train or a plane, I'll find him. Within an hour, I'll have all of his family and friends and other known associates or romantic interests under scrutiny or surveillance. And I'll have my network of informants canvassing the fleabags in the district."

"So you intend to use your Secret Service assets."

"It's why you hired me. This man now represents a credible threat against the president of the United States."

"Very well, then. Do not fail me, Agent Spoke."

"Have I ever?"

A beep signified the commlink was severed on the other end. Spoke did his personal business, flushed, and washed his hands in the still-running water. He turned off the faucet and dried on a hand towel, then wiped everything he'd touched. He went back into the bedroom, where Cynthia was just rolling out of bed.

Last night, she said she was going to call in sick today so she could spend more time with him. He had the day off, so they planned to get to know each other better. She was a mid-thirties marketing executive, and he was a mid-thirties Secret Service agent. At least, that's what he told her.

He was and he wasn't.

He could just see an outline of her lithe body in the darkened room as she stood and stretched. Obviously comfortable moving about in the darkness, she approached him. She was just reaching out her arms to wrap him up in a hug when he steeled the fingers of his right hand and jabbed her hard in the belly just below her sternum.

She expelled her breath with a pained gasp and folded to the floor in the fetal position, struggling to breathe. August Spoke stepped over her writhing form and turned on a table lamp. He dressed quickly and retrieved a suppressor from his pocket. He screwed it onto his service gun after pulling it from its shoulder holster, turned, and looked at his girlfriend of one week.

He'd never dated a Black woman before. In fact, last night had been the first time she'd felt comfortable enough to take him home with her.

The sex had been wonderful, he recalled with a smile.

No first-time jitters. Their bodies fit together like they were made for each other. They'd explored and played and loved and laughed and slept. Then, they did it all over again. Twice more.

This morning, though, he saw her differently. She was now a witness, a loose end. With the stakes of the operation now heightened, Cynthia Manford was now evidence.

Without a thought or feeling to the contrary, August Spoke shot her in the head, collected the expended shell, and unscrewed the suppressor. By habit of both his careers—Secret Service agent and covert assassin—he wiped everything he'd touched in the room, using the same hand towel from the bathroom. When the police arrived, they would find no clue to his identity. He'd taken precautions during sex so there would be no DNA on or in Cynthia's body.

With one final visual canvas of the room, Spoke searched again for any evidence the police might find. There was none. He grabbed her purse and emptied the contents on the bed. He grabbed her cash—a couple hundred dollars—and left the rest. He took one more glance around, appreciating her expensive art. It consisted mostly of African figurines, sculptures, and paintings. He wiped everything again, stepped over her body, and left her apartment. When he closed the door behind him, he quietly forced it open again to make the scene look like a robbery. He left the building discretely through the stairwell, careful to avoid looking into any security cameras.

CHAPTER 3

CARL STOOD FACING AARON MCGRATH—DIRECTOR of the Terror Event Response agency—in the barren desert, and a mixture of raw-edged feelings tore through his gut. He wanted to kill the government agent for what the man had done to his son, and he had no doubt McGrath felt the same way about him because of what he'd done to his daughter. Neither acted on those feelings, for they shared a more important mission. They both wanted to know what Melissa Mallory's captors had done to her and why. They both wanted to punish those people on behalf of the teen girl and her mother, President Shirley Mallory.

For Carl, punishing the girl's kidnappers was the only way he could justify, in his own mind, all the carnage and destruction he'd caused over the past week. He suspected McGrath felt the same. They'd both hurt a lot of people. They both had a lot of pain and suffering to answer for.

An hour earlier, Carl had been shot, and a painful bruise throbbed across the high middle part of his back. He still wore all his tactical gear from the rescue, including his armored vest, so he couldn't get his fingers onto the area to try massaging some of the soreness away. They said getting shot in the vest felt like a mule kick. Carl disagreed, even though he'd never been kicked by a mule. When the drug lord's thug stitched him across the back with his Uzi, the vest stopped the bullets, but it felt like armor-piercing projectiles were punching through the vest and into his body. He took the bullets meant for the girl, though, and she lived. That was all that mattered.

He didn't much feel like a hero, but that's what heroes did, at least in the movies—take bullets and save teenage girls.

Carl had survived his thirty-day stint as a terrorist-turned-hero. He'd gone into combat for the first time in his life at the age of fifty-three. He'd had a gunfight with a drug cartel and lived to talk about it. Overall, his terrorist body count now stood at nearly forty, including FBI agents, cops, other covert government agents, and drug thugs, and he wasn't done with the killing yet.

Carl was exhausted. He wanted a long nap after a long shower after a long, full-body massage, but he wasn't going to get any of that. The one thing he was *not* going to do was complain—not in front of Aaron McGrath.

He looked nothing like Carl had imagined. He was tall and slender with close-cut, stately, salt-and-pepper hair and fashionable wire-rim, round glasses. He wore a black turtleneck shirt over blue jeans, and his black flight jacket was unzipped midway to his belt. Despite his advanced age—Carl guessed he was in his mid-sixties—McGrath's eyes held the same intensity he'd seen in other covert agents he'd battled over the past month.

He took a deep breath, set his mind to the mission, and faced his former nemesis and now mission-critical partner. Carl looked Aaron McGrath in the eyes and said, "The general that flew us up here, El Patron, didn't just happen by the exchange zone. He wanted his money back. Reyes was just a tool, a pawn who got out of control. Maybe he had his own agenda. I don't know."

Aaron McGrath squinted at Carl and lifted an eyebrow. "El Patron was on US soil?"

Carl nodded. "He all but confessed to funding the kidnapping through people he called his investors. He knew about the Delta recovery team you had on standby. He knew exactly where they were located, what their response time was, and what their rules of engagement were. And he said he knows for a fact that the president's people don't know his identity." Carl paused to let McGrath digest his information.

"That's why you wanted to be off comm."

Carl nodded. "You thought I wanted to have a man-to-man fistfight to settle our differences?"

McGrath said nothing. Both men had removed their miniature comm devices from their ears. Aside from McGrath's transport chopper idling five hundred feet away—its engine droning, blades swishing the air—there wasn't a human within a mile of them. The president's *Marine One* helicopter and its armada of army escort choppers had left after retrieving Melissa Mallory. Now, Carl Johnson and McGrath had the empty desert two miles north of the Columbus border crossing all to themselves. It was the border crossing Carl and his mercenaries had used for the mission to retrieve the president's daughter.

Carl said, "I had trouble understanding how a bunch of drug thugs could have pulled off the kidnapping against even a tiny contingent of Secret Service agents."

The senior covert agent nodded and pulled a smartphone from his pants pocket. He dialed a number and touched the tab for the speaker.

"Palmer," came a voice Carl recognized from the government's covert op station in Virginia.

"Code alpha-six."

"Stand by."

The line was silent for a while, and Carl got the feeling the code was an instruction for her to clear her command center of nonessential people. While he waited, he watched McGrath's square jaw muscles work. All the death and destruction they had caused over the past few days of fighting each other had now brought them to the brink of an alliance. They had both been pawns in a larger conflict choreographed by an unknown, common adversary.

Agent Palmer's voice returned. For some reason, her voice filled Carl with calmness. Despite the fact he had been at odds with the government for a month, he still trusted Palmer. She was the only one he trusted.

"COMSEC level alpha-six is active, Director McGrath. This channel is restricted to the two of us. It is not being recorded on the mission records."

McGrath said, "Johnson has confirmed an executive-level leak in the US government."

Carl added, "And El Patron's investors are very highly placed in the Mexican government."

Palmer said, "Continue."

Carl summarized his encounter with the general during his rescue of Melissa. "I think Melissa's kidnapping wasn't about money. That was just the cover. They did something to her. Drugged her up or something. I think they intended to release her all along, but she's not the endgame. We need to know what they did to her and why." His mind raced ahead, planning a path forward. "And we need to know *who* they are."

"Agreed," McGrath said.

Agent Palmer said, "Carl, what is your interest in this going forward?"

Carl took a deep breath and kicked at a tuft of grass. It was true that he had almost half a billion US dollars and a presidential pardon. He could retire and disappear anywhere in the world now.

"These people who financed the general led us down this path." Carl paused. "They hurt that girl. And me. And a lot of other people. I'd like to see them pay."

"As would I," McGrath said. "If you can ID El Patron, I can put the full might of the US intel apparatus on finding all his known associates."

"Mm-hmm." Carl looked south, envisioning another operation on Mexican soil. "That would certainly be the efficient government way to handle it."

"You have something else in mind?" McGrath said.

Carl nodded. "These people have eyes and ears in your camp at a high level, and they use the same playbook that you use." He turned to face McGrath again and looked him straight in the eye. "I use a different playbook."

"We've noticed." McGrath studied him for a moment with gray, emotionless eyes. "What would you do, Mr. Johnson?"

"I'd do something a bit more…public."

McGrath notched an eyebrow in question.

Carl said, "If I had a missile right now, I'd smoke that El Patron mu'fucker's helicopter and see what prominent people on both sides of the border go into hiding. Then your intel apparatus can locate them, and I can go have a chat with them." He shrugged. "He can't be more than a couple hundred miles away yet."

Apparently, the government man approved of his strategy. Carl listened to a lot of tactical jargon as Aaron McGrath authorized one of the fighter jets that flew the president's CAP—Combat Air Patrol—to break formation. A moment later, an explosive sound blasted over the desert as the fighter slammed through the sound barrier. Carl looked up. He couldn't see the plane, but he saw its white contrail far above. A few seconds later, he saw a bright flash as two more smoke trails sped away from the first.

McGrath said, "Consider El Patron smoked, along with his escort chopper. What do you need for this next phase of the mission?"

Though he was still following the twin contrails into the distance, Carl was considering the near future in terms of logistics, weapons, and manpower.

"I need Agent Palmer on my team out here. I have a feeling the people we're going after will make Alfonso Reyes and his crew look like rookies. We better do it right this time."

"Agreed."

"Can you conference Mr. Garcia on this call?"

McGrath nodded, and Carl gave him the number.

"Go for Garcia," the young man answered.

Carl couldn't help but smile. The kid had his mission jargon solid.

"Sitrep," Carl demanded.

"Boss! I thought we lost you!"

"Almost did." Carl gave Garcia a quick mission summary. "Our mission is not over yet. Have Mercs Three and Four go back to the trade site and get Alfonso Reyes."

"He shot your son, Boss. You didn't kill him?"

"I want something worse than death for that man." Carl paused and looked McGrath in the eye. To Garcia, he said, "I'm going to let our new allies interrogate him the way they interrogated me."

Garcia said, "Whoa. Remind me never to make you angry, Boss."

"He knows some of El Patron's people," Carl said. "It might be helpful if we knew them too."

The TER director nodded.

Garcia said, "I'll take care of it."

"Then have Mercs Three and Four stay in-country to provide security for Luisa and Julia Reyes. If El Patron contacted his network, those two ladies are in imminent danger." Carl had basically traded those two ladies for Melissa Mallory. He hadn't liked it, but it was what he'd had to do to get the president's daughter to safety. Now, he had to do right by those ladies.

"Copy that."

"Set up another op center ASAP. New equipment, new phones, everything. I'll contact you when I arrive in Albuquerque this afternoon." Carl nodded to McGrath.

After cutting the connection to Garcia, McGrath regarded Carl. "I continue to wonder how an untrained civilian like yourself has been so successful in this arena."

"I *am* trained, Aaron." He gazed at his nemesis. "I was trained by the best in the business—you and your government killers." Carl took a deep breath, then looked away and changed the subject. "How are Special Agent Cummings and her daughter?"

"Their injuries were…psychological." McGrath looked into the distance, but Carl could tell he was reviewing the carnage Carl had left in his path. "With treatment, they should recover in time." Then the man cast those empty eyes on Carl again.

Carl nodded. He knew he'd never be able to forgive himself for what he did to them. "Anita?"

McGrath paused for a long time, and Carl knew the man was fighting the same internal emotional battle he was. Anita was McGrath's daughter, and Carl had almost killed her to get to him.

"She's alive." McGrath paused, then seemed to switch mental gears. "Proceed with the new mission when you are ready, Mr. Johnson."

"I'm ready now."

"Good hunting." With that, the government agent simply pivoted and walked off toward the army helicopter idling in the distance. He didn't offer Carl a ride, and Carl wouldn't have accepted if he had.

Carl simply turned and began his 200-mile hike toward Albuquerque, still fully decked out in black tactical body armor and weaponry.

A half hour later, a different army chopper landed nearby and ferried him north to the Albuquerque airport. The crew chief gave him a duffle bag for his tactical gear and weapons, and he shook the man's hand in thanks. He made the hour-long hike to reach downtown and grabbed one of several old SUVs his team of mercenaries had hidden in various parking structures. Carl checked into a run-down motel on Central Avenue, the kind he'd become comfortable with in his new life of nonexistence. He'd been off the grid for just over a month.

The hotel room smelled of stale cigarettes, and the shower was barely hot enough to be called warm. The showerhead was clogged with years of mineral deposits and sprayed water practically everywhere except on him. He lay on the bed for several hours, but sleep was fitful. It seemed every time he closed his eyes, he saw either his son's bleeding body or the faces of the men and women he had victimized during his war of vengeance. Finally realizing he would get no sleep, he dressed in clothes he'd bought at a dollar store and prepared to drive over to Old Town for dinner at the High Noon Saloon and Restaurant.

It was cool outside, so he put on a jacket, but he hesitated at the door. He felt an overwhelming sense of danger. He didn't know what he was walking into or whom to trust. He got the distinct feeling he was being tracked or followed.

So he pulled his shoulder holster and Glock from his duffle.

CHAPTER 4

1700 MST, THURSDAY
ALBUQUERQUE, NM

COSTAS DRAKE SAT WITH VICENTE Orizaga at the tiny table in his nondescript motel room near the far east end of Central Avenue in Albuquerque. Both men leaned close to the secure satellite cell phone sitting on the table. The volume was low to prevent anyone else from hearing the conversation, though no one else was in the room. The rest of his twenty-man team—the Unit—was camped in the two adjacent rooms.

The heavily encrypted signal made the caller sound like he was on the opposite side of the planet, but he could easily have been in the same Albuquerque hotel. Costas Drake was a former military man and high-level CIA wet-work specialist, but he wasn't one of the half a dozen people in the country privileged to know the identity of the person called Rainman.

He'd known Rainman was planning something huge. That was why he let the man recruit him months ago. Not until now, when the plan was in the final stages of implementation, had Rainman finally revealed the true scope of his operation.

After hearing his boss's objective, he concluded first and foremost that he'd better have a Plan B. So many things had to go right, and so many pieces of Rainman's bizarre puzzle had to fit together precisely that Drake had trouble seeing how the man could possibly hope for success.

If Rainman was successful, in three days, he would pull off the biggest coup in the history of the world. If he failed, there would be nowhere on the planet he, nor anyone associated with him, could hide. That was why Costas Drake had privately begun to formulate an emergency exit strategy. Already, he'd pooled together money and several new identities in case he had to flee.

The electronically altered voice of Rainman said, "You have the list, Mr. Drake?"

"Roger that. I have ten individuals to be terminated."

"I assume your teams are prepared to deploy."

"Affirmative. I have three six-man teams ready to deploy on all fronts with a two-man team on standby," Drake said. "All we are waiting for is your order."

"The order is now given. I want dead bodies, Mr. Drake, and a lot of them. Women and children. Coordinate your strikes to begin just before midnight tomorrow." The electronic voice paused, then said, "That is, tomorrow night midnight, not tonight midnight."

"Understood. Tomorrow night midnight, not tonight."

"Mr. Garcia may have to be hit earlier, so be ready to move on that front immediately, as soon as we have his identity and location."

Drake was intimately familiar with the timetable since he had developed all the tactical aspects of the assault plans. They were going for a one-two knockout punch that would send the entire country reeling in shock. First, the president would be hit, though he wasn't sure how Rainman was going to pull that off. Then, Drake's unit would assault the civilians on the kill list.

"Roger that. It will look like the American Terrorist eliminated his own man first, then the civilians. We'll plant the encrypted cell phone at the scene. Aaron McGrath's personal number is programmed in, and our computer has synthesized a threatening ultimatum in Johnson's voice and will send it to McGrath's voice mail. The recording will be 82 percent accurate. It'll pass preliminary tests by FBI analysts and should easily support the conclusion we want them to draw. It will look like Johnson is at war with the government again. But…"

"You have a question?"

Drake hesitated. "Aaron McGrath is an extremely dangerous and well-connected man. He's a veteran of the wet-work business. I recommend him to be the first person we eliminate. My two-man team can be in Virginia by nightfall tonight—"

"McGrath is being dealt with. When you begin your operation, he will be a nonfactor. The important issue is that the FBI currently does not know the full involvement of Carl Johnson in the operation to rescue the president's daughter. The details of the operation were classified and restricted to the TER agency only. Neither the FBI director nor the local SAC of the Albuquerque field office has specific knowledge of that operation. Besides, I don't care if they really *believe* Johnson is going rogue again. I just want them to buy into the possibility for twenty-eight hours. That's all we need. The FBI will spend time and manpower chasing false leads. After that, it will be too late for them or anyone else to do anything to stop us." Rainman paused. "And gentlemen, I need this to look particularly gruesome."

"Understood," Drake said. "I have men who will do the deed. The women will be—"

"Not just the women," Rainman said. "The girls too. And the baby. We need to paint a vicious and brutal picture of the American Terrorist in action, something so despicable that it will shock the country and polarize everyone, including the FBI. I want everyone blinded to all other possibilities for twenty-eight hours."

Costas Drake was silent for a moment as he and Vicente Orizaga looked at each other across the tiny table in the darkened room. Drake had conducted such unscrupulous missions before, sometimes under orders, and sometimes just for the thrill of hearing his victims' screams. But his victims had always been men and women, or at least teenage kids. What Rainman was ordering him to do was beyond despicable. Not that it mattered. His unit was being paid extraordinarily well. They'd do what they were told to do, even if it involved children.

Vicente Orizaga, though, wasn't an operator. He was a money man. To his credit, the man didn't flinch at the unspoken orders. He merely nodded.

"Understood," Drake said. "But if this goes sideways—"

"I'm paying you to make sure it doesn't," Rainman's scrambled voice commanded. "We do this right, the Terror Event Response agency will be effectively neutralized, and Carl Johnson will be the most hunted man in the world this time, not just in the US."

Drake snorted. "Or we will become TER targets. Because if we mess this up, *we* will be the subjects of the manhunt."

"Speaking of a manhunt," Rainman continued, "I've just received intel from my sources that Johnson is flying into Mexico City tomorrow, about noon, on a government covert ops jet. I believe he is going after the Triad. Have Mr. Orizaga hire a team for surveillance only. I have assets in the region who will terminate Mr. Johnson as soon as you give me the location of him and his team."

Orizaga said, "It is an easy matter to have the authorities arrest them as soon as they land."

"Negative. Johnson already has mercenaries in-country. They all need to be eliminated, preferably at the same time. Johnson has proven to be a master of contingency planning. We cannot take the risk that he has organized his team into independent cells with separate missions. In order to eliminate his team members, we must first identify them."

Orizaga spoke in heavily accented English. "My people can interrogate Johnson."

Rainman laughed, but the scrambler converted the sound into something more resembling a hacking cough. "Carl Johnson was interrogated by TER people for eleven days last month, using the most effective techniques known to man, and he never broke. His travel companion is a TER operator named Nancy Palmer, and she most definitely will not break. Have your team follow Johnson to his op center, but be careful. Palmer was almost a Navy SEAL, and she will no doubt spot any careless surveillance."

Drake grunted. "*Almost* a Navy SEAL. Johnson is going to have to do better than *almost*."

"This woman was due to graduate at the top of her class...*of men*."

Now Drake chuckled. "Maybe I'll enroll her in my school—teach her some of my tricks."

"I'm sure that's what one of her classmates and an instructor were thinking when they jumped her in the shower...right before she killed them with her bare hands. They tried to rape her. Tried to teach her that SEAL training was no place for a woman. Needless to say, they were not successful. There was no official report of the event, but I'm told that one of the men—and I don't want to visualize how she did it—died from a bar of soap lodged deep inside his throat." Rainman's electronic voice paused. "She has been described as extremely lethal, and we now know what Carl Johnson can do, so take no unnecessary risks. If your team must engage, you have shoot-on-sight authorization for both of them. Otherwise, let my assets handle the termination."

There was a pause, and Drake decided he was supposed to say something, perhaps acknowledge Rainman's discourse.

Before he could utter a syllable, Rainman continued, "Mr. Orizaga, are our benefactors in the Triad ready to move on the Mexican government?"

"They are. Four days from now, the border between my country and yours will no longer exist." Orizaga glanced at Drake, then said, "I still can't believe we're really going to kill the president of the United States."

"That's only the beginning, gentlemen." Rainman chuckled, but again, the electronic alteration of his voice made it sound like he was coughing up phlegm. "Shirley Mallory is already dead. She just doesn't know it yet."

CHAPTER 5

2000 EST, THURSDAY
WASHINGTON, DC

MARCUS AURELIO SAT IN THE darkened lobby of a run-down, cash-only hotel and contemplated his situation. One moment, he was on top of the world. The next, he was a dead man walking. It was amazing how many people took for granted the expectation that their lives would follow some kind of master plan. His plan was simple. Get a first-class education, serve his country, advance upward, maybe become president someday. Getting killed prematurely was not part of the plan. What a difference twelve hours can make.

He was a smart man. He had multiple degrees by the age of twenty-three. He had twin BS degrees in economics and statistics. He also held an MA in political science and had just begun studies for his PhD in the same field. Everyone who had ever met him knew he would go far in politics. In addition to his razor-sharp mind that could win virtually any debate on any topic, he was also empathetic and a genuinely nice guy, which was rare in DC. He also had two secrets, one that guaranteed him success in his career advancement, and another that would surely derail his career.

His first secret was known to only a few, and it was the primary reason he'd snagged an internship with the president's chief of staff, Martine Scallow. It was also the reason he was now running for his life.

Marcus Aurelio had a photographic memory. His memory wasn't truly eidetic, in that he didn't recall every detail of everything he'd seen—sights, sounds, smells, where a person was standing at a particular moment, or what they were wearing. His photographic memory was limited only to the written word. Simply put, he could recall every word of every book he'd ever read—ever—since the first picture book he'd picked up at age two. He could instantly recite every web page and every email he'd read. He remembered it all. What made his gift even more remarkable was that he *comprehended* everything he'd ever read. The subject matter was irrelevant. He was an expert on many topics, from science and physics to music theory and history. The subject he loved most, of course, was politics.

All he had to do to instantly remember an item of text was to get a glance at it. He didn't have to study a document or even fully read a document. If his eyes caught a glance, he could then study and read the text in his brain long after the document was removed from his sight.

It was such a glimpse at the face of his boss's smartphone that had ended his life. The device was, of course, encrypted, but once that encoded signal reached the display, it could be read by anyone.

Scallow had walked into his office that morning not knowing Marcus was already at his desk, working on an assignment.

Marcus glanced up briefly and muttered his standard greeting. "Morning, Martine."

Scallow had been startled and stuck his smartphone in his pocket quickly. The move seemed forced and secretive, so naturally, Marcus's brain almost subconsciously began to decipher what his eyes had glimpsed for that tiny fraction of a second, even though the four-inch display of the device was more than ten feet distant.

Two and a half minutes later, Marcus gasped as his brain finished its interpretation. He tried to maintain an air of nonchalance, but he could feel his boss's eyes on him the whole morning, even though the man was locked in his office.

Marcus worked until ten—the time he normally took his midmorning break—then let the other staffers know he was going for coffee, the same as he did every day. Except he never got his coffee, and he never went back to the office. Instead, he bypassed the White House cafeteria and walked right out the employee side entrance. He continued past the security barriers, caught a cab, and went into hiding.

Like all of Scallow's full-time staffers, Marcus was cleared for the highest levels of classified information because his job required it. He knew the First Daughter had been kidnapped on US soil by the drug cartel leader from Mexico, and he knew the terrorist, Carl Johnson, had agreed to participate in the rescue operation. That was why what he'd seen on his boss's smartphone screen confused him initially.

Bobcat released on schedule. Mexico on board next phase. Urgent! Relocate to secure bunker before POTUS returns to DC.

Bobcat was the Secret Service's code name for Melissa Mallory, the First Daughter. POTUS was the standard acronym for president of the United States.

The meaning to the cryptic text message was instantly clear to Marcus.

Bobcat released on schedule.

The conclusion of the rescue effort was planned and *known* before the rescue mission had even been launched. And if the president's chief of staff knew of the scheduled release before it happened, then he was complicit in the planning of the kidnap operation.

The president's chief of staff conspired with a foreign country and other Americans to kidnap the First Daughter! Or maybe not.

Marcus admitted to himself that there were holes in his theory. There were other possible explanations to someone having foreknowledge of the rescue operation. Perhaps there was a dual mission, and maybe the other effort had negotiated Bobcat's release before, or even during, the rescue operation. That possibility was more plausible than the conspiracy angle, except for one small detail.

Urgent! Relocate to the secure bunker…

The only real reasons Marcus could think of to hide in a bunker were security and safety. Therefore, the conspiracy involving the kidnapping of the president's daughter was part of a larger plan. That plan was moving to the next phase, which involved moving Martine Scallow, the president's chief of staff—and no doubt other key personnel—to a secure bunker *before the president returned to the Capitol*. The question now in Marcus's mind was *why?*

Marcus knew if he were wrong, people would simply wonder why he had not returned to work. But if he was right, and he was convinced that he was, then he had every reason to fear for his life. Martine Scallow was a very powerful man in DC circles. His influence was not limited to White House activities.

Normally, without any hard evidence—written copy or electronic file—a person's word would just be considered hearsay in any court of law, not that this particular conspiracy would ever find its way into any court in the land. There were, however, many cases where the testimony of a person with photographic or eidetic memory was admissible as legal evidence.

That's why he knew men would be hunting him, men who worked for the chief of staff or whoever that man worked for. If he was right about the conspiracy, they would kill him, no question. There was only one man he could turn to for help—one man to whom he had absolutely no connection outside of an experimental one-night stand five months ago. He called the man from the filthy hotel lobby's phone since he'd abandoned his own cell phone hours ago.

"Peoples," came an official-sounding reply.

He wasn't supposed to know that Stephen Peoples worked for the Terror Event Response agency, but they'd exchanged many secrets that night.

"Stephen," he whispered. "I need you."

"Marcus? Is that you? Christ, I thought we agreed you wouldn't call me anymore."

"Stephen, I'm in trouble. I don't have anyone else to call. I know who leaked information in the First Daughter's kidnapping."

"Goddammit, not on an open phone line, Marcus!" Peoples paused on the other end of the connection, and Marcus pictured him rushing into a room where he could talk in private.

The fact that Peoples hadn't denied his statement told Marcus the TER was at least investigating the possibility of treason within the US government. It didn't take a rocket scientist to conclude the only realistic way a highly trained group—and a group of drug-related thugs would never be *that* highly trained—could overcome the First Family's Secret Service detail was if the opposing force knew Bobcat's protection protocols, exact transportation route, security detail composition, armored car specifications, and comm channel codes.

"Where are you, Marcus?" Peoples finally said. "I'll send a car for you."

"No! They'll find me. You have to meet me somewhere. There's no way they know about you."

Peoples seemed to consider that. "I agree. Get in a cab and head out to my condo. You still remember where it is?"

"You're still out near Andrews Air Force Base, right? How could I forget? Best night of my life."

"Yeah, well, just get your ass over there."

For a moment, Marcus heard genuine tenderness in the man's voice, and he wished somehow they'd been able to make it work. Except for the part where the man had a wife and a couple of children.

Stephen Peoples returned to business. "Don't stop anywhere until you get to my place. I'll meet you in…" In his mind's eye, Marcus saw the agent checking a wristwatch. "About forty-five minutes."

Marcus replaced the old tabletop phone's receiver in the cradle and turned to leave. He almost walked right into a man who had magically appeared in the space behind him. He'd been scanning the small room for any sign of surveillance, but he hadn't seen anyone enter or leave the lobby. Now this man appeared as if from thin air.

He wore jeans and a black turtleneck sweater under a lightweight windbreaker.

He's crazy, Marcus thought, *because it's damned cold outside.*

The temperature was in the low thirties, but the wind was screaming through the city, making it seem much colder. The man wore a black head glove, and his eyes were hidden behind stylish, teardrop-shaped black shades.

"Hello, Marcus," the man said.

He pulled his shades off and revealed emotionless black eyes that stabbed right into Marcus's soul. Despite the heavy overcoat Marcus wore, he felt a chill slide up his spine. The intruder took a step forward, intimately into his personal bubble, and Marcus bit down on his bottom lip to keep it from trembling.

The man said, "My name is August Spoke. What say you and I take a little ride?"

The question was asked in a gentle way, and Marcus Aurelio was just entertaining the thought of running when he looked past the man and saw a sight that completely deflated his tiny balloon of hope. The sight told him in no uncertain terms that fleeing would be a futile gesture. Two more men—each a bigger man than he and August Spoke combined—hovered in the doorway. He realized at that moment that he was going to die.

For a moment, Marcus entertained the emotion of disbelief. It seemed utterly impossible anyone could have followed him or otherwise tracked him through the seedy part of DC.

Agent Spoke put his arm around Marcus's shoulder and guided him toward the door. "Why don't we begin our discussion with who you were just talking to on the phone?"

CHAPTER 6

1805 MST, THURSDAY
ALBUQUERQUE, NM

CARL JOHNSON KNEW SOMEDAY HE'D have to face a situation where his previous *ordinary* life would clash with his new *extraordinary* existence. He figured he'd run into his friends from his previous life and would have to deal with how they would react to the news stories painting him—correctly—as a terrorist. He'd often wondered if they would avoid him or treat him like a leper, not knowing how to deal with the *new* Carl Johnson.

He particularly wondered how Randal Cunningham—his best friend of twenty-five years—would react. Would the man hug him, or would he steer his kids and grandkids away from him? They'd known each other's children almost since the kids were born. They'd used each other as emergency contacts over the years. They'd taken each other's kids to the emergency room when one or the other was out of town on business trips. They'd practically raised each other's kids, and he loved that man's children and grandchildren like they were his own.

As it turned out, it was not the potentially awkward reunion with former friends that highlighted the severe contrast between the old Carl Johnson and the new. Instead, the evening he returned to Albuquerque, he found himself quite unexpectedly involved with a completely unknown person.

A month ago, he wouldn't have—*couldn't* have—gotten involved. Now, he was different. He was a badass, but not because of any special training, unless one called being tortured by the government a form of special training. He was no longer *just a guy*.

He was an *old* guy by badass standards, approaching fifty-four years of age. He was five-foot-nine, 170 pounds, and though he was very fit for his age, he hadn't had a fistfight in almost twenty years. He could still count all his rumbles in his entire life on one hand.

Until last month, he was just a guy. Not a big guy. Not a tough guy. Not a hoodlum. Not a thug. Not someone you'd tell your kids not to talk to if you met him on the street, and definitely not someone you thought might shoot you or cut your throat if given sufficient reason.

Now, Carl was *that* guy.

He sat in the hole-in-the-wall restaurant in Old Town, sipping his lemon water and waiting for his dinner to be delivered. He had been contemplating the reasoning behind the Melissa Mallory kidnapping and the involvement of high-ranking military personnel—US or Mexican, or both—when the young woman he was destined to help, the woman who was to bridge the expanse between the old and new Carl Johnson, walked into the dining room.

The place was less of a restaurant and more of a bar. The bar had an informal dining room attached to it. It was the kind of place where you could enjoy happy hour, then go into the next room and choose from a limited number of dinner entrées when you were done partying. Flat-screen TVs were mounted high on the walls around the room, but the volume of each TV was turned down.

CNN was playing snippets of the president's speech in front of Congress. Shirley Mallory had left her stricken daughter at the Las Cruces hospital, flown across the country, and given her well-advertised speech to Congress—all in the space of ten hours. Carl neither knew nor cared about the subject of that speech. He'd never been much interested in politics beyond voting. In fact, he'd voted Republican this time only because a woman candidate was different. Just like he'd voted for the Black Democrat.

Different had to be better, right?

Carl's attention from the TV was diverted as soon as his destiny entered the restaurant. She was a striking young woman. He quickly realized she had the same effect on the other dozen patrons. She removed her knee-length black leather coat in the archway between the foyer and the dining room and handed it to the hostess to hang up. From his table across the room, Carl watched her walk across the room. She was stunningly attractive, maybe twenty-five, maybe thirty. She had mocha-caramel skin, and her face was framed by jet-black straight hair a little shorter on the right side of her face than the left. She had an exotic-looking, narrow face and full lips adorned with glossy, cherry red lipstick. She had high cheekbones, lovely hazel eyes, and a narrow nose.

Carl made eye contact with her and smiled. When she smiled back at him, her whole face lit up like he was the most wonderful sight she had seen all day. Her smile was dazzling and revealed a full set of perfect white teeth. He instantly forgot she had to be at least twenty years younger than he, maybe more.

She hesitated like she was going to change course to visit his table—or maybe that was just his imagination because that's what he wanted to happen—and he had half-risen from his seat when her friends in the corner near the fireplace called to her. She turned partly away, gave her three girlfriends the same radiant smile she had just given him, and headed to their table. Even as she moved away, she cast him another glance and a shy smile. He interpreted it as an invitation, so he continued rising from his chair with the intent of going over to introduce himself.

As his gaze danced down and back up over her lithe figure, he thought she could be the poster girl for the IBTC—what a previous girlfriend had announced was the Itty-Bitty Titty Committee—but he wasn't at all discouraged. She was slender and petite, and she wore a very short black miniskirt. In her five-inch black heels, she looked about as tall as he was. The young woman wore a sleeveless brown leopard pattern silk blouse. Her miniskirt was tight on her round but narrow butt and revealed strong legs with toned thighs and well-defined calf muscles. Her black handbag was one of those stylish things she probably bought on Fifth Avenue in New York City.

He examined her profile and backside as she sauntered over to join her friends. He had just taken his first step in her direction when he heard the foyer door slam open, accompanied by lewd comments. The unseen hostess squealed, and three hoodlums strutted into the dining room. All three were big guys, and each one outweighed Carl easily by fifty pounds.

The alpha dog of the clan seemed to be the Black guy with the massive chest and even more massive gut. He was short, barely five and a half feet tall, but his biceps were huge—as thick as Carl's thighs. His accomplices were White and Hispanic and equally massive, though taller than the alpha dog.

The Black guy said, "Where'd that faggot go?"

The woman Carl had been just about to chat with looked toward the archway, as did everyone else in the dining room, including Carl. Alpha dog made eye contact with the woman, and the three young men gangsta-walked toward her.

Carl froze, then slowly returned to his seat. *No way. No fucking way she's a dude!*

She gasped. "Oh my God!" Her voice was husky and sensuously deep—too soft and tender for a guy, but deep for a girl.

He checked her out again as the hoodlums went over to her, but he still couldn't see it. Maybe the boy had surgery or something, but he sure looked like a girl to Carl. Maybe the thugs knew him. Otherwise, he couldn't imagine how they would see through his appearance.

He thought about helping her when the guys started pushing her around, but he decided not to get involved. A strong genetic distaste somehow hard-wired into his DNA told him that a man—even a feminine man or a gay man—should be able to stand up for himself. That thought was so tightly woven into Carl's gut reaction, he didn't feel any sympathy as the boy-girl tried to evade the three bullies, each one of which more than doubled her weight.

The three men surrounded her while her three dinner friends cowered behind their table. One had the presence of mind to work on her cell phone, presumably calling for emergency help.

The White guy said something about her "fake-ass hair," and he grabbed her hair and yanked. But the hair wasn't fake, and his tug sent the boy-girl tumbling facedown on top of the nearest table. As she sprawled across the top of the table, the Hispanic guy stepped behind her and grabbed her hips, then mimed like he was butt-fucking her. Then the Black guy pulled her upright by the arm and ripped her miniskirt off.

She wore a pink thong, and her tight, slender butt was as perfect as

Carl had ever seen on a woman. But when she snatched at her skirt, she briefly faced Carl, and all doubt vanished.

The girl was packing a bulge inside her thong.

The Black guy held the skirt high with his left hand, and when the boy-girl reached for it, the hoodlum punched him hard in the belly. His breath erupted with an abbreviated scream, and he doubled over, both arms folded across his stomach. He took a step backward and wobbled on his stilettos for a second, then folded right down on his butt and rolled onto his side. He gasped in pain, mouth wide open and trying to get air, and tucked his knees up to his chest in the fetal position.

If the bullies had stopped right then and left, Carl would have done nothing. They'd had their fun. But they didn't stop. The Black guy kicked the boy-girl in the back, and the White guy kicked him in the butt. The Hispanic guy hauled his leg back like he was going to kick a field goal. He was aiming for his face and looked like he was getting ready to put his full two-hundred-plus pounds into the kick.

Carl jumped up and pulled his Glock from his shoulder holster under the windbreaker he wore. It was an unwieldy weapon with the attached suppressor, but he aimed quickly. He gave no shouts, threats, or warnings. Carl simply and calmly pulled the trigger.

The boy-girl's three girlfriends—if they were, in fact, girls—had all screamed in anticipation of that final kick, so no one heard the suppressed gunshot. Everyone just saw the man tumble sideways right before his foot contacted the fallen boy-girl's face. The bully's kick missed, and he fell dead.

His accomplices both exclaimed, "What the fuck?"

The White guy was the first to see Carl's gun. "Oh shit!" he hollered, running for the door.

Carl gave him no warning either. He didn't shout any cop phrases like "Freeze!" or "Stop right there!" or "Show me your hands!" He had no witty retorts for the fleeing hoodlum. The man got only two steps toward the archway when Carl shot him high in the back, between his shoulders. The bullet's impact knocked the man off-balance, and he bounced off one side of the archway leading to the hostess station. He landed faceup with his eyes wide open, but he lay motionless.

Even before the second bully hit the floor, Carl had his Glock aimed solidly between the eyes of the Black guy, but the man wasn't intimidated. Carl noticed his eyes were slightly glazed and thought maybe he was too high to realize he *should* be afraid.

"You a faggot too?" Alpha Dog leered.

"Doesn't matter, does it? Because I'm a man with a gun," Carl said. He felt an abrupt rush of anger wash over him as he spoke.

"Well, whatchu gon' do, bitch?" the guy said, taking a step toward Carl. "It's easy to shoot a man in the back. You got the balls to do me face-to-face?"

Carl pulled the trigger. It wasn't like in the movies where the bad guy's body gets launched backward by the impact of the shot. The bullet didn't blast out the backside of his skull and splatter gore everywhere. The bullet entered the man's brainpan and stayed put. Alpha Dog's head snapped back, and he folded to the floor right where he'd stood.

Carl packed his gun away and looked around. Everyone was stunned. They stared at him like *he* was the monster. Many took a step back like he was more dangerous than the hoodlum guys, which was arguably true.

Carl pulled out his handkerchief and wiped his water glass free of fingerprints. Next, he wiped his utensils, the back of his chair, and any other surface at his table that he had touched. While it was true that after saving the president's daughter, Shirley Mallory directed the FBI to put a *do not detain* notation in his file, he figured the cops were on their way to the restaurant by now, and they likely wouldn't know about that notation until they got him downtown and booked him. The best option was not to be there when they showed up and not to leave any obvious evidence of his involvement. Besides, if he was in jail for a day or two, he couldn't get to his business in Mexico.

He started to leave, then noticed one of the boy-girl's girlfriends was kneeling beside him. He was still writhing on the floor, gasping, not able to get air. The guy had hit him hard, and Carl knew he could suffocate if he didn't stop panicking. The girlfriend just started crying and clearly didn't know what to do.

Carl made a snap decision, knowing he had maybe two minutes before cops swarmed the restaurant and cordoned off the immediate area. Shots had been fired, so the cops would show up with SWAT. He couldn't be inside that cordon when it closed.

He stepped over to the boy-girl and raised him upright by his shoulders. He slapped at Carl weakly, but Carl just hugged his head against his left shoulder. He whispered to him, "You're safe. It's okay. I'm not going to hurt you." He tilted the man's face toward the ceiling and told him to try to breathe through his nose with quick, shallow breaths.

The boy-girl's eyes were wild and full of fear the way a person would be when they think they are dying. But when Carl just smiled at him and said he would be all right in a minute, that he just had the wind knocked out of him, he calmed down a bit. He closed his eyes for a moment to concentrate on breathing, and Carl saw he had perfectly applied makeup. His long eyelashes were real, not fake.

He tried to breathe like Carl had told him to, though Carl figured there might still be the danger of serious internal injury. Alpha Dog had put a lot of power into his punch. Still, when he opened his eyes, Carl wanted him to see confidence in his eyes to help him get past the panic.

The boy-girl grabbed Carl's arm and shoulder, and Carl held him tight, then pressed his right hand firmly just below his sternum. His stomach muscles fluttered with spasms, but after a few seconds of gentle massage, he started breathing slower and slightly deeper.

Carl felt like he was out of time.

He looked at the girlfriend, wanting to give her instructions, but she was useless. She just knelt there, still sobbing. Neither of her other two friends had shaken themselves free of their shock, either. So Carl made another snap decision. He had to take the young man with him.

He told the girlfriend to grab his skirt and get his coat and follow him outside, but the girlfriend didn't move. Carl guided the injured boy-girl's right arm around his neck and picked him up—he couldn't have weighed more than a buck-ten—and carried him out of the restaurant. He got him into the passenger seat of his old SUV, still naked from the waist down except for the pink thong. Carl didn't bother with the seat belt. He slammed the door and ran around to the driver's side, jumped behind the wheel, and got the old SUV started.

His unintended passenger leaned forward in the seat and rocked forward and back, clutching his stomach and moaning. Carl heard him gasping as he struggled to breathe and cry at the same time.

Already, he could hear multiple sirens approaching, and he knew every on-duty cop in the city would be converging on Old Town. Several cops and an entire SWAT team had lost their lives in Carl's private war against the FBI a week ago, and every cop in the state knew who he was. His picture was burned into their memories, and he couldn't risk taking the chance that one of them wouldn't shoot him on sight.

Oops, sorry, Madam President. He had a gun, and we forgot you told us not to arrest him.

Carl burned rubber getting out of the parking lot. He knew all the side streets and alleys leading into and out of Old Town, so he made his way quickly to Central without passing any cops, then headed west until he arrived at his run-down motel. He parked in front of the door and scanned the area until he was sure no one was giving him any undue attention. He carried the boy-girl into his room.

He was still struggling to breathe, though he wasn't gasping as much. He laid him gently on the bed on his back and pulled the threadbare blanket over him. The slender young man rolled onto his side and curled up again, clutching his stomach. He moaned and sucked in air. Carl stroked his cheek and smoothed his hair away from his face.

"I know it hurts, but you'll be okay in a while. I'm going to get some ice for the bruising," he said. "I'll be right back."

Eyes closed, the boy-girl just nodded.

The motel was a square U-shaped building with the open end of the U facing Central Avenue. The ice and Coke machines were located midway along the center leg of the U, in the laundry room, and could only be accessed with his room key. Carl held up a small plastic trash bag he'd brought from his room and filled it with ice. When he got back to his room, the boy-girl was silent, and for a moment, he seemed to have fallen asleep. Carl grabbed a white towel that looked like it had been in use since before the turn of the new century and sat on the bed. The young man opened his pretty hazel eyes and watched him. Carl felt like he was gazing into a lovely girl's face.

Carl pulled back the blanket and told him to roll onto his back. "I'm going to raise up your blouse so I can put ice on your tummy, okay?"

At the boy-girl's nod, Carl gently pushed his silk blouse up. He could see his bra was padded, making him look like he had small breasts when he didn't.

"I'm not a doctor, but it doesn't look like you have any broken ribs." He could see a slight discoloration—a deep purple tint—in his flawless caramel brown skin. "But you're going to be sore for a few days. When you get home, I want you to take a bunch of Ibuprofen, okay? Then ice your bruises every day." He laid the thin towel across the young fellow's upper belly so the bag of ice wouldn't freeze his skin, then gently put the ice in place. "Let me know if that's too cold."

The boy-girl nodded again, and Carl smiled at him. He pulled the blanket back over his lower body. Looking at him up close, Carl could tell he was a lot younger than he originally thought, maybe twenty, so Carl instinctively shifted into the role of parent. As he looked at the young man lying before him, Carl felt a deep sense of guilt and shame. He could have—*should have*—stopped the assault sooner. Instead, he had allowed his own prejudice to prevent him from doing what he knew was the right thing. It shouldn't have mattered that the victim was a gay boy or a cross-dresser, or whatever. None of that mattered. He should have acted sooner. If he had, he could have defused the situation without killing those men. Not that he cared one whit about those bullies.

He reflected on his *new* self. The one defining factor that made him a badass was that he didn't care about killing. Somehow, he'd lost the moral distinction that prevented *normal* citizens from killing other people, just in the last month. Everyone in a modern civilized society knew killing or hurting people was wrong. It was fraught with consequences, and people were conditioned to avoid it, to feel guilty about doing it. Even cops, FBI agents, and military soldiers—though trained to use deadly force when necessary—sought to avoid it unless there was absolutely no other choice.

Up until last month, Carl was the same as the millions of other citizens. Now, he was different. The thing that made people normal—a moral compass—was now missing from his soul. In the last month, he'd killed cops, FBI agents, federal officers, drug cartel members, and even a foreign army officer. None of it bothered him in the slightest.

Less than an hour ago, he shot those three men, *not* because he wanted to do the right thing and save a boy-girl from being assaulted. He killed them because he was angry *at them*. He killed them because they were bullies. Now, he acknowledged he'd killed them for the wrong reason.

That the victim was ultimately saved was a fringe benefit. That was why he felt guilty. It should have been about the boy-girl, but it hadn't been.

Carl stroked the smooth skin of the young man's cheek with his palm. "What's your name?"

"Rainey Livingston."

"I'm Carl. I'm sorry this happened to you. I should have stopped it sooner." He hesitated a long moment, then said, "The same kind of thing happened to me, Rainey. I got done in by bullies recently. It's why I carry this."

Carl patted the shoulder holster inside his jacket. In his case, it was the TER agents who kidnapped and tortured him for information, and they had enjoyed his pain a little too much. He remembered the smug doctor smiling as he went about his task to inflict unimaginable chemical and electrical pain on Carl. He smiled at the memory. That doctor had been the first man he'd killed with his bare hands, and it hadn't been all that hard, either physically or morally. In fact, it felt good. It felt *real* good.

"What you're feeling right now," he said gently. "It will pass in time."

He wasn't completely convinced he was telling the truth. In reality, one had to let go of the anger and the feeling of helplessness and vulnerability for it to pass completely. Clearly, Carl hadn't let go of his own emotions yet. His experience was too recent.

He looked at Rainey again and was surprised at the sudden well of emotion he felt. It had been the same with the president's daughter after rescuing her, and it had been the same with Julia Reyes, the innocent stepdaughter of the drug lord who kidnapped Melissa. Maybe that kind of empathic connection was his superpower. Maybe his mission in life was to save kids, or something like that.

A lot of people say they'd kill someone who messed with their kids, but normal people don't have the skills or the tools to actually do the deed. Normal people couldn't step outside their moral fabric. Carl could. Without hesitation, the *new* Carl Johnson could kill anyone who messed with his kids or with anyone else of importance to him. He wasn't afraid of getting shot or killed. He wasn't afraid of anything. He couldn't be hurt anymore. He warmed at the thought of having an empathic superpower. He could envision the comic book written about him in a couple years.

Some superheroes had energy beams or Hulk strength. Carl, on the other hand, had a broken moral compass and an emotional detachment to match his empathic superpower, enabling him to kill some people without remorse and save others.

Crazy. When he refocused on his new companion, he found Rainey watching him. He smiled again. "Roll over and let me check your back."

He wanted to make sure Rainey didn't need to be in the emergency room. He pulled the ice bag from his belly and removed the towel. Rainey grimaced when he rolled onto his belly, and again when Carl's fingers probed the wounds where the men had kicked him in the middle of his back and on his tailbone.

The back wound was a fist-sized bruise. The discoloration would last a few days, but the pain would likely recede in a day or two. The tailbone injury was more serious. The man had kicked Rainey hard enough to cause a two-inch gash. The blanket had almost stopped the bleeding, but when he rolled over, the gash reopened. Carl held a corner of the towel against the cut and kept pressure on. Rainey might need stitches.

After a few minutes, Rainey started trembling, and Carl realized he was crying. He seemed so feminine that it was hard for Carl not to think of him as a young woman.

"God, I'm so stupid," he said between sobs. "Why did they beat me up?"

Carl pulled Rainey's head and shoulders onto his lap and hugged him. He stroked his hair and rubbed his shoulders and neck as Rainey pulled his legs up. He cried for a long time, but Carl knew it wasn't because of the assault or the pain of his beating. It was because there was no meaning to the violence. It was because he had been powerless to stop what had happened. Carl understood those feelings of vulnerability intimately.

Finally, Carl said, "They did it because they could. Because they were bigger and stronger than you are. They did it because they didn't think anyone would stop them."

Why it had happened to Rainey was no different from why the US government had done what they had to Carl. The government had the law on its side, and it was bigger than he was. They tortured him because they could. Because no one would, or could, stop them.

Until he fought back. Until he started killing and torturing them in return, doing the same thing to them and being labeled a terrorist because of it.

He shuddered at the thought of what those bullies might have done to Rainey if he hadn't been there. If he had let that man kick Rainey in the face, the young man might have died, or he could have been disfigured or crippled for life.

He supposed it was just human nature that the strong preyed on the weak. Maybe that was Carl's new purpose in life—to protect the weak. Save the kids. Maybe that was why his dark side had been brought out by his transition into the abyss. He liked the intense emotional attachment he felt for Rainey, Melissa Mallory, and Julia Reyes. He liked being able to help them. He liked being an empathic superhero. It gave him a purpose. It channeled the anger that sought to consume him, and he desperately needed an outlet for that anger.

CHAPTER 7

2030 EST, THURSDAY
WASHINGTON, DC

AUGUST SPOKE TOUCHED HIS FOREFINGER to his earpiece to activate it and waited for Rainman to respond.

"Report."

"As Mr. Scallow surmised, the intern didn't obtain any electronic copies of the email or any other documents, and they didn't write anything else down."

"You must be absolutely sure of this."

Spoke glanced at the dead intern beside him. "I am sure."

He and the dead man occupied the second bench seat of the old minivan. The intern's boyfriend, who had not been hard to find soon after Aurelio had gone missing, lay bound and gagged on the first bench seat. Spoke's two imposing muscle-bound men sat in the front seats. It took only the brief application of severe pain to the boyfriend for the intern to open up. At that point, Agent Spoke got answers to all his questions in the ten minutes it took the driver to get the minivan to a relatively deserted stretch of industrial shoreline.

They pulled into the parking lot behind a boat shop. There were shoreline berths where the shop employees could tow a customer's boat purchase down a ramp and into the water of the Potomac. The driver pulled the minivan to the head of one of the ramps. Eventually, the vehicle and the bodies would be found, but not within Rainman's one-day window of vulnerability.

"How in the world did you find him?"

Spoke smiled in the darkness. "It's easy to find a needle in a haystack if you have a very sensitive magnetometer."

Rainman clearly didn't get the metal detector humor because he remained silent, so Spoke said, "I knew where to look. There are very few places in this city where one can truly disappear. Those motels are in the seedy part of town, and a nicely groomed White man like our intern stuck out like a sore thumb. People remembered seeing him. He was not hard to find at all."

Rainman said, "Conclusions?"

"He called a man named Stephen Peoples. They had a one-night stand a few months ago. Peoples is, or was, gay curious. He's married with children, but he felt the need to try something different. Apparently, his curiosity was satisfied, much to Marcus Aurelio's discontent, because Peoples broke it off real quick and told our boy not to call ever again."

Spoke paused, but Rainman must have recognized the pause for the silent concern that it broadcasted.

"Don't make me ask the question."

"Stephen Peoples is a fairly high-level field agent with the Terror Event Response agency. If I eliminate him, we will have a trail of missing people that may form a trend. The TER has a lot of smart thinkers that do nothing but look for trends, and with the events of the last week, they're on high alert over there."

"Agreed. Meanwhile, are all witnesses disposed of?"

Spoke looked out the side window and made a good show of passing his gaze over the dark water of the river like he cared what was out there. He felt the driver's gaze on him in the rearview mirror. He'd hired the two guys, but not for any contribution they might add to his hunt or to the interrogation of the intern. He was well capable of attending to those tasks himself. He hired them simply because they looked threatening when he did not.

He wasn't at all dissatisfied with his outward appearance. He stood a shade under the six-foot mark and weighed one-sixty. Plain and simple, he was well-trained and extremely capable, but he just didn't look scary. The two guys he'd hired looked very scary. Both weighed well over 250 pounds. He brought them along so the intern, when they found him, wouldn't try to run, scream, or put up a fight.

The muscle had accomplished the task. Their mere presence had sobered Aurelio quickly, and Spoke had sensed the exact moment when the man surrendered—right after he looked over Spoke's shoulder and saw the men in the doorway of the fleabag hotel.

"Stand by."

Spoke still held the silenced gun he'd used on the boyfriend's knee-caps. He shifted his aim and fired two shots through the headrests of both front seats. He had anticipated this particular task, so he'd hand-packed his nine-millimeter shells extra light on the powder. The two men's heads snapped forward, but both bullets stayed inside their skulls. There was no mess to clean up. Not that it mattered. He was simply going to let the minivan roll into the river and sink.

"The task has now been completed."

"Good," Rainman said.

All four men were now dead, each shot through the head. He got out of the minivan through the passenger sliding door and walked around to the driver's door. He opened it and hit the electric switches to roll down all the windows, then went to the back and popped open the rear hatch. It wouldn't take the vehicle long to sink with the interior air evacuating through the open windows and hatch.

Spoke went back to the open driver's door and pressed his foot on the brake pedal, put the console-mounted gearshift into neutral, and stepped back. As he watched the minivan roll down the ramp and gently into the water, he unscrewed the suppressor from the disposable, untraceable gun and tossed both pieces into the water, as far away from the shore as possible. Then, he peeled off his latex gloves and dropped them into the water. They were immediately swept away by the slow-moving current.

"What do you want me to do about Agent Peoples?"

"Leave him to me. We'll kill two birds with one stone."

August Spoke had no idea what that meant, but he wasn't about to question his orders. Besides, the beep in his ear informed him Rainman had closed the channel.

CHAPTER 8

"THERE'S A CAB PULLING UP out front, Miss Palmer," Agent Stephen Peoples said. "That might be Director McGrath." The "three hours late" part remained unsaid.

The security warning had chimed from Peoples' position at the management console, and Agent Nancy Palmer ceased pacing the floor between the wall monitors and the three analyst workstations. In the time she'd known McGrath, he'd never been so much as ten seconds late for a meeting. Now, he was late for his shift by three hours and fifteen minutes. And he hadn't answered his cell.

She said, "Have the guard issue challenge protocols, just in case."

Peoples had known that particular security safeguard was going to be put into play, and Palmer noticed he'd already started to transmit the order to the guard's terminal even before she finished giving the instruction. It was standard access policy when someone was unexpected or late in arriving.

Normally, personnel were admitted into the secure facility after checking their government ID cards that were embedded with a biometric chip. Those were extremely hard to forge or duplicate, but not totally impossible.

A person's biometric data—height, weight, eye color, blood type, photo, and even a digital voice recording and DNA sample—was stored on the chip. Not only could a person be positively identified on-site, but that data could also be compared with stored data on some of the government's most secure computer networks. Trending data was also constantly updated for each biometric ID card. For example, a person couldn't enter one facility if they hadn't been logged out of another facility. Similarly, a person couldn't log out of a facility in Virginia, then log into a facility in California an hour later. The personnel computers would easily track those trends and raise red flags.

Since no system was completely infallible, a protocol of security challenges was developed for each field office when it opened, and that data was *not* stored off-site in any DOD computer. Retinal scans and fingerprints were matched. Five security questions were asked, and each question had two answers—one normal answer and another answer to be used in duress. Advanced algorithms would measure the stress level of the person being challenged. Minute levels of agitation would be detected by a presumed impostor who was *almost* sure he had the right answers.

Aaron McGrath passed his challenge perfectly and was admitted into the facility. When he entered the living room of the house serving as the ops center, Palmer froze in mid-pace and stared at the man. Monroe, who was on duty with Peoples, stopped giving his report and gawked at McGrath.

"Whoa, Boss. You look like shit…um, sir." Monroe stood and stepped beside McGrath. "You want a Red Bull, or maybe some strong coffee?"

"Coffee would be good."

Monroe started to step past the man but hesitated and pointed at the man's chest. "You're, um…you're missing a button there, Boss."

Palmer eyed the man with concern. His striped button-down shirt's collar button was mismatched into the next lower buttonhole, and the V-neck pullover sleeveless sweater was pulled more over his right shoulder than his left, like he'd pulled it on and forgotten to even out the shoulder seams. His shirt cuffs were unbuttoned, and one was rolled up to his forearm while the other hung loose at his wrist. He looked like he'd slept in his clothes.

McGrath's hair was a mess by normal standards, and his eyes were red with deep shadows and bags under both.

Peoples eyed McGrath as he walked into the op center. He walked slowly, like he was tired or in pain.

Palmer said, "You don't look so good, Aaron."

After Melissa was delivered to the hospital at Las Cruces, McGrath and the president had been driven to Holloman Air Force Base, where they had boarded Air Force One to get back east in time for her six-o'clock speech to Congress.

"I was supposed to be at the president's speech, but instead, I spent most of the evening hugging the toilet bowl. I must have picked up a bug out there in New Mexico. My doctor gave me some homeopathic remedies, though." He held up his small carry-on.

McGrath noticed Peoples and frowned. "I thought Tim Fredericks had the duty tonight."

Agent Stephen Peoples nodded and said, "Agent Fredericks was in an accident on the way in. He's in the emergency room. I got called to fill in about two hours ago."

McGrath seemed to have trouble concentrating, but he still picked up on the doubt that was clear in Peoples's voice. "Explain."

Peoples hesitated. "I just don't believe in coincidences."

He gave no further details, so Palmer said, "Tell him what you told me."

The man shook his head. "I got a call last night from an associate I haven't seen in five months, and he was scared out of his mind. Claimed he knew who leaked info to the First Daughter's kidnappers."

Palmer narrowed her eyes and looked at McGrath, but he seemed not to be able to focus on the obvious conclusions he himself had suggested on his flight across the country on *Air Force One*.

"Go on," she said to Peoples.

"I told him to get in a cab and meet me at my apartment, but he never showed. He was an intern for Martine Scallow, but now that man is also unaccounted for."

McGrath said, "The president's chief of staff is missing?"

Agent Peoples nodded. "All of the rest of his staffers are where they should be, or at least, they were as of 2300 hours last night."

McGrath was slow in responding, so Palmer said, "Keep working on that angle. See if those two show up somewhere. First thing in the morning, run a location check on all key government personnel." She glanced at McGrath. "Copy me on any other missing persons or any other anomalies."

She turned to McGrath, who said, "What's your status, Nancy?"

"My plane departs in two hours, and I'll be in Albuquerque a little over three hours later. If Johnson keeps his word, I'll depart for Mexico City with him aboard at 0900 and touch down three hours after that."

McGrath nodded. "You don't expect him to show tomorrow, do you?"

"I'm concerned about his rage."

"We need intel, Nancy. We can't allow Johnson to interfere with our mission objectives or go off the reservation on this op. There's too much at stake."

"I agree that his unpredictability has been a pain in the ass when he's been the target of our ops, but he's also been a game changer for us when he's on our side." She fell silent for a moment, then shrugged. "I'll just have to make sure he stays on our side."

"You like him, don't you?" McGrath said.

"I *understand* him, and I think he can help us beyond his role as a look-alike for the drug lord."

McGrath nodded. "Still, he's a loose cannon. If he goes rogue, you'll have to eliminate him. Will you be okay with that?"

"No, I won't. But if it needs to be done, I will do it."

Monroe arrived with a steaming cup of instant coffee. McGrath reached for it, but his hand was shaking so badly, he almost couldn't grab it. His jerky motions splashed nearly a third of the liquid onto the floor before he finally got control. He took a sip and noticed Palmer watching him.

"Nerves," he said. "That medicine must have me wired."

"Maybe you should rest. Agent Peoples can take up the slack while I'm gone."

McGrath smiled. "I'll be okay once I get a little of this gourmet coffee in me."

Palmer chuckled. "Sip it sparingly. That stuff's government-issue—two dollars a pound gourmet blend. Comes in a cheap-ass five-gallon corrugated can with a black-and-white label pasted on it to camouflage its true value."

They both shared a quiet laugh, and McGrath's eyes adopted a distant gaze. She could tell he was thinking about Johnson.

"You like him too, don't you?" she said.

"I know what he's going through."

"We killed his kid, Aaron. He didn't kill yours, even when he could have. Hell, if he was half the terrorist we thought he was, he would have killed her."

"I know, Nancy. I don't want to have to kill him, but if he doesn't play by the rules, he will become expendable."

CHAPTER 9

0115 MST, FRIDAY

ALBUQUERQUE, NM

CARL SAT ON THE EDGE of the bed as Rainey slept on his side, next to him. Soon, the fatigue of the previous day's events caught up with him, and he felt his head nodding into sleep. He curled up on the bed behind Rainey and held him. Several times, Rainey jerked in his sleep like he was having nightmares, and a couple of times, he made a keening sound like he was trying to scream in his dreams. Each time, Carl woke up, held him tight, and talked to him gently until he quieted down.

Just before sunrise, they prepared to leave the motel. Carl wrapped Rainey in the blanket and dropped him at the house of one of his friends. He had wanted Carl to take him home so he could introduce him to his folks, but Carl declined. He said only that he didn't want to encounter the police and didn't explain further.

In truth, he didn't want to have to explain to Rainey's people that their boy had been with a terrorist all night. While Carl was no longer labeled as such, he knew he was, in fact, still *that guy*. You didn't become a bad person, then suddenly turn good again just for one good deed or just because the president declared you untouchable.

Carl got out of the SUV and walked around to open the passenger door just like he would for a woman. After climbing out with the blanket tied around his waist, long legs peeking from the dragging folds of cloth, Rainey wrapped his arms around Carl's neck. He leaned into Carl just like a girl would and hugged him for a long time. He gave Carl a shy kiss on the cheek. Carl watched the boy-girl sashay up the short concrete walkway toward the front door, trailing much of the blanket.

Carl then headed immediately toward the airport, but not without a detour to his storage shed to pick up a duffel bag containing a terrorist's most powerful weapon—cash. After a quick breakfast, Carl drove around to the west side of Albuquerque International Sunport, to the cargo gate, arriving just shy of nine o'clock. He always found it curious why the Sunport was classified as an international airport when he'd heard it had no direct international connections. He'd heard all international connections were made through other, larger airports in cities like Denver, Houston, Phoenix, and Dallas.

Carl found it ironic that he pulled in at the very same gate where his mercenaries had ambushed Special Agent Cummings and her elite TER commandos three days ago. He showed his driver's license to the civilian gate guard who was clearly expecting him, thanks to advance notice from McGrath's TER team, and he was directed to a parking area near the cargo hangar. Moments later, he was boarding Palmer's Gulfstream, likely the same jet that had delivered the elite kill squad his mercs had terminated.

Agent Nancy Palmer met him at the top of the stairs. He'd only met her once, during his aborted attempt to find and kill Director McGrath in Virginia two days ago. She'd been decked out from head to toe in black tactical gear and had intercepted him. Now, she was dressed in civilian clothes, and he did that man thing—his gaze drifted down along the curves of her slender physique and back up again—as he climbed the steps to enter the plane.

She wore faded, tight denim pants, and the first button of her light blue, button-down shirt was open, which Carl found enticing even though she wasn't very ample in the chest or showing any cleavage. Over the shirt, she wore a dark blue, pinstripe blazer. All in all, she looked like a business executive on vacation who didn't know how to dress for a vacation.

She wasn't what he would describe as beautiful, but she was definitely attractive. She carried herself like a professional athlete. She looked strong, and her body seemed well-toned. He found himself feeling a bizarre and embarrassing attraction to this woman, who undoubtedly had a major role in the decisions leading to his son's death.

"And do you approve?" she said. Her voice grated with a sound that was more like a dangerous whisper than a spoken word.

At the top of the steps, Carl leaned sideways and looked behind her, then glanced behind himself as if looking for someone. He said, "Pardon me for staring, but I was expecting a kick-ass government commando all dressed up in tactical gear. Where is Agent Palmer, anyway?"

She gave him a sarcastic look. "Very funny."

Carl smiled and reached out his hand, which she shook. Her grip was firm, her skin warm. He fought his programmed greeting of "It's nice to see you again," because it was not. Looking into her eyes, he could see all the people involved in the killing of his son, Mark. She must have sensed his thoughts because her demeanor changed instantly as the smile faded from his face. He quickly released her hand.

She said, "I'll give you the nickel tour before we depart."

Without waiting for his acknowledgment, Palmer walked past the passenger area to the modified closets in the rear half of the plane. Carl followed, dumping his duffel bag on a seat. When he caught up with Palmer, she explained the various storage compartments and narrow closets, all of which were hardened steel appliances that opened with a ten-digit code. She had him commit the code to memory.

On the left wall immediately behind the passenger seats was the restroom. Beyond that was a full-length closet that held a single wicked-looking sniper rifle with a folded bipod assembly under the barrel and an oversized scope. Palmer called the weapon a Barrett M107, a 50-cal shooter that pretty much destroyed anything it was fired at.

"Any halfway decent sniper could hit a target up to a thousand yards with that weapon," she said. "A true professional could 'reach out and touch someone' a mile away."

"You mean reach out and kill someone," Carl said.

"Same difference."

"I assume you are such a professional?"

"I am."

She was looking at him, and he found her gaze too intense to match.

He tried to appear calm and appraised the Barrett again. "That looks like the same sniper rifle Merc Four used yesterday to save my ass."

Palmer nodded. "Same model. I like to dress mine up a little nicer, though." She pointed at the bulbous laser optics on the top rail. "You know, 'cause I'm a girl and all."

Carl looked at the assassin again. "You enjoy all this gun shit, don't you?"

"I was a Navy SEAL." She shrugged. "Of course, I like guns." Then she gave him a girlie smile, and her nose crinkled up a bit. "I like knives too."

Beyond the sniper closet was another storage unit that held a variety of automatic weapons, including Uzis, micro-Uzis, P90s, and the folding-stock PDW—the computer-designed personal defense weapon that fired six-millimeter armor-piercing rounds. She said it was her favorite for urban warfare when she needed instant stopping power in crowded spaces. She said it was like the P90 urban street fighter, but lighter in weight and quieter, with less recoil. "All in all, it is a better killer," she said, "and you don't have to mess around with a top-mounted magazine."

"Sista needs to get a life," Carl said.

On the opposite side of the aisle, Palmer showed Carl the closets that held ammunition, first aid kits, MRE rations, a variety of black handguns and suppressors, infrared and night vision headsets, black metal hand-cuffs and white plastic zip cuffs, telescopic carbon-composite police batons and pepper spray, and an assortment of grenades—frag, explosive, and flash-bang. In the bottom drawer were six high-performance combat parachutes.

She ended the tour with a quip about how easy the parachutes were to use. "Just strap it on and jump out of the plane. When you pull the cord, they practically fly themselves. Well, until you hit the ground."

Carl didn't laugh.

Palmer nodded toward the cockpit. "Let me introduce you to Air Force Colonel Vesario Reichert. He's the Air Force pilot that retired El Patron yesterday. Only the best of the best qualify to fly CAP for the president. With our help, the administration spun the incident as a training accident, but the colonel would have had to face disciplinary action, even after a long and decorated career. He's now temporarily assigned to the TER."

CAP, Carl recalled, was the acronym for Combat Air Patrol. They were the special detachment that flew cover for *Air Force One* whenever the president was in the air.

Carl followed Palmer forward. As he entered the cockpit, both pilots turned toward him. Colonel Reichert was a slender man, maybe five-eleven or six feet tall, and he was a few shades darker than Carl. He had intense green eyes that had likely stolen the hearts of many women in his younger days. The colonel gave Carl a brief head-nod when they made eye contact.

"Nice bit of work yesterday, Colonel," Carl said. "I can't begin to describe how much that general deserved to have a missile smoked up his ass."

"I've been briefed on your exploits also," he said, half talking over his shoulder and half attending to his flight preparations. "Killing those cartel druggies and bringing the First Daughter back was no easy task, I'm sure. Pretty impressive for a civvy."

The copilot, whom Palmer introduced as David Blick, eyed Carl like he was an enemy he was being forced by circumstances to work with.

Which pretty much summed up their current situation.

Carl took a guess at the man's hostility. "Second trip to Albuquerque this week?"

He figured the guy was comrades-in-arms with the elite commandos Carl's mercs had dispatched three days ago. He'd no doubt also heard how Carl had kept the commando leader alive and hacked his head off while the man was still conscious, partly for revenge and partly to unnerve the man's boss, Aaron McGrath. Not as obvious to anyone but Carl, it was partly to prove to himself and the US government agents that he could be as ruthless as they were. It was part of his transition from normal civilian to most wanted terrorist.

"Those were damn good men," the copilot said.

"I'm sure they were, but they were overconfident and cocky. They thought I was going to lie down and die because they'd been doing this longer than I or because their guns were bigger. But killing is a nasty business, Mr. Blick, and I've come to learn that we don't retire from the business of killing. We keep killing until we get killed, period." He looked at the deck carpet for a long moment. "But it's a chosen career field. It's not like those guys didn't have a choice whether or not to kill my son and come hunting me."

Carl turned away from the man. He'd been seduced by all the government ops mumbo-jumbo and the tech toys and weapons. He'd almost forgotten why he was in this mess. With his recollection clear again, he recalled that these people were not his friends. At best, he was going into this mission and would soon be surrounded by enemies of varying degrees of definition. Any of them could turn on him in a heartbeat if it fit the government's objectives. He had to work with some of his enemies, like Palmer and her crew, to accomplish his personal mission. Others, like the entity called the Triad that controlled El Patron, were to be dispatched with extreme prejudice.

His enemies were directly responsible for Mark's death. His task wouldn't be complete until he avenged his son. And Melissa Mallory. He saw Agent Palmer studying him, but he walked past without acknowledging her and took a seat in the cabin after stuffing his duffel beneath his seat. He reminded himself that Nancy Palmer was not his friend. She was a government agent, and he had no doubt whatsoever that she would kill him if it fit the government's agenda.

He began to formulate his own contingency to eliminate her if the necessity arose. He'd have to do it without weapons and without any kind of hand-to-hand combat.

How do you kill a badass Navy SEAL?

CHAPTER 10

NANCY PALMER WATCHED JOHNSON MOVE silently by her, a storm of dark emotions trailing in his wake like a tangible cloud. The man wasn't just angry. His emotions went a lot deeper. At one moment, he seemed fine until the copilot's words triggered Johnson's sudden emotional change. As he passed, she could feel his anger and his hatred radiating like heat from a lava flow.

He seemed like two separate and distinct men contained within the same shroud of skin. One was polite and caring, a charming gentleman she'd caught checking her out and flirting with her. He seemed kindhearted and carefree about things, and she wondered if she'd glimpsed the remnants of his personality from *before*. The other Carl Johnson was a raging man, full of raw pain. She could see by his quick change of persona that he was barely keeping his rage under control.

She could relate to his rage. It was a monster, but it was also a powerful motivator. It was, in fact, her reason for joining the military and becoming an elite covert operator in the war on terror. Learning her twin sister was killed five thousand miles away by a terrorist bomb would pale, she knew, to Carl's pain of watching his adult child being murdered right in front of him. She could only wonder how Johnson kept hold of his sanity, though she figured an argument could be made that he hadn't.

Rage could be an efficient tool if used properly. It had served her extremely well for the last few years, and it had enabled Johnson, an untrained amateur, to accomplish deeds over the last thirty days that fully trained operators might not have been able to handle. So far, Johnson was able to keep his monster on a tight leash, using gut instinct instead of training to control the rage. He seemed to be able to analyze a scenario and plan out a tactical response before letting his monster roam free. He'd been tested under fire and performed well.

If he were ever prosecuted for his actions, that very ability to analyze and plan would mean the difference between a plea of insanity and full-intent murder. There was no doubt in Palmer's mind which side of the line Johnson would fall. To make matters worse, Johnson seemed to be fully aware of what he was doing and what his punishment would be if he were caught.

And he didn't care.

Regardless, he was an extremely valuable asset for the previous mission to rescue Melissa Mallory and for the current mission to prosecute her abductors. Not many operators could have pulled off an ad hoc rescue of the president's daughter the way Johnson had, and he conducted his operations—against the FBI and the elite TER agents sent to kill him—with flawless planning and execution.

He'd found illegal funding and materiel and mercenaries to conduct his operations. For thirty days, he stayed several steps ahead of a government that had billions of dollars of intel assets with which to find him.

The TER could never predict what he might do next because he simply acted on whatever impulse popped into his mind at any given moment. He was an amateur that didn't operate by any predictable rules of engagement. They couldn't profile him, so they couldn't anticipate him.

Any of his mercenaries could have simply completed the initial assignment, taken their money, and run, but all had remained in his service. Carl Johnson had become their leader, and they were fiercely loyal.

Carl Johnson was an engineer and a project manager in his former career. Before last month, he sold real estate. He had been a captain in the Air Force, but only as a research engineer. He had no military combat training.

Nancy Palmer knew she helped create Johnson's monster, and she knew he knew it. How a civilian in his circumstance could stand to look her in the eye—or work with her or McGrath on this mission—was beyond her understanding. She wondered what his motivation was.

Why is he so intent to find and kill the men who kidnapped Melissa Mallory? Why does he even care about the president's daughter or what larger agenda her kidnappers have?

Palmer considered these things as she watched Johnson take a seat near the rear of the jet. He didn't sulk about or flop himself into his seat in anger. He was calm and controlled in all his movements. He reminded her of many of her operators. Like a trained professional, he was tense and primed for instant action. His gaze darted about as he absorbed the details of everything around him.

There was no first-class section, as the entire business jet was luxurious. The front section was, however, more spaciously appointed. At the beginning of the section were four luxurious leather seats—two mounted on each side of the aircraft, one behind the other. A sturdy table could unfold from the wall in front of each seat, and all four seats could swivel to enable a group conference. Next were three rows of four equally luxurious leather seats, also positioned in twos on each side of the jet. Those seats did not swivel.

Johnson sat in the window seat of the middle row on the starboard side of the jet. He fastened his seat belt and stared out the window into the featureless desert beyond the cargo hangar. Well, it seemed featureless to Palmer. She'd been to Arizona and New Mexico a handful of times over the years but had yet to see anything of redeeming value in the landscape.

Behind her, Reichert and Blick exchanged their preflight code talk. Then the colonel did the same with the control tower.

"We're cleared for priority takeoff when you're ready, Agent Palmer. Direct route straight to General Roberto Fierro Villalobos International Airport in Chihuahua, Mexico."

"We're ready now, so please proceed."

"Roger that. Distance is about 450 miles. Gate-to-gate flight time is approximately one hour twenty-two minutes with priority clearances on both ends."

"Very well."

Only the starboard door was opened, so she hit the button that engaged an electric motor somewhere in the deck below her feet. The stairs rose and folded in half, the lower half smoothly against the upper half, which then folded into the doorway of the bulkhead. It whined to a close, and she slid the locking lever counterclockwise to latch the door. She took a step toward the cockpit with the intention of sitting in the crew jump seat behind the copilot, then reversed her course at the last moment and sat in the seat beside Johnson.

His eyes were closed, and if he knew she was there, he gave no indication. She didn't even know whether or not he was awake until half an hour into the flight when he started muttering words she couldn't make sense of. He clutched at the armrests on both sides of his seat and jerked his head away from the window. Eyes wide open, he stared ahead, a thousand miles in front of the cockpit window.

She'd seen the look of shock and trauma many times in the eyes of soldiers. His was the look of a person who had seen something that a human should not see—done something a human should not do.

Tentatively, Palmer reached out and laid her right palm on Johnson's left forearm and was shocked at what she felt. He was in great shape for a fifty-three-year-old man. When she touched his arm, though, he was so tense, his sinewy muscles felt like cords of steel. She could feel him trembling. In the blink of an eye, he moved so quickly she almost struck him in defense.

His right hand shot across his body and gripped her hand, and he shouted, "Don't leave me! Mark, don't go!"

His fingers dug into her wrist like a vise grip, and he slowly turned his to face her. In his eyes, she saw pure, unadulterated hatred, and she thought he had finally lost the battle of control. She tensed, expecting his attack.

Carl blinked rapidly three times, and the hatred was replaced by raw pain. He relaxed his grip on her wrist. She let go of his arm and started to slowly pull her hand away. He surprised her by wrapping his fingers around her palm and holding her hand in place. He relaxed in his seat and turned his face toward the window again.

After a few minutes, he said, "It's always the same nightmare." He seemed to have difficulty putting his thoughts into words. "I get to him before Reyes drives up, but he doesn't know what's coming. I try to pull him back inside the lobby, behind the metal door, but he always pulls his arm away and turns to start walking away from me. Then he dies. Every time I close my eyes. Over and over again. He just pulls away from me and dies."

After a while, Johnson released her hand, but she decided not to let go of his arm. She imagined she was doing some good, helping him control his monster. She remembered the calming effect of her hand on his shoulder during his meeting with President Mallory in Virginia earlier in the week, when he'd been grieving his son's death even as he hoped for ways to kill Aaron McGrath.

President Mallory had squashed those hopes, and now, whatever closure Johnson sought was bottled up inside him. He seemed ready to explode, though he was visibly relaxing at her touch. She watched tears roll down his cheek, and for a long while, he seemed on the verge of sobbing.

He said, "I always imagined I would build this portfolio of apartments and mini storage buildings as my retirement nest egg. I already own three. I figured when I died, I'd leave millions of dollars of assets to my son so he'd live comfortably." Johnson turned toward her and wiped the tears from his eyes with his palm. "What's the point of all that now?"

She knew he wasn't looking for an answer, so she gave him none.

"What's the point of living, Agent Palmer, if not for our children?"

"Call me Nancy."

He turned away. "I don't want to call you *Nancy*." He said her name like it was a curse word, and his voice was as hard as steel. After a few moments, he continued with a gentler tone, "Do you suppose there's anything else after this fucked-up life that we live? Some kind of afterlife where I'm going to be forgiven after all the people I've killed?"

"God forgives us all."

"*You* believe in God?" Johnson almost chuckled. "You kill people for a living, Agent Palmer. How the fuck can your God forgive you for that?"

"I kill to protect people."

Johnson faced the window again. "I suppose that's the difference between you and me. I just want to kill people."

She tried to understand his pain and empathize with his loss, but she'd had a hand in creating that loss, as did Aaron McGrath and President Mallory. Sooner or later, if Johnson lived long enough, he'd have to find some kind of closure. If he was lucky, he'd learn that killing would never alleviate his pain.

If, as Aaron surmised, closure caused him to turn on the TER or the president, it would be Palmer's task to put him down. She desperately hoped it wouldn't come to that. She had a feeling deep inside that Johnson was one of the good guys.

If he could just keep his monster under control.

He lacked the training to compartmentalize his pain. As a result, he was a grenade, and the pin was already pulled. Worse, he was in danger of crossing over to the dark side and finding solace in the mere act of killing.

"Mr. Johnson," she began. "Carl." She paused, then spoke softly, "Killing without purpose makes you no better than the men you're hunting."

Johnson started to object, but Palmer tightened her grip on his arm and raised her left hand to silence him.

"Let me help you. I can show you how to…" She hated sounding so clinical about the business of pain and death. "I can show you how to compartmentalize your pain to allow you a better chance to complete your mission."

He turned from the window and looked at her. "Okay," he said. "And while you're at it, you can teach me how to be a better killer. I've been lucky up to now, but luck won't always be enough."

Palmer nodded and removed her hand from his arm. She felt a strange bond with the man. He seemed to know his emotional turmoil was a weakness, yet he didn't try to hide his vulnerability from her. He was letting her know he needed her. It was part of his magnetism, and she figured that was part of the reason his mercenaries fought for him. She also felt drawn to him because of it.

Men didn't like to show or even admit having a weakness, especially not to a woman. Johnson was different, though. He seemed fully aware of his strengths and weaknesses. In many ways, he reminded her of her boss, Aaron McGrath. He wasn't quite as old as McGrath, though both were attractive and fit, and both were mentally reserved, intelligent quick thinkers, and decisive. But that's where the comparison ended.

Johnson possessed an additional skill set she hadn't seen in other male leaders. She hadn't seen it in female leaders either, though most women in command positions knew they had to mimic the male command style, or they'd never be placed *by men* into command positions.

Even the current president of the United States played the man's game exceedingly well. Once elected, a president has an administration to help run the country's affairs, the power players of which are predominantly male. There was no room for a woman's touch in the presidency.

As much as Palmer admired Shirley Mallory, she knew a woman could only inject a limited amount of herself into her command style. While the president led her administration, she had to play by the rules or face losing the confidence of the men. Besides, the rest of the world was mostly run by men, so they dictated the rules of the game. Palmer wasn't bitter about it. She simply understood the landscape on which she operated.

Carl Johnson wasn't following the rules of government service or covert ops, or perhaps he was just making up his own rules. Either way, she found his deviance appealing. Johnson was emotionally gentle and possessed a tenderness that counter-balanced his ruthlessness. He let her comfort him because he knew he needed *her* strength to remain strong himself. Regardless of the outcome of their current mission, Johnson would either find closure or he wouldn't.

Suddenly, she didn't want to kill this man.

CHAPTER 11

0930 MST, FRIDAY

CARL HEARD ONLY THE BARELY audible buzz of the engines in the rear of the plane. There was no chatter of passengers and no inquiries from flight attendants. There was only peace and quiet.

He was very conscious of the closeness of Agent Palmer. With his eyes closed, he studied her. She wore no perfume, nor did he detect any fragrance from soap or shower gel. His senses remembered a hint of mint-flavored toothpaste he had breathed in when she stood close to him earlier, explaining the various weapons in the locked cabinets. Now she wanted to teach him lessons of emotional compartmentalization.

What the hell am I supposed to do with all that nonsense?

With sixteen available seats on the spacious plane, not counting the cockpit jump seat he'd seen when talking to the pilots, he and Palmer continued to sit next to each other throughout the flight. It seemed almost childish that the reason neither of them moved was because the truce they had formed might then be shattered.

His left arm and her right arm shared the center armrest, and their arms touched for the duration, sometimes sliding millimeters against each other as they breathed or as the plane rode minor air turbulence. He refused to break that contact with her. He found it impossible to hate Palmer, just as he had discovered he could not hate McGrath or the president. Instead, he revisited his bizarre attraction to the woman through their physical contact and wondered if she felt the same.

Not likely, he thought.

If he messed up this op or even stepped out of line, she'd cut him loose for good. That was the kind of soldier she was. Still, he allowed himself to enjoy a brief respite from what seemed like a continual six-week span of violence. He kept his breath steady, not wanting to betray his feelings and spoil the moment.

Eventually, he opened his eyes, and in his side vision, he saw Agent Palmer watching him. He smiled.

"What?" she said.

Carl turned to face her as much as his seat would allow. Her face was slender, her cheekbones prominent. Her blue eyes could look both innocent and pretty, or dangerous and deadly. She had that deadpan gaze down pat, though, and it lent an intense look to her face. Her blond hair was short and straight. It was a practical, low-maintenance hairstyle.

She had what he referred to as young skin. Her face was smooth and unblemished, with no lines, wrinkles, or scars. Her nose was narrow, and her lips were medium—not thin but not full. She wore no makeup, eyeliner, color, or any of the things that women seemed to think were necessary to be pretty.

Agent Palmer was a plain woman. She was attractive in a kick-your-ass kind of way, and that's what Carl found attractive about her. That, and her extreme fitness. He remembered grabbing her arm and recalled now how strong she felt. She had not yielded. He'd always had a special attraction to physically fit women.

"How old are you, Nancy?"

The barest hint of softness touched the corners of her eyes when he used her first name, and he could tell she was struggling not to smile. "Twenty-seven."

Which made him almost twice her age. His smile broadened, and suddenly, she couldn't hold back her smile either.

She slapped his arm playfully. "What?"

Carl chuckled and turned forward in his seat. He wondered if there was a girlie woman hidden deep inside her, maybe one with a sense of humor. He wondered in what kind of world a woman like Nancy Palmer and a man like himself might connect. He remembered sensing a deep vulnerability in her when they first met in Virginia, but then he shook his head. "Nothing. Just an old man's fantasy."

Colonel Reichert came on the intercom and announced they were half an hour out from General Robert Fierro Villalobos International Airport. Carl's smile faded, and his mind shifted gears as he looked forward to the mission ahead of them.

Carl tried to get a sense of where they were in relation to the border of Mexico and both New Mexico and Texas, so he concentrated on the memory of an iPad map he'd seen yesterday morning during his rescue mission. New Mexico's border with Mexico was minuscule, while the Texas border with Mexico stretched in a twelve-hundred-mile wavering line from the northwest to the southeast. He could picture the Gulfstream jet turning left and reentering US airspace in less than half an hour. That meant they were still within reach of US covert assets if their unknown adversary had them to deploy against them. If their adversary had such assets, then he or she also probably had the capability of knowing where they were and where they were heading.

He grunted.

Palmer's smile disappeared, and she said, "What are you thinking?"

Carl shifted his gaze to the right, which had him staring out the window. He felt a discomfort in his gut. "I feel like I'm running around a blind corner not knowing who's around there waiting to shoot me in the head."

He faced Palmer again, and her gaze darkened as she absorbed the implication that he didn't trust her.

He shook his head. "No, it's not you. It's not about trust."

One of the things he'd quickly learned about Agent Palmer was that the two of them seemed to be instinctively of one mind, sharing similar thoughts, though he wasn't quite sure how he'd come to that conclusion. He just *felt* it.

"But what if there's somebody *like you* on the other side?" he asked. "We still don't know who we're up against. What if there's a *McGrath* over there running the op? I keep thinking about Melissa's kidnapping. I keep thinking there's no way some drug cartel hit men could take out Melissa's security detail without inside help. Somebody powerful or highly placed must be working against us."

Palmer nodded. "We've come to the same conclusion. There must have been an informant."

Carl nodded and felt a deep sense of satisfaction that he and Palmer were indeed on the same wavelength.

She continued, "Aaron and I agree that this implies someone very high in the government is involved in the kidnapping and…"

Carl waited. He got the feeling Palmer was going to disclose some kind of secret or classified information. He didn't push her. She had to know he and his team needed all available information to succeed in their mission.

Finally, she said, "The president's chief of staff, Martine Scallow, went missing right after one of his interns contacted us about information regarding someone who may be behind the information leak."

"What does the chief of staff do?"

"He basically runs the White House operations and staff. He's the gatekeeper to the president. He controls her schedule and coordinates who has access to her in terms of meetings. Some chiefs of staff historically had a lot of clout, and some had none. Scallow is one of the more power-ful chiefs the White House has seen. Even the directors of the three-letter intel shops and the chair of the joint chiefs have to get Scallow's approval of their agenda to see President Mallory."

Carl nodded. "Has the intern been questioned?"

"He's missing too."

"So the intern is likely dead, and either Martine Scallow knew that information also and was killed, or he *is* the source." Carl paused. "And El Patron was afraid of someone equally powerful in his government. The Triad has to be very powerful to scare a veteran general." Carl thought for a moment, then said, "Is Scallow powerful enough to manipulate the Secret Service?"

"Manipulate? No. He doesn't have that kind of control. To manipu-late the Secret Service would require him to enlist the director or assistant director. However, if someone like Scallow had a cooperative Secret Service agent providing him information, then yes, he could pull it off."

"Sounds like this whole thing couldn't be just one person. Sounds more like a conspiracy, but who would benefit from kidnapping the presi-dent's daughter? Who in the government would take such a huge risk by providing this kind of intel to the Triad?"

Palmer said, "That's your line of business, right? Investment 101. High risk must equal high reward, or why make the investment, right?"

"High reward." Carl pondered El Patron's disclosure before he died about the Triad needing a monetary return on their investment. He recalled his own conclusion that this entire event must be about more than money. "So what if they know we're coming?"

"Mm-hmm. What do you want to do?"

Carl looked out the window again, but he wasn't seeing the landscape far below. He was instead formulating a plan. "Let's give 'em a head fake."

CHAPTER 12

1130 MST, FRIDAY
ALBUQUERQUE, NM

COSTAS DRAKE AND VICENTE ORIZAGA again sat on opposite sides of the tiny hotel room dining table. Blackout curtains were in place, and no lights lit the room. They had barely moved except to use the bathroom and to order out for food. The room smelled like a mixture of pepperoni pizza and Chinese takeout.

In the adjoining two motel rooms, the twenty-man unit was similarly camped out. Everyone was under strict orders to remain sequestered in the rooms. Drake didn't want to risk any of his team being seen in public. The other rooms were crowded and uncomfortable, but he knew all of his men had endured far worse during combat operations.

He and Orizaga hunched over the satellite cell phone and strained to hear Rainman's electronic voice through the speaker. The volume was turned so low that both men had to concentrate hard.

"Your team at the Chihuahua airport has the terrorist in custody?"

"No, sir," Drake said. "His plane went down in some mountainous ravines about eighty miles north of the airport."

"Went down."

There was no question mark in his voice when Rainman repeated the words with slow deliberation. Drake got the feeling his boss was deciding whether or not to believe the report. Or perhaps the man was revising his mission plan based on the news of Johnson's demise.

Fifteen seconds passed before Rainman spoke again. "This could work in our favor. Proceed as planned with your operation against your local targets tonight, but disregard Mr. Garcia. With Johnson out of the picture, Garcia is irrelevant. Recover Johnson's body from the wreckage and plant it on-site as planned. We can still blame our operations on the terrorist. The fact that he's dead is icing on the cake. Questions?"

Drake looked across the table at Orizaga, who shook his head. "None."

"Good," Rainman said. "Mr. Orizaga, thank you for personally supervising the delivery of the product and its formula, and for financing Mr. Drake and the Unit. Providing that layer of isolation between my planners and Mr. Drake's operations has ensured there are no traceable financial connections to what we are about to do."

A warning tingle sizzled up and down Drake's spine. With such an audacious plan, operational security was paramount, and the possibility that Rainman would consider Orizaga and himself to be loose ends was a very real scenario.

Rainman continued, "Please proceed back to Mexico and arrange an in-person meeting for me with the Triad to formalize our partnership three days from now. At that point, you will be a very wealthy man. The Triad will control Mexico and all of Central America, and they will share in the control of the rest of the western hemisphere. Just to be thorough, I think it's appropriate to destroy all records pertaining to this transaction. Understood?"

"*Si, señor*. I understand. This will be done."

Rainman disconnected the call on his end, and Drake blew out a breath he'd been holding for some time.

Orizaga said, "Do you think it was wise to omit the fact that the search parties have not located the wreckage yet?"

"It has only been an hour since the crash. Besides, I thought he was going to bite our heads off because of this new snag in the plan."

"He still may if we don't find the body."

CHAPTER 13

1135 MST, FRIDAY
NUEVO CASAS GRANDES, MEXICO

CARL DISEMBARKED THE PLANE IN a closed hangar building at the municipal airport in Nuevo Casas Grandes. It was the same airport he and his mercs drove by yesterday morning on the way to Alfonso Reyes's compound to rescue the president's daughter. The airport superintendent stood at the foot of the starboard door stairway, smiling widely. Carl held his twenty-five-pound duffel out but didn't let go when the airfield controller grabbed it greedily.

"This is one million dollars, US," Carl said. "You have a family, right? A wife and some children?"

The superintendent had a confused look on his face and responded in heavily accented English. "What does that have to do with anything?"

Carl suddenly made his voice hard. "I just want to make sure you understand what will happen to them if you fail to make sure my plane stays safe. No police and no army. If I encounter any surprises, I'll take *all* of your family from you, including your in-laws and cousins. Even family you never knew you had. Everybody."

Carl's assumption was that in a country where drug lords like Alfonso Reyes and high-ranking generals like El Patron wielded substantial power and control, a small airport superintendent in the sparsely populated part of the country would be accustomed and susceptible to such threats.

"Am I clear?" Carl said.

"*Si, señor*. You are very clear. There will be no surprises."

"Thank you." He let go of the duffel. "Our rental car is ready?"

The man nodded toward the office a dozen paces away. "Through the office, there is an exit door. Your car waits there."

Agent Palmer had come down the stairs behind him, so he followed her into the office at the near end of the big hangar. His legs were still a bit shaky after the pilot's crazy maneuver. With Palmer's approval, Carl had told the pilot he wanted to disappear from radar and land at the municipal airport instead of Chihuahua.

"Piece of cake," Reichert had said.

In the time it took for Carl and Agent Palmer to get back to their seats and buckle in, the colonel had put in an emergency distress call. Something about failed electrical and hydraulic systems. Halfway through his transmission, he'd rolled the Gulfstream into a steep nosedive.

As Carl had watched the ground approach much too fast, he'd regretted his change of tactics. Before the pilot pulled out of the maneuver, they were so close to the ground that Carl could see individual farmhouses, trucks, and even shrubs. Right before the plane plowed into the desert, the pilot pulled up in a maneuver that Carl had been certain would tear the wings right off the plane. The plane had leveled out thirty feet above the ground, still moving at tremendous speed.

Carl hollered up into the cockpit, "Damn, Colonel! Where'd you learn how to fly? In the Navy?" He'd swallowed his queasiness and glanced over at the agent seated beside him.

She smiled. "You okay?"

"You enjoyed that, didn't you?"

Agent Palmer had shrugged. "Part of the business. But we can go back up and grab your stomach if you want."

Carl had grunted and looked out the window as the near-barren landscape flashed by beneath the plane. "Very funny, Miss Bunny."

Now, the Gulfstream was stuffed into a hangar where it would be serviced, refueled, and kept hidden from prying eyes in orbit, if there were any satellites searching for them.

Carl wasn't just being paranoid. He had ordered the change in the game plan to keep whoever *might* be tracking them off-balance. He felt ten times more exposed in this mission than in the relatively uncomplicated operation to rescue the president's daughter. This time, he felt like he was playing chess against an unknown adversary whose capabilities he could only guess at. Maybe the pilots and Agent Palmer felt secure in their technology, but Carl had no such feelings of comfort.

They departed the Nuevo Casas Grandes municipal airport a little after eleven. Carl let Palmer drive their rental car. The SUV was a small, modern crossover with all the bells and whistles, like navigation, an iPod dock, and even seat warmers. It tried to be a cool, young-person sporty car and a small-family, sleek minivan at the same time. The back seat lacked legroom, but copilot David Blick occupied the rear seat by himself, and he was not a big man. Colonel Reichert had remained at the municipal airport to supervise the servicing of the plane.

Carl studied Agent Palmer while she drove, admiring the way her intense blue eyes kept scanning the land to her front and sides. He had noticed her constant eye movement when he first got on the plane and had tried to mimic her actions. Now, every fifteen seconds or so, she glanced in the mirrors—left mirror, center mirror, right mirror, then center again, then left again.

She seemed completely aware of her entire environment, always examining and noticing things, so Carl felt safe in her presence. He was driven by a need for justice or vengeance—he wasn't sure which—but he knew without doubt that the mission would succeed or fail because of Palmer's capabilities and not his own. Even though she was dressed in civilian clothes, he could tell by looking at her and by the way she moved, she was dangerous. In fact, she looked no less lethal in civvies than she'd looked in her black commando outfit two days ago.

As observant as she was, it shouldn't have surprised him that she noticed him looking at her. When she glanced at him, he felt a curious mixture of anger, attraction, and intrigue. He wondered how such a woman had become a deadly government agent. He wondered what she was *before*.

A couple of hours into the drive, Palmer let Blick drive and told Carl to join her in the back seat. She pulled her black canvas carry-on from the tiny trunk space behind the bench seat. When she opened it, Carl saw that it contained a variety of weapons and high-tech gear. She pulled a padded box from the bag and gave him a comm device. It was the same kind of ear device he'd seen her wearing in Virginia.

Carl was amazed by how tiny the in-ear communicators were and how securely they fit into the ear. They had rubber barbs that held them in place in the ear canal but were so comfortable, he didn't even feel its presence. Despite their small size, the devices were able to transmit and receive encrypted signals from a satellite that she said was dedicated to their mission. It was parked in a geostationary orbit a couple hundred miles above Mexico.

She tapped a couple of links on her tablet computer, and young Mr. Garcia came online immediately, as did a man named Agent Peoples at Palmer's TER op center, somewhere in Virginia.

Carl watched Agent Palmer work her tech magic as she coordinated the various support personnel. Her efficiency calmed his jitters that seemed to increase as they approached their destination.

He recalled her calming effect on him when he'd thought he was going to lose it after waking from the nightmare. Indeed, at that instant of waking on the plane, he didn't know quite where he was. He thought he was back at the scene of Mark's murder, and instead of Agent Klipser choreographing the hit and Alfonso Reyes pulling the trigger, somehow, for an instant, it became Agent Palmer doing the deed. In that instant, he wanted nothing more than to kill her, but he quickly realized she wasn't the person to bear his wrath. She seemed to know what he was feeling, and he could see an understanding in her eyes. The touch of her hand on his arm had calmed him. If not for that tender gesture, he would have tried to act on his impulse. That was how wired and out of control he was.

It wouldn't have mattered, he knew, because he sensed she was more than capable of defending herself. *A female Navy SEAL! Damn!*

He would have wrecked the tenuous truce allowing them to conduct the operation together. It would have compromised the mission, and the mission was all that mattered.

And he would have gotten his ass kicked at thirty thousand feet…by a girl!

Carl removed the communicator from his ear. "Thank you, Nancy," he whispered. "For stabilizing me on the plane. It helped, and I need that kind of help."

She looked at him and nodded but seemed to have trouble holding his gaze. In that moment, he understood the struggle she was facing. He'd seen that look before, never in battle, but in life, in relationships, and in sports. It was the look of someone who doesn't want to hurt your feelings but knows their words or actions would do exactly that.

The woman had orders to kill him if he deviated from, or jeopardized, the TER's mission objectives. Of that, he had no doubt. In fact, he accepted the reality of her dilemma. She was conflicted because she liked him. He could tell. It may not be a romantic attraction, he thought, but it was a connection beyond what was required of the mission.

He gave her his Yoda voice. "Sense the conflict within you, I do." She looked away, and he said, "We're both killers, you and I, but the difference between me and your kind is that I know who my enemies are. It's clear and simple for me, and the bad guys don't change on the whims of politics or mission objectives. I know who I have to kill, and I don't have a problem doing it. I don't take orders regarding it, so I have no conflicts about it."

"I know you're not my enemy *right now*, Carl. But what about later? What about a year from now?" She let him consider the implications of her words. "There were half a dozen people involved in the op that killed Mark. The president and Aaron and I…we *all* made the decision. What happens next year, or next decade, when you decide we *are* the enemy?"

Carl felt suddenly sobered as she finally broached the subject. He'd wanted—*needed*—to talk about it, but he hadn't been able to find the inner strength. In a way, it was a relief that she did it for him. He looked away, sucked in a deep breath, and let it out slowly.

"Believe me, I've run those same questions through my mind hundreds of times. Thousands of times. I blame Aaron McGrath more than you or the president for what happened to my son, and I keep trying and failing to find some other outcome to the last thirty days. I keep looking for some other decision that he could have made, some other *thing* I could have done, where Mark doesn't die, given what we knew at the time. But I just can't see it." He clasped his palms together and worked his fingers. "I'm just going to have to find a way to live with it."

"But can you live with working with me, with thinking every time you look at me that I'm partly to blame?"

He looked her in the eyes and said, "I guess I'll have to, won't I?" He lowered his gaze again and said, "You know, Nancy, what really hurts is knowing that the person who's really to blame is me."

She looked confused.

Carl nodded. "I baited Agent Klipser to get him to kill me because I knew the torture would never end. I'd never have been able to give him the information he needed, and he'd never have accepted that he had the wrong guy. And he almost did kill me. But if I hadn't defied him, Mark would still be alive. If I had held out on that table for another day, maybe two, Klipser would have finally realized I wasn't the guy. He'd have had to since that's when the first ransom demand came in." He went back to twiddling his fingers. "But I wasn't strong enough."

Palmer nodded. "Carl, a Navy SEAL couldn't have survived what you went through. That's why we developed the new interrogation regime…to break operators who might have been trained to resist harsh interrogations."

He looked at her. "So why didn't you stop the torture? Why didn't you reach the only possible conclusion and decide I was innocent?"

She looked him dead in the eyes and said, "Because we thought you were Alfonso Reyes. Because the odds of two unrelated men looking exactly alike were too astronomical to believe. Because you both even had the same kind of dental surgery. The only real difference between you two is that he wore glasses, and you've had laser eye surgery." She looked out the window, but Carl knew she wasn't seeing the passing landscape. When she looked back at him, her eyes had watered a bit, and that surprised him. "Carl, I'm truly sorry for what we did to you. To your son."

"I know." He sighed. "So, how do you do it, Nancy? You've been through what I'm going through. I can see it in your eyes. How do you pretend it doesn't hurt until after your mission is complete? How do you pack all that stuff away and ignore the pain and the anger?"

They talked about emotional compartmentalization until they reached the compound, but Carl got the feeling Palmer's methods involved mental trickery rather than mental toughness. She talked about building vaults inside the mind and locking away contents until he was at a time and place where he could give the emotions due consideration. She talked about pretending the event—the pain—belonged to someone else or never happened. She talked about being on the outside of the event looking in, being clinical about the event, and analyzing it from a spectator's perspective.

Mental trickery. Psyche myself into believing I'm tougher than I really am.

Nevertheless, Carl absorbed the woman's wisdom. He accepted that she was an expert in the art of war, killing, and compartmentalizing, and he listened to her until they approached the fortified wrought-iron gate of the Reyes compound.

Carl put his earpiece back in and discovered that Mr. Garcia had called ahead to warn the mercs of their arrival, but Carl and Palmer were still met by the business end of several automatic weapons. Carl was pleased to see Garcia had recruited a dozen new mercs. They looked the same as his original mercs—lean, wiry men probably with less-than-honorable discharges. They looked like men who lived for the adrenaline rush and the excitement of killing someone, anyone.

Trent Englebaum, referred to as Merc Three, had taken the leadership position over the new security guys. He exchanged words with one of the two heavily armed men at the gate. The heavy metal structure slid open just long enough for Blick to drive through.

Carl and Palmer got out while Blick parked the SUV inside the security fence near the gate. Carl liked what he saw. At least half a dozen mercenaries, all heavily armed and dressed in full tactical gear, patrolled the expansive property. And those were just the men he could see. Clearly, young Mr. Garcia had interpreted Carl's concern over the safety of the Reyes ladies properly and had deployed sufficient cash to ensure their protection.

He was just getting ready to greet Merc Three when Agent Peoples's voice in his earpiece made a startling announcement. President Mallory had just been admitted to Mountain View Regional Medical Center outside Las Cruces, where Melissa was being treated. After her speech to Congress, she'd flown back to New Mexico to be near her daughter. While being briefed by Melissa's doctors, the president became nauseous. Minutes later, she had a mild seizure and fainted. She was now reported to be in a coma.

Carl stopped in his tracks and looked at Palmer. "Those are basically the same symptoms Melissa had." Palmer nodded, and he added, "That can't be a coincidence."

Merc Three approached, and he and Carl bumped forearms. Three said, "Nice work yesterday, out there in the desert with Reyes and his crew, Boss. Real nice. Never seen a civvy get shot and still take care of business like that."

Three was a slender fellow and stood an inch taller than Carl. He had a serious face with dark eyes, shallow cheeks, and several days of razor stubble. He gave Palmer a quick up-and-down appraisal.

"So, do we trust her?" Three said with a head-nod at Palmer, like she wasn't standing an arm's length away.

Carl answered the way he thought a combat leader should. "I thought we covered that a couple days ago."

"*Riiiight.*" The man dragged out the word and nodded with a glance at Palmer. "We trust her to look after the government's interests."

Palmer said, "In this op, my interests and yours coincide."

Three looked at Carl and raised his eyebrows in question, and Carl noticed the change the mercenary had evolved through over the last seven days. He and the other three mercenaries, two of which died during this week's op, had simply hired on for the money. They craved the excitement and had initially shown disdain for Carl, who was, in their minds, merely a civilian with no combat experience and no teeth to his command presence.

That is, until his ambush dispatched the FBI SWAT team. And the elite TER tactical team.

Carl had made several more tough calls under pressure, and as a result, the mercenaries, following his instructions, had prevailed numerous times against highly trained adversaries in over-matched contests. He had earned their respect and their trust. Indeed, while Mr. Garcia had procured the services of a dozen more mercenaries, Carl was certain they only signed on because of the endorsement of Carl's two surviving mercs.

Carl nodded. "She's on our side." He paused a beat and smiled. "This week."

"Well," Three said casually. "Welcome temporarily to the team, Agent Palmer." He gave her a fist bump. To Carl, he said, "Do we have intel?"

Through their earpieces, Peoples said, "Yes, we do."

"Let's have a meeting," Carl said, looking around. "Where's Four?"

"She's coordinating a tactical defensive plan up at the house."

Three half-turned to Palmer, who followed the two men. "By the way, we received your equipment delivery this morning. A C-130 flying the colors of the Mexican Air Force air-dropped some containers out behind the house."

"A C-130?" Carl said. "Those planes were antique when I joined the Air Force thirty-five years ago."

Palmer said, "The local air guard doesn't have C-17s in its inventory, so we had to go old-school."

Merc Three chuckled. "You gonna let her get away with that, Boss? She just called you old-school."

Carl chuckled and turned toward the house. *Technically, I am old-school.*

Three added, "By the way, I don't know if you've heard, but we've got satellite support, so except for the new security boys, we're all on sat-comm now. Moving up in the world, eh, Boss?"

Carl nodded. The fact that McGrath had the clout to have a billion-dollar national security satellite asset retasked for this mission gave Carl a significant boost of confidence. Still, his paranoia lurked deep in the back of his brain.

"I want a low-tech backup plan in case we lose the satellite or have to go dark for any reason."

Three said, "You expecting trouble, Boss?"

Carl shrugged. They did, after all, lose their drone two days ago during the rescue mission to the most unexpected of circumstances.

"The shit never hits the fan when people are expecting it."

CHAPTER 14

1345 MST, FRIDAY
NORTHERN MEXICO

CARL AND AGENT PALMER WALKED a hundred yards to the front entrance of the Reyes mansion while Merc Three remained behind and handed out assignments to the gate guards. The estate of the now-captured Alfonso Reyes was located on an isolated strip of beachfront land that dipped lazily down to the water. The ten-foot-high black wrought-iron security fence surrounded the house on all four sides, though the property extended all the way down to the water and for another half mile to the north and south.

The beach faced due west, and the emerald water of the Gulf of California stretched away as far as he could see, though Carl knew Baja California sat directly west over the horizon. There was very little wave action out there, and the glass surface was dotted with yachts and fishing trawlers. The beach in front of Carl was pristine white sand, which stretched away to the south. A hundred yards to the north, rocky cliffs rose abruptly and dropped straight into the water.

On the drive from the municipal airport, Palmer had called their destination San Carlos, the seaward end of a place called Guaymas. The area wasn't completely uninhabited, but because of the huge amount of land owned by Reyes, there were no nearby structures or neighbors.

Carl was so captivated by the sight of the water, the beach, and the cliffs that he wobbled into Palmer. He reached out a hand and touched her lower back to keep himself moving in the right direction while he gazed at the scenery. He subconsciously adjusted his direction, guided by the contact of his fingertips against her back, just like a comfortable couple would do. After a few seconds, he realized what he was doing, snatched his hand away, and turned his attention back to his destination.

"Sorry."

Palmer gave him a sly sideways look and said, "It didn't hurt much."

Merc Four greeted them at the door. She and Carl bumped forearms, then she smiled and looked at Agent Palmer. "Hey, Nance."

Palmer smiled slightly. "Cassiopeia Englebaum." She stepped forward, and they hugged like old-school buddies for a moment. "Good to see you again."

Carl said, "I'd forgotten that was your name." He'd only ever referred to her as Merc Four.

Merc Four shrugged and gave him a hard smile. "What can I say? I didn't pick either one of those damn names. It was my pappy and my hubby. Bastards, both of 'em."

Carl glanced between the two female warriors. "So, you two know each other?"

"Nance and I shot it out in an all-services sniper competition a couple years ago."

Palmer said, "Only a handful of *men* on the planet could have made those shots like Cassy did from over a mile away yesterday, but when I read the after-action report and saw three tangos were hit inside of five seconds, I knew that was Cassy's handiwork."

"Tangos?" Carl said.

Palmer nodded. "Tango is the military's phonetic word for the letter T, and target starts with a T."

"I got it," Carl said. "So 'tango' is for 'target.' " He notched his eyebrows with renewed respect for his female mercenary. *Three kill shots within the space of five seconds…from a mile away!*

Despite the fact that her long-distance shooting had saved his life, he didn't know the details and wouldn't have understood their significance until just that moment when Palmer put things into proper perspective.

Merc Four said, "I always hoped we might work together again, Nance."

"*You* went to the dark side, Cassy, not me."

"Yeah, damn husband's a bad influence."

From a hundred feet away, Merc Three said, "Hey, I can hear you." He tapped his ear, where his comm device was.

The two women shared a quiet laugh. Something told Carl it was Four that could have been the bad influence on her husband. She just looked reckless, like she was addicted to adventure. Maybe they were both already bad when they met.

The word of their arrival had obviously reached the main house because the front door flew open, and eleven-year-old Julia Reyes—who pronounced her name in Spanish as *Hoo-lia*—ran down the steps. She was the stepdaughter of Carl's look-alike, Alfonso Reyes, but she didn't seem to mind his resemblance to her stepfather. After all, Reyes would have killed her along with her mother if Carl hadn't intervened. The girl raced toward him, her long braid flopping behind her head, and literally jumped into his arms with the reckless abandon of a child who knew he would catch her.

Catch her he did, then he wrapped her up in a long hug and gave her a kiss on her forehead. He instantly forgot about his mission and felt his heart melt at the presence of the young girl. As he hugged the girl, he caught Agent Palmer's gaze. She looked at him with concern but made no comment. Carl followed her gaze from Julia to her mother.

Luisa Reyes was the wife of the drug lord who had kidnapped Melissa Mallory. He was an abusive husband and an equally terrible stepfather. Carl could tell Luisa both loved and hated him because of his resemblance to her husband. Julia had inexplicably bonded with him the previous morning, and he with her. He respected her, understood her, and showed her love without conditions or judgment. He was like that with kids *before*. He was surprised and relieved to see that this part of him hadn't been destroyed by his terrorist persona.

The girl wrapped her arms around his torso and buried her cheek against his chest. He walked up the steps awkwardly, the girl sort of crab-walking backward with him.

"I knew you'd come back, Carl," she said.

She was bilingual and spoke English almost flawlessly. They hobbled together to the top of the half dozen steps, and he pried her away finally.

He cupped her cheeks in his palms, smiled down at her, and kissed her again on the forehead.

She said excitedly, "Are you gonna take us to America with you?"

"Either that, or I may just stay here with you."

The girl rattled off the Spanish translation to her mother, who now stood in the doorway. Luisa's gaze passed over Carl, Palmer, and Merc Three. Carl could clearly see that she could not separate him from her look-alike husband as easily as her daughter could. He stepped up to her and hugged her briefly, then kissed her on the cheek.

One fact of life that he knew with certainty was that a man cannot have a relationship of any kind with a girl-child without having a relationship with her mother. As he gazed into Luisa's eyes, he knew he could never have a relationship with this woman. Inner conflict swept over her countenance like alternating sunshine and storm clouds.

They had no history together, but he knew her love for him was because he had proven he would not hurt her and because he showed genuine affection for her daughter—something her husband rarely did. The hatred was because he looked exactly like her husband, and she'd always be reminded of the look-alike's abuse.

Carl understood her discomfort and was warmed as the woman managed a forced smile and even returned his hug. She was a beautiful woman by any measure. She stood about five feet five and was a petite, curvy woman with a rich cocoa skin color. She had sharp, high cheekbones and a wide mouth with full lips and dark brown eyes that were probably friendly to everyone but Carl. Her daughter looked just like her, except in an adolescent package.

Even as Julia wrapped her arms around him again, Merc Four's voice interrupted his reunion. "Let us know when the love fest is over, Boss, so we can get to business."

As everyone except the new mercs passed through the foyer and into the huge living room, Carl untangled himself from Julia's arms again and told her he'd hang out with her and her mother shortly. The two Reyes ladies went upstairs, and Carl turned his attention to Agent Palmer as Merc Three came through the foyer.

Everyone looked at Carl like he was supposed to say something. He nodded at Agent Palmer to start the briefing.

"Agent Peoples," she said. "What's your status?"

"We're fully operational on this end."

"Is Director McGrath on his feet yet?"

"Negative. His bug seems to have completely taken him out of the game."

"Bug?" Carl said.

Palmer nodded. "He thinks he picked up something at the hospital yesterday. Stephen, is there any word on Chief of Staff Martine Scallow or his intern?"

"Nothing yet."

Palmer clarified for Carl and his team. "Both have gone missing. The intern, a young man named Marcus Aurelio, contacted Agent Peoples yesterday claiming to have information about who may have provided classified information to Melissa's kidnappers. Agent Peoples arranged a meeting, but the intern never showed, and now, Martine Scallow has also dropped off the radar."

Agent Peoples added, "Our operating assumption is that Scallow and his intern somehow discovered the traitor's identity and have been targeted."

Palmer said, "Are any other personnel missing?"

"I've got analysts at the main office looking into that. It's a big government, but I should have something within the hour."

"Have your analysts start at the top and work their way down."

"Roger that. Top-down."

There was a moment of silence, then Carl said, "Okay, you're up, Four. What's our defensive situation here?"

He listened while Merc Four explained weapons status and placement and her tactical plans, but most of the military jargon went in one ear and out the other. He'd watched plenty of war movies and action flicks, but in the real world, he didn't speak that language. She talked about assault paths, choke points, defensive measures, counterattacks, and evac routes.

Four continued, saying, "Apparently, Reyes was a bit paranoid. He has a helicopter parked out back. Looks like a modified EC14—a luxury Mercedes twin-engine taxi that seats eight. Probably set him back a nifty eight million."

Merc Three said, "Pocket change for a guy like Reyes."

Carl corrected him. "Pocket change for a guy like me now, since I have all of his $500 million."

"Four hundred eighty-seven million and change," Garcia added. "To be precise."

Three waved a hand through the air. "Who's counting pennies?"

Carl looked at Merc Four. "You were saying?"

"We also have Reyes's armored personnel carrier hidden in an underground bunker on the other side of that hill out yonder." Four pointed out the window, where a fifty-foot grassy knoll swept down to the surf beyond the expansive house. "Reyes owns everything you can see along the beach for a mile total and a quarter mile inland. The underground bunker is actually serviced by a tunnel leading from the basement garage of the house to the inland road. A couple of armored cars are parked in the basement garage just in case an emergency evac is needed."

She spent considerable time outlining their escape plan, noting that it wouldn't be difficult for their adversary to figure out the disposition of Carl's defensive forces since they were on land and stationary. They had to be prepared for the very real possibility that a determined force of significant size could overrun the estate, especially if accompanied by one or more armed choppers. Everyone had to be prepared for an immediate evacuation at the first sound of the alarm or the first sign of attack.

Merc Four outlined the equipment provided by Mr. Garcia's suppliers and by Agent Palmer's TER resources. They had what was called a man-portable short-range radar unit. Its range was limited by its low power, but that was countered by the advantage of its emissions not being detectable by any force more than two or three miles away. They also had half a dozen antiaircraft missiles to combat helicopters or low-flying fighters. They had armor-piercing RPGs, two miniguns to discourage a ground assault, and a brand spanking new truck-mounted 50-cal machine gun for antipersonnel work.

When it was time to abandon the mansion, they could use the armored SUVs in the basement garage, Reyes's armored speedboat tied down at the dock, or the topside APC—armored personnel carrier.

He sensed Four was primarily reviewing the plan for her husband's clarification and to bring Palmer up to date. The review also gave Carl reassurance that the dozen mercenaries on guard could handle a sizable invasion force, at least until the civilians could be evacuated. Palmer nodded as Four concluded.

Palmer looked at Carl and said, "All right, I recommend everyone get rested and fed while we wait for actionable intel from Agent Peoples. You never know when your next meal or nap will come."

Everyone left the main room to attend to their own manner of rest or food. Carl took an energy bar from his duffel and sat out on the veranda facing the beach. The heat from the sun soothed him and helped him relax, and he allowed his eyes to become hypnotized by the slight undulations on the surface of the water offshore. Even though the temperature was in the low eighties, there was a slight breeze out of the west that kept him cool.

He tried to practice Palmer's suggestions about putting specific memories into compartments, but the effort only slid the faces he didn't want to see across the inner view screen of his mind, like a picture slide show. He saw the girl he almost tortured, Lisette Cummings, as well as her mother. He saw the battered and bloody face of Anita Chapman. He saw the bullet-ridden corpse of his son, Mark, and the blood pooling beneath his body on the concrete in front of the young man's apartment.

Like an intrusion of light into darkness, Carl saw the smiling face of Julia Reyes. Next, he envisioned the two kids he had saved, Melissa Mallory and Rainey, and a feeling of warmth spread through him. He'd done something good by those three kids, and the warmth he felt gave him purpose. It balanced the evil he felt he was becoming.

He took a deep breath and focused on a luxury yacht slowly cruising by a quarter mile off the coast. Two of the black-clad mercs on fence patrol studied the yacht through binoculars for a moment, then continued their patrol. Carl took one last look around and went back inside, intending to find an empty bedroom suite to do an hour of yoga, then take a shower, then get a meal. He decided on one of the two downstairs suites rather than upstairs, where the mercs were bunked, and headed toward the room farthest from the living room.

He opened the door and stepped in, then froze. There she stood, right in front of him, stark naked.

CHAPTER 15

1420 MST, FRIDAY
NORTHERN MEXICO

"WE HAVE DISCOVERED THE IDENTITY and other personal information of El Patron," Agent Peoples said over the comm channel.

Carl nodded to the team gathered before him in the living room. "Excellent."

"Analysis of his financial records shows that his accountant is an individual recently flagged by Homeland Defense as a possible terror suspect based on the substantial size of several recent cash transactions to and from offshore accounts operated by US dummy corporations. This accountant, Vicente Orizaga, has recently brokered several indeterminate deals, each over one hundred million US dollars. Cash was moved roughly every four months since February of last year. His personal account shows that he took a 2 percent fee in each of the three transactions. We're working on tracing the ownership of these corporations, but that may take some time.

"Mr. Orizaga has also been known to manage transactions for several prominent Mexican political leaders and influential action groups. Queries we've made to high-profile international accountant groups indicate that if the Triad was looking for a CPA, Orizaga is the one they'd use. We believe the Triad is a collection of three very wealthy power brokers, but that conclusion is partly based on Orizaga's recent transactions. We have no specific records of their identities, so we have no actionable intel yet."

Palmer said, "What is the likelihood that Orizaga is involved with the kidnapping of the First Daughter?"

Peoples said, "There is no evidence yet, but computer analysis gives a 38 percent probability that he is involved."

"I'd double that probability," Carl said. When everyone looked at him, he said, "You've got some entity, probably this Triad, who invests several hundred million on *something* with the same CPA that works for an army general, who was definitely involved with Alfonso Reyes, who kidnapped Melissa Mallory, and twice demanded $250 million in ransom."

Carl paused while his audience absorbed his interpretation. "The general was deathly afraid of these investors—and I use the term *investors* only because that's the term the general used with me. So I figure the ransom money was his opportunity to pay them back for some kind of short-term loan, plus interest."

Peoples objected. "It doesn't take $500 million, or even a tenth of that, to organize and fund a kidnapping operation. Not even if the target is the First Daughter."

"Precisely," Carl agreed. "Kinda makes me wonder what *does* cost several hundred million. And why the hell would they try for such a high-risk target like the president's daughter? I mean, seriously, there's got to be people or kids you can kidnap to raise that kind of money and not have to go up against the Secret Service."

Palmer added, "You're suggesting Melissa Mallory was essential to the operation?"

Carl shrugged. "Maybe they demanded a ransom just to make it *seem* like a kidnapping. Maybe they were trying to cover up a different objective. I don't know." He looked around the room. "At the exchange site yesterday, Alfonso Reyes decided to shaft the general and his investors and tried to keep the money. He gave his man the order to kill Melissa, and his own wife and daughter."

Palmer nodded and said, "So, maybe Reyes was just a tool. Maybe he wasn't part of the larger plan. Maybe he had his own agenda."

Carl nodded. "Something changed. Something happened to upset the master plan. The general's plan *and* Reyes's plan."

"Not some*thing*," Palmer said. "Some*one*."

She stopped talking, and everyone stared at Carl. He got the feeling he was the focus of a secret that everyone but him knew.

"What?" he said.

Palmer said, "*You* happened, Carl."

Carl looked up at the ceiling for a moment, struggling to keep the imagery of Mark's death in its assigned vault until later. Finally, he scanned the room. "So, maybe Alfonso Reyes was under orders to release Melissa all along. And I nearly fucked the whole thing up by involving Reyes's wife and child." Carl's gaze went to infinity as he recalled the confrontation. "Reyes lost his composure and tried to kill the girl because of me."

Merc Four shook her head. "You saved her by taking that shot in the back."

"Hell, the whole op nearly went to shit *because* I was involved. If anyone else had went to get her yesterday, the trade would have gone smoothly."

Palmer shook her head. "I'm having trouble believing that. We went over your scenario from every possible angle, and it made absolute sense."

"Just like your analysis led to…" Carl looked at Palmer and swallowed the words he really wanted to say. *To my son's death.* Instead, he closed his eyes and said, "To everyone believing *I* was Alfonso Reyes."

Agent Peoples said, "I've read all the after-action reports, so maybe a fresh perspective might help?"

Carl took a deep breath and nodded.

Agent Palmer said, "Go ahead."

"Clearly, the general and his people anticipated a double-cross from Reyes because he showed up with offensive assets. His assets were likely prepped long before the trade site was specified, and he was airborne before your people were in place, Mr. Johnson. He knew something about Reyes that we don't know. I'm thinking Reyes planned to kill Melissa all along. Even if he couldn't escape, he knew the general wouldn't kill him because that man wanted his money back. I think Reyes saw an opportunity to blame the whole thing on Johnson. Melissa Mallory was destined to die, except Johnson took the bullets for her. It's extremely likely that if another retrieval team had gone down there, Melissa would have died."

Everyone was silent for a moment.

Carl said, "Okay, so except for Reyes's double-cross, Melissa was originally supposed to be released. Why?"

Palmer echoed his concern. "What's worth the risk of being hunted forever by US covert forces?"

Merc Three said, "Unless you had inside information and knew the US wouldn't be hunting you."

Four added, "Who has the power to stop a manhunt?"

Palmer shook her head. "No one. The president has majority support in the House and the Senate. Once Congress agrees to a covert war, only the president can stop it."

Carl said, "So, the question I think we should be asking is not why Melissa was released, but why she was *taken.*"

"Well," Merc Four slapped her knees and stood up. "Why don't we go ask this Orizaga fellow? Worst case, we make a mistake but find out he's not involved. And the world has one less money-laundering accountant after we kick his ass. Best case, he points us to someone else involved at a higher level. Hell, maybe he can give us the Triad's identities."

"I like the way you think." Carl gave the female merc a sly grin. "Agent Peoples, does Orizaga have an office around here?"

There was a pause, and Carl imagined Agent Peoples consulting with his analysts.

"He has no office, but according to his business registration documents, he's a home-based freelancer. His home is an old, fourteen-thousand-square-foot plantation house on six hundred acres about a two-hour drive north of your current location. Twenty miles west-northwest of Hermosillo. Satellite maps show it's pretty barren country."

Carl stood. "Well, let's go say hello."

"Actually," Peoples said. "I've just been told Señor Orizaga is in Albuquerque. He is registered at the Hyatt Downtown. He checked in three days ago, but no one has seen or heard from him since. His current whereabouts are unknown."

"Another missing person," Carl said. "Interesting."

Palmer said, "Is his house vacant, then?"

Peoples said, "Negative. Records show he has three generations of family members living at the residence."

Merc Three said, "So a daytime covert entry is not possible. I recommend three mercenaries, plus myself, go along to keep the family and any security under control while you two"—he pointed two fingers at Carl and Palmer—"check his office safe and computer for relevant information."

Peoples objected, "This is an off-the-books op. That rendition protocol expired when Melissa was brought back across the border. We can't risk US involvement in an illegal home invasion."

"The American Terrorist has his own operational protocols," Carl said.

"But Agent Palmer—"

"Has no authority on this team outside of being an observer. The US is absolved of involvement in this op in case things do go south." He looked over to the government agent for approval.

"Agreed," she said.

Carl added, "Besides, too many coincidental things are happening very quickly, and we need answers."

"I agree," Palmer said. "Let's go see what we can learn. Agent Peoples, can you—"

"Stand by."

Mr. Garcia's voice came on the line. "So what's our backup plan, Boss?"

"Backup plan?" Palmer said.

Garcia said, "You know, for when the shit hits the proverbial fan."

Carl chuckled. "On your end, Mr. Garcia, the fallback plan remains the same. Drop everything, grab the family, and get the hell outa town. On this end, if things go sideways, we'll rally back at the airport."

Peoples came back on. "I just received an update on President Mallory's condition. She remains in a coma as a result of her seizure. We couldn't wake Director McGrath, so we called an ambulance."

Suddenly, Carl gasped at the impossible. "Fuck *me!*" he said. "This whole thing wasn't about a kidnapping. This was about assassinating the president of the United States! And they used her daughter to do it."

CHAPTER 16

1530 MST, FRIDAY
NORTHERN MEXICO

MERC FOUR NARROWED HER EYES. "Are you suggesting they used the president's daughter as a carrier to infect her mother?"

"If they did, it's an incredibly fast-acting agent," Palmer said. "It's been—what?—a day between when she got her daughter back and her seizure?"

Three shook his head. "That can't be it. Reyes's men handled her at the trade site yesterday, and none of them wore any kind of protective breathing gear. Not even gloves." He pointed at Carl. "And you touched her too, but you're not sick."

Palmer said, "Maybe it's some kind of DNA cocktail. The president and Aaron McGrath are her parents, and they're both sick."

"Well, they're not dead yet," Carl said. "If it's a biological or chemical agent, then there's an antidote for it. I say we continue the mission and find out what Orizaga knows." He looked around and found the others nodding.

"Mr. Blick, can you fly a helicopter?"

"I can fly anything."

"Let's get moving then."

Aboard Alfonso Reyes's luxury helicopter, no one spoke during most of the thirty-minute trip northward. Carl kept his thoughts focused on his son's life and death, on Melissa Mallory's rescue, and on the elaborate ruse to assassinate America's first female president. He watched the shadows lengthen on the ground that passed beneath the chopper. The blue-green water of the Gulf turned to hues of yellow, orange, and red in line with the setting sun. They had maybe half an hour remaining before sunset.

He glanced out the right window at the city of Hermosillo. Lights were coming on, and he could see the neon signage of many international brands. He couldn't read the words on the bright signs, but he recognized the logos—Walmart, McDonald's, Home Depot, Dairy Queen, and IHOP.

"Agent Peoples, are you with us?"

"I am."

"What do we know about this city?"

"Hermosillo is the capital of the state of Sonora. It is also the sixteenth largest city in Mexico. It has a population of about eight hundred thousand, give or take, and its primary business sector is manufacturing. Cars mostly, but also electronics—televisions and cell phones and IT-related computer equipment."

Carl said, "So, if something says *Made in Mexico,* it probably comes from here."

"Well, I'm not sure—"

"Doesn't matter. Please continue."

"Hermosillo and all of the state of Sonora is on Mountain Standard Time. The altitude of Hermosillo is about seven hundred feet above sea level. The area has had fairly explosive growth in the last few years at 2.5 percent per year, so the population is putting pressure on the infrastructure. The water table is now lower than sea level, and salt-water creep into the water supply is a constant problem. The average low temperature for December is fifty degrees at night, while the average high temperature during the daytime is seventy-seven. Right now, the temperature is eighty-two, and lately, the nighttime temperature has been in the low sixties.

"Vicente Orizaga's homestead is located in a wide valley, in a somewhat hilly part of the country. The roads in the area are unpaved, and his nearest neighbor is five miles to the north in a completely separate valley. I might add that the local airport—General Ignacio Pesqueira Garcia International, which features mostly flights to other Mexican airports and a few flights to Phoenix and Los Angeles—is like your airport in Albuquerque. It doubles as an air force base."

My airport?

Carl pondered that for a moment as the helicopter approached the Orizaga plantation from the southwestern quadrant. He'd arrived in Albuquerque when he was twenty-eight and had lived there for the better part of twenty-five years. Albuquerque was home for him. *Before.* He wondered where home would be in the future. So much had changed for him in the last thirty days. Even though the president had pardoned him for his terrorist activities, everyone he loved and nearly everyone who knew him lived in Albuquerque. They wouldn't forget what he'd done, who he'd become.

Mark moved out from Alabama after graduating high school and lived with Carl for three years. Then he lived on his own for another nine years, just across town. Carl knew that if he stayed in Albuquerque now, he'd see Mark's face at every restaurant they'd ever visited—every theater, every store, and every park.

Carl felt someone touch his arm, and he jerked away. In that same instant, his sojourn into deep thought ended, and he realized he was clutching the armrests of his seat with a death grip. He didn't realize he had closed his eyes, but when he opened them and looked around, he noticed everyone in the helicopter except the pilot was looking at him. It was Agent Palmer who had touched his arm and brought him back to the here and now.

Merc Three said, "You okay, Boss?"

Carl grunted at the man. "No, I'm not okay. I was thinking about my dead son." He took a deep breath and looked out his window at the approaching homestead. "Getting myself motivated."

Palmer said, "Agent Peoples, ping the property. See if there are any cell phones, landlines, or internet connections."

The agent did not answer.

"Stephen, are you there?"

There was a click and a momentary squeal that was barely audible, then the comm channel was silent.

CHAPTER 17

TER Agent Stephen Peoples was the senior of the two analysts on duty, the other being Monroe Petrelli. Technically, he was a field agent, but he had been reassigned as McGrath's second-in-command after Agent Fredericks's accident the previous day. Since Aaron McGrath was incapacitated, Peoples was now serving as the TER commander for the ongoing mission to find and punish the people responsible for kidnapping the president's daughter.

The mission had taken on an entirely new dimension with Johnson's premise that the kidnapping of Melissa Mallory had been a clever ruse to use her as a carrier to infect—to *assassinate*—the president. The premise was so far-fetched as to be almost without credibility. Still, Peoples knew he had to pass up the chain of command any and every possibility, no matter how ridiculous it sounded. Problem was, he had only the word of a known terrorist who was consulting on McGrath's operation.

Peoples found it unfathomable that a senior military officer from a neighboring ally would be hip-deep in the plot. And for a high-level official in the US government to be complicit in such a plot—according to the intern, Marcus Aurelio—was beyond incredible.

Peoples paused in his discussion with Palmer's tactical team. He sat at the management workstation behind Monroe's analyst station and read the two new alerts that just came in over the classified net.

He had reviewed TER agency protocol regarding who he was to

report to. Technically, every TER commander reported directly to the TER director, and the director reported only to the president. McGrath was both event commander and TER director, and now he was incapacitated, as was the president.

It followed that Peoples, as acting mission commander, should report to an assistant director in the TER chain of command. However, Vice President Walter Breen disagreed in his phone call half an hour ago. The vice president's logic was that Peoples, as a replacement commander in McGrath's operation, should report directly to Breen in the absence of the president. Peoples was not comfortable with that conclusion without researching the protocol regulations, and that's exactly what he told the vice president.

There were several levels of senior assistant directors in the TER chain of command, but what complicated his circumstance was that McGrath himself was personally involved in the operation. The man was, in fact, operating several levels below his own pay grade, but his director stamp was all over this operation. Now, Peoples had to figure out whether or not his new position included all the perceived director-level authorities McGrath had previously established in this particular terror event.

The TER regs were crystal clear about one thing. It was his prerogative as a TER mission commander to validate his reporting chain of command, and he could tell Vice President Breen knew it. So the man didn't push the issue. He reluctantly gave Peoples time to research the proper procedure and advised him to keep the issue in-house—which meant *to himself.* Breen said there were extraordinarily sensitive classified details that Breen knew and Peoples needed to know to continue his op.

Peoples was wary of the cloak-and-dagger claim of additional sensitive information. The TER had access to all classified intel from every source in the country, including the Department of Defense, the Central Intelligence Agency, and all other federal, state, and local police departments. It was impossible to believe the vice president would have access to information not already available to Agent Peoples. The TER had access to *everything,* but Peoples was senior enough to understand the mechanics of politics. Vice President Breen wanted control of the operation. He was making a power play. Peoples had no problem with that, as long as it didn't require him to break any protocols. He knew he would yield to the vice president, but he still had an hour to call him back.

Upon hearing the news that McGrath's condition had worsened, the vice president had ordered Peoples to call paramedics. Just now, the flash intel traffic indicated the CDC (Centers for Disease Control and Prevention), working with USAMRIID (United States Army Medical Research Institute for Infectious Diseases), verified the complete quarantine by National Guard personnel of the hospital in south-central New Mexico, where the president and her daughter were being treated. The town of Las Cruces had been isolated as well.

The next intel flash announced a similar quarantine order was instituted at Andrews Air Force Base in Maryland after the entire flight crew of *Marine One* had been stricken by bouts of nausea. Yet another quarantine order had been issued for Holloman Air Force Base near Las Cruces, where *Air Force One* was now parked. Several members of both flight crews had been hospitalized with seizures, and two had died within the hour as a result of what was being reported as a complete neurological collapse. In addition, an outbreak was being reported at a combat helicopter squadron on the army base in El Paso.

Even as Peoples read the reports, mentally preparing a quick summary for Agent Palmer, a chime echoed from his workstation, and he pulled up the notification window. Two paramedics were at the front door with a gurney. He used his wireless mouse to approve access for the medics. The notification window showed the ceiling-mounted security camera view inside the front door, and Peoples watched the TER guard open the door. He then returned his attention to the report on the quarantines. He was just about to turn and toss his first question to Monroe when he heard the analyst gasp. He heard the familiar popping sound of a Taser gun being activated.

Peoples knew instantly the TER op station had been breached. The paramedics were not who they appeared to be, and he had let them in. Instinct and training took over immediately as he pivoted back toward his management station and reached for the emergency alert button wired into everyone's desk. The alarm would sound back at the TER agency headquarters, and within minutes, a SWAT team would arrive to determine the extent of the incursion, and if necessary, they would use deadly force to retake the facility. More important, all computer and communication assets of the station would immediately be purged. That action would prevent the compromise of comm circuits and classified information by the invading force.

It took Peoples barely half a second to reach the button, but an instant before his plunging palm made contact, he felt an unbearable pain rip through his body. He crashed into the workstation, missing the button, and his body hit the floor. The fiery pain receded, but he was still aware of the spasms continuing to ripple through him as a result of his electrified nerves.

He heard the clap of a suppressed gunshot and knew his analyst was dead. He saw a pair of boots appear near his head. One of the boots shoved roughly at his shoulder, pushing him from his side onto his back. He looked up at the paramedic impostor, then focused on the gun the man held. It was pointed at his face.

The man said, "Your boy Marcus says hello."

Agent Stephen Peoples focused on the black orifice of the weapon pointed at his head and actually saw the flash of white light that marked the end of his life.

CHAPTER 18

1742 EST, FRIDAY
UNDISCLOSED TER OP STATION, VIRGINIA

THE PARAMEDIC IMPOSTOR SPOKE TO the empty room. "Rainman, this is Spoke. The TER op station assigned to the Melissa Mallory event is secure."

"Sterilize the station. With Johnson dead, we no longer need that asset."

Spoke sat at Agent Peoples's management console and previewed the activity log as Rainman gave instructions. He worked the keyboard and mouse with latex-gloved hands.

"Hmm," Agent Spoke said. "Now, *this* is interesting."

"Yes?"

"Sir, I'm looking through the last hour of log entries, and it appears Johnson is not dead."

"We were told his plane crashed. Drake's in-country Unit personnel reviewed the radar track. The plane went down."

"The plane may have gone below radar coverage, but it did not crash. He and a small party just left the Reyes compound. They're heading for Vicente Orizaga's homestead."

There was a long silence.

"Bastard is crafty. I'll give him that." Rainman paused. "Very well. Sever the satellite comm circuits into and out of central Mexico. But keep the secondary channel to Albuquerque open. I want you to keep Mr.

Garcia on a tight leash. He may be able to provide us with intel on John-son's movements before we eliminate him later this evening."

The second paramedic impostor entered the living room that served as the operations center of the safe house. That man had just returned from the back of the house and his assignment to kill the other guard.

Rainman's voice continued, "Attempt to back-trace Garcia's location. Unit personnel in Albuquerque are standing by for his coordinates."

"Understood."

"When you have Garcia's location, evacuate McGrath's operations center and burn the house."

"What about Aaron McGrath?"

"What's his condition?"

Spoke skimmed a few entries on the monitor. "Still unconscious, ac-cording to the log."

"He is likely in a coma from which he will not recover, but I don't want to take the chance that he might regain consciousness, even tempo-rarily. Have you touched him or anyone else?"

"Negative. Your orders were quite clear."

There was a long pause on the channel, and Spoke waited patiently.

Rainman said, "Fine. Leave McGrath in the house when you burn it."

"There's something else, sir."

Rainman waited, then said, "Well, don't make me beg."

"Yes, sir. I was doing a keyword search of the logs and audio record-ings." He didn't know any way to sugarcoat what he'd found, so he just said it. "You're not going to like this, but several keywords regarding the chief of staff have had recent activity. It looks like Agent Peoples was co-ordinating with the TER main office at Bolling Air Force Base to log the current locations of all senior government personnel. No doubt they're looking for other officials with whereabouts unknown."

"I will be on that list, along with my primary supporters. By moving everyone to the bunker, I may have moved too soon on that front."

"Johnson also posited the theory that Melissa's kidnapping was planned as a method to infect the president and assassinate her."

"Fuck!"

There was a loud noise in the background, and Spoke envisioned Rainman pounding a fist on a table. Rainman took a deep breath and cursed again. Spoke could never remember his handler losing his composure like that.

"Who the hell is this guy? Are we sure Carl Johnson was only a civilian? Could he possibly have been a deep-cover operator or military intelligence?"

Spoke shook his head, though he knew Rainman couldn't see the gesture. "Everything we know about him, everything the TER and the CIA knows, says he's just a real estate broker. He's a former Air Force officer and engineer. No combat training, no command experience, no covert operations." Spoke paused. "He's just crazy lucky, sir."

"*Lucky?* He killed or injured thirty highly trained federal officers and field agents last week with only a couple mercenaries. He found someone to hack into the secure FBI system, and he stole and laundered $500 million into untraceable offshore accounts. Where the hell is he finding this kind of talent? How does a civilian even know what kind of talent to look for?"

Spoke remained silent.

"Hell, he single-handedly almost blew our entire operation by going down there to rescue the girl. He killed Reyes and made a deal with our man, El Patron, then convinced Aaron McGrath to order a decorated Air Force combat pilot to fire a missile *across the border* and kill our guy. Ten months of planning almost went up in smoke because of one man. One lousy fucking civilian."

August Spoke said, "Actually, sir, Alfonso Reyes was not killed. My keyword search on his name shows that he was delivered by Johnson's mercs to the in-country CIA station chief, who transported him last night to the TER facility in Virginia for interrogation."

Rainman was silent for so long, Spoke thought he had disconnected the channel. Finally, the man gave his instructions. "August," he said quietly. "*This. Man. Must. Die.* He is your top priority now. I don't care how you do it or how much collateral damage is required. Carl Johnson is dangerous. Find him and kill him!"

"Understood."

The comm channel beeped its disconnection tone, and Spoke sat motionless at the terminal for a moment, then continued reviewing TER reports and files. When he finished, he knew exactly how and why

Johnson had become so successful as the American Terrorist. The man created his own rules of war. He was unpredictable and hadn't yet been successfully profiled by the best law enforcement people in the country.

So how do you kill a man who has nothing left to live for and doesn't care if he lives or dies?

CHAPTER 19

"**W**HAT THE HELL JUST HAPPENED?" Carl said.

All contact had instantly been lost with the TER op station, with Mr. Garcia in Albuquerque and with the mercs at the Reyes mansion.

Palmer said, "I don't know, but this is not good."

Carl had spoken quietly in his surprise over the sudden disconnection. Still getting used to not having to shout like everyone did in helicopters in the movies, he was surprised again by the fact that she heard him. But like everything else Reyes had owned, the Mercedes aircraft was top of the line. Eight million dollars' worth of comfort in a helicopter included a nearly silent and very plush interior. The seat cushions were memory foam and covered in supple, beige leather. There were four rows of seats behind the pilot, two abreast. There was an empty row directly behind Carl and Palmer, and three of the new mercs occupied the last two rows while Merc Three sat in the copilot seat at the front right.

Merc Three turned in the copilot seat and said, "You got that right. You gave us a broke-ass satellite!"

Palmer shook her head. "Satellites don't break. One of the reasons they're so expensive is because they're exhaustively tested and built from the highest quality components available. The government doesn't go with the lowest bidder on these. They do it right. Even if our channel did fail, it would have been immediately switched to one of a dozen backup circuits. We wouldn't even have lost a millisecond of comm."

Carl said, "You're implying someone repositioned the satellite or just turned off our channel?"

Merc Three said, "Who would do that?"

Palmer said, "A better question is who *could* do that. Very few people have the authority to preempt a TER operation or retask a classified satellite. That kind of authority comes from way up."

Carl narrowed his eyes. "How high up?"

Palmer hesitated. "Higher than Aaron McGrath, and he answers directly to the president."

"Well, shit," Merc Three muttered. "Are you telling me we're getting butt-fucked by the president after saving her girl?"

Carl shook his head. "Shirley Mallory is in a coma."

Three said, "At least, that's what they're telling us."

Carl added, "What about the chief of staff? He's either missing or in hiding. Does he have that kind of authority?"

Three said, "I'm not really up to date on political hierarchy. How high up is the chief of staff?"

Carl said, "Right up next to the president. Literally."

"Higher than the vice president?"

"Negative," Palmer said. "If something happens to the president, the vice president becomes president, and the chief of staff becomes the new president's chief, unless he is replaced. Basically, the chief of staff is the manager of the White House staff and is the president's executive assistant. There are some that describe the typical chief of staff as being the *co-president*, or the gatekeeper to the president, because of the control and influence that person has.

"The chief of staff controls not only the president's schedule, but they also control who is allowed to see the president. Some of the chiefs of staff of past administrations have even met with senior administration officials *for* the president—from the intelligence chiefs, to the heads of the military departments, to other lesser departments. From that perspective, the chief of staff has enormous influence. Martine Scallow's influence is in the upper-middle range of that power regime. Certainly, all director-level department heads have to go through Scallow to see President

Mallory, but he rarely meets with senior political officials in her place. Although, he has probably held some of her meetings during this crisis with her daughter."

Carl digested her information. "It sounds like you're saying Scallow is a very powerful person with a lot of influence, but maybe not with the authority to command the kinds of activities we've seen arrayed against us."

Palmer nodded.

Three said, "Well, maybe he's using his powerful influence to command people who do have authority to do these things."

Palmer nodded again. "That means he could be the information leak behind Melissa's kidnapping, or someone he controls could be."

Carl nodded. "And he disappeared, either right before or right after his intern called Agent Peoples."

Merc Three said, "Well, who's in charge up there now? The VP? Can we warn him somehow? Maybe he's next on Scallow's hit list."

"We're just guessing about things and people that we really don't know anything about," Carl said. "Maybe whoever this is thought we'd interpret it as a signal to abandon the mission." He looked at Agent Palmer, and she shook her head.

"A mission cancellation would come through TER channels," she said.

Carl said, "That means the satellite comms were shut down intentionally by someone outside the Terror Event Response agency."

Palmer said, "Or by a new authority in control of the TER."

Merc Three said, "If they wanted to terminate the mission, all they had to do was give the order to Miss Government Agent here. She'd terminate the mission and us."

Carl glanced at Agent Palmer, and she gave him a down-up head-nod. He could see in her eyes she'd do it too.

She wouldn't like it. He saw that in her eyes too. *But she'd follow orders. And she wouldn't hesitate. With her, the mission always came first. Whatever the mission happened to be. No matter what the mission morphed into.*

Palmer said, "Except they'd need the satellite link to relay that order."

Carl broke the long silence that followed by saying, "So they're trying to isolate us. Why?"

No one said anything.

"We *really* need to know who our enemy is in our own government."

"At this point, *who* it is doesn't really matter," Palmer said. "Based on what El Patron said to Carl, we've been assuming he and his associates had high-level informants or partners in our government. They confirmed that when they jammed our comms."

Merc Three said, "In which case, we're fucked because we're going into this mission blind now."

Palmer nodded. "Worst case, they've compromised TER, and we no longer have government support."

"In which case, we're *royally* fucked because they now know everything the TER op center knows about why we're down here." Merc Three cursed some more. "We're in a foreign country, without support, and our visas were just expired. You know what I'm saying?"

Carl said, "Okay, so now they know we didn't crash. Took 'em long enough." He considered several mission options in his mind for a moment. "But I can think of an even worse scenario."

Everyone looked at him.

Carl pulled the tiny comm device from his ear and seemed to study it as he continued, "What if they only disabled the receive circuit on these things but left the transmit circuit live and can hear every word we say?"

Merc Three said, "Hell, what if they can track us with these things? You know, like GPS or something." He pulled his comm out, as did everyone else.

Everyone dropped their device to the carpeted floor, and stomping sounds echoed throughout the interior for several seconds.

Carl nodded. "So, McGrath's team is no longer calling the shots."

Merc Three grunted. "We *think* McGrath is no longer calling the shots."

"Maybe," Carl said. "Whoever is in control wants us to cease and desist. That tells me we're on the right track."

"It's not McGrath," Palmer said. "I promise you that. But whoever they are, we're a threat to them."

Three nodded. "If they really want us isolated, the first thing they'll do is notify Mexican authorities. They'll manufacture some kind of story about how dangerous we are, and they'll send the big guns after us."

Palmer agreed. "If they've shut down my op center, they'll also go after Mr. Garcia because they'll assume that you and he have a backup method to communicate."

"There is no backup communication plan other than by cell phone, so as long as I don't call him, there's no chance they'll find him," Carl said. "I told him about this quote my pops used to say. 'When the shit hits the fan, get out of the fan business.' As soon as we went dark, Garcia automatically packed his bags, grabbed his family and some money, and left the city."

Merc Three said, "Maybe we should head back. If they're trying to terminate this mission, the first thing they'll do is hit the Reyes house and send out a team to greet us at our destination."

Carl looked out the window at the approaching homestead. It was early evening, and lengthening shadows from the nearby hills were crawling across the valley floor. The homestead was well-lit by perimeter and interior lights. The sky was still bright overhead, and full darkness was still maybe thirty minutes away.

He turned his attention back to his team, glancing from Merc Three to Palmer and back. He turned sideways in his seat and gazed at the other three intense-looking mercenaries behind him. One was a Black man about Carl's complexion. The second was many shades darker than Carl. The third was a short, brown-eyed redhead who looked like he could win the Arkansas hog-wrestling championship. Everyone seemed to be waiting for him to decide, so he made the only call he knew was viable.

"Their action plan or their timetable is vulnerable. They think we can do some damage or shed some unwanted scrutiny on their plan. They'll know I won't be discouraged. So they'll keep trying to stop us until they succeed. If there is a strike planned against the Reyes mansion, we can't get back there in time to make a difference, and I'm pretty certain Merc Four will have arrived at the same conclusions that we have. I'm guessing she's already taking precautions." He glanced forward at Three, who nodded. "We need answers, and those answers are potentially right below us."

Palmer nodded. "Our adversary likely knows we're on the way to Orizaga's house."

Three said, "And they won't be sending luxury helicopters after us."

Carl remembered El Patron's spectacular arrival at the hostage exchange site in an army helicopter troopship. He was accompanied by a gunship that blew their surveillance drone out of the sky and killed Merc Two with simultaneous missile strikes. That kind of firepower would make short work of their luxury helicopter if it came to a fight.

He knew their adversaries wouldn't send under-matched rent-a-cops, either. He didn't know for sure, but he was guessing that Mexico had SWAT cops as well-trained as their US counterparts. They probably had Mexican anti-terrorist soldiers like Delta or SEALs in their army too. The question in Carl's mind was how long it would take their adversary to convince the Mexican government to deploy forces against them.

"Well," Carl said with a shrug. "Nobody said war was fair." He looked around the cabin again. "Anybody wants out, there's the door." He thumbed toward the passenger slider beside him, even though they were still flying five hundred feet up.

One of the mercs behind him said, "Hoo-wah!"

To Agent Palmer, he said, "We need intel, so let's go get some."

She nodded. He raised his voice a bit to address the helicopter pilot. "Full speed ahead to Orizaga's house. We continue with the mission."

CHAPTER 20

1615 MST, FRIDAY
ALBUQUERQUE, NM

GARCIA LAID HIS TRAVEL BAG near the front door and opened the door leading out of the office. He peeked out into the hall to make sure it was empty and reached up to throw the self-destruct switch. The destruct wasn't anything that would blow up the building. It was merely a small heat charge that would generate a high enough temperature to melt the laptop he'd been using. There was a short time delay so he could get out of the condo in case something actually caught on fire or exploded.

The office was on the fourth floor at the west end of the Gold Street Lofts, a mixed-use collection of luxury lofts built on top of commercial store space in the middle of Downtown Albuquerque. Over 80 percent of the building was still vacant after the Great Recession, which made it an ideal location for an operations center. The office, which was really a residential condo, was leased from its owner for cash.

Like all the other condos in the building, Garcia's was a semi-custom unit that the owner had bought at the height of the real estate bubble. Also, like many of the other condo owners, the man found himself with an over-priced asset he couldn't afford to keep and couldn't sell when that bubble had burst. It was completely unfurnished, except for Garcia's portable computer, desk, chair, and cot.

The computer equipment had been procured on the recommendation of Carl's ex-CIA tech hacker—a man with an expensive drug habit to support. Henry Erickson had been caught in a sting operation. He'd tried to bully a supplier into providing him with merchandise by using his status as a CIA officer. Except he didn't know the supplier was an informant.

After the operations of the past week culminating in the rescue of the First Daughter, Erickson had been given a few days off. Garcia recalled Carl had decided the hacker would not be needed for the current operation since they now had TER support. After all, a drug-addict computer wizard was a security breach waiting to happen.

Garcia was manning Carl's operations center alone. It meant long hours away from his wife and new baby, but he didn't mind. He was a mega-millionaire countless times over, thanks to helping Carl swindle the US government and Alfonso Reyes's drug cartel collectively out of half a billion dollars.

The large, black touch-pad Garcia just hovered his hand over was the activation switch for the equipment-melting charge. He was just about to apply pressure when the chime from the computer reestablishing a TER comm circuit froze him. He slowly closed the door and cautiously walked over to his workstation. He tapped a key to get rid of the screen saver, and the blank blue screen asked for his password. He typed in a long complex password, and an unfamiliar face appeared on the wall screen display.

"Mr. Garcia, there you are. I dropped your comm channel for a minute."

"More like *five* minutes," he said skeptically. "Who the hell are you?"

"Oh, sorry." The man on the screen was busy pounding his fingers on his keyboard. "I'm Spoke, August Spoke."

He said it like "Bond, James Bond," like Garcia was supposed to be amused. He wasn't. A serious breach of comm security had occurred, and he was primed for anything suspicious, but the new man certainly looked like a geek analyst. He was young and wiry, and he had black, spiky hair up top. He wore a "Save the Whales" black tee, and his left arm was covered with intense vampire tattoos. Monroe had looked pretty much the same, except without the tattoos.

"What happened to Monroe and Agent Peoples?"

"Yeah, they're dropping like flies around here. Peoples had a seizure just like the prez and Mr. McGrath, but Monroe's got some wicked nausea and, you know, the runs. He's in bad shape. I don't think we're gonna see him again for a while."

Wicked nausea? Do people really talk like that back East?

Garcia said, "So what's up with comms?"

"Well, your circuit went down because Peoples fell over on his computer and spilled his Red Bull into the computer fan casing. They're using networked PCs here instead of multiple terminals hooked into a big central server. Keeps operational security local, you know? Anyway, his PC was the one commanding the satellite. When he shorted out the machine, it may have retasked the satellite by default. Probably took out the satellite comm channel or reset it or something. It's an NSA asset, so I'm checking with them now. We'll probably be back up in a few minutes."

The man took a sip from a can of Red Bull, and Garcia wondered why the man would be drinking anything near his computer after what had happened with Peoples.

Spoke said, "Anything new on your end?"

"Carl and Palmer and a few mercs are en route to Orizaga's home office looking for information about what was done to the First Daughter and the president. They're also searching for intel about the other high-level players that might be involved, both in Mexico and here in the US."

Spoke nodded. "Yes, I have most of that in my event logs, but not their departure time."

Garcia told him.

"Got it." Spoke did more keyboard work, then looked into the camera on top of his desk monitor. "Okay, why don't we reconnect every fifteen minutes to update each other? I'll let you know how the satellite situation is going down there, and you can update me if Mr. Johnson makes contact by cell, okay?"

"Will do."

Spoke signed off, and Garcia sat back in his chair. Every instinct in his body told him something was wrong, but he couldn't put a finger on anything specific. He looked over at his travel bag on the floor next to the door. He was certainly relieved the commlink had been reestablished at least with TER, but he was worried about Carl.

They had no backup communication plan other than the one-time-use cell phone Carl had taken with him. Since cell signals were too easily traced, cell phone contact was to be saved for an emergency. So Garcia figured there was no emergency. Either that, or the op was blown and Carl was dead.

He settled back to wait.

CHAPTER 21

AUGUST SPOKE PUSHED THE CAN of Red Bull aside. It was a nasty drink to someone who rarely put anything other than water into his biological machine. He pulled off his itchy spiked-hair wig and massaged his scalp beneath a military-style buzz haircut. Then, he scratched at the irritating adhesive of the fake arm tattoos. It was amazing what kind of disguise props could be found in DC at a moment's notice.

He activated his earpiece with a touch of his index finger. "Rainman, this is Spoke."

"Go ahead."

"Johnson is leading a team to Orizaga's plantation. They left half an hour ago. I figure their ETA is an hour from now, perhaps a little more."

Rainman was silent for a moment. "That gives us time to get there first. Retask the Unit detachment from the airport."

"I recommend we use the local military, sir. Agent Palmer had a defensive package air-dropped to the Reyes property this morning. Among other assets, they have antiaircraft missiles. That tells me they're ready to repel an air assault, and you can be certain she won't have a problem firing on the Unit, though she likely won't engage local forces. I figure you don't want Unit assets involved in an air war down there at this point. Perhaps Mr. Orizaga can arrange for his people to send an army contingent out and set up a well-concealed ambush. The international airport outside Hermosillo doubles as an air force base, and they keep soldiers stationed there for security. They can be on-site at Orizaga's house in a little more than half an hour."

"Good thinking. Proceed with that. Make sure Orizaga's office is searched and all intel removed. And tell Drake to make sure Johnson is really dead this time. I want no survivors among Johnson's group."

"Understood. May I recommend a backup plan…in case Drake is not as efficient as you need him to be?"

"Go ahead."

"Authorize an immediate strike against Reyes's beachfront property. We have a boat in the Gulf near the property. Johnson has proven himself to be lucky and very resourceful, but without his assets at the Reyes estate, if he or any member of his team survives, they will be completely isolated. Then, as soon as we locate and eliminate Mr. Garcia, the Johnson team will have zero support assets."

"I like the way you think, Mr. Spoke. I was going to give you that authorization. I want the house decimated and everyone inside killed."

CHAPTER 22

1620 MST, FRIDAY
HERMOSILLO, NORTHERN MEXICO

CARL FELT LIKE A BADASS as he stalked across the lawn toward Orizaga's house. It was amazing how thirty hours had changed his life. Yesterday morning, he'd worn black tactical gear to get the girl, but he was unseasoned in real combat. He'd been afraid of failure yesterday. Today, he was not afraid. He'd led men and women into combat, he'd had to perform under fire, and he'd been shot. He was confident in his capabilities and knew his limitations.

The helicopter ride from the Reyes mansion had taken a little less than an hour. At first, the pilot kept the luxury chopper at a modest cruising speed and altitude. After the comm circuit went down, the chopper hugged the ground at a slower speed so they'd avoid ambush. Carl wasn't happy his team was on its own with the mission, but he certainly preferred knowing rather than *not* knowing.

Palmer walked beside him. From his side vision, he watched the woman move. She more resembled a stalking lioness than a commando. In fact, it was her movements that he was emulating. Her gaze kept darting around, and she held a very deadly looking automatic weapon in a casual but ready position, its business end loosely pointed at the ground a few feet in front of her. It was one of the six-millimeter armor-piercing PDW automatic rifles, the personal defense weapon she'd shown him on the Gulfstream.

All the team, including the pilot, wore black tactical gear. Palmer had also fitted Carl with combat specs, which were light-gray tinted goggles that looked more like athletic gear a cyclist would wear to keep the wind and bugs out of his eyes. The side edges were tapered like teardrops that wrapped toward his ears, giving him excellent peripheral vision. He also wore a Kevlar combat helmet with a black matte finish. It looked just like the ones the FBI SWAT team wore a month ago, when they'd kicked his ass in front of the Starbucks in Downtown Albuquerque at the start of his detour down Terrorist Lane.

One of the mercenaries stayed with the helicopter to secure their exit ride. There was no perimeter security fence, so Mr. Blick had set the helicopter down a couple hundred feet beyond the back of the huge house. Carl could tell this was a completely different kind of estate from Reyes's. Its owner lived in a different world, more reserved and less flamboyant, and he worked in a different kind of business from his clients. There were no armed guards patrolling outside, and there were no armored cars or machine gun personnel carriers.

The huge house looked like an old adobe structure that had been remodeled into a fairly modern, two-story house with several wings added on in recent years. The exterior stucco looked fairly new, and the windows and French doors were high-end wood-frame appliances. The sand-gray color of the house blended well with the natural growth of the valley.

Merc Four and the other two mercs had already rushed into the huge estate house to secure the family members and any security guards. Those three were also tasked with confiscating all cell phones and cutting phone lines to the house. There were only two guards—what Merc Three called rent-a-cops—on the property, and they surrendered quickly and quietly when the well-armed, black-clad commandos stormed the house.

Carl and Agent Palmer approached the back door. They had agreed she would take the lead, but she hesitated and lightly grabbed his arm. She stared at him for a moment, and everything about her told him she was a killer. The way she focused her deadpan gaze on him, her posture, and the way she held her weapon all told him how deadly she was. Then her gaze softened and danced back and forth between his eyes.

"In the bedroom." That was all she said, and he took the hint.

"Yeah, I got it. It never happened. Let's go in."

"But it *did* happen." She kept ahold of his arm, but her grip was surprisingly gentle.

He had entered the bedroom suite, not knowing she was in there. Just out of the shower, Palmer was naked. She'd been drying herself, but the towel did little to hide her body. He'd stood frozen for several long seconds, then turned away.

"Sorry, I was looking for a room to do some yoga. I didn't know you were in here."

"That's okay," she said quickly.

He'd fantasized that she hadn't wanted him to leave, so he didn't. When he looked back at her, she had let the towel fall away. He'd closed the door and turned to face her. He didn't intend to approach her, but the heat that flashed through his body took control. She met him halfway, and they kissed feverishly. She had wrapped her arms around his neck, fingers clawing into his shoulders, and he had grabbed her butt and pressed her into him…

For all of three seconds.

Their comm units had beeped in their ears, and the spell was broken.

"Agent Palmer, I have actionable intel," Peoples said. "Are Johnson and the others still on the channel?" They had separated, though neither wanted to, and Carl had gone into the living room.

He tried to blink away the memory. Her bare skin had been hot from the shower, soft and smooth. Her muscles were tight in his grip.

Carl said, "Yes, it did happen, but I know it shouldn't have."

She nodded and let go of his arm. "The men I meet don't live in my world."

Translation: Normal men can't handle a badass killer like Agent Palmer. Beyond sex, she probably wouldn't be able to find any kind of comfort or support from someone not in her line of work. Carl got the feeling the woman standing in front of him, lovely though she was, lived a very lonely existence.

"Thank you for that," he said.

She cocked her head a bit. "For what?"

"For being…gentle…about rejecting me." He smiled to break the tense moment.

"I haven't rejected you yet." She smiled in return and nodded toward the door.

Once inside the house, Carl fell in behind Palmer. She moved carefully and quickly with the stock of her PDW glued to her shoulder. Her gaze followed the front and rear aim sights on the weapon as the rifle proceeded her into each room. He waited by each doorway as she gave the rooms they passed a quick interior scan and hollered, "Clear!"

Carl basically protected her rear, staying in the hallway with his Glock pointed at the floor. The mercs still considered him a rookie, even though he'd shot the Glock the day before and now had combat experience. He hadn't been given an automatic rifle because, as Palmer had said, a combat scenario was no time for learning how to use a new weapon.

Carl crab-walked sideways in Palmer's wake. He tried to mimic her catlike movements and settled quickly into a practice of rotating from side to side every few steps and scanning behind him and in front as they moved through the hallways. Like Palmer, he kept a wall at his back, but he was careful not to actually make contact with the walls. He noticed Palmer did the same thing. Neither wanted to make any scraping noise. He knew that, while the exterior of the house looked like an old, remodeled adobe, the inside was all two-by-four frame construction covered by half-inch drywall. Bullets would blow right through that stuff if they rubbed their gear against it or leaned against it, and it creaked.

It wouldn't be like in the movies, where the heroes could duck out of the way as neat little holes in the wall chased them around corners. He'd actually tried to sell a house that had felt the touch of a drive-by shooting in Albuquerque's Westside. Inside the house, the drywall had literally exploded from the bullet impacts, leaving dust and debris and two-by-four wood splinters everywhere. The bullets passed through the stucco, the drywall, and the multiple walls of the house before blasting out the back and into the next house. There was literally no place to hide from bullets in a house unless it had an old metal bathtub.

Whenever Palmer came to a doorway or a blind hallway, she hollered, "One!" This was her numerical designation for this op. If a friendly was nearby, he would holler back his own number designation so the two wouldn't shoot each other. The amazingly simple method of identification made a lot of sense to Carl, as an opposing force couldn't possibly guess at which numbers his group would be using.

Carl was designated as Zero. He wanted to think it was because he was the leader of the band, but he knew it was more likely because he had limited combat experience. He'd been lucky in his free-for-all engagements where *everyone* was his enemy. Now, though, the home invasion required true combat experience, quick thinking, and restraint, and he understood his limitation.

There was a lot of screaming and harsh language inside while the commandos forced everyone out into the front yard, but there was no violence. There were perhaps a dozen children on the property, and the adults weren't willing to risk their safety.

The mercs know their crowd-control business, Carl thought as he moved through the house to the front foyer.

He saw out through the wide-open, double front door that the mercs had rounded up everyone a dozen paces away. Everyone was grouped together, and all had been made to deposit their cell phones in a pile in front of the group. One merc stood guard over the collection of occupants while the other two prowled inside and outside, looking for stragglers.

Those three mercs were designated as Three—because that was Trent Englebaum's previous designation—and Nine and Twelve. Numbers were staggered, Palmer had said, just to mix things up. An opposing force might just assume there were at least twelve in their force and might hesitate to engage them. Or they might call out the wrong number and get shot for their troubles. If they didn't call out a number, they'd still get shot.

The team cleared the house quickly and found Orizaga's office on the second floor of the northwest wing, near the front of the estate. The room was probably close to eight hundred square feet. It was richly appointed in dark red hardwoods, and an exotic black wood trim wrapped around the room at the three-foot level. Below the wood, the wall was dressed in rich cloth wallpaper with thick stripes in red, brown, and green. Above the wainscot, the wall looked like finely brushed plaster painted beige.

The wall to the right of the door held a huge floor-to-ceiling window covered partly by sheer drapes. The wall opposite the door held a six-section sliding glass door that led to an expansive balcony, complete with a bamboo cocktail table and two matching, cushioned recliners. The wall to the left of the entry door held a massive built-in bookshelf constructed of the same fine black wood as the wainscot. The shelves were filled with books. The only anomaly in the wall of shelves was a huge black safe mounted midway along the wall with the top of the safe about shoulder height. The access panel held a digital keypad instead of the typical round combination knob.

A massive desk occupied the center of the room, equidistant from the entry door and the balcony. Carl knew next to nothing about exotic woods, but the reddish-black desk looked extremely expensive. Its surfaces held a brilliant sheen that highlighted its subdued wood grain. The top of the desk was immaculately empty of everything except three large flat-screen monitors.

Carl could tell a laptop was missing because the charger cable snaked around the front, where a person would sit. Carl followed the cable and discovered the cord was still plugged into a flush-mounted receptacle in the honey oak floor. Orizaga also had a tower computer beside the desk. Carl circled the desk, finally standing behind the very comfortable-looking, black leather chair. The computer equipment sat on the floor on the left side of the desk. He pulled out a tray on well-oiled rollers from under the desk and found a wireless keyboard and mouse. He hit a key, and the displays lit up two seconds later. The center screen held a login password box. He grunted his disappointment.

Over his shoulder, Palmer said, "We don't have time to try to guess what his password is." She made her way directly to the safe.

"I'll find someone who knows the password." He pivoted and headed toward the door. "Zero!" he hollered.

There was no response, so he raised his Glock and moved quickly into the hallway, prepared to shoot anyone he saw. He knew no one was going to voluntarily give up the password, so he tried to psyche himself into getting ready for the task of convincing someone to cooperate. Tried to convince himself that it was nothing he hadn't already done in the previous weeks. Told himself it wasn't anything he wouldn't do again in the near future. He had to release his monster from its designated compartment. He felt a sense of excitement along with the dread. Carl hated his monster, but he also loved it, for it gave him confidence and strength. His monster made him feel alive.

He walked quickly out the front door, toward the gaggle of family members and groundskeepers huddled together under the watchful eye of Merc Three. Carl approached the group, holding his Glock at his side, and stood by Three's side.

"Which one of these people is Mrs. Orizaga?"

"No clue, Boss. I don't speak the language."

"Let's see if they speak my language, then."

With his left hand, he peeled open the Velcro tape holding the combat goggles firmly to his face. The lenses were practically clear, but he wanted the adults to clearly see the conviction in his eyes. He stuffed the goggles in the left thigh cargo pocket of his black fatigues and slowly walked around the group of about twenty people. Their eyes followed him as he moved.

Four of the people were workers, dressed in cheap gray work pants and shirts. Those men all wore gray caps, maybe to shade their eyes from the sun while they worked or maybe as a sort of informal work uniform. Two of the women were similarly dressed in maid's uniforms of gray and white striped skirts and blouses.

There was an elderly woman and an elderly man, three women who were maybe in their mid-thirties to mid-forties, and the rest were children ranging in age from maybe five to fifteen. Everyone looked scared except for one of the women. She was Mrs. Orizaga, Carl knew instantly. She was the kind of trophy wife a middle-aged accountant with mega-millions in the bank would keep.

She was a light-skinned, lovely woman with curvy hips, a narrow waist, and large breasts. Her face was extraordinarily fine. She wore expensive clothing. While the rest of the group followed him with their eyes until they could no longer see him without turning their heads, this woman twisted to watch him as he moved around the side of the group. She knew she was his target, and she wasn't about to let him step up behind her and intimidate her. By her defiant attitude, Carl could tell she was accustomed to dealing with, or at least seeing, dangerous men.

Several of the younger children whimpered and huddled closer to the older children and adults as Carl stepped into their midst. Mrs. Orizaga had turned completely around to face him. She gazed at Carl through hazel eyes. She was as tall as he was, and they faced each other from a closeness of only twelve inches. Without breaking eye contact, he placed the business end of his Glock against the head of the elderly woman who stood directly to her right.

The beautiful woman gasped, but the older woman did not. The elder woman rested a bony hand on the handle of a pull-along cart holding her oxygen bottle. Plastic tubing turned into a small cannula beneath the old woman's nose. She was leaning heavily on the handle of the cart for balance. Carl could tell the old woman was expending a lot of energy simply standing up.

To the defiant woman, Carl said, "You are Mrs. Orizaga, are you not?"

"I am." She seemed to square her shoulders a bit with the statement. She did not scare easily, he had to give her that. "You're an American. You cannot do this."

"I am Carl Johnson, also known as the American Terrorist," Carl replied. He saw her flinch. "You know I *will* do this." He paused while she considered his revelation. "My president and her sixteen-year-old daughter are in the hospital because of men your husband works for. I will kill everyone here if you don't tell me what I want to know." Carl paused for a moment, then said, "I want the password for his computer system."

"Please, I don't know—"

Carl pulled the trigger, and the explosion of sound set off shrieks and screams of terror. The elder woman folded to the grass. Mrs. Orizaga screamed too, and she turned to kneel at the dead woman's side, but Carl grabbed her by the hair and yanked her sideways. Carl shifted his aim, and together, he and Mrs. Orizaga faced one of the younger children. He aimed at the child's face.

Mrs. Orizaga shouted something in Spanish.

Carl whispered in her ear, "I can do this all day, lady." He tensed his arm. "What is the password?"

"I just told you!"

"In English, please."

"I can't. You have to enter it in Spanish."

"Then say it again."

She muttered a word or phrase that sounded like it took twenty letters to spell.

"Come with me," Carl said. He released her hair, took a firm grasp on her upper arm, and led her back toward the front entrance of the house. As he scanned the property, he saw Agent Palmer watching him from the window of the office.

Carl led Mrs. Orizaga up the stairs and toward the corner entry to the hallway leading to the office. Almost as an afterthought, as he stepped around the corner, he hollered, "Zero!"

"One!"

But it was a man's voice.

CHAPTER 23

1629 MST, FRIDAY
NORTHERN MEXICO

M RS. ORIZAGA HAD ACTUALLY CROSSED the threshold of the corner and became partly visible to the man around the corner, so when Carl yanked her back toward him, her left arm and leg remained in sight of the gunman for a moment before following the rest of her body to safety. She looked like a cartoon caricature, her arms, legs, and hair flailing.

Clouds of drywall dust and two-by-four studs exploded in front of them as the gunman's bullets chewed into the wall inches from their bodies. Carl pulled the woman down to the floor and fired five shots through the wall to where he knew the gunman had to be standing. Then, he reached around the corner and emptied his Glock into the space, pulling the trigger as fast as he could. When there was no return fire, he peeked into the hallway. The man was down. He let go of Mrs. Orizaga just long enough to eject his spent magazine and replace it with a fresh one from his vest. He dragged Mrs. Orizaga along with him and approached the gunman.

From far ahead, he heard another yell. "One!" It was Palmer's voice this time.

"Zero!"

She came into the hallway with her weapon at the ready while Carl examined the dead man. Of the seventeen-round clip he had fired off, only one bullet had hit home. He'd scored in the center of the man's forehead.

Carl rough-handled Mrs. Orizaga toward her husband's office at the end of the hall. He walked right past Palmer without looking at her and shoved Mrs. Orizaga into the office. He could feel Agent Palmer's eyes on him as he moved past her. He and the woman stopped behind the desk, and Carl pointed at the keyboard. She entered the password, and the screen unlocked.

Palmer said, "Write it down so I can verify it."

The woman wrote it down, and Carl locked the screen and unlocked it. He put his gun on the desk and told Mrs. Orizaga to sit on the floor beside the desk. She didn't move, so he shoved her back into the corner where the bookshelf wall met the French door wall. The woman trembled, but it was with anger, Carl saw, not fear. He set about his task of scanning the hard drive of the computer.

Mrs. Orizaga glared at Carl and said, "If it's the last thing I ever do, I will hunt you down and kill every last member of your family."

Carl, hunched over the keyboard, looked sideways at her. "You know what?" he said. He picked up his Glock, stepped over to her, and placed the barrel against her belly. "Your husband and his people already did that."

He pulled the trigger, and the sound of the shot echoed in the big room. She flopped back against the wall as if punched, then slid slowly down the wall of shelves until she fell into a sitting position and over sideways. Her mouth held the shape of an O as if expressing surprise.

Carl glared down at the woman for a moment more. "Fucker," he said.

As he uttered the word, he felt a chill of exhilaration spread through his body. He recognized it as the same feeling he experienced while he was hack-sawing Agent Klipser's head from his body a week ago. That feeling had been a combination of vindication and hatred. And thrill.

Carl shoved his gun back into its holster on his thigh. He went back to the desk and resumed his scan of the computer's file directory. He glanced behind him when he heard a click at the wall, where Palmer was working, and he saw her pull open the wall safe. She pocketed an electronic device she had been using, reached into the small box, and pulled out a folder.

She thumbed through the stack and said, "I've got something here called Operation Trojan Horse."

"Not a very original name," Carl said.

"Yes, but it's an ominous name for an operation involving the president's daughter."

Carl scrolled through Orizaga's computer files. "I see about eighty gigs of movies here and a bunch of PDF files. It's all in a folder called Operation Unity. It's all in English too." He looked over at Agent Palmer. "Like it was intended for English-speaking clients, not Spanish speakers. And here's a subfolder also called Operation Trojan Horse."

"The plan to kidnap and infect Melissa Mallory?"

"It fits." Carl nodded. "Damn, Nancy." He continued to scroll. "This looks big. Real big. There are spreadsheets, presentation files, and PDFs here. And there are videos with gigabyte file sizes." He looked up. "This isn't the kind of material you prep for an audience of one, or even for a small group." He scanned some more. "These presentations and reports include tables of contents and executive summaries." Finally, he stood. "This material is intended for a substantial group, maybe a dozen or two participants. This is a massive program plan, and they've been at this for a long time."

Palmer came over to the desk and plopped the folder in front of him. "Carl, you're not going to like this."

Carl picked up the folder and scanned through several loose sheets of printed pages and two thick reports. "Well, fuck me sideways. I thought your TER reports were super-classified."

"They are usually above 'eyes only' and restricted to TER commanders, directors, and the president's senior staff. Not even the classified congressional oversight committees see these."

"I bet the chief of staff sees them."

"Or the vice president, or a number of other senior personnel who could email classified copies with no one suspecting anything."

"Scallow's intern learned who it was."

"Maybe he went to his boss and told him, then they both were killed or captured."

Carl nodded. "Maybe Mr. Scallow is our adversary and had his people kill his intern. Then he went into hiding."

"That's possible, but before Agent Peoples went off-line, we never learned who else, if anyone, might be missing."

"We were getting close," Carl said. "And we didn't know it. That's why they shut us down."

Palmer began summarizing the other documents from the safe. "These are after-action reports covering everything that happened over the past thirty days. Everything that happened involving *you*."

Carl narrowed his eyes. "Why the hell do these people care about me? I switched sides and helped the government."

Carl felt like a lab rat, a guinea pig. He looked at the computer screen again. Seeing files dating back over ten months validated his assessment of the complexity of his adversary's plan.

He shook his head forcefully. *There's no way anyone could have set me up from the beginning. No way anyone could have built an entire operation to kidnap Melissa Mallory around the freak coincidence of me looking like Alfonso Reyes. No way anyone could have predicted I would go insane and declare war on the US government.* He shook his head again, finally shaking off the disbelief running through his mind, and returned his full attention to searching for answers.

"Huh," he said. "Well, ain't this something?" He looked sideways at the agent and suddenly smiled, but there was no humor in his expression.

"What are you thinking?"

He nodded. "I know who we're up against."

CHAPTER 24

"I MAY NOT KNOW EXACTLY WHO they are," Carl said, "and I can't put faces to them yet, but I know *what* they are."

Palmer remained silent, waiting for him to continue.

"I've got the same feeling in my bones now, as I had two weeks ago when I was looking for Aaron McGrath. I didn't know who he was either, but my gut told me he was a high-power, covert agency guy. I thought maybe CIA or something like that. These guys have to be like your TER agency, probably just with different letters. They'd have to be to have access to these kinds of classified reports, right?" He leaned over the keyboard and nodded at the center monitor. "The dates on these videos and the various files go back many months, but I only got involved last month because of a fluke, a mistake of identity.

"I'm nobody to these guys. I'm a gnat on the back of an elephant. I'm just a squirrel trying to get a nut. There's no way in hell these guys could have developed a yearlong plan for whatever it is they're trying to do and then have a program goal of finding someone like me who looks like Alfonso Reyes. There's no way they could have anticipated last year that I, or someone like me, would ever get involved. So," he said with confidence as he straightened up, "I figure this group is composed of a crew of operational planners just like the TER has. They've got a high-ranking director, a *McGrath equivalent*, and they've got a behind-the-scenes leader, probably someone who stands to benefit the most from a successful outcome of the plan. And they've got a heavy hitter—a power broker who can make things happen and who has high-level connections here and in the US—just like El Patron was for the Triad."

Palmer said, "That makes sense. Given that framework, I nominate the chief of staff for the power broker. He's got a lot of influence, but not the authority. But he could get a lot done if he had someone else above him with a lot of power or money, or both."

"Who might that be?"

She shrugged. "Could be anyone from a high-ranking administration official, like the vice president or the secretary of state, to a top-level three-letter director, to a mega-billionaire civilian."

"Well, they're adapting their plan by the day and by the hour to account for what we're doing. And they're pretty good at it too. They have an almost instantaneous response time."

Palmer said, "If that's the case, we'd better change things up a bit because they know where we are. They'll be sending a covert wet-work team for us. If they already have in-country assets, we should expect them at any moment. An operation like this without boots-on-the-ground muscle is just spitting in the wind."

"I think they're going to use your TER operators as their muscle. They've got control of your tech and probably your op center too."

"They probably won't use TER field agents, but they certainly can hire out the fieldwork to the same kind of independent contractors the three-letter agencies use."

"Okay, but what is the Mexican play in this op? Why would the Mexican government, or people highly connected with the government, risk involvement in an op like this? What do they gain?"

"I don't know, Carl, but there's a *very* small circle of people with the power to run an op against Aaron McGrath or the president. And they couldn't do it without people inside the president's own staff. So, if Martine Scallow isn't helping them, then he's dead. He's well-connected, and I can't see *anyone* running a high-level op like this without his buy-in." She glanced sideways at him. "They'd also need high-level involvement at the CIA because they're the kings of the covert operations world. We use them too, for field support, because they have the equipment and trained personnel to carry out ops anywhere in the world. In addition, they'd need unrestricted access to certain NSA surveillance assets, so they probably have someone high in that chain of command too."

Carl said, "We've been taking a defensive posture up to now. Maybe we should open up a second front on these mu'fuckers. Target number one is Martine Scallow."

"Even if we find him, he can order the Secret Service to protect him. They'll never let you get close."

"Reyes got close and took the girl."

"That's because Reyes had an insider."

"I have you."

They both leaned their palms on the desktop at nearly the same instant.

"Carl, you overestimate my value."

They stood nearly shoulder to shoulder, leaning on the desk. He looked sideways at her, and she looked sideways at him.

"I trust you, Nancy. I don't know why, but I just do. I sense you're one of the good guys. I believe you'll do the right thing by Shirley Mallory and not just blindly follow orders from higher up." He pulled a memory from the back corner of his brain. "Thirty-five years ago, as a butter-bar lieutenant, I took an oath to defend the Constitution against all enemies, foreign and domestic. I'm guessing you did the same more recently."

She nodded, and they fell silent for a while. Carl considered the commitment they both seemed to have just made. Palmer stuck a USB thumb drive in the side of the keyboard, and Carl dragged the entire Operation Unity folder, with all of its video files, document files, and subfolders, onto the thumb drive.

Palmer paused, then pointed at a page in the folder on the desk. "Look at this sheet." She laid it in front of him.

He noticed the title of the page first: Task List.

"What the hell?" he said as he scanned the contents of the page.

The page held only the names of people he had become intimately familiar with over the past two weeks during his war with the US government. FBI Special Agent Lenore Cummings was at the top of the list, along with her daughter, Lisette. Cummings's mother was on the list too. Anita McGrath Chapman was also on the list with her husband and four children.

"What the hell does this mean?" He could scarcely believe what he was seeing.

Palmer nodded. "A task list is operator-speak for people to terminate with extreme prejudice."

Carl looked at the last name on the list: Garcia, NFN. He knew NFN was a government acronym, and it was easy enough to figure out—No First Name. He'd encountered its cousin, NMI for No Middle Initial, back in his Air Force days—as in Johnson, Carl NMI.

"This is a government *hit* list?"

Palmer shook her head. "Not government. It's our adversary's hit list."

"But why? Except for Cummings, these people are all civilians, non-combatants. They're innocent victims of my road rage last week. Well," he said with a grimace. "I guess, technically, Mr. Garcia is a terrorist, like me." He looked at the list again. "They're going to murder *children?* And who or what is this *Unit?*"

He saw a notation at the bottom of the sheet, under the names and addresses, with a recommendation to prioritize the targets as listed. It was signed by someone named Costas Drake, and he was listed as the commander of the Unit.

Palmer said, "Think about what this means." She paused, but Carl had no new insight. He was still dazed by the discovery of the list. Palmer said, "This task list means that someone is going to finish what you thought you needed to do last week." She pushed off from the desk and stood up straight. "And they're going to frame you for it."

Carl took a deep breath and lowered his head. "I don't know why these guys have such a hard-on for me, but whatever it is, I just got all these people killed."

"Carl, this isn't a random footnote in a report or some kind of attempt to punish you. This is an ongoing operation, and it has been in planning for many months. Melissa's kidnapping was the opening salvo. But this part," she said, pointing at the task list. "This has to be a new development. Something is happening soon, and you're going to be the fall guy. If they're successful, the whole world will be looking for *you* and not *them.*"

Carl nodded.

She continued, "So we're no longer just trying to find out what they did to Melissa Mallory. That was part of a larger plan, which we need to understand and stop."

Carl looked up at the agent and nodded. "But what could murdering these people possibly have to do with trying to assassinate the president?"

CHAPTER 25

Cassiopeia Englebaum, also known as Mercenary Number Four—or Merc Four for short—examined the yacht parked a half mile offshore simply because it was *still there*. She'd noticed the boat cruising slowly to the north about half an hour after the boss left. Now, it was just sitting there with its portside anchor cable extended into the water.

By habit, she was paranoid about such things. She was, after all, an illegal mercenary. In that business, one never knew when the authorities would find you until they actually knocked down the door. Since she was engaged in an active operation, she preferred to call her paranoia by its other name—situational awareness.

Besides, everyone was on high alert since the comm went down. One instant, the op center agent was in mid-sentence, and the next, there was only dead silence on the channel. Carl Johnson would continue his mission. Four wasn't quite sure how she knew that, but she did. She and her husband had only known Johnson for a week, but they'd come to know how he operated. Whenever an unknown factor or a new challenge was introduced into the mission, Johnson was one to charge full speed ahead, even when retreating was the smart thing to do. Four was convinced that was why he was still alive.

If Johnson were here, Four thought, *he'd probably already have ordered the yacht nuked with an RPG on general principles because it is an unexplained anomaly.* So Merc Four was prepared to do just that. On the other hand, a stationary fifty-foot yacht anchored off the private beach was generally not cause for alarm, according to Mrs. Reyes.

Julia Reyes, or *Hoolia,* as she pronounced her name, had translated while her mother explained that everyone in the region knew the mansion belonged to her late husband. Alfonso Reyes was well-known as a globe-trotting philanthropist, along with his reputation as the leader of a drug cartel. It was not uncommon for boats to park off the coast so tourists could watch the house with binoculars. Everyone wanted to get a glimpse of the flamboyant, charitable playboy.

Merc Four took a liking to Julia and easily saw why the boss was so attached to her, despite only knowing her a couple days. She was cheerful and inquisitive, always smiling and asking questions.

Four took a liking to Luisa Reyes as well, but for different reasons. Luisa was petite and curvy and brown, just like Merc Four liked her women. She and her husband had a fairly open relationship, but they had long since agreed only Four was allowed side partners, not her husband. And Four's partners were only women, which made it agreeable to her husband because she often let him watch or even participate. She had considered confessing her interest in Luisa to her husband when he returned, but once when she caught Luisa's gaze and smiled, the woman had simply looked away. There was clearly no mutual interest.

Merc Four considered the interpersonal dynamics of their mercenary fan club. Johnson was smitten with his new pseudo-daughter, Julia. When he first met the girl during their failed first attempt to find Melissa Mallory, he took to giving the girl full-body hugs, holding her, and kissing her forehead like he was afraid to ever let go of her. Like he *needed* another kid. But when he hugged her mother an hour ago, it was a friend-zone, half-sideways, no-frontal-contact hug. It was also clear to see that Luisa Reyes both loved and hated Carl, this new man in her daughter's life who looked almost exactly like her late husband.

What a storm of emotional turmoil Luisa must be feeling, Four thought, *every time she looked at the man.* Four had the hots for Luisa even though Luisa had the hots for Johnson, and he clearly had the hots for Nancy Palmer, Four's longtime friend.

Merc Four considered the psychological quagmire of the group's interpersonal dynamics. Luisa Reyes was in love with the man who delivered her husband to the TER, and the boss was in love with the TER agent instrumental in the death of his son and who helped run the op to kill Johnson as well.

For her part, Nancy Palmer was a blank slate. She was completely unreadable. She didn't have an interest in anyone, but that didn't surprise Four. She'd known Nancy for three years since their shooting competition. During the competition and after, she'd tried to bond with Nancy, but the woman warrior kept her emotions completely walled off. She had no friends and no attachments and seemed comfortable maintaining her life that way.

Merc Four abandoned her fantasy relationship with Luisa Reyes and continued to allow Julia to follow her around like she was the girl's gun-toting role model. Maybe the girl considered it all simply a big adventure she'd tell her kids about in a couple decades.

When Johnson was around, the girl clearly loved the way he let her cling to him. He wasn't quite a father figure or a big brother, and he definitely wasn't a role model.

To say the girl is love-struck is probably not accurate either, Four thought. *It might be more like a preteen crush on a guy she thinks can protect her and keep her safe.*

Johnson seemed to have a unique sense of righteousness about him. When he promised something, you could take that to the bank. Relying on someone's word was rare in Four's business.

Julia didn't seem to understand how dangerous Johnson really was. He was a raw, open wound. You never knew if he was going to hug you or kill you…or kill your family. Four realized that was not the kind of dynamic an eleven-year-old girl would understand or even care about. Johnson made her feel safe, and that's all that mattered to her.

In the beginning, all Merc Four and her husband cared about was that the terrorist paid extremely well. A lot of jobs they'd taken in the last couple of years were bodyguard gigs, driving legal or illegal bigwigs around. Mostly, they just stood around looking dangerous, but every now and then, they took a gig where they actually got to do some gun work. Just three months ago, they escorted a drug shipment across Texas. There was a little dust-up at the end, and some shots were fired, so they'd had to leave the country for a while.

The odds were the two of them against ten, and six of the ten had died. When you have elite army training and expensive high-tech black-market weapons with low-light and infrared scopes, two commandos could hold off a hundred times that many when all the opposition had were shotguns and chrome-grip pistols. There was never really any danger on that gig, and there most certainly was no adrenaline rush like they'd been seeking.

They'd hid down in Mexico, where Mr. Garcia's network came calling with the promise of real action and crazy money. Two thousand a week for six weeks minimum!

The boss had more than delivered on his promise of action and adrenaline. At first, Four and Three were completely happy with grabbing a couple grand while some lunatic civvy who'd lost his son declared war on the FBI. But the way he'd lured those assault teams into that building and blown them to hell had earned the respect of both her and her husband. Then, there was the way he planned and directed the ambush of that elite TER team. And they had prevailed! She was ready to follow that man into any battle now.

She shivered involuntarily as she recalled watching the video of what he did to the TER survivor. He literally hacked the man's head off while he was *still alive!* She couldn't have done that. Hell, her husband couldn't have done that.

The boss excited her because he wasn't a desk commander. He'd gotten into the shit with them. He promised action and delivered. Not once or twice, but three times now. Merc Four always knew this was how she wanted to go out—fighting a big fight against a big enemy. Kicking butts and taking names.

The boss scared her too. She sure didn't want to be on the receiving end of his wrath. In her military career, she'd seen lots of field commanders, softies and badasses alike. She'd been sent on lots of missions with her units, pursuing crazed despots or protecting civilians against them, or training third-world soldiers how to fight them.

After her military career, she'd worked as a mercenary for those same kinds of bad men—drug runners, flesh traffickers, hit squads. All those men—military or civilian, soft or hard—had some degree of *badness* in them. But she'd never truly seen a man as driven as the boss. Johnson was both righteous and evil at the same time—a crazy combination for one who was called a terrorist. He wasn't bad only to maintain a reputation or only when his henchmen were around. He was bad through and through.

She'd always wondered where bad men—or women—came from, or what kind of kids they were, or how or when or where they learned how to be bad or do bad things. Carl Johnson was a perfect example of the origin of a bad man. She could easily see that he'd been a gentleman and a loving father *before*. She'd seen him turn. She'd seen him cut his teeth on violence. In the space of a week, he'd morphed into a stone-cold killer. He'd been forged by the actions of the US government.

Then, crazily enough, he launched his team into a rescue mission for the very people he wanted to kill and who wanted him dead. In a month, Johnson was transformed from an ordinary civilian into a terrorist monster. Then in another day, *a single day*, he transformed into a hero.

Johnson was no ordinary hero. At the exchange site where he'd rescued the First Daughter, he took bullets in the vest for the girl. He'd hugged and kissed Julia like his own daughter, but only two days earlier, he'd almost stuck a scalpel in the chest of that FBI agent's daughter to get her mother to reveal the TER director's identity. Four had actually held her breath until he pulled the blade away from the girl.

Merc Four shook away the memories and turned her attention to her Barrett M107 sniper rifle. She smiled as she recalled actually showing Julia how to sight through the powerful scope and pull the trigger on the unloaded weapon.

It wasn't unloaded now. The safety was on, but it was ready for action with a full mag of 50-cal rounds inserted. It sat ready for use on a fancy brushed steel, bar-height dining table that had been moved into the formal living room. A short bipod was attached under the front end of the long barrel.

Four decided to examine the yacht again, more to discount it as a threat than for any other reason. It was unnecessary since half the patrolling mercenary guards were no doubt watching it also, but she looked it over again anyway.

It wasn't like a covert kill team could storm the beach from the boat, not even after dark. The mercs at the estate had clear fields of fire across the expansive property in all directions, and the beach itself was an empty kill zone with no cover if someone were to foolishly try that tactic. Any adequately prepared assault force would correctly assume the mercs would also have night vision devices. And the assaulting force had to scale or destroy the sturdy security fence. That wasn't something they could do covertly.

No, Four thought. *An assault will come from the air.*

Before she stuck her eye behind the scope of the big sniper rifle, she glanced at the laptop sitting on the table next to the weapon. Its screen showed a circular radar sweep. A USB dongle stuck out of the right side of the machine and was wirelessly connected to a portable radar transceiver the mercs had mounted on the roof of the mansion. The low-power beam only reached out a couple of miles, but it would give a few precious minutes of warning for any impending air assault. A straight line extended from the center of the display to the outer edge and continuously rotated around the center point every two seconds. The screen was empty. There was really no need to monitor the screen, as the laptop had several different audible alarms that would indicate an airborne radar return signal, as well as active jamming or interruption of the wireless connection. As Four glanced at the screen anyway, the line continued its rotation, leaving no blips behind it.

Four leaned over behind the rifle and sighted through the scope and the glass panes of the French doors facing a huge brick patio on the beachfront side of the house. Trendy sheer curtains hung from two hooks at the top of each door. Earlier, Four had pulled back one of the curtains a bit and used a clip pin shaped like a flower to hold the curtain. She had enough clear window to see the yacht.

The boat jumped into focus through the powerful scope. The vessel was mostly dark with only a couple of lights on near the front, where she knew the pilot would be. The brilliant yellow-orange skyline marking the setting of the sun just minutes earlier provided a beautiful backdrop for the boat.

Merc Four was just getting ready to activate the thermal imaging lens when she heard the patter of feet and soft voices whispering behind her. She turned just as Mrs. Reyes reached for the light switch.

"Please don't turn on the light."

The woman withdrew her hand, then she and her daughter gasped as they realized Four was hovering over the very deadly looking rifle.

"It's okay," she said. "I'm just looking at the boat anchored out there."

Julia said, "Can I look?"

"Sure, sweetie, come on over and take a peek." Mrs. Reyes looked like she was about to object, so Four said, "It's not a bother, and it's perfectly safe."

She pushed a button on the left side of the weapon, and the magazine dropped out into her waiting palm. She made sure the chamber was clear and stepped aside as the girl moved to the table.

Julia looked excited and scared at the prospect of touching the weapon, even though Merc Four had let her handle it earlier. Four showed her again how to balance the rifle on the bipod, raising or lowering the stock with her right eye at the scope so she could see through.

Julia said, "Wow! The boat looks so close. And I see a man looking at us too."

"You do?" She didn't see anyone a moment ago. Merc Four gently nudged Julia aside and said, "Here, let me see."

She gazed through the scope and saw the man. The sun was just touching the horizon behind a distant hazy cloud, but the sky around the setting globe was aflame in hues of yellow and red. The man was a shadow against the fading sunset, and Four felt a chill as she realized the yacht was anchored in the exact position necessary to make it difficult for anyone at the estate to see the boat clearly. Four's experienced eyes could still see the watcher was outfitted in black combat gear, same as hers. He held a large pair of powerful military-spec binoculars to his face.

By habit borne of many years of combat, Merc Four carefully slid the magazine into place and prepped for a shot, even as she studied the commando on the yacht. The man lowered the glasses and looked over his shoulder like he was searching for something.

In the sky. "Fuck *me!*"

There were only two reasons why the man would blatantly study them in the open when he hadn't moments ago. Either he didn't care that they knew he was there, or there was nothing they could do about it. Or both.

"Cover your ears, Sweetie!"

Julia did, then Four took the shot. The sniper rifle exploded with sound, the glass window shattered, and she watched the commando disappear from the deck of the boat, presumably launched into the water on the opposite side. Then she yelled at the top of her voice.

"Incoming!"

CHAPTER 26

1702 MST, FRIDAY
THE REYES ESTATE, NORTHERN MEXICO

A SPLIT SECOND LATER, MERC FOUR heard the laptop emit a shrill tone. It wasn't the high-pitched tone reserved for fast movers, like supersonic, high-flying aircraft or missiles. It was the low-pitched tone, indicating a slow-moving target, such as a helicopter gunship, a fighter, or bomber flying a few hundred knots. She saw the single blip on the laptop's short-range radar screen. It was an inbound cruise missile. It had to be.

We're fucked!

But that was impossible. The only military force within a thousand miles that could deploy a cruise missile was the US Navy. Why would the Navy waste a million-dollar weapon just to destroy a house? A helicopter gunship could do the same with generic air-to-ground missiles without risk and for a far lower price tag. Merc Four also knew all missile explosives displayed a distinctive blast pattern and left behind specific chemical residue that could be easily traced and identified. The US government might as well take out an ad on CNN and announce to the world that they just launched an attack against a foreign country—an ally.

Four picked Julia up by the waist and headed down the hall toward the door to the basement, grabbing Luisa by the arm as she ran past her. The two off-duty mercs clamored out of their rooms and raced down the stairs. Both were fastening straps on their combat vests with one hand while carrying assault rifles with the other.

Four yelled, "Everyone into the basement! Now!"

Once Merc Four was well into the hallway, she put Julia down to run under her own power. The two mercs followed the three women to the back of the house. In mid-stride, Merc Four kicked the crash bar and sent the steel door crashing against the concrete wall to the stairwell. She ran down the steps three at a time. Behind her, the Reyes ladies yelped as the two mercs lifted them off their feet because they weren't running fast enough. The last man through slammed the metal barrier door behind him.

Four's brain worked overtime. The cruise missile's speed was maybe four or five hundred knots. The portable radar range was two, maybe three miles max. That meant they had at most half a minute to live.

The guys outside wouldn't even have time to reach the front door. The evac plan was to abandon the property through the escape tunnels under the house. But even if the mercs outside knew a cruise missile was coming, even if they knew enough to run *away* from the house, they had absolutely zero chance of getting out of the blast radius. When the missile hit, the compressive shock wave from the high-explosive warhead would crush anything and anyone within a hundred meters in a microsecond. Good news was that the mercs wouldn't suffer.

The counter in Merc Four's head said ten seconds had passed as she hit the bottom of the two-level flight of concrete steps. She saw that the basement really could be more accurately described as an underground garage. Ahead, she saw two armored SUVs parked beside the entrance to the escape tunnel leading away from the mansion.

Fifteen seconds left!

She got in and cranked the key that was already in the ignition, and the big engine roared in the confined space. She put the big car in gear, got the nose turned into the tunnel, and stopped. While she waited for the others to rush in, she fastened her seat belt.

Ten seconds left!

The last door closed, and she floored the gas pedal. A squeal of rubber echoed in the tunnel before the tires caught, and the overpowered SUV raced into the darkness, pinning the occupants against their seats.

"Seat belts!" she hollered over the engine noise that seemed to be refocused from the close concrete walls of the tunnel back into the cabin of the SUV.

Five seconds!

The tunnel was only a quarter mile long, but she knew they weren't going to make it to the other end. When the blast wave hit, it was going to rip right through their tunnel and send them tumbling through the confined area. Maybe launch them into orbit out the other end.

She was wrong. They'd gone maybe halfway through the tunnel when the missile hit, and the tremendous blast collapsed the tunnel right on top of them.

CHAPTER 27

1702 MST, FRIDAY
ALBUQUERQUE, NM

"**R**IGHT NOW, I'M MINDING THE shop all by myself," Spoke said. "Well, me and the guards, but they don't do analyst work. Monroe is sleeping off his nausea upstairs, and paramedics came for McGrath and Peoples about five minutes ago." He sighed. "I just hope my replacement gets here by dinnertime. I'm starving, and day-old donuts and bagels just don't cut it. Know what I'm sayin'?"

Garcia watched the man on his monitor and acknowledged that he was, like the other government geek he'd been talking with, a true multi-tasker. The man chuckled, did keyboard work, chewed gum, and talked, all at the same time.

"By the way, I'm August," Spoke said. "So, what's your first name, Mr. Garcia?"

Garcia found the question a bit curious, but not because the analyst asked it. It was the way he asked. He asked while not looking at the camera, but he seemed a little too insistent—like he was anxious to know but trying *not* to seem anxious. And that set Garcia's spine tingling in warning. Again. He wasn't quite sure what it was about Agent Spoke that felt creepy. The man had dark beady eyes, and his face was hard with sharp features. Garcia felt like a mouse in front of a snake that wasn't yet hungry. He felt like the snake was just playing with his food for the moment.

He thought about the analyst's question. Garcia wasn't his real name.

On his first meeting with Carl, before he knew the man as Carl Johnson and before Carl was labeled the American Terrorist, they had a quick job interview on the loading docks behind a store at the west end of Central.

"So, what's your name," Carl had said almost three weeks ago.

"Garcia. And yours?"

"Smith."

They'd had a brief chuckle over that irony. Garcia and Smith were two of the most common surnames in Spanish and English. He'd known Carl only as Mr. Smith for the duration of their first operation until the FBI leaked his real name to the media. In fact, Carl still knew him only as Mr. Garcia. Just yesterday, Garcia asked Carl why he had never asked his real name and had been startled by Carl's reply.

"Mr. Garcia, we're still in the fan business, and the shit can still hit the fan and splatter. If I get taken and tortured again, you don't want me giving up your real name. Call it operational security."

A part of Garcia believed his boss. He still called his mercenaries only by their number designations. Another part thought it might be Carl's way of not getting too close. Garcia recognized that the man was still trying to come to terms with losing his son. Keeping his distance was part of his recovery process, but Garcia sensed that Carl liked him—sort of like a mentor would feel toward a favorite pupil. He also suspected Carl didn't want to let anyone get close to him that he might lose again.

In the end, Garcia had never given Carl a first name or even his real surname. He was simply Garcia or Mr. Garcia.

"James," he said in response to Spoke's question. He felt pressured to answer, like it was a test or something.

"James *Garcia?*" Spoke tented his eyebrows like he didn't believe him.

"Dude, in Spanish. *Jaime.*" Garcia pronounced it *High-meh.* Jaime was equally as generic in Spanish as James was in English.

The emptiness returned to Spoke's eyes, and Garcia could tell the man didn't believe him. None of the other analysts had asked him for his first name. They hadn't needed to know, and they didn't even care to whom they were speaking. Why did this analyst care?

Spoke didn't press the issue. He continued his updates with almost robotic precision. He promised to report again in fifteen minutes, then disconnected. It occurred to Garcia at that moment that Spoke hadn't given him any more information this time than he had in his two previous updates.

He was being punked. He was sure of it. Something on the government side of the operation had changed. Now he was certain the satellite link with Carl had been severed intentionally, and for some reason, the beady-eyed guy named August Spoke—if that was even his real name— seemed to be teasing him along.

Again, the young Mr. Garcia looked over at his small duffel by the door. He thought about Carl. It was time to leave. Right now.

Get out of the fan business.

Still, he hesitated. He had a gut feeling Carl was in trouble and needed him. He couldn't abandon him. He genuinely liked the man and felt he had to be there for him.

So he waited.

CHAPTER 28

1918 EST, FRIDAY
UNDISCLOSED TER OP STATION, VIRGINIA

SPOKE TOUCHED THE EARPIECE WITH his left index finger. "Rainman, this is Spoke."

"Go ahead."

"Mr. Garcia is getting suspicious. I recommend eliminating him ASAP."

"Why do you think he's suspicious?"

Spoke frowned. It was typical of Rainman to question all assessments, especially regarding security matters. He always wanted all the raw background data as if to see if he would arrive at the same conclusion. The gut feeling of field experience, however, was often hard to translate into raw data. He knew the stakes of the operation and understood Rainman's need for information, though.

"I asked him for his first name, and he gave Jaime."

"Hmm. Spanish for James. A very generic name."

"As is Garcia. I've run his face through all national and international databases with facial recognition algorithms and have had no hits. I've also begun a scan of the national driver's license database for a matching photo, but that will take some time. I'm checking Interpol too. Maybe this man is a Mexican national, has dual citizenship, or is an illegal alien."

Rainman said, "It occurs to me that for Garcia to have made the kind of financial transactions he has made for Johnson, then he must have access to a network, either here in the US or, more likely, in Mexico, that can move large sums of money electronically, without raising red flags and without traceability."

"Just like Vicente Orizaga does for us."

"Except the TER found Orizaga before we could intervene. They could not find Garcia."

"Orizaga has gotten careless in recent months. As for Mr. Garcia, his ex-government hacker is using what we call the Shadow-Net. It evolved from the TOR Project, which itself was an offshoot of a classified US Navy program that provided internet research free from surveillance and tracking. The Shadow-Net is extremely difficult to penetrate; however, the NSA facility in Colorado does much more than monitor cell phones. We've traced Garcia's computer network, but if he relocates or reconfigures his system, we'll lose him and have to start over. That's another reason I think we should move on him ASAP."

"I find it increasingly disturbing that Carl Johnson can be more efficient than the TER. I don't want to underestimate him the way McGrath and his people did."

Rainman fell silent, so Spoke said, "Moving the kind of money Garcia has moved and procuring the kind of material he has procured is no easy task, sir. I doubt he could accomplish that alone."

"Precisely. Have Mr. Orizaga engage his associates in the Triad to investigate a possible connection in their own neighborhood. Maybe they already know about their local competition. It occurs to me that Garcia would also need specialized black-market acquisition talent to provide the kinds of logistics and mercenary support he has."

"And regarding a preemptive strike on Garcia?"

Rainman paused. "Deploy Drake's team and keep the building under surveillance, but I want to wait until we identify Garcia's infrastructure, just in case he or Johnson elude us. Then make a soft entry. See if the Unit can take him alive. If he's running Johnson's financial transactions from that computer, then he must have the account numbers and access codes, either in his head or on the computer. They're holding half a billion dollars of the Triad's money. Grabbing that will cripple his operation and might give us some leverage in our future negotiations with them. Confiscate his hardware."

"And if he resists or creates a scenario where the Unit might be compromised?"

"No police can be involved at this point," Rainman said. "Taking him alive is preferable to dead, but dead is also acceptable."

"Understood."

Rainman added, "Keep the current timetable to hit the others after midnight. We need that angle to serve as a distraction because we're still vulnerable for seventy-two more hours. After that, it won't matter what the world believes."

Spoke nodded to the empty room. "Maybe Johnson is infected. He was with the girl when she went active."

"That was more than twenty-eight hours ago. Obviously, he's not infected, or he'd be dead or in a coma by now, same as the president and Aaron McGrath."

Spoke nodded again, mentally kicking himself for such a simple oversight. "I'll get you your seventy-two hours."

"See that you do."

CHAPTER 29

THE ROOM HAD DARKENED CONSIDERABLY as the sun set behind the huge estate. Neither Carl nor Palmer had turned on a light in the office. The progress indicator for the file transfer had just registered 100 percent when Carl heard the yell through the office patio door he'd opened exactly for that purpose.

"Incoming!"

He and Palmer both looked out the center of the window wall in front of them. They both saw a flash of fire and a smoke trail heading toward the house.

Heading straight for them—right at the office where they stood.

Palmer snatched the thumb drive out of the computer and yelled, "Go!"

Carl raced through the open office door and was all the way down the hall at the back of the house, with Palmer right on his heels, when the rocket hit. There was a loud clap of sound and a concussive blast of air that blew out windows throughout the huge house. As far as Carl could tell, most of the blast damage was localized to the front wing of the house. There was no fireball, but that entire section of the house collapsed instantly.

Before they landed, they'd all agreed that since they had no heavy weaponry beyond a couple of shoulder-held RPGs on the helicopter, their only reasonable course of action was a full retreat if the house was assaulted by any sizable force. When Carl and Palmer tore out through the back door, the other three mercs were already in a full-on sprint toward the luxury chopper two hundred feet away.

The pilot had kept the engine idling. As Carl closed the distance, the rotors began slicing through the air rapidly with a swishing sound, reaching takeoff speed in seconds. The merc who had been left behind for security had prepped the two RPGs and scanned the sky all around through binoculars.

As everyone converged on the chopper, the merc who had been on lookout duty on the roof shouted, "I saw two troop trucks and a handful of Jeeps, one with a roof-mounted 50-cal."

They all piled into the chopper, and the security merc said, "No air assault, Boss. We got lucky this time!" He started prepping his RPGs for storage, but Carl grabbed him and pulled him aboard.

"Leave that stuff!" To the pilot, he said, "Get us out of here and hug the ground."

As soon as the rear door closed, the pilot lifted off and raced the chopper just a few feet above the ground with the nose tilted down for max speed. Carl couldn't see the arriving force beyond the house, which meant they couldn't see Carl's chopper.

Carl watched the ground race by not even ten feet below. Right when it looked like the pilot was going to plow into the near hillside, the helicopter rapidly gained altitude, crested the hill, and dropped back down on the other side. Carl breathed a sigh of relief.

He mentally tuned into the quiet hum of the engine as the helicopter lifted higher into the sky some distance away from the Orizaga estate. He looked into the darkness outside the portside window and could feel the gazes of each of his team members on him. All of the mercs had seen him kill the old woman or heard about it immediately afterward.

Still facing the window, looking at the bright lights of the receding city of Hermosillo, he said, "The president and her daughter are in the hospital dying, and I'll do whatever it takes to save them. If I have to kill a hundred people or a thousand, I'll do it."

He said the words, but he didn't feel the truth of his own conviction.

Palmer seemed to sense his struggle. She touched his shoulder and whispered, "Compartmentalize."

He turned to face her. "I crossed the line, Nancy."

She shook her head. "You did what needed to be done. If you hadn't, we would not have the intel we came here for." She patted a Velcro pocket on her combat vest, where the thumb drive rested.

"I murdered an old woman for a bunch of files." The question he was trying to delay answering was how many lives were the president and her daughter worth?

"Hey, Boss," Merc Three said from the copilot's seat.

Carl turned his gaze on the man.

"I don't think I could have done what you did, but I know you had to pick someone."

Palmer said, "It was a mission-critical decision. She was the oldest, and she was already on life support." Palmer paused. "She was the right choice. She was the only choice."

Carl heard a near-silent "Hoo-wah" from behind him and figured it was an ex-military macho man's way of giving support. He glanced around the cabin and nodded. Then he turned back to the growing darkness outside. After a few moments, he turned and looked at Palmer for a long time. Her assessment was clinical and heartless, but he knew she was right.

"What have I become?" he said. Agent Palmer said nothing, so he continued, "It was easier this time."

She nodded.

"It was too easy. If Mrs. Orizaga hadn't given up the password…" He pondered whether to say it out loud or not. "I already had my next two targets picked." His gaze became distant. "I would have killed them all, Nancy. The kids too. To save the president, I would have done it."

Carl gripped the armrests of his seat so tightly his arms trembled. Agent Palmer reached over and laid her palm on his forearm. This time, there was no comfort in her touch. It didn't steady him. She only reminded him of how ill-prepared he was for this kind of life.

He was being swept along by events, and those events were changing him, reshaping him. His monster was taking over, driving him insane, and guiding him into the deepest, blackest part of the abyss. How much killing was too much? He thought about Aaron McGrath for a moment and wondered how long that man would fight the battle. He realized

McGrath would fight until the end. At that moment, Carl realized he had to be clinical like Palmer and McGrath. He had to pack his feelings away and accomplish the mission. His gaze grew hard.

Merc Three said, "You gonna be okay, Boss?"

"No," he said. "I'm going to see that old woman's face in my mind for the rest of my life."

Right next to my son's face. And Lenore Cummings. And her daughter, Lisette. And Anita Chapman. All of them forever reminding me how badly I fucked things up.

He looked back at Palmer. "How can someone compartmentalize that?"

She said nothing.

He pulled out his cell phone and stared at it for a moment. Then he looked at Palmer.

She said, "By your own rules, you can only use that cell once. Is whoever you're going to call *that* emergency?"

"McGrath needs to know his family is on a kill list."

Agent Palmer raised her eyebrow at his statement, and he knew what she was thinking. Director McGrath and he had declared war on each other last week. They'd hurt each other in the worst possible way, and now, Carl was reaching out to save McGrath's family.

He dialed the number Palmer gave him, and a coarse voice immediately answered, "Go for McGrath."

"You don't sound too good."

"Johnson." McGrath hacked for a long while, then said, "What's your situation?"

"We've been butt-fucked by an unknown adversary high up in the government. He or she is well positioned, protected, and has extensive resources."

"Agreed."

"There's no easy way to say this, but Nancy found a kill list with your daughter and her family on it. Can you get a team to her?"

McGrath hacked again. "Negative. I'm out of the game. Don't know how long I've been asleep. I remember someone trying to wake me, but…"

Carl had put the cell phone on speaker, and he and Palmer listened to the man cough until he was breathless.

"Something has changed, Johnson. I think someone's here—"

McGrath's voice was replaced by a rapid beeping tone. The call terminated. Carl looked at Palmer, then removed the battery from the cell.

Merc Three said, "What do you want to do, Boss?"

"The only thing we *can* do." He glanced around the cabin. "We fight until we can't. Our adversary has a team somewhere. He or she has staff members, assistants, and suppliers. These people have families too. Everybody does. We'll find them and use them."

Palmer narrowed her eyes. "Are you sure you want to go down that path, Carl?"

Carl grunted and looked forward. "I'm already going down that path. Have been for three weeks. I knew when I stepped into the abyss, there was no turning back. I never truly understood what that meant until today."

Until I killed that old woman.

He looked at Merc Three and at each of his mercs behind him. He knew they were seeing his doubt, but he also wanted them to see his resolve.

Finally, he rested his gaze on the agent sitting next to him. "Our adversary has already established the rules of engagement by using a sixteen-year-old girl to try to kill the president. The kid gloves are off. Nothing and nobody is off-limits." Carl sucked in a deep breath and let it out slowly. "Me and these guys"—he waggled a finger around the cabin—"we're terrorists, Nancy. The question is, can *you* go down this path with us?"

Palmer shrugged and said, "It's a good bet that I've already been classified as a traitor and a terrorist right along with you."

Carl nodded. "Then let's escalate. Let's give 'em something new to think about."

CHAPTER 30

"RAINMAN, THIS IS SPOKE."

"Go ahead."

"We have identified Mr. Garcia. His true name is Daniel Ortega. He's a naturalized US citizen originally from Mexico City. He's related to the well-known Ortega family, with extensive connections to black-market weapons and mercenaries, as well as offshore financing institutions and forgery operations. He has a wife and a newborn child in Albuquerque."

"Instruct the Unit to take him at his office at once. The intel on his computers will likely prove valuable. See if he'll voluntarily give up his account codes. If so, terminate him. If not, deliver him to the TER interrogation facility in Virginia."

"Very well. And what of the operations underway in Mexico, sir?"

"Reyes's beachfront house was completely destroyed, though Johnson's team still needs to be dealt with. They left Orizaga's home right before the army contingent arrived." Rainman's voice paused for a one-count. "In a helicopter."

Spoke expected that rebuke. "There was no record that Alfonso Reyes kept a helicopter at the house or that he even owned one," he lied.

The record had been on the audio recording of Johnson's conversation with Agent Peoples, but Spoke hadn't reviewed that recording until after his previous report, where he recommended using local military personnel rather than the fast-response Unit team from the airport. At that point, it was too late to do anything about the plan.

Rainman said, "Neither errors nor excuses will be tolerated."

Spoke paused. "Understood."

"Carl Johnson and what remains of his team are running out of options and assets in-country. They'll try to make contact with Garcia or possibly with the Ortega family for assistance. Have Orizaga move his local army assets against the Ortega family wherever they may be. I want them eliminated. All of them. If we can't find Johnson's team, then I want to leave them nowhere to turn for help."

CHAPTER 31

THE LANDSCAPE PASSING BENEATH THE helicopter was almost pitch black, except for the occasional lit homestead. Carl had asked the pilot to drop down below radar level and fly without running lights. The luxury helicopter skimmed low over the ground at full speed. They had no warning of the disaster until they were almost right over the site of the mansion. In his mind, Carl had been expecting to see the mansion destroyed and burning. As the helicopter flashed over the site, he realized there was no structure left to burn. All he saw in the near darkness was a huge dark pit. The building, its landscape, the security fence, the parked cars, and the APC had all been scraped from the earth. All that remained was a crater.

His heart leaped into his throat, and all he could think about was Julia Reyes. He gasped at the thought of losing her and absently reached out for Palmer's hand. He needed her stabilization more than anything at that particular moment.

"They got out," Palmer whispered. "We had an evac plan."

"No." Carl shook his head and looked out the window. "We didn't have a plan for *that*."

He let go of her hand, then leaned back in his seat and shifted his gaze to the horizon. A long line of blue and red strobe lights of emergency vehicles approached from several miles inland.

They had discussed the possibility of encountering a rogue army unit under the control of another high-ranking officer who might have replaced El Patron. They had defensive weapons to handle a low-level conflict like that, even if it involved a helicopter air assault or air force jets. But no one in their group—neither Carl, his mercs, nor his TER tactical support office—had anticipated this level of engagement. He drew valuable conclusions from what he saw.

The destruction below wasn't the result of a missile barrage from a helicopter gunship. Though Carl was a rookie in the business of war, he could easily tell the crater he now gazed into was the result of a single strike.

"Nancy," he said, "what kind of weapon is powerful enough to completely obliterate an eight-thousand-square-foot building, leaving no trace of the structure, and leave a crater that big?" He already thought he knew the answer.

Merc Three answered instead. "A fucking cruise missile would do that."

Palmer added, "With a high-explosive warhead. They'd want complete destruction, so they wouldn't use a drone-mounted smart bomb. That wouldn't have enough yield."

Carl nodded and glanced at the agent beside him. "I'm guessing Mexico doesn't possess cruise missiles."

In the dim light of the cabin, he saw Palmer shake her head. "None that I'm aware of."

"So our adversary can order a US Navy vessel somewhere to launch a cruise missile to destroy private property in a friendly nation." Carl shivered as he considered the power wielded by the adversary, then told the pilot, "Maintain radio silence, fly low, and continue back to the airport. That's our rally point. If there were survivors down there, that's where they'll go."

The Reyes ladies and the mercs probably never even knew what hit them. That's the way the US military operated.

Shock and awe.

All their adversary had to do was convince senior government officials that a credible terrorist threat existed at the location of the mansion.

We've located Carl Johnson, the American Terrorist who kidnapped the First Daughter. He has a sizable mercenary force, and we have ac-

tionable intel indicating he is preparing for another strike on US soil. There are zero friendlies at the location.

Palmer added, "And our adversary can order the execution of civilian women and children within our own borders."

Carl looked at Palmer. "Would a TER assault team kill civilians if ordered?"

"Never." She shook her head. "None of Aaron's directors or commanders would ever follow that kind of order, no matter who issued it. Nor would the SEALs, Delta, or the CIA wet-work teams."

Carl nodded. "So our adversary likely has an illegal kill squad in the US. Probably mercenaries. They're in New Mexico right now, preparing to murder women and children to make it look like I did it."

Palmer added, "So what are we going to do about it?"

"Excuse me?" Merc Three said. He looked around the cabin and made a finger movement like he was counting people. "I don't know if you all are keeping score, but we just got our asses handed to us on a silver fucking platter. My wife is down there in that fucking crater along with the rest of our goddamn team!"

Carl turned and spoke quietly to him. "My son is in that crater too, Trent, and if we don't somehow fix this, more innocent women and children, including the president and her daughter, are going to be in there too."

"But what *can* we do against this kind of adversary? This guy commands US military assets!"

Carl spoke loud enough for everyone, including the pilot, to hear him. "They're not going to stop hunting us. They're not going to assume we're dead. I wouldn't. They hit us hard, gave us a bloody nose, so we hit them back. We hunt them down and kill them before they kill us."

"News flash," Merc Three said from the front seat. "We're fighting the US *fucking* government. By definition, that makes *us* the bad guys."

"That's not news to me," Carl said. He looked over at Palmer. "You know the address of McGrath's op center in Virginia?"

She told him. "You're going to terminate him?" Her voice held surprise.

He gave her a devious smile, but he wasn't sure she saw it in the dark cabin.

"But why?" she continued. "He doesn't know what our next plan is. Hell, *we* don't even know what our next move is."

"Naw, Sista. He's an asset, and we need him. He implied that his op center is no longer secure, so I'm going to have Mr. Garcia send mercs out there to rescue him. Then I'm going to save his family." Carl paused. "And then he'll owe me. Forever."

CHAPTER 32

Y OUNG MR. GARCIA'S FEAR MANIFESTED itself as a knot in the pit of his stomach. He now knew the new TER guy, August Spoke, was the enemy. His gut had told him that fact hours ago, but his brain hadn't listened. The whole operation had transitioned from what Garcia could consider *normal* into something that didn't seem very governmental at all. He now saw the government trying to run a complex infiltration op in a foreign country to find out who kidnapped the president's daughter with only *one* agent on the other end handling everything.

How long does it take to fix a damned satellite or get a new one into position or whatever the government does with those things up there? With an op this important, you'd think they'd pull out all the stops to support the mission.

When Garcia thought about it from that perspective, nothing made sense anymore. The new agent named Spoke had somehow reeled him into the change of procedures, slowly stringing him along while giving him nothing in return. But that's what government agents did, wasn't it? They lied, if necessary, to achieve their mission.

If he'd followed Carl's protocol, he and his family would be on the road right then, with a couple million dollars in two duffel bags and a bazillion more in offshore accounts. He should have turned his back like his boss had told him to, yet he hadn't. He couldn't abandon the op center because he'd had a panicked feeling that Carl needed him. He had to be there…just in case.

On the plus side, he'd been able to act on Carl's text message, and he had just dispatched a three-man team from Mexico to the address in Carl's text. They'd be in position to extract Director McGrath in a couple hours. But now, it was time for Garcia to leave.

He would set up a new private operation center without government involvement or interference. Then if Carl needed assistance, he could provide support.

He went over to the wall, where all his dozens of backup smartphones were connected to chargers. He selected one and entered a brief text to his wife. She also had a one-time-use phone that she never used. It simply sat connected to a charger on the dining room table.

Get ready.

That was their emergency code. It didn't mean to get ready. It meant, "Get out now!" It meant pack nothing, not even baby supplies, and meet him at their prearranged rendezvous place.

He hit send, but the device immediately beeped at him. When he looked at the face, it gave him an error message: *Message not sent.*

He narrowed his eyes at the cell, then noticed the signal strength indicator in the upper corner showed no bars. He grabbed the second cell and discovered the same condition. Two others at his feet showed the same.

"Fuck!"

Garcia turned off the phone and raced to the door. He punched the self-destruct button and grabbed his duffel. He was rewarded by a flash of heat behind him and heard the sizzle of plastic and metal melting. Within two seconds, the innards of the computer were a molten puddle of ooze on the metal table. The circuit breaker on the power strip feeding the equipment quickly tripped as the computer's melting power supply shorted.

He yanked the door open and ran full speed down the hall to the elevator. He cursed himself with every footstep. He should have done what Carl told him to do. He should have gotten out sooner. Somehow, Agent Spoke had found his op center. The fact that they were blocking cell signals confirmed what Merc Two told everyone last week.

"Before they breach, they'll block all cell transmissions and landlines so we can't communicate. Then, they'll shut off the power. Then, they'll come in shooting."

The mercenary had been wrong. The invaders hadn't revealed their presence by shutting off the power. They were already in the building. Panic spurred him to run faster. The elevator was still in operation because the "up" arrow above the door was lit. He could hear the elevator's mechanism purring.

Fuck! They're coming up in the elevator!

Garcia ran past the elevator to the nearest fire escape stairs. It was actually farthest from his unit, so he hoped—no, he prayed—if they were also coming up the stairs, they would choose the fire escape closest to his unit at the other end of the hall. He realized the futility of his prayer as soon as he opened the fire escape door.

He eased the heavy metal door open slowly and quietly, half expecting a barrage of gunfire to welcome him. Instead, he noticed two things almost simultaneously. The electronic locks on the doors were normally card-operated. The doors could be opened from the inside simply with a push bar like he'd just done. From within the stairwell, though, only people who lived on each floor could open their door, and only with a card key. The indicator light on the key panel was always red except when it shone green for two seconds after a card swipe. Now, however, the green light was constantly on, and it stared him in the face. The assault team, whoever they were—cops, SWAT, FBI, covert government agents—had disabled all the stairwell locks with a master command. The second thing he noticed was the trample of boots echoing in the stairwell, coming up from below.

He was trapped.

CHAPTER 33

1815 MST, FRIDAY
ALBUQUERQUE, NM

WITH THE FIRE DOOR OPEN just enough to stick his head through, Garcia listened to multiple sets of combat boots pounding quickly up the stairs. The reverberating echo in the silent fire escape made it sound like a whole SWAT army was coming up, but Garcia figured it was probably only three or four. After all, the deployed force would also have teams coming up the other fire escape stairwell and the elevator.

They were close, maybe just below him on the third-floor landing. If he stayed in the hallway or in the condo, he was dead. The chime of the elevator arriving at the fourth floor reminded him he had no choice but to enter the stairwell. He pushed the door open a bit more and slid through. Then, he realized the pounding boots had suddenly stopped.

Shit! They heard the elevator chime through the open door!

In his mind, Garcia pictured the leader holding up his fist to stop his team members. He pictured them straining to hear something, anything. So he froze in the stairwell with his hand holding the big metal door open. He couldn't let it go because the hiss of hydraulic air would betray the door closing.

There was only one direction for him to flee—up—but he dared not move. The slightest squeak of his shoes on the concrete floor would betray him, as would the rustle of the denim fabric of his pants rubbing together as he moved forward. So he froze until he heard someone speaking.

"Copy that," the voice below him said. "Almost in position." The voice took a different tone and said, "Let's go."

The boots pounded the concrete again, and Garcia let go of the door, hoping the echo of boots would cover the sound of the massive door closing and his footsteps. Fortunately, because the building's upper floors were all residential, the metal fire escape doors were cushioned against the frame by rubber molding. The door closed with a barely audible bump that was lost in the boot noise.

Garcia got himself around the turn of the steps halfway between the fourth floor and the fifth and waited. There was a moment of silence as the unseen assault force gathered at the fire door.

"Go!"

The force moved quickly through the doorway, but before the door closed behind them, Garcia heard a voice trail up the hallway, saying, "Copy that. Reengage all locks and secure the building."

Shit!

A moment ago, he'd been trapped in the hallway. Now, he was trapped in the stairwell. He heard a chorus of electrical clicks as the fire door locks engaged in the stairwell. At the fifth-floor landing in front of him, he heard the sound of the locking mechanism, which was accompanied by the green light extinguishing and the red light illuminating at the fire door.

He had no choice now. He had to go down to the first floor. That was the only door that was always unlocked in accordance with fire regulations to let people get out safely. He didn't want to go down there because he knew there would be someone on guard, but he couldn't stay where he was.

When the force discovered the melted computer equipment and realized he was not in the condo—they probably were making the discovery at that exact moment—they'd canvas the entire building. They'd go up first to clear the fifth floor. Then they'd make their way downward, clearing each floor as they descended. When that happened, he'd better be out of the building.

He unzipped his small duffel bag and pulled out the gun. It was a Glock, but Garcia found no comfort having possession of the weapon. He'd fired guns over the years growing up in Mexico, but he wasn't fooling himself into believing he could survive a gunfight with the force in the building searching for him. The problem was, if there was a man downstairs on guard, he wouldn't get out of the building *without* a gunfight. And as soon as the shooting started, the force would be all over him.

He looked the weapon over and decided quickly that a gun wasn't going to help him in his current situation. He put it back in his bag and ran quickly down the stairs. He tried the fire doors on each level as he passed, even though all the red indicator lights were lit, and they were all locked as he expected. At the bottom of the stairwell, he stopped and peered through the small window in the door. The window was too small for any person to fit through, and even if it had been large enough, it was laced with thin wire, making the window virtually penetration-proof.

The condo building butted up against a public parking structure, but the portion of the ground-level parking area reserved for condo residents was fenced off from the public parking areas. Somehow, the assault force had gained access through the card-access gate, and two big black SUVs were parked haphazardly in that area.

Even if Garcia managed to sneak past the single guard that he saw, he'd still be trapped inside the fenced area. There was one access gate for cars and another, smaller pedestrian gate, but the guard was stationed close to both. Garcia couldn't get through either one unnoticed. The guard was glancing around, but he was still facing away from the fire exit. At first, Garcia didn't understand until he heard the voice in the stairwell above, accompanied again by the thunder of fast-moving boots.

"On our way down!"

The guard looked down and began fiddling around. Garcia realized the man was zipping his fly. He'd been peeing up against Garcia's car, which was parked right next to one of the black SUVs.

Garcia smoothly and quietly eased the fire door open and gently let it close. He stepped one pace to the right and crouched between the concrete wall and the small trash compactor. It wasn't much of a hiding place, but it was somewhat in the shadows, and no one would see him unless they were actually looking right at the compactor.

He grabbed the gun from his bag again. His goal wasn't to win a battle. On the contrary, when he started shooting, they'd shoot to kill. He knew what the government had done to Carl. He knew of the *harsh interrogation* methods used. There was no way in hell he was going to let them strap him to that table and torture him.

The fire door burst open. The first man stopped and held the door for ten more men, and he talked on an unseen radio at the same time. He was close enough for Garcia to touch his leg. If the man even glanced in his direction, he'd be found.

"He was long gone, Mr. Drake." There was a long pause. "Negative on the hardware. He triggered a heat charge. There was nothing left but a puddle of plastic fused to the table." Another pause. "The heat was intense. They knew eventually someone would find them. They were prepared."

The speaker released the door after the last man exited, then said, "Copy that. He's got maybe a five-minute head start on us. Have local PD cordon off a three-block radius around his house. He lives in what is called the South Valley. We're fifteen minutes out."

The black-clad force loaded into the two SUVs, and the gate opened as they pulled in front of its motion sensor.

Still concealed, Garcia reached into his duffel and pulled out a cell phone. He had three bars, so the assault force had turned off their jammer. He sent the same brief text message to his wife's one-time-use phone: *Get ready.*

This time, the text message went through.

Their prearranged meeting place, Lumpy's, was their favorite burger joint out on the west end of Central Avenue. It was a mile from their home, so he knew she'd be out of the cordoned area.

If she left right now. If, unlike Garcia, she followed Carl's instructions.

CHAPTER 34

2105 MST, FRIDAY
ALBUQUERQUE, NM

T HE *ADVERSARY* WANTED SPECIAL AGENT Cummings and Anita Chapman and their families dead, so Carl wanted them alive. Their deaths figured into the adversary's plans somehow. Maybe it was as simple as Palmer thought—the adversary wanted to make the kill look like Carl was resurfacing as the terrorist. Maybe it was true that his opponent was using one of his tricks—throwing a head fake at the world so law enforcement would be preoccupied with Carl while his opponent roamed free to complete his plans, whatever those were.

Carl didn't think the events could be viewed so simply, though. There was a reason for what the adversary was doing, even though Carl didn't know what that reason was. Nevertheless, he wanted to negate whatever advantage his opponent was seeking. He wanted to force him or her to adapt and possibly make a mistake.

Besides, he felt responsible for the targets' lives. It was because of Carl that they were on the kill list. They weren't combatants. They didn't deserve to be pawns in his war with the adversary.

Two days ago, Carl found the whole process of transiting the southern border of the United States rather mundane. He had simply driven across the border at the Columbus, New Mexico, Port Of Entry in plain sight, using a disguise that matched his fake-but-legitimate ID and passport. He'd returned with the president's daughter aboard the helicopter belonging to the now-deceased El Patron.

This morning, he'd flown south across the border, compliments of the covert TER agency. Now, he had just returned to Albuquerque on the same government plane. Colonel Vesario Reichert, the Gulfstream's pilot, told him they were listed as a private jet bound for Houston from Mexico City, even though they didn't leave from that airport. As soon as they were airborne, the superintendent Carl had paid off altered their flight plan, and they were given permission to fly directly into Albuquerque.

It sounded easy enough, but Carl still wasn't convinced the feds wouldn't be waiting for him at the cargo hangar when they landed. His worrying was for naught because the customs officer that met the plane at the cargo hangar allowed him through with barely a perfunctory glance at his passport and a few questions about what he was bringing into the country.

He retrieved his SUV from the cargo hangar parking lot and left the airport through the south gate while the colonel, also with a false identity, stayed with the plane and got it refueled. A few minutes later, Carl merged his SUV onto northbound I-25.

Sooner or later, Carl knew the adversary would see through his deception. The adversary wouldn't expect him to fly back to Albuquerque in the middle of a mission, but every hour his plane sat at the airport increased his risk of discovery.

Suddenly, his paranoia kicked into overdrive, and he wondered if his adversary hadn't somehow marked his SUV while he was gone. Maybe someone had attached an electronic transmitter to the car on the premise that he or someone else on his Albuquerque team would retrieve the vehicle. Maybe they were tracking him right now.

He pulled off the highway and wound his way through downtown, pulling in and out of parking garages and through alleys, until he parked in the underground garage of the Hyatt. He parked right next to his open-air Jeep that was still parked there, though he was mildly surprised the FBI hadn't confiscated the vehicle when they thought he was the drug lord. It seemed like so much longer than a month since they had first arrested him and turned him over to the TER for interrogation.

Carl got out and walked up the exit ramp and out of the garage. He walked east a bit, crossed the street, and entered another parking garage. He found Mr. Garcia's backup cars and noted they were exactly as he'd told Garcia to purchase. They were all old, nondescript SUVs with faded paint, dents, and scratches. All were legally purchased and properly registered with the state Motor Vehicle Department. He selected one at random and found the keys in the most obvious place—above the visor—and left the parking garage.

He detoured to the far west end of Central Avenue to grab another duffel of cash from his storage unit. If he got to them in time, his survivors would need the cash. It was at that moment Carl realized his operation had completely unraveled, and he was left with virtually no usable assets. He still had the contents of the storage shed, but he had no local team members to rely on for support. He felt exposed and vulnerable because he wasn't a trained field agent like Palmer or the mercs. He was a thinker, a big-picture guy, not an experienced tactical combatant. He was in it up to his eyeballs.

He still had the four mercs he'd left along with Agent Palmer, but they were a million miles away in Mexico. They were tasked with locating the president's chief of staff and figuring out who the adversary was. When he returned to Mexico, Carl needed a plan to eliminate that person, but he knew a team of six was really inadequate for that task.

Merc Four and her men were dead. They had failed to rendezvous at the municipal airport. Carl felt another pang of heartache as he thought about Julia Reyes's pretty smile and her hugs. Her mother had made her own decisions by becoming mixed up in the mess with her husband long before Carl came into the picture, but Julia was innocent. She didn't deserve the life she'd been given. Ultimately, he knew their deaths were his fault. He should have expected his adversary to bring the big guns to the party. He should have had a contingency for that possible outcome.

It was also entirely possible he would never see Mr. Garcia again. He felt an attachment to the young man. He was going to miss him. Garcia was like a protégé. The young man had been the first man he had hired after his son was killed.

Before he'd gone on his mission of revenge.

Before he started murdering FBI agents and covert government operators.

Before he became the American Terrorist.

If he discounted the moral and ethical implications of his illegal operations, somehow Garcia had become his last connection to that previous life before the killing and revenge had started.

Carl made his way back to northbound I-25 and headed toward Santa Fe. He figured the Chapmans would be less capable of displaying hostility toward him than Special Agent Cummings, so he decided to go for them first. Anita Chapman wasn't going to be happy to see him again, not after what he did to her. Her husband wasn't going to be happy either.

CHAPTER 35

CARL DROVE THE SPEED LIMIT, taking almost an hour to get to Santa Fe. He easily found the Chapman house in the east part of town up near Canyon Road, where the well-to-do folks lived. The address had been efficiently included on the task list.

He appreciated the fact that in this part of town, the roads were rarely straight for any significant distance. That meant anyone trying to conduct surveillance on him, or on the Chapman house, would have to be in close proximity, which raised their potential for exposure.

Carl saw nothing suspicious as he parked along a street with no sidewalk. He had changed into civilian clothes on the plane, then changed back into his black tactical gear at the storage unit. Glancing around his old SUV again, he checked his Glock, pulled the suppressor from a Velcro pocket on his vest, and screwed it onto the end of his gun.

Like many older sections of Albuquerque and Santa Fe comprised mostly of adobe homes, the Chapmans' home had an alley behind it—a throwback to times when garages and carriage houses were accessed from the back of houses. Carl walked quietly along the alley behind the Chapman house and paused at the gate leading into their backyard. He looked up and back. Almost as an afterthought, he thumbed the release lever on his Glock, let the magazine fall out of the handgrip and into his left palm, held it up in the dim light, and reassured himself the mag was full. He slid the mag back in and quietly snapped it into place with his palm. The wall was thick adobe, a six-footer, so he couldn't see over it. Good news was no one could see him approach until he was actually in the backyard. He eased the gate open a bit and slid through, his handgun pointed at the ground near his feet.

He wasn't too concerned about the husband. Despite the violence he had put the family through just three days ago, these were *normal* people who went through their lives feeling insulated from people like Carl. Their gate wasn't locked, and the drapes in the expansive family room windows facing him from fifty feet away were wide open. He wouldn't be surprised if the patio door was unlocked. That's how normal people lived. Even when their lives were touched by violence, they assumed lightning never struck twice.

The backyard was expensively landscaped with gravel, sand, natural trees, and shrubs. There was no grass. The high moon lit the yard, and Carl moved easily among the shadows until he stood next to the sliding patio door. He pushed the handle, and the extra-wide door slid open an inch. He felt heat waft through the crack.

He scanned the patio once more before making his entrance and understood why the door was unlocked. A huge pile of firewood was neatly stacked just off the far side of the concrete slab. The cloudless sky had allowed the temperature to plummet down below twenty degrees—a perfect night for a roaring fire in the corner kiva fireplace.

Even as he contemplated whether to sneak in quietly or to move in fast, Anita's teenage son went over and stoked the fire. It blazed up almost immediately, and Carl heard the snaps and pops as tiny nodules of sap in the soft pine logs blasted with mini-explosions of smoke and sparks. Carl couldn't clearly see Anita because she was seated on the couch, on the other side of her husband, but he could see the two-year-old in her lap clapping gleefully, and two of Anita's smaller children—they looked like twin girls—were cheering and laughing on the floor just in front of her.

Carl risked another peek to see the whole room and where everyone was in it. Todd rose from the long, plush couch, and Carl's gaze followed the man as he went into the kitchen. Then he looked back at Anita, and his breath caught in his throat at the sight of her. She saw him at the same instant and screamed.

Tried to scream.

Carl pushed the big glass door open easily and stepped inside as Anita uttered more of a croak than a scream. Her mouth was held nearly shut by the metal contraption strapped around her head. A black strap stretched around the back of her head, and another stretched over the top of her head and beneath her jaw. Another forehead strap was attached to the over-the-head strap and was held against Anita's forehead with a cushion pad. A single, slender metal bar was attached to the forehead strap and extended down to her chin, following the contours of her face, nose, and mouth. It was held against her chin with another cushion pad.

A horizontal, inflexible wire attached from the vertical bar and the ends of the wire arms disappeared into her jawbones at the edges of her mouth. The whole apparatus, Carl knew, was to prevent her jaws and facial bones from healing crooked and disfiguring her after the beating she had received at his hands.

My God! I did that to her.

He shuddered as he relived the memory, and for the briefest moment, he forgot about the teenager tending to the fire.

Until the boy grunted.

Carl saw the chunk of wood coming at his head from the extreme edge of his peripheral vision, and at the last fraction of a second, he did his *Matrix* move. He leaned backward and to the side, arms flung out to either side, and the dry feathered bark of the wood actually brushed his nose. The small log flew through the space his head had just occupied, hit the far wall ten feet to Carl's left, and stuck in the drywall.

Slowly bringing himself upright, Carl looked at the young man and pointed the Glock at him, but he kept his finger off the trigger. He had no intention of shooting anyone, but the sight of a handgun with a huge suppressor on the barrel was a scary sight for most *normal* folks. It had the desired effect on the teen, and his eyes flared wide.

"Nice throw, kid. Now sit your ass down."

The teen did as he was told but glared at Carl all the way over to the couch. No doubt he was recalling Mr. Garcia's three men who had taken the family hostage. He sat next to his mom, and to Carl's surprise, Anita Chapman passed the two-year-old from her lap to her son, stood, and walked over to Carl. She stood silently before him for a few seconds.

She was a pitiful sight. One eye was still half closed and discolored, though most of the swelling from his beating had obviously gone down. She had a string of tiny butterfly bandages stuck to her left eyebrow, where he had struck her repeatedly with the butt of his gun while trying to get her into the basement safe that was to be her prison cell. She still wore a clear plastic nose guard taped to her cheeks.

If she'd just gotten in the vault like I told her…

She gazed at him through green eyes. Her short brown hair was laced through with blond streaks and was plastered against her head by the metal-and-strap face brace. She looked about forty or so, pleasantly plump with a round face that had probably been oval three or four kids ago.

"My father told me about your son." She looked at him for a long torturous time, then said, "So have you changed your mind and come to kill me and my family?"

Carl was silent. He wanted to apologize, but he knew there weren't enough words in the universe that would make her forgive him for what he'd done to her.

"Well?" she hissed as she watched him examine her brace. "Are you pleased with your handiwork?"

She looked up at him because she was half a head shorter. He could tell she was afraid, but she stood there, not moving or trembling.

Finally, he could take the silence no longer. He looked away. The sight of her laying on the floor of the steel vault, her face a bloody mess, haunted him. All because he wanted revenge on her father, Aaron McGrath.

"No," he said quietly. "I'm ashamed." His voice cracked.

Her eyebrows rose in surprise. It clearly wasn't the reaction she was expecting. "Then why are you here? We're no threat to you."

Carl heard a toilet flush, and a few seconds later, Todd reentered the family room. As soon as he saw Carl, he looked quickly at the couch to see that the kids were safe.

He stepped quickly around the long couch and the coffee table, passing in front of the fireplace, and froze when he saw the gun in Carl's grip, pointed at the floor. "What the hell is this?" he demanded. "Haven't you done enough?"

Carl wagged his arm a bit, lightly slapping the gun against his leg in warning when it appeared Todd was going to try to be a hero. He was a big guy, but he was soft. He was a homebody, a family guy, a *normal* guy. At the sight of the gun, he stayed where he was.

Anita reached out and laid her left hand on Carl's right forearm. "Please don't hurt my family. Please."

She paused for a moment, and Carl thought her breath smelled like coffee. He glanced over her right shoulder and saw her cup sitting next to a big bowl of popcorn dead center of the coffee table. Of course, with the brace on her head she probably couldn't open her mouth wide enough to eat any kind of solid food.

She continued, "It's me you want. I'll go willingly. Just don't hurt them."

Anita's eyes watered as she pleaded, but Carl took a deep breath to steady himself and to get rid of the guilt.

"Sista, if I'd come here to kill someone, they'd be dead already." He considered how to explain his purpose there but opted for the truth. "Your father is in trouble, and some bad men are coming after you and your family."

Anita took her hand from his arm and made a croaking sound that would have been a laugh of ridicule if the brace weren't keeping her mouth mostly closed. "*Bad* men?"

"Okay," Carl said. "*Worse* men." She looked like she was going to argue, but he held up a hand to silence her, speaking loud enough for everyone to hear. "Look, President Mallory's daughter was kidnapped by a man that looked like me, so Aaron and his people thought it was me. That's how all this started."

He felt somewhat vindicated that McGrath had confessed his error to his daughter, if not to him. "There are powerful people in our government and in the Mexican government behind the kidnapping, and your father and I are mixed up in this mess. Those people want you and your kids dead—I don't know why—so I want you alive. It's as simple as that. So you can come with me and live, or you can stay here and die. And don't take all night thinking about it."

Todd said, "How the hell do you expect us to trust you after what you did to us—to *her*?"

"Your trust is irrelevant," Carl said. "I'm leaving here in sixty seconds. Live or die?"

He packed his Glock into the shoulder holster Merc Three had modified to accommodate the suppressor. He pulled the key to his SUV from his left pants pocket.

"Yo, kid. You know how to drive?" The teen nodded, so Carl tossed him the keys. "At the end of the alley and to the right is a late-model SUV with dark tinted windows and faded white paint. Drive it up the alley and stop right beside the gate." Carl thumbed over his shoulder. "Wait for us there, but do *not* use the horn."

Anita, her husband, and her son all looked at each other. Finally, she and Todd both nodded, and their son ran through the open patio door.

Carl said to the adults, "Bundle up the kids in coats and let's go. Right now!"

The parents jumped into motion, and in half a minute, the two twin girls and the toddler had hats, gloves, and coats on. They all looked like a family getting ready to go out and play in the snow, except there was no snow outside. Just freezing cold.

Anita said, "Todd, grab as much food and water as you can carry."

Carl shook his head. "Negative on that. I have emergency supplies in the car. And no cell phones, laptops, tablets, or iPods. All those electronic gadgets can be tracked. And no ID cards, wallets, credit cards, or ATM cards. If for any reason you get stopped by police, and they enter you into their computer, the bad guys—the *worse* guys—will instantly know where you are because all your accounts are probably already flagged."

Carl hustled them out into the backyard, where he heard the SUV idling in the alley. He held Todd back and told him to unfasten the propane tank from the grill, open the cock, and toss the tank near the fireplace.

"I'm not leaving you alone with my family, you bastard."

Carl just grunted at him. "Fine. Get in the car, and I'll torch the house. When the *worse* guys get here and your house is on fire, it will take them some time to discover that you're not inside. It might give us a decent head start."

Carl pulled a thick envelope from his inner jacket pocket and handed it to Todd. Todd just stood there while he set about disconnecting the propane tank.

"Jesus!" the man said, rifling through the hundred-dollar bills. "How much is in here?"

"Fifty thousand. There's more in the car. Because from now until it's safe, you can't go to your bank or do any kind of online banking or withdrawals of any kind. You have to stay completely off the grid."

Todd walked backward toward the rear gate. "What's to stop me from just driving off and leaving your ass here?"

"Because I know how to stay off the grid, and you don't." He heaved the heavy metal canister to the patio door. "Without my help, the men looking for you will find you in less than a day."

Carl opened the valve and heard the satisfying hiss of escaping gas. He turned the canister onto its side and rolled it across the carpeted floor toward the fireplace. He and Todd Chapman ran to the gate.

The explosion was less than dramatic. There was merely a slight whoosh as the escaping gas ignited. Because the patio door remained wide open, the overpressure wave from the mild explosion easily escaped the house without blowing out any windows. Most of the family room caught fire immediately, and Carl knew the whole house would be engulfed within minutes.

Todd jumped into the front passenger seat, and Carl jumped into the first row behind him and his son. When he pulled the door closed behind him, he found himself thinking the car looked more like a family minivan than an SUV. There was an uncomfortable moment when Carl realized he had landed himself on the bench seat next to Anita. Her twin six-year-old daughters occupied the rear bench seat.

The teen looked back at him from the driver's seat and said, "Where to?"

Carl said, "I'll drive. Let's you and I trade seats."

He didn't want to take the chance of getting stopped by cops for letting a teen driver with no ID handle the car. Besides, he needed to get away from Anita. His guilt was almost unbearable.

Todd said, "So where are we going?"

"To Albuquerque," Carl said. "I have to save another woman who wants to kill me even more than you do."

CHAPTER 36

ARL PULLED THE SUV OVER two blocks east of Cummings's house in East Downtown Albuquerque just past midnight. He'd taken a two-hour detour east of Santa Fe, then went south, ending up on I-40 some thirty miles east of Albuquerque. Back in Albuquerque, he wound around the residential streets until he was certain no one was trailing him. He stopped the car northeast of Broadway and Central, left the engine running, and gave Todd Chapman specific instructions. Then he took off on foot.

As he walked along the quiet streets trying to avoid the pools of light cast by the occasional overhead streetlights, he considered how he could approach FBI Special Agent Lenore Cummings. She wasn't going to be any happier to see him again than Anita Chapman and her family were. Carl knew that for a fact. The difference was that the FBI agent had the skills and the tools to fight while the Chapmans did not. Cummings wouldn't be amenable to any kind of discussion. Of that, he had absolutely zero doubt. She'd kick his ass if she had the opportunity, or she'd shoot him if she had a gun handy.

He'd strapped that woman to a table naked and humiliated her. He'd given her all kinds of visualizations of what he could do to her daughter. He'd even strapped Lisette to a table right next to her and almost cut into the girl's chest with a scalpel to make the agent give up Director Mc-Grath's location.

In the end, he almost killed the girl in a blind rage. He'd wanted to very badly, just to punish the FBI agent for her role in his son's death. He wanted to make her feel what he felt, just like he'd wanted to kill Anita Chapman to punish her father. But he hadn't been able to do the deed. He couldn't kill Cummings's child or McGrath's adult child. Fact was, he knew his mercy wouldn't garner him any karma points with the special agent just as it had not with Anita.

No, Cummings won't talk. She'll take action. She'll try to kill me first chance she gets.

His next thought was to try entering quietly and taking her daughter hostage again—hold a gun to the girl's head. Surely, that would make a mother hesitate and make her listen to reason, but this particular mother was highly trained. She might sense he wasn't prepared to kill the girl any more now than he had been three days ago. Besides, he was unwilling to put that girl through that kind of hell again.

As he approached her street, he realized his decision had been made for him. He spotted a big black SUV parked on the street to his right. It had a government license plate, and that stopped Carl in his tracks for a moment. He nodded to himself as he realized he'd just learned something new about his adversary. His opponent could command the use of government assets, even if the personnel, as Palmer figured, were mercenaries. The assault force wanted to remain undetected, so they'd parked on the next street.

He approached the vehicle, crossing the street at an angle the way someone would if they were simply on their way home after the midnight shift. Then, he realized what a rookie he was. If they'd left someone in the truck, that guy would see him coming. He closed his eyes and cursed himself silently. Nevertheless, he was committed. He couldn't change his path now because that too would alert any watcher left behind in the truck.

Carl sauntered past the driver's door, then at the last second, he spun back and pulled his Glock in the same motion. He aimed two-handed but found the driver's seat empty. He couldn't see into the back because the other windows were heavily tinted. He took a deep breath to steady his nerves and reached for the door handle. It was unlocked, and the door opened easily, but no explosion of gunfire greeted him. The vehicle was empty. On a hunch, Carl checked the ignition and found the key missing. He pulled down the sun visor, and the key dropped onto the seat. He snatched the key, tossed it into the shrubs across the street, quietly closed the truck door, and headed back to the corner to make his way over to Cummings's street. When the kill squad tried to escape, they'd have to walk.

The FBI agent's house was third from the corner, on the west side of the street. He paused at the house on the corner. For a brief moment, Carl thought about avoiding the confrontation. He was a fifty-three-year-old rookie, not a combat veteran. He thought about removing his suppressor and firing a few shots in the air to give Cummings the warning she needed. No sooner had the thought crossed his mind, he realized all that would do was let the commandos know he was in the area. They wouldn't abandon their mission. They'd simply accelerate. Cummings was a federal cop, so she had her firearm with her, but she was outgunned, warning or not.

Carl took a deep breath to steel his nerves. The corner house featured a long, six-foot-tall brick wall along the north side of the backyard. Carl slid into the bushes at the end of the brick wall almost at the front of the house, where the yard wrapped around the side a bit. He remained still and silent for a few seconds and strained his senses for any sign of movement near him.

He heard a whining sound behind him and saw a dog lying on its side next to the chain-link fence that connected the brick wall to the house. In the moonlight, he could see its flank was covered in blood and knew at least one member of the assault team had crouched exactly where he was now.

He climbed the fence as quickly and quietly as he could and knelt beside the dying animal for a moment. The old mutt gazed at him through puppy-dog eyes and whimpered again, but Carl could do nothing for the animal. Even a suppressed gunshot to end the pup's pain would echo in the near-silent night.

He continued through the backyard and climbed over the sidewall of the next house. He paused and listened, then approached the wall to Cummings's house. He grabbed the top of the wall and slowly did a chin-up until his eyes cleared the top, and he looked into the yard. Nothing moved.

The FBI agent had a nice Victorian house with a fairly large backyard. While most of the restored Victorians in East Downtown were red or painted brick with wrap-around porches—trimmed in vibrant colors of green, white, mauve, or even yellow—Cummings's house looked light blue or gray in the moonlight. Wide slats of horizontal vinyl siding covered the outside of her house.

He'd seen lots of old Victorian houses in Ohio two decades before, when he'd been stationed at Wright-Patt. In fact, he knew that in the early 1900s, a lot of folks moved to Albuquerque from back east and had built their homes in the eastern Victorian style. This was in what was known as New Town. Back then, New Town was the eastern edge of Albuquerque, the frontier. Downtown was its neighbor to the west, and a mile west of Downtown was the enclave still known as Old Town, which featured the native adobe-style home.

New Town, Downtown, Old Town—that was all there was to Albu-querque a hundred years ago. Over the decades, New Town was absorbed into Downtown, becoming known in recent years as the hip and trendy East Downtown.

While the colors of the Victorians and the front facades looked different, Carl knew the interior layouts were all fairly similar. Most had porches, front and back, some stretching the full width of the house and some not. The front entry doors of most of the homes evenly bisected the width of the houses. Most of the homes were two-story, as was Cummings's house, and most of the front doors led not into a foyer, but directly into a wide hallway that featured a staircase up to the second floor. Typically, the bedrooms and a bathroom were upstairs, and the living areas and kitchen were downstairs.

As Carl peeked over the wall, he noticed Cummings's house lacked a back porch. Instead, it had an expansive deck on the back with a shiny steel cooking grill shining in the moonlight. There was a minimal amount of grass beyond the deck, and some shrubs and a couple of trees stood guard next to the back cinder block wall.

On the side of the house near Carl's wall was a small sitting patio with a metal lattice table and two matching chairs. He assumed the furniture was black, though he couldn't be sure since they were in deep shadows. The sitting patio was lined with foot-high planter boxes, though all the plants were in hibernation for the winter. The patio door was a glass

French door, and it was ajar, having been forced open without breaking the glass.

Carl completed his chin-up, scrabbling over the top of the wall far less gracefully than the heroes in the movies. He landed awkwardly but on his feet, then crept through the open glass door. He squatted just inside the door, and his attention was drawn straight ahead toward voices coming from a room on the opposite side of the house. He heard a man's voice and a no-nonsense woman's voice he instantly recognized as Lenore Cummings.

He crept silently toward the voices and heard the wood floor creaking above his head. It was a stealthy creak, slow and deliberate, like his own. Someone was searching the upstairs rooms to see which were occupied. From his previous research on the agent earlier in the week, Carl knew she lived with her mother and her daughter. There was no man in Cummings's life, yet the creaking floor sounded to Carl like a heavy person moving about cautiously.

Carl could tell Cummings's house had been modified from its original layout. The living room, where he now crept, and the dining room and kitchen had all been combined into one open living space with all the walls removed. He knew from experience that at least one of those walls would have been load-bearing back in the day, so thick laminated wood beams would have been inserted above the downstairs ceiling to support the upper floor. It hadn't been done well enough, which was why he heard the flooring above his head creaking. Also, the wall between the hallway and the living room had been removed. With that wall removed, the stairs seemed to sit inside the living room. The staircase itself had been remodeled into a trendy fixture with metal steps and metal railings, with see-through lattice below the banister to make sure kids didn't fall over the sides. It was very modern and chic. The front door on Carl's left was almost directly in front of the staircase.

Carl approached a set of solid wood double doors to the left of the front door, as one would perceive it upon entering the house. He approached out of view of the occupants because the left door of the set was closed, and the right half was open just wide enough for a person—maybe a mercenary—to slide through sideways.

Pulling his silenced Glock from his shoulder holster, Carl eased into the doorway and saw the doors led into Cummings's bedroom, likely a former reading or family room now remodeled into the master bedroom suite. She sat upright in her king-size bed located under a large window. With her table lamp on, he could see that her blanket covered her lower body, and she was wearing a high-necked, white cotton nightgown.

"You!" she said as she saw Carl in the doorway.

The commando, who stood in front of the left half of the double door set, had his back almost completely toward Carl. The man chuckled. "Like I'm going to fall for that trick."

Carl said, "You should have."

Just as the commando started to turn toward his voice, he shot him in the side of his neck, just below the edge of his combat helmet. The bullet tore out through the other side of his neck accompanied by a minimal squirt of blood, and the man collapsed where he stood.

There was a sudden movement from upstairs, like maybe someone twisting in surprise at the sound from below, so Carl knew the other commandos knew that something had gone wrong with their plan. After all, a suppressed gunshot was only silent compared to an unsuppressed shot, but it was still quite loud in a quiet house in the dead of night.

Carl ran up the metal stairs three steps at a time. A girl's squeal of fright reached his ears, and he grabbed the metal banister at the top to fling his momentum back in the opposite direction, toward where he now knew the girl's bedroom was—right over her mother's.

He burst through her closed door with a kick that shattered the wood jamb and ripped the top hinge right out of the wall. The commando had a hand over Lisette's mouth and was trying to manhandle the kicking girl into a firmer grasp, so he was totally unprepared for Carl's violent entrance. Carl shot him right through the left lens of his acrylic combat goggles. He fell back and released the girl, and Carl simply grabbed her hand and literally dragged her into the hallway.

"Let's go! Your mom is waiting downstairs."

To his surprise, she didn't argue, scream, or resist. They had just gotten to the back of the hall at the top of the stairs when Carl realized he'd made a critical error. The creeping sound he'd heard when he'd first entered through the patio door had come from the room above the living room—not from Lisette's room.

Even as he realized his mistake, four things happened at almost the exact same instant. First, Carl got to the top of the stairs with the girl at his side at the same time that Agent Cummings arrived at the bottom of the stairs. She lined up the sights of her MP5 right between Carl's eyes.

Then, the *second* thing happened.

The door opened across the hall from Lisette's room, and a commando took aim. Without thinking, Carl spun in front of the child as flame erupted from the man's weapon.

For the second time in a week, Carl took bullets in the back of his combat vest. The multiple impacts pushed him and the girl against the wall. She squealed as they bounced off hard. He fell flat on his back with the girl still in his grasp.

Then, the *third* thing happened.

CHAPTER 37

CARL'S MOMENTUM ROLLED HIM OVER on top of the girl and almost down the first step of the stairs. When Carl looked up, he saw the commando looking right at him. His weapon was aimed at Carl's head as he pulled the trigger again at point-blank range.

But he missed.

Cummings had fired a brief salvo that peppered the steel railing in front of the killer a millisecond before he'd fired. She'd missed since she didn't have a clear shot, but sparks had flashed in every direction, and the commando flinched as he fired.

Carl felt the heat as the man's bullets zipped by his left shoulder. He shot the man five times—twice in the neck and three times in the face.

Then, the *fourth* thing happened.

Right after Cummings fired at the commando, she took two steps back to get a better angle on the guy. She raised her MP5 to fire, even as Carl shot the man dead, and the front door exploded inward. Carl saw the FBI agent knocked off her feet by the blast, and her weapon slid across the highly polished wood floor.

Still on his belly with the girl protected beneath him, Carl aimed at the three black-clad commandos who stormed through the blown-out doorway. They all held some kind of futuristic-looking, short-barreled weapon with smooth rounded features that was barely longer than the width of a man's shoulders. There was no magazine extending downward beneath the weapon.

The first man in aimed at Cummings, so Carl shot that man first. His shot bounced off the top of the man's Kevlar helmet, and the man screamed in pain and fell back. Carl rose up on one knee, firing in a two-handed position until his gun was empty. Shaking and breathing deeply, he picked himself and Lisette up and led her by the hand cautiously down the stairs.

He saw Cummings get to her feet, and he said, "There could be as many as two more unaccounted for if their SUV had been crammed to the gills with shooters, or maybe they had another team in a different SUV parked somewhere else."

Cummings grabbed her MP5 and hugged her daughter. "Reload, Johnson!" she said.

Carl looked around, suddenly not able to breathe. He felt dizzy and disoriented. He looked down at his Glock as if the weapon was responsible for the victory and not him. Everyone was dead. He did it. He survived his first gunfight against six professional soldiers.

I won! Six!

"Reload!" the agent repeated. "You're empty. Like you said, there may be more."

Absently, he thumbed the release and let the expended magazine drop out. He felt for another from his vest and palmed it into place. Then, he scanned the three dead men. Their Kevlar helmets were pickled with multiple bullet impact dimples. Two of the troops had acrylic face shields instead of goggles, and those shields were now totally destroyed.

"Christ, Johnson! You killed them all with headshots!"

"*Fuck me!*" he whispered.

"Swear jar," Lisette said quietly.

Carl tried to lean against the railing of the stairs, but he grimaced at the movement. His back erupted in pain.

"We were very lucky," Cummings said. "These three had P90s."

He looked at her, tented his eyebrows, and shook his head, unsure what she meant.

"They use 5.7x28mm cartridges. Armor-piercing. The bullets would have punched right through that vest you're wearing. They're designed to tumble around inside a target to make a bigger internal wound. You get shot by one of those, you'll go into shock immediately. You're going down, and you're not getting back up. If the guy upstairs had a P90 instead of an MP5, we'd all be dead right now."

Carl took a deep breath and tried to will the grogginess away. "So why did these guys have them and the guys upstairs didn't?"

"Because you don't need armor-piercing rounds to shoot women in their beds. The P90s were for the mop-up crew, so they could deal with any bodyguards or law enforcement wearing body armor." She glared at him, and he could see competing emotions shifting across her countenance. She said, "Why are you here?"

He looked at her, then at her girl. Under his gaze, Lisette shrank back behind her mother. The lanky girl wore pink cotton pajamas with a cartoon character he didn't recognize on the front. He looked at the agent again, aware of the weapon in her grasp. He had to give her an answer that she found acceptable, or she was going to use that weapon. He could see that in her eyes. So he settled on the truth.

"You're on a kill list, Agent Cummings. Your daughter too. And your mom and Anita Chapman and her family."

"But why are *you* here? Why do you even care?"

He started to confess that he felt deeply ashamed at what he'd put her and her daughter through three days ago, but he sensed she wouldn't be able to match that bit of humanity with the terrorist she knew him to be.

"Someone—my adversary—wants you dead, so I want you alive. They're going to blame your murder on me. I don't know why yet, and we don't have time to discuss it now. So get your coats and let's move."

As he looked again at the dead bodies, he found it amazing that he had not missed a single shot. With the exception of Alfonso Reyes a couple days ago, and Mrs. Orizaga and her mother today, he hadn't fired a handgun in almost thirty years since Air Force Officer Training School. And yet, he'd scored all seventeen shots in the head, face, or neck.

"Where *is* your mother?" he asked.

"She drove out to Flagstaff to visit her sister."

Carl nodded. "She's probably safe, then. I get the feeling that this op is centered around me, in New Mexico and Mexico."

Cummings grabbed a dead man's P90. She seemed to consider something about the weapon, then tossed it aside and kept the MP5. She led her daughter into her bedroom and returned, wearing a jacket and holding a handful of magazines from the dead commando in there. She stuffed the extra mags in her jacket pocket and slung the MP5 over her shoulder.

Carl said, "Seems to me that a P90 would come in handy if we run into more of these guys."

"The MP5 uses nine-millimeter rounds, and in a pinch, we can get that ammo pretty much anywhere. The P90 is a better killing weapon, but it uses controlled military ammo that we can't get more of. Better to stick with common weapons with inexpensive and interchangeable rounds."

"Whatever. Let's go."

As Cummings got her daughter into a coat from the closet adjacent to the door, Carl heard one of the commandos groan. It was the first man through the door that Carl had hit with a ricochet off his helmet. Somehow, the man had survived Carl's second bullet, a direct shot through his face shield. The lower portion of his jaw was a mess. Carl rolled the commando from his side and onto his back. He had military gear and unkempt hair showing under his combat helmet, and he wore a blood-soaked bushy mustache and a scruffy beard. He looked like one of Carl's mercenaries, which gave Carl an idea.

He knelt beside the man and said, "You work for money, so there's no need for you to die here. Tell me who you work for." He knew the grunt soldier wouldn't know who the adversary was, but his boss or commander might know.

"The Unit."

"Your injury isn't critical." It was. "If you want to live, give me a name."

"They're going to kill you."

"Mm-hmm." Carl glanced around at the bodies. "Yep, they're doing pretty good so far. Give me a name."

In the commando's eyes, Carl saw certain inevitability. The man knew he was going to die, so Carl didn't bother asking for any further information.

Calmly, he aimed his Glock between the man's eyes. "Last chance."

The man said nothing, so Carl pulled the trigger. He stood and looked over at Cummings and her daughter. They both stood there staring at him.

"What?" he said with a shrug. "That's what he was going to do to you, so fuck him."

"Swear jar," Lisette said again, but this time, it was a whisper without conviction. It was accompanied by a little temper tantrum, a quick stomping of her feet, like she was more interested in getting him to stop cussing rather than collecting revenue for her swear jar.

He turned toward the door. He felt oddly safe, figuring if there were other commandos in the area, they would have joined the fray already. Either that, or the remainder had bugged out when their op went south to avoid law enforcement. Someone had to have reported all the gunfire.

Cummings and her daughter stepped near the blasted-out doorway, but they stayed just out of arm's reach from Carl. Lisette was a comical sight, dressed in her pajamas, furry snow boots, and a snow coat. The girl had a muffler wrapped around her neck and wore a thickly knit hat and mittens.

Now that the shock of the home intrusion and the gunfight had waned, Carl saw abject fear in the girl's eyes. She recognized him now. She remembered what he'd done to her, and he found it difficult to look her in the eye. He saw equal amounts of curiosity and animosity in Lenore's eyes. He could tell his previous explanation was marginally sufficient. She needed more. He pulled loose a couple Velcro tabs on his combat vest and stuck his left fist as far up his back as he could reach. He grunted as he tried to massage the bruises from today and two days ago.

"This is the second time I've taken bullets for a girl." He closed his eyes for a moment, then turned to face Cummings. "Melissa Mallory was the other. Thursday morning." Lenore Cummings tented her eyebrows in confusion, and he nodded. "This was all about the president's daughter. Alfonso Reyes kidnapped the girl, and because I look like him, McGrath's people thought it was me."

"Oh my God," Cummings whispered quietly. "Your son…"

"Collateral damage." He sighed. "Aaron McGrath used my son as bait. He thought he had leverage on Reyes."

They were both silent for a few seconds.

"After everything that happened, after everything I'd done, I went down to Mexico to rescue Melissa. Try to put all this behind me. I saved the girl and brought her back home." He took a breath. "Turns out, it isn't quite over."

"I'm sorry about your son."

He nodded. "I know." He looked her in the eye. "So is McGrath." He took a deep breath. "This was all one big misunderstanding." *A clusterfuck,* he recalled, *was the old saying in the military.* "That's why I'm here. Melissa Mallory and her mom are still in danger. And…" He paused again and glanced at Cummings. "I have to find a way to make this right. For what I've done to people."

Carl pulled out a cell phone and typed a single word into the text app: *Go.*

It was his code word for the Chapmans. If he sent "Come," that meant he was under duress, and they were to leave the area immediately. "Go" meant the opposite. Not even ten seconds later, headlights brightened the street and slowly approached Cummings's house. While waiting, Carl stared out the door, but he was looking back in time, not seeing the street.

"A month ago, I was just a regular guy. I was nobody. Now look at me." He looked at the dead bodies on the floor. "Look at what I've become." He waved a hand around the room, and his gaze rested finally on Lisette. "Look at what I've done…to you."

He couldn't explain how a fifty-three-year-old program manager and real estate broker could take out a squad of professional killers without missing a shot. Granted, he had luck and surprise on his side—again—but there was no way he should have won that engagement. He'd turned into a killing machine.

"You've become a truly evil man, Mr. Johnson. I have no doubt about that," Cummings said. "But you took bullets meant for my daughter. A mother doesn't forget that kind of thing."

"I wish I could just go home to my son and be innocent like 99 percent of the rest of the population. Just be a normal guy again."

Never going to happen. You chose the abyss, dude, and now you have to live there.

Outside, the Chapmans pulled up, and he felt seriousness come over him again. He knew he had to get his head back in the game. He took a deep breath and checked his Glock. Cummings prepped her MP5.

"You." Carl nodded at Lisette. "Grab onto the back of my vest and stay behind me."

But the girl shook her head and stayed behind her mom.

"Look, I know you're scared and you hate me, and you should. But that man…" Carl head-nodded up to the top of the stairs. "He was aiming at you, Lisette. Not me. They want you and your mom dead, and they'll try again. But if you're holding onto me, my vest and my body will protect you. The bullets won't go through my vest and me, okay?"

The girl nodded, but still hesitated.

Her mother said, "It's okay, sweetie. Go ahead."

Carl turned toward the open doorway and felt the girl grab onto his vest. "Okay, now I don't think there's any bad guys left because I think we got all of them. But if there are, and if I get shot, you just stay behind me and try to hold me between you and whoever is shooting, okay?" He glanced back and saw her nod. "Use me as a shield until you get to the car. You ready, Agent?"

"Let's go. I got the left side."

"I got right."

The three of them moved cautiously across the yard to the curb. The SUV looked abandoned. In fact, Carl had to concentrate to recognize Todd's head and torso smartly hunched over behind the steering wheel. He was as low as he could get in case bullets started flying. The front passenger door was slightly ajar, as was the passenger door.

Carl squatted and crab-walked sideways like he'd seen Palmer do, and his gun was stuck out in front of him in a two-handed grip. He scanned the street and the adjacent yards. The trio had covered half the distance to the SUV when the nightmare suddenly continued.

Cummings said, "I have movement! At the corner! He's coming fast!"

CHAPTER 38

0020 MST, SATURDAY
ALBUQUERQUE, NM

CUMMINGS SAID, "SWEETIE, RUN FOR the car!"

Carl added, "Go, Lisette! Go fast!"

The gangly girl let go of Carl's vest and ran. Her two bow-tied, blond pigtails bounced outside her knit winter hat.

"Clear this side!" Cummings said.

"Go. I'll cover."

The agent's front yard had no wall, fence, or trees. It was a wide and deep expanse of brown grass that was probably a well-tended yard in the spring and summer. Carl knelt to one knee and took aim as the runner approached up the sidewalk. There was no streetlight between Cummings's house and the corner, so all Carl saw was a running shadow. He aimed at the man's head to avoid his body armor and was just about to pull the trigger when he heard Cummings's harsh whisper.

"Jogger! Female!"

Carl stood suddenly and whipped his gun behind his back just as the jogger seemed to notice him. She waved.

He waved his left hand and said, "Hey, neighbor! Whassup?"

She waved again, and as she ran closer, he saw in the dim light that she wore earbuds under her black sweatband. She'd probably heard his voice but didn't hear what he'd said, so she just waved a second time, then ran past him.

Carl took a last look around as he hurried to the SUV. The passenger door slammed shut, and he jumped in the front and slammed the door, then glanced back to make sure everyone was inside.

He slapped Todd on the shoulder and said, "Go!"

The man put the pedal to the metal, and the SUV shot forward.

Carl said, "Make your way back to Central, then go east out of town. I have a safe house about sixty miles east of Albuquerque."

Todd Chapman gasped like he'd heard something from a movie. "You have a *safe* house? Who the hell *are* you?"

"I'm a fucking terrorist, Todd. Of course I have a safe house."

"Swear jar," Lisette said.

Cummings said, "Language."

Carl turned sideways in his seat and looked at her.

"Children," she said.

He looked at the kids behind her who were also looking at him. He nodded. "Sorry."

Carl studied the pitiful crew. They were all dressed like they were hastily rushed out of their homes with no time to prepare. Their entire world had suddenly erupted in violence, and they were all scared out of their wits. Cummings had crowded her daughter on the back bench with the Chapman teen and his twin six-year-old sisters, while Cummings sat on the second bench next to Anita.

Cummings said, "Hi, Anita. We met at your father's house in Virginia last year. I'm Lenore Cummings. I was interviewing for an assignment."

Anita Chapman nodded, "I remember you."

The two women hugged awkwardly because of Anita's metal jaw brace.

Carl caught the gaze of the Chapman teen. "Can you shoot, kid?"

"My name's not *kid*."

"I don't know your name, so just answer the question."

The boy hesitated, then said, "I can shoot."

Carl ripped open the Velcro straps on his armor vest, shrugged out of it, and passed it back to the teen. He said, "Put that on when we hit the interstate. If the adults go down, you'll be the last one standing who can protect the children."

Cummings turned in her seat. "What have you fired?"

The boy said, "A shotgun, a semiautomatic M-16, and a 357 chrome-grip."

She said, "If I go down, grab my MP5. It's like the M-16, but not as loud and has less kick. It has a faster firing rate, though, so you'll rip right through a magazine on full auto in about two seconds flat. When it's time to shoot, keep the selector switch on semi, okay?"

The teen nodded.

Cummings turned back forward and looked at Carl for a few seconds. "What is this about? Why are these men coming after us?"

Carl took a deep breath. "Remember I told you Director McGrath and his people mistook me for the Mexican cartel leader who kidnapped the president's daughter?"

Cummings nodded.

"Well, Alfonso Reyes and his crew did something to Melissa while she was in captivity for over a month. Right after I got her back, she had some kind of seizure. I discovered track marks on her arms from multiple injections."

Todd looked over. "You're working *with* them now? With the government?"

Carl ignored him. To Cummings, he repeated, "They did something to her. Gave her some kind of DNA-specific virus or something. Hours later, President Mallory collapsed in a coma." He nodded at Anita. "Your father has it too."

Carl turned forward in his seat as Todd guided the SUV onto I-40 eastbound. He gazed out the windshield at the cluster of uptown office buildings and restaurants sliding by on the left. There was very little traffic on the interstate at that hour. Carl considered his own progression from innocent civilian to domestic terrorist. He'd redefined who his enemies were, and McGrath and Shirley Mallory were not among them.

Carl said to Todd Chapman, "Let me have the phone I gave you." He took the battery out and tossed the phone and the battery out the window." A few minutes later, he said, "We've all been manipulated, caught up in a masterfully planned plot to assassinate the first woman president. I'm going to find out who my adversary is so I can learn why he thinks it's okay to kill children."

CHAPTER 39

NANCY PALMER STUMBLED OUT OF the tiny bathroom and resumed her seat by the wall opposite the desk. Just the effort of walking took an enormous amount of energy, or so it seemed. Her entire body ached. Every muscle screamed with fatigue. Even breathing seemed like a chore. She could never recall being so tired and sore in her life.

The smell from the over-used bathroom permeated the entire office. Half a dozen people had been getting sick in there for three or four hours. Everyone was sick. At first, they attempted to maintain some sense of cleanliness in the bathroom. Each person used the facility and cleaned up after themselves. That courtesy, however, was the first casualty of the virus. Other symptoms developed very fast. First, the Reyes ladies and the mercs started complaining of migraine-like headaches. Then, nausea struck everyone nearly at the same time. Then came shakes and seizures, both mild and severe. Then came loss of control of bodily functions.

Over the last hour, only a couple of people made it to the bathroom in time, and several were too weak and sickened to even try. Palmer was now the only person with any mobility other than the copilot, David Blick, who had yet to show any symptoms.

Unlike everyone else, Blick contracted the virus only a few hours ago when he'd helped Merc Four drag in the wounded from the Reyes compound. They'd been trapped underground near the end of the escape tunnel for several hours before finally managing to extricate their SUV. With Merc Four driving, they made their way to the Nuevo Casas Grandes airport.

Blick leaned with his butt against the desk facing her. He stood as still as a statue, and she guessed he was in shock, perhaps unwilling to accept what was happening to them. He might not be helpful when she came up with a plan. So far, though, there was no plan.

For a moment, she watched the tiny television sitting atop the file cabinet in the corner beside the desk. Everything was so clear now, but they had been so wrong before. She knew who their adversary was, and she knew he had beaten them. He'd sent her and Carl off on a wild goose chase completely unrelated to the real endgame. The game was over. It had been over for a long time. They just hadn't seen it. The adversary had head-faked them.

Palmer looked down at the series of reports she'd brought back from Orizaga's safe. The collection of documents on her tiny table was just the tip of the iceberg. She'd also skimmed the data on the thumb drive over the hours since Carl's departure and came away with a clear strategic picture of what they were really up against.

The virus was not, in fact, a DNA-targeted concoction aimed at the president. Someone on Carl's team had unknowingly brought the virus to the meeting earlier that day. Of that, she had no doubt, but she had no idea who it might have been. The adversary had found a way to infect someone. The documents stated that the onset of symptoms began as early as six hours or as late as fifteen hours after infection. Everyone, including herself, began getting sick at right about the ten-hour point.

That meant Carl had the virus too and was probably sick at that very moment. The report stated the virus was spread only by touch, and Carl had hugged, fist-bumped, or shaken hands with everyone at the meeting. And she'd kissed him. He was definitely infected. She wondered if he even knew what was happening to him.

He'd had time to prevent the murder of those families before becoming ill, although she had no idea if he had actually done so. He'd blindly charged back to Albuquerque to rescue women and children without a plan and without any way to recruit the kind of talent he would need to go up against trained unit killers. That was his methodology, always doing the unexpected—the insane. Create a plan on the move. Keep the opponent guessing and rocking back on their heels. That was how he had been so successful against the TER and the FBI for over a month.

In the operation-planning arena, Carl could analyze what-if scenarios in his head while an op was ongoing. He didn't have to write things down or discuss them. He rivaled Aaron McGrath in that regard, able to change the direction of an op in real time, even as new parameters were presented. He was always two or three steps ahead of his opponent.

The good news was there had been no mention on the international CNN channel of a high-profile murder spree in Albuquerque. If the Unit wanted to blame the murders on Carl, she was sure they'd make a spectacle of it. They had not done so.

Palmer wondered if Carl had touched any of the people he rescued. He had the Contagion. There was no doubt about that. If he was as sick as she was, with deteriorating mobility, then there was no one remaining who even had a chance to do anything about the terrible plan she had uncovered. That thought reinforced just how hopeless their situation was. The adversary had won.

She seriously considered just putting her head down on the table and letting the fatigue take her, just for a short while. She needed rest, but she resisted the desire to just give up and go to sleep. If she closed her eyes, she might never wake up again. There had to be a way to salvage the mission. There was always a way. She just had to find it.

The reports identified the viral research facility hidden in the perfect location *in plain sight*. It was in a normal office building right in the middle of downtown Chihuahua City, maybe two hundred road miles from their municipal airport.

The city of Chihuahua was a modern city, the capital of the state of Chihuahua, and home to slightly less than a million people. Its airport, while labeled international, featured only flights around Mexico and a few US airports. Those connections gave Chihuahua access to every major city in the world. As a result, its economy was thriving.

A precision strike on the office building where the lab was located was out of the question, even if the virus was contained or fully destroyed in the strike. The collateral damage of even a nighttime hit on that building would be enormous because it was surrounded by high-rise apartment buildings. Casualties would count into the thousands, and the destruction would run into tens of billions of dollars.

Contagion, as the Melissa Mallory virus was called privately by the Triad, was harmless if released because it was transmitted only by physical touch. It could not survive floating in the air outside of a human host. But that was not the only deadly bug being developed at the lab. She shuddered at the thought of the other pathogen, the airborne cousin to Contagion, being released into the atmosphere.

According to the report, the office building with the lab had a state-of-the-art security system and a highly trained security staff. A covert assault on the building would likely fail because resistance in the building would be fierce. Such an operation had to be coordinated through political and military channels, so the adversary would see a ground or air assault coming from miles away. He'd get the virus and the antidote out and destroy any remaining evidence long before the lab was breached.

As her eyes began to close, Palmer realized her awareness was floating away, like when you begin to see crazy mental creations indicating you're just beginning to start dreaming. She snapped her eyes open and shook her head side to side, which only served to exacerbate the intense headache she felt. It seemed as though her brain was literally rattling around, painfully bouncing off the walls of her skull.

Any team sent to destroy the virus had to accomplish the deed from inside the building. They had to be invited in. A heavily armed assault team couldn't do that. Palmer and her sick mercenaries couldn't do that. Carl Johnson, the American Terrorist, couldn't do that, even if not stricken by the virus.

But Alfonso Reyes could.

CHAPTER 40

"**W**HAT THE HELL DO YOU mean, they *all* escaped?"

Costas Drake cringed as the anger in Rainman's electronically altered voice exploded from the satellite cell phone. He had a right to be angry. Drake's Unit personnel had performed miserably.

Orizaga said, "Clearly, he found your task list among the reports in my safe. Perhaps Mr. Garcia has been in contact with him since then and was able to mobilize a rescue."

August Spoke's voice came on the line. "I seriously doubt Mr. Garcia's network has fast access to the kind of talent deployed at Special Agent Cummings's house. If he did, Johnson would have used this talent before. Evidence at the scene indicates one man was deployed, and he was no mercenary. He was a pro."

"It couldn't have been only one man," Drake argued. "My men are highly trained. Johnson must have engaged a team of elite ex-Special Forces men."

"FBI's crime scene investigators have been all over the house for the last four hours," Spoke replied. "With the exception of a wild spray from an MP5, a single generic nine-millimeter handgun was the only weapon used by the opposing force. All kill shots were fired from the same weapon. Seventeen hits, zero misses, all headshots. CSI says one of your Unit fired a triple tap upstairs. However, there were no impact holes in the walls anywhere upstairs. Your man hit his target, but this guy still managed to take out the entire six-man squad."

Drake added, "Agent Spoke, in the CIA covert ops, we fire ten thousand rounds a month to maintain our shooting skills at their peak. I know you guys in the Secret Service do the same thing. But even I couldn't have taken out six Unit men by myself in the heat of an assault, certainly not all with headshots."

Rainman interrupted, "Christ! Are you saying Johnson has found himself a Delta commando or a SEAL?" When the man paused, Drake found himself wondering if Johnson had sent his almost-SEAL, Agent Nancy Palmer, to prevent the task list from being fulfilled.

Spoke said, "No, sir. Professionals at that level don't shoot Glocks. That's a rookie gun. I think it was Johnson. He was issued a Glock by one of his mercs last week. I recall reading that in the TER after-action reports. I think he found the task list in Orizaga's safe and somehow smuggled his way back north of the border to intervene."

"Johnson?" Drake could hardly believe his ears. "He's a fucking civilian with no military training!"

"Maybe," Spoke said. "Or maybe not. Don't forget, he *has* been highly effective."

Rainman let out deep breaths that the electronic scrambling converted to a wheezing sound. "If he's not the amateur we figured him to be, he is a major risk I had not previously factored into my plans. He can subvert everything I have worked for."

He paused, and Drake had the feeling Rainman was creating a new path in his plan even before he spoke the details.

"Johnson has minimal assets now, so information will be his most powerful weapon. Gentlemen, I don't need to remind you that we're still vulnerable until President Mallory dies. So he still has a forty-eight-hour window to do some damage."

Rainman was silent for a long while, but Drake knew not to interrupt the man's thought process.

Finally, he continued, "August, I have a special task for you, which we'll discuss off-line. Have your man wrap up things at the op station. I want you to leave immediately for my location. Mr. Orizaga, I want you on the first plane back to Mexico."

"My flight to Los Angeles is scheduled to depart at nine o'clock, and my connection will get me into Hermosillo at noon."

"I didn't ask when your flight is scheduled to depart. I said I want you on the first plane back to Mexico. Am I clear?"

"Be careful, Rainman," Orizaga said. "Do not confuse me with the rest of your hired help."

Drake saw a warning look in his liaison's eyes that he hadn't seen before. Orizaga was getting pressure from Rainman and, no doubt, from the Triad. It was Johnson-the-amateur against the world, and by some impossible turn of events, Johnson had the upper hand. The man was making everyone feel the heat.

"Mr. Orizaga," Rainman said, "if we don't stop Carl Johnson from interfering, there won't be any difference between you, me, and my hired help. We will *all* be wanted criminals. Or we'll be dead. I need you to coordinate with our friends in the Triad. I want to move up my timeline."

"*Before* the president dies?"

"If Johnson was able to access the Triad files from your computer, then he knows about the antidote. He'll try to use Agent Cummings for her FBI contacts, I'm sure, and Anita Chapman has media contacts around the world. By blaming him for those murders, we would have discredited Johnson so no one would listen. We'll have to do that a different way now. As soon as your plane departs Albuquerque, I will be grounding all US air traffic. And as soon as you cross the border, I'm going to announce the viral outbreak in New Mexico and on the east coast, and I'm going to blame all that on Johnson. I'll then seal all US borders, and the Air Force will turn back all inbound and outbound flights, with force if necessary. So make sure you do not miss your flight. Mr. Drake, I'm going to have the director of the FBI assign you as my personal liaison to the Albuquerque field office. You will have direct command over all FBI assets and operations in the hunt for the terrorist and his accomplices."

"Understood," Drake said. "What about Johnson? He could be here in Albuquerque or back in Mexico by now."

"Doesn't matter. When I close the border, he will be trapped on whichever side he happens to be. We'll ramp up the hunt by involving international law enforcement. Last week, he was wanted for kidnapping the First Daughter. In about an hour, he'll be wanted for using a biological weapon to assassinate the president."

CHAPTER 41

0845 MST, SATURDAY
ALBUQUERQUE, NM

ARL, IN DISGUISE, MADE HIS way back to the south cargo entrance of the Sunport and was allowed access. The colonel already had the engines powered up and was waiting for him at the door.

"Sit up front with me, Johnson," Reichert said when Carl boarded. "I want it to look like we have two pilots. Safety regs."

He pulled off his dreadlocks wig and did as the colonel requested. It was a rare treat because he got to hear the chatter pilots exchange with the control tower, and the view of the wide expanse of empty land beyond the runways was spectacular from the cockpit. He also got to see the procession of airplanes snaking from the terminals and along the taxiways on the north side of the tarmac. Five planes lined up on the north side of the west end of the main east-west runway, and Carl's Gulfstream waited patiently on the south side taxiway not even fifty feet from the group of larger planes.

He scanned the Sunport runway system. There were markers, lights, and painted strips on the ground seeming to point in every direction. It was such a jumble that Carl figured only trained pilots and traffic directors could make sense of it.

The morning sun shone brightly out of a crisp and clear, flawless blue sky, and Carl was reminded of why he fell in love with New Mexico so many years ago. The first time he visited, almost thirty years past, he'd stepped off the plane, walked out the front door of the airport, and noticed the big blue sky that seemed to go on forever. It stretched from the impos-ing Sandia Mountains in the east all the way to the volcanoes many miles to the west. The blue canopy capped the entire length of the high-desert paradise known as the Rio Grande Valley.

As he reflected on the last twenty-four hours, it occurred to Carl that his adversary was literally nipping at his heels. At the safe house, where he'd taken Cummings and the Chapmans, young Mr. Garcia said he'd barely escaped the op center alive. The adversary had traced their heavily encrypted data link and neutralized the op center. McGrath's had been similarly compromised. A cruise missile had been deployed against his team in a foreign country and killed half his team members. Sooner or later, the US intelligence machine would find him on behalf of the adver-sary. Then the US military would pound him into dust.

At first, Carl rated his chances of survival at zero. He had a single TER agent, and only four of his mercenaries had survived the missile attack. On the other hand, even though the adversary obviously commanded the US military and law enforcement assets, Carl had to acknowledge he wasn't completely helpless. He had a helicopter and a Gulfstream jet for transportation, along with a couple pilots, and the jet was stocked full of high-tech covert ops weaponry.

At least the task list targets were safe. Special Agent Cummings knew the business of finding fugitives, and she knew the resources the Unit would bring to bear. She could keep them hidden.

"We're number two for takeoff," Reichert said, and nodded ahead of the plane. "But I'm not liking that."

Carl saw what looked like a black police car driving across the airport grounds. Its red and blue strobes were flashing, and it sped toward the midway point of the main runway.

"If it blocks the runway, there's no way we'll get off." Reichert looked to the right. "Here comes another one."

Carl leaned forward and saw a second airport security car pull up to the taxiway. There was a 737 at the front of the line. It was number one for takeoff. Another Gulfstream showing the logo of AeroMéxico sat behind that plane, and a second 737 was lined up behind that one. The security cars pulled to a stop in front of the second 737.

Reichert said, "Well, that's it then. They're onto us."

"They're definitely onto *something*," Carl said. "But I don't think they're onto us."

"Can't be a coincidence, arriving like this right when we're in line to take off."

"But look at those cars. They're just sitting there, and each has only a single occupant."

"Doesn't take more than two cars to block a runway."

"This is a military base also, Colonel. If they were onto *me*, they would have sent a lot more than two cars. They would have sent them all. Tanks and APCs too. This place would be swarming with Air Force Security Police combat troops, city cops, FBI, and SWAT."

The first 737 was given permission to take off. With a roar, the big plane sped down the runway and lifted into the air. Moments later, Carl heard the tower direct Reichert to taxi into position. Thirty seconds later, they raced down the runway.

A few minutes into the flight, the colonel said, "That was close. That other Gulfstream was the last plane allowed off the ground. The Sunport is now closed, and I just heard every airport in the country is closed. All planes in the air will be allowed to continue to their destinations. All inbound international flights are being redirected to airports outside the US."

Carl said, "A nationwide shutdown." He looked over at the pilot. "That's unexpected. So, somehow the game has changed again, and now our adversary is reacting. We need to be prepared to do the same." He thought for a moment. "You know, I've never seen an AeroMéxico plane at the Sunport before. In fact, I've never seen *any* international planes here before. I once heard there are no direct international flights to or from Albuquerque, but I don't know if it's true."

Reichert said, "I'm not following you."

"Just before Agent Peoples went off-line yesterday, he said Vicente Orizaga would be returning from Albuquerque this morning. Bet you a dollar that was his plane."

"I'll see your dollar and raise you one. You're presuming a connection between his takeoff and the airports getting shut down." Carl nodded, then Reichert continued, "I don't buy it. If he's working for the adversary, he would be allowed to fly out anytime."

"Not if they wanted to keep his involvement secret. Make his plane the last one up, then close the borders. His is just another plane in the sky."

"In that case," Reichert said, easing the throttles forward a bit more. "We'd better get across the border before he does, or we might find ourselves getting turned back."

"Agreed."

An hour and a half later, shortly after beginning his approach to the airport at Chihuahua City, the colonel again radioed an emergency. This time, he called in a starboard engine fault and requested to be diverted to the much closer Nuevo Casas Grandes municipal airport.

Carl recalled that the municipal airport had relatively little traffic, maybe only a dozen flights a day, and mostly to the other regional airports around Mexico. In fact, it catered primarily to town jumpers, which were mostly propeller planes and private helicopters. Colonel Reichert had previously related to Carl that the airport superintendent did not take bribes, so Carl's gracious offering of cash was considered a retainer for services to be rendered at some point in the near future. The superintendent had the two-person control tower direct the Gulfstream into the same hangar as yesterday.

The hangar doors closed behind the plane as the engines spooled down. Carl grabbed the door's locking lever and rotated it a quarter turn clockwise. The door unlatched, and he waited while it unfolded slowly on its near-silent electrical motor, then he stepped down onto the door's built-in steps and found himself alone on the concrete hangar floor. He was mildly surprised that none of his team was present to greet him. Perhaps they were busy or had moved on to other mission business.

The colonel came down the stairs after him and began his after-flight inspection of the airplane. Carl left him to that and strode toward the office door at the north end of the hangar. He pulled the office door open, and the metal from an improperly aligned doorframe grated loudly. He froze.

Before his brain truly recognized what he was seeing, his body reacted to the smell of sickness and death. He gagged and sucked in a breath through his mouth to avoid the smell. Then his brain digested what his eyes saw.

They're sick. They're all sick!

Against that backdrop of misery, though, he nearly jumped with joy at the sight of Julia Reyes. Luisa Reyes sat on the floor in the left corner of the office with her head hanging chin-to-chest. Julia was sprawled across her lap, and her eyes were open. Her face brightened for a second at the sight of Carl, but her attempt to rise produced only a twitch in one of her arms.

Some primal instinct deep in the back of Carl's brain told him not to enter the room, but a swelling of love and sorrow at the pitiful sight of his girl made him enter, nonetheless.

Besides, he rationalized, *if whatever afflicted everyone was airborne, then I've already taken in a lungful as soon as I opened the door.*

He made a beeline for the girl, scanning the room as he moved. Mercs Three and Four sat sprawled arm-in-arm on a couch against the left wall. Three made a feeble attempt to get up, but he couldn't seem to muster enough strength to do more than move his feet into position. He failed to even lean forward, then gave up, his head flopping back against the back of the couch. He moaned while he breathed. Carl heard Merc Four's ragged breathing, but she was unconscious.

Of all the dozen mercs guarding the Reyes mansion, only two surviving mercs lay on the floor. One was unconscious and had blood-soaked wraps around his skull, his upper right thigh, and his right arm near the armpit. Parts of his black fatigues had been cut away when the dressings were applied, but the dressings were so thoroughly caked with dried blood, Carl got the impression the man hadn't been attended to in several hours.

The other merc also lay faceup, but his eyes were wide open, and he wasn't breathing. His limbs were splayed out, and his body was twisted like he'd had some kind of severe seizure. One hand was frozen with its fingers clawing at the concrete floor, while the other clawed at the air near his head. The other three mercs that Carl had left with Agent Palmer to support the next op were sprawled on the floor of the office. Two were dead, eyes wide open, and the third was curled into the fetal position. He moaned and shuddered with each raspy breath.

Only David Blick seemed in control of his faculties. He sat alone at the desk against the wall opposite the door. He looked like he was just waking from a deep sleep and rose from his chair a full two seconds after Carl pulled open the door. Carl had already crossed the room and squatted beside Julia.

"Stay away from her," the man shouted, pointing at Julia. "She's infected! We're all infected."

Carl ignored him. He felt an overwhelming need to hug the girl as she gazed up at him with her innocent brown eyes. He pulled her up by the shoulders, and her head lolled back as he settled her into his lap. He picked up a half-empty bottle of water that had been knocked over sideways. Julia moaned as he snuggled her against his chest, and she watched him as he tilted her head back and brought the bottle to her mouth. He fed her tiny sips, but she was barely strong enough to swallow. Most of the water dripped down her chin.

Though Julia was almost a teen, she reminded Carl of a heart-warming memory from thirty years ago when he'd fed his newborn baby, Mark, a milk bottle. Like a baby, Julia seemed so helpless, and her arms sat limp in her lap. But she gazed into his eyes with such love as he coaxed tiny bits of water into her mouth. He smiled and kissed her forehead.

Blick said, "You've just signed your own death warrant, Mr. Johnson. You now have twenty-eight hours to live."

Carl glanced over at the pilot. "Where's Agent Palmer?" The man issued a head-nod toward the restroom, and Carl said, "She's sick too?"

Blick nodded. "Everyone is sick. You are too, now."

"Sick with what?"

"A virus."

"I've only been gone a day," Carl muttered. "What the hell kind of virus takes *everyone* down that fast?"

Carl turned his attention back to Julia in his lap. He pulled a small packet of liquid power gel from one of the mercs' discarded combat vests and tore off the tip. Then he slowly squeezed the five-hundred-calorie meal, little by little, into Julia's mouth and let her drink a few more sips of water.

Like a wilted flower receiving a little bit of rainwater, Julia regained some strength as he fed her. Slowly, she became able to take deeper breaths. She raised one of her hands and rested it on Carl's thigh. He was deeply concerned about her weak condition. He was no doctor, but he couldn't fathom how she and the others had deteriorated so severely. They were all fine yesterday.

He laid Julia back on her mother's lap and tried to get Luisa to take some gel and water, but that task was hopeless. She floated in and out of consciousness, but when she was awake, she barely had the strength to keep her eyes open. She needed to be in a hospital. They all needed to be given water and food intravenously, but as soon as they were admitted to any hospital, the Unit would discover their location. Any computer record containing any of their names, or maybe American foreigners in general, would raise a red flag. Best case, the Unit would send in a small hit squad posing as medical staff to assassinate them. Worst case, they'd bomb the entire building and kill everyone in the hospital. Maybe they'd get the Navy to launch another cruise missile. Maybe they'd tell the military decision-makers they thought the target was a terrorist compound.

Carl stood and shook his head. He'd gotten careless, and now he was infected. It was a stupid mistake, and one that Aaron McGrath would never have made. Love was never an excuse to sacrifice the mission, and Carl had done exactly that.

"Where did you all catch this bug?"

David Blick had sat back down at the small metal desk and laid his head on his folded arms. He didn't answer.

Carl realized the only way he could save this team was to find some kind of private hospital that wouldn't report their presence or their condition. Maybe the superintendent could help. He hadn't betrayed them to the authorities, so maybe he knew someone who would quietly set up a special care wing in their home. Any amount of supplies could be purchased with a sufficient amount of money.

The Gulfstream pilot, Colonel Vesario Reichert, entered the office and froze in the doorway just as Carl had.

"Christ Almighty!"

Carl had just stood up when he heard the bathroom door squeak open. Agent Palmer stumbled out. She was still dressed in her black combat gear, but her skin was flushed a deep red, and a sheen of perspiration covered her face and neck. She wobbled toward a chair against the wall, but it was clear to Carl she was going to miss the chair.

Carl and Reichert reacted at the same moment, crossing the room to her, but Carl palmed the air in front of the colonel. "Stay back. She's infected. So am I."

Carl grabbed Palmer and bore most of her weight as he helped her into a chair against the wall near the bathroom door.

As he kept her from falling over, she whispered in his ear, "It's you, Carl. You're the carrier."

CHAPTER 42

1030 MST, SATURDAY

NORTHERN MEXICO

ARL LOOKED AT THE AGENT, but she was nearly unconscious. Next to her chair was a simple, metal foldaway table with a laptop on it. The computer was closed, and several sheets of paper with neatly printed writing on them sat on top of it. Palmer's head lolled chin-to-chest, and she muttered incoherently, so Carl picked up the handwritten pages and started reading. His breath caught in his throat several times as he read what Agent Palmer had to know was her last mission report.

> Melissa Mallory is *Patient Zero*
> Virus designed to become active upon ingestion of a sedative
> Virus spread by touch
> Victims become contagious within minutes of exposure
> Attacks central nervous system, leads to complete neurological failure
> Phase 1: 28-hr gestation, 25% fatalities, 75% coma
> Phase 2: 72-hr period, 100% fatalities
> Antidote effective any time before death
> Antidote deadly if given to uninfected

He read deeper into Palmer's report again. The part that chilled him was that months of clinical trials on hundreds of human test subjects—homeless people and prisoners with no rights—had been conducted to perfect the virus and to maximize its lethality. Then, a sixteen-year-old girl was used as bait to carry the Contagion to the president. There was something about the virus that was nagging at the back of his brain. He turned back to the first page and stopped on the second bullet.

Virus designed to become active upon ingestion of a sedative.

"So that's how they did it," he muttered to himself.

Melissa had been injected multiple times over the last week of her captivity with designer stimulant drugs. Those made her severely agitated at the trade site, and it made her need a sedative to settle her after her rescue. The president's doctor had unknowingly started the viral outbreak.

Carl had some of that sedative also. Melissa wouldn't take a shot, so Carl told the doctor to mix it with juice. Then, Carl drank a sip of that juice to prove to her it wasn't poison because she wouldn't drink it otherwise. He sat with the girl in his lap for a few minutes before she went to sleep. He held her hand and touched her cheek.

The activation of the virus was nearly instantaneous, according to the reports, and the results of the clinical trials were definitive. Every exposed test subject—every single one of them—either died after twenty-eight hours or went into a coma. There were no anomalies, and there were zero exceptions.

So why am I not sick? How could Agent Palmer think I'm the carrier?

As he reviewed the chain of events in his mind, he recalled very clearly that no one had touched Melissa after she had the sedative. But she was already infected with a latent form of the virus when she consumed the sedative activation agent.

I had the activation agent inside me before Melissa gave me the virus.

Carl looked up from the report and focused his gaze on the seated pilot. "Mr. Blick, when did you get infected?"

The man answered without raising his head, and his muffled voice echoed softly off the metal desktop. "I helped carry one of the wounded mercs when they arrived late last night. About twelve hours ago. I've got a little less than sixteen hours until I enter phase two. Well, that is, if I don't die in phase one."

Carl looked at Reichert. "How are you feeling?"

The colonel shrugged. "I've had a badass headache since last night and had a bout of nausea this morning before you got to the airport."

"She says I'm the carrier," Carl said. "I shook hands with the superintendent here when I gave him his fee."

Reichert nodded. "I shook his hand yesterday and this morning." Reichert looked at Agent Palmer.

Carl knew he was realizing he would soon be in the same state as she was. Carl reviewed Palmer's summary sheets again. He said, "There is an antidote over in Mexico City. It's in an office building, in the same lab where the virus was developed. I have to go get it."

Blick said, "Look around, Mr. Johnson. Your team is incapacitated. How do you plan to run an op with no combat support?" The man looked at the colonel and shrugged. "All you have is Colonel Reichert and myself, and I've been out of the military over twenty years. I can't even remember when I last fired a handgun. And my gut tells me the people who created this virus are not going to want to part with the antidote."

"I'll have to convince them otherwise." Carl added, "You know what they say when we're up against long odds. We'll either find a way, or we'll make one."

He heard his own words, but he knew he was merely posturing with empty bravado. He had no plan. His gaze settled on the old television mounted on top of the gray metal file cabinet in the corner next to the desk. It caught his eye for two reasons. First, it was a museum piece, a chunky cathode ray tube device he hadn't seen in well over twenty years. Second, it featured a CNN news report describing a military quarantine of Washington, DC. The US Capitol was described as the site of a massive viral infection.

Carl turned up the volume, but the commentary was in Spanish, so he turned the volume back down. He read the English ticker at the bottom and found that he, Carl Johnson, was being blamed for the outbreak. The report said there was no country to retaliate against with the massive might of the US military—no terrorist organization to attack—because the outbreak was a domestic attack. The plan was cleverly implemented by the American Terrorist, a disgruntled citizen whose son was accidentally killed in an FBI raid the previous month.

Carl's picture was flashed up on the screen. He recognized it from one of his real estate websites. The crawling ticker claimed Johnson had been driven insane with grief and blamed the president and everyone else in the government for the death of his son. Johnson had reportedly kidnapped and infected the president's daughter, who then spread the infection.

Carl stuck his hands in his pockets, looked down at the floor, and shook his head. Three weeks ago, he did blame the president, the FBI, and the rest of the government for his son's death. More recently, he'd come to understand the government wasn't his enemy.

The real, now-captive kidnapper, Alfonso Reyes, had used inside information to fight his way past Melissa Mallory's Secret Service security detail with a heavily armed assault squad well over a month ago. All of the girl's security detail had been killed in the kidnapping assault.

How could anyone believe a grieving father would ever be able to defeat the elite protection professionals of the Secret Service and kidnap the First Daughter? And where would a man with no previous biological experience, no underworld contacts, and no money find such a viral agent or fund its development?

But no one was asking those questions, at least not yet. The media and the FBI had their target. Carl Johnson was guilty because his adversary said they had irrefutable evidence of his complicity. No one was questioning the evidence. Eventually, his background would be scrutinized by the intelligence agencies, and they'd find the holes, but the president would be long dead by then. And that, Carl realized, was the genius of the plan. The adversary did not have to prove his evidence even existed.

Even as the futility of his situation tumbled through his brain, he watched the vice president's sound bite interview. The scrolling English ticker at the bottom of the screen said the man promised to get to the bottom of this deadly attack on America. He promised no lengthy trial for the American Terrorist, but he instead advocated quick and extreme justice.

"But that justice will have to wait," he said.

He was going to immediately assume the duties of president since the country was effectively without leadership. The clip above the ticker showed President Mallory shaking hands and sharing cheek kisses with nearly everyone in Congress after she addressed the nation. She had unwittingly spread the virus to virtually the entire legislative branch of the government, and within a few hours, those people had infected the remainder of the executive and judicial branches.

Much of the senior military staff was also incapacitated. Twenty-five percent of those infected had succumbed to severe strokes and seizures in a massive die-off twenty-eight hours after the speech. The rest—100 percent of everyone who had touched the president or who had touched someone who had touched the president—were infected and in comas.

Vice President Breen was quoted on the CNN ticker as saying he would show the world the US was "strong and stable, and that the country was not weakened by the attack." Then he issued a strong warning against any nation that sought to take advantage of the terror attack. The military was put on high alert, and the borders were sealed until the spread of the virus was contained and the crisis had passed.

All air traffic was grounded, and any aircraft attempting to leave or enter US airspace would be shot down to prevent possible spread of the virus. Martial law was in effect across the nation, and the population was ordered to remain off the streets. Washington DC was on lockdown, as was Las Cruces and Holloman Air Force Base. In addition, numerous outbreaks were being reported in Albuquerque and its neighboring cities that were within easy reach by air travel—Dallas, Los Angeles, Phoenix, and Denver.

The ticker said Vice President Breen and the CDC were doing everything in their power to defeat this terror attack. Already, existing vaccines were being tested on the virus. Based on initial test results, a vaccine would be available to the public within a few days.

A few days…

According to Palmer's summary sheet, the president would be dead in a few days. Shirley Mallory had been infected just over two days ago. She survived the first culling of the twenty-eight-hour phase one period, and now, she remained in the seventy-two-hour phase two period of coma. That meant Mallory and her daughter had less than forty-five hours to live. The US government leadership who had survived phase one had maybe sixty hours to live. Everyone else Carl had touched also had about that long. Carl closed his eyes and shook his head. The war had been over before anyone had even known a battle was raging.

Or had it?

Carl turned to face Colonel Reichert. "Vice President Walter Breen is our adversary. He's the one person who stands to benefit most from

President Mallory's death. But Melissa's kidnapping isn't only about assassinating the president. This is nothing less than a total takeover of America in a bloodless coup."

To the rest of the world, Vice President Breen was a hero. He'd survived the terror attack. The ticker said he'd been out with stomach discomfort the day of the president's speech. Now, he had taken swift and decisive action. He promised salvation and victory in just a few short days.

The colonel started to speak, but Merc Four began coughing. Her body stiffened in a brief and violent seizure, then relaxed. For a moment, Carl thought he had witnessed her death, but she took a shuddering breath and coughed again.

"On the plane, you said something had changed, and I think it was *you*," Reichert said. Carl looked at him and nodded, so the man said, "Agent Palmer said the adversary wanted to blame the gruesome murder of Special Agent Cummings and the other civilians on you to keep attention focused on you and not on him."

Carl nodded. "You're implying that was a critical part of his plan, which makes sense. According to Palmer's data"—Carl waved the set of papers he held—"the president is expected to die in seventy-two hours. All Breen has to do is wait until then to become president, but now he's rushing it."

Reichert shrugged. "He must be vulnerable. He must think you can hurt him." The colonel paused. "And there's something else too."

"What's that?"

"There's no way a cure could be synthesized in"—he did the two-finger quote-unquote gesture—"a few days. I have a friend at USAM-RIID, the army research center that works with the CDC on viruses that can be weaponized. We always discuss what-if scenarios and how the CDC battles natural or man-made biological pathogens. It literally takes hundreds of man-hours just to identify the various components of a new virus. Then it takes days to isolate those components and discover its transmission vectors—you know, how it spreads, how fast, and how virulent it is. After that, it takes weeks to develop counteragents. They test all those agents, in hundreds of culture dishes each, to determine the best way to kill the new virus. And once that cure is found, it would take months for the nation's *entire* pharmaceutical industry to mass-produce and distribute inoculations for the millions of people infected or at risk in this country, not to mention the billions at risk all over the world."

Carl nodded. "Okay, that makes a lot of sense from a logistics point of view. So, you're suggesting that even if they're close to discovering a cure, as CNN is reporting, they'd still be *months* away from distribution?"

Reichert nodded.

Carl saw the full picture. He said, "So Breen already has a stockpile of the antidote and plans to hold back its release until the president and the rest of the government die. He plans to take the oath of the presidency, and a company whose CEO is on his team miraculously steps forward with a vaccine that cures this Contagion. He's keeping the media focused on me, so they won't question a miracle cure."

Reichert nodded again. "And once Breen has consolidated his power, the answers to those questions will be moot."

Carl continued to read the scrolling ticker. New details were constantly released by the VP's office and by the CDC regarding the outbreak. The vice president was being heralded by the media as the first truly transparent leader in history. Though Breen was locked up in a top-secret bunker, he was providing the media with detailed information as soon as it became available. He said he wanted the nation and the world to know exactly what he was doing to combat the evil menace that had attacked the fabric of freedom.

The entire flight crews of both *Marine One* and *Air Force One* had been hospitalized yesterday afternoon with a variety of symptoms ranging from severe headaches to nausea to seizures. About one in four had died as a result of complications that were still not clearly understood.

The military had responded quickly to quarantine Andrews Air Force Base, and the CDC immediately deployed personnel who were already in the nation's capital on a mock training exercise to assess the Contagion. "They responded so quickly," said the vice president, "it was believed that all infected personnel and exposed family members had been located and were receiving care."

"Mock training exercise, my ass." Colonel Reichert snorted his contempt at the tiny TV. "I bet a month's salary someone high up at the CDC is in on this with the VP."

"That was my thought as well," Carl said with a nod. "Using me as the scapegoat for this whole affair was simply an accidental opportunity he grabbed."

"I agree. The logistics and planning of this whole affair must go back many months. He has high-level help and lots of it."

Carl took a deep breath and blew it out. "So trying to locate and dispatch everyone involved is not feasible."

Reichert shook his head. "It's well documented that hunting and killing is your forte, so he'll have a contingency for that."

The colonel head-nodded at the TV screen, where the picture showed a map of the city of Las Cruces. An inset showed an exploded view of the Mountain View Regional Medical Center, where the president and her daughter were being treated. National Guard personnel had quickly locked down both the hospital and Las Cruces to prevent the catastrophic spread of the disease. However, pockets of outbreaks in and around Albuquerque, and other nearby cities, were not contained. The CDC had deployed a rapid-response containment team to those cities, but several thousand cases of the virus already had been reported. CNN medical experts estimated that tens of thousands more cases went unreported as infected people failed to realize the significance of their symptoms. Infected people had almost two days to travel around the country and the world, spreading the virus before airports were shut down.

The colonel said, "I find it interesting that the National Guard has so quickly quarantined Las Cruces, yet no such military activity is happening around Albuquerque."

"You're suggesting Breen anticipated and planned for this?"

Reichert nodded. "He planned for a possible outbreak in Las Cruces because he knew that's where the president's daughter would be taken for treatment. Likewise for DC."

"Which means he knows about this." Carl held up Palmer's notes. "How it spreads and how dangerous it is."

"Except he didn't anticipate you becoming a carrier and starting an additional epidemic in Albuquerque." He paused, and Carl got the feeling Reichert was getting ready to drop the bomb. The pilot said, "It takes weeks to organize the logistics of a week-long military deployment, especially for the National Guard. Hundreds of personnel have to be assigned, dozens of military transport vehicles must be prepped, and thousands of gallons of fuel need to get requisitioned. This is a real operation, so they'd need weapons and ammunition, tons of food, hundreds of tents, dozens of portable latrines, and miles of razor wire for security fences we see there." Reichert pointed at the television, where CNN showed the military detachment camped behind the security fence. He continued, "Not to mention all the biohazard suits needed for a containment operation of this nature."

Carl nodded his understanding. "You can't just throw weekend warriors, or even regular marines or army soldiers, into biohazard suits and tell them to stand guard. They have to be trained how to eat, sleep, and pee in a bio-hostile environment."

"That's right. National Guard troops are there simply to provide perimeter security, and trained specialists have no doubt sequestered everyone inside the hospital. For an operational deployment of this magnitude, the vice president can't just call up a general he knew from back in his military days. A significant number of leaders very high in the military chain of command must also be involved." Colonel Reichert paused for a moment, then summarized, "We're not facing some power-hungry madman trying to take over a third-world nation. The vice president is running a well-funded and well-planned coup. This war is over, Johnson. He's already won."

As he watched the CNN ticker, Carl felt equal parts anger and fear growing inside him as he absorbed the news that he was being blamed for the entire event. This was so much larger than the killing spree he'd embarked on earlier in the week. He was no longer seen merely as a deranged lunatic targeting federal agents. He was no longer just a domestic terrorist. Now, he would forever be known as the man who had unleashed a deadly weapon of mass destruction with the intent to destroy the US government. And in two days, he would be immortalized as the man who had murdered a sitting president—the first *woman* president—of the United States. What the shadow government was accusing him of doing was far worse than crashing planes into the World Trade Center.

Colonel Reichert echoed the thoughts running through his mind. "The country is lost. The world is going to be a very different place when Walter Breen takes the oath of the presidency."

Carl took a step forward and swept the television off the filing cabinet. It crashed against the far wall with an explosion of glass and plastic. He walked across the room and knelt on one knee beside Palmer's chair like he was proposing marriage. He listened to her ragged breathing for a moment, then gently lifted her chin. Her eyes fluttered open, and she tried to focus on him, but she barely had the strength.

She took a deep breath, and Carl leaned forward like he was hugging her. He rested her chin on his left shoulder and whispered in her ear.

"Nancy, I'm sorry I did this to you."

She replied weakly, "Stop feeling sorry for me, bitch, and go get the antidote."

He chuckled softly in her ear. "I love it when you talk like a sailor." He leaned back and cupped her chin, serious again. She tried to say something, but no words came.

"I need you, Nancy. I don't know how to beat these guys."

She managed to raise her left arm and placed her hand on his shoulder. "You've come this far," she said.

She gave his shoulder a light squeeze, and Carl wondered how much of her reserve strength that gesture stole from her. Her arm flopped back down on her lap. Palmer took a couple of deep breaths as she summoned her last dregs of energy.

"Aaron and I…we never could catch you"—she paused to catch her breath—"because we couldn't think like you. You stayed…ahead of us, kept us guessing. Didn't give us time…to analyze and anticipate." She nodded with her eyes closed. "Do that now, and you'll beat them. You have to…be the American Terrorist to win against Breen…and the Triad." She paused again and said, "Do the unexpected. *Be. Carl. Johnson.*"

CHAPTER 43

1135 MST, SATURDAY

NORTHERN MEXICO

CARL SAT IN THE RIGHT pilot seat of the sleek luxury helicopter as he again approached Vicente Orizaga's homestead outside
Hermosillo. He gazed to his right, out the window of his door, but
this time, the landscape passing beneath the craft held no beauty for him.
Too much had happened. Too many people had died or were going to
die unless he saved them, and he didn't know if he could. To save the
president, he had to get the antidote and remain free. He could not be
captured, even if it meant sacrificing his team members, along with Luisa
and Julia Reyes.

Carl's breath caught in his throat as he thought about Rainey. Carl had
hugged and comforted him, treating his cuts and bruises after his assault.
Rainey was well past the twenty-eight-hour mark, and his friends at the
house where Carl took him were right at that critical point. He wondered if
Rainey was still alive, maybe in a coma in a hospital somewhere. Maybe
someone took him to a hospital at the onset of a seizure or nausea. Maybe
he died at home, alone. He wondered about his family and friends.

*How many are dying because of me right this minute, even as these
thoughts tumble through my brain?*

He considered just how bleak the situation was for himself and his
team. Normally, infected people who survived into phase two could live
in a coma for the full seventy-two hours of the second phase, but none of

his team would last that long. They wouldn't be kept clean like victims would be in a hospital. They wouldn't have intravenous food and fluids.

The airport superintendent was pushing twenty-four or twenty-five hours since he shook Carl's hand, and Carl wondered how many people that man had touched afterward. He had undoubtedly infected his own family, along with the families of other personnel at the airport. Eventually, someone would drop at the airport, or local hospitals would begin seeing the symptoms of the Contagion. Authorities would inevitably see the similarities with the American epidemic. Police, army, and the Mexican equivalent of the CDC would descend upon the municipal airport. When that happened, Carl's team would be held in isolation until they died. Or if the Unit arrived first, there would be no isolation.

Carl figured he had as many as six hours or as few as three hours until the municipal airport was quarantined. If he took more than six hours to obtain the antidote, his team would die, and he would only be able to save himself. He found himself wondering if the antidote would even have any effect on a carrier.

Suddenly, Carl was faced with the prospect of living the rest of his life as an incurable carrier of a deadly disease. Living an isolated life, not being able to touch anyone ever again, was only slightly more horrifying than living on the run, labeled as the terrorist who killed the president and all of the US government. He tried to dismiss the tidal wave of negative thoughts so he could concentrate on the mission at hand. He had to obtain the antidote.

When he'd told Colonel Reichert of his plan to return north across the border, the pilot simply nodded. "You like suicide missions, don't you?"

"Dude, you've got one usable day remaining in the rest of your life. You have something better to do with that day than save Shirley Mallory?"

"Well, since you put it that way."

Carl turned his attention to the inside of the helicopter. There was no obvious difference in the two pilot positions. The panel in front of him and above his head held the same control stick and the exact same configuration of knobs, levers, buttons, computerized lights, gauges, and indicators that David Blick was using to fly the aircraft.

The sleek, luxury aircraft featured four doors. The two front seats had car-like doors that opened outward on front hinges, and the cabin door on each side of the passenger cabin was configured like a minivan sliding car door. When closed and latched, almost none of the outside sound could be heard inside the cabin. Even the engine noise was dampened almost completely. Carl could only hear a soft, high-pitched whine accompanying a comfortable rumble he could just barely feel through the chair arms and soles of his combat boots.

Carl gazed out the front windshield at the house in the distance below. He sucked in a deep breath as the aircraft approached the house, where he'd robbed the owner of critical project information and killed his wife and the elderly woman. He was sure to receive an unpleasant welcome, but he forced himself to believe the man would decide not to kill him until he returned the half-billion dollars to Orizaga's investors. It seemed reasonable to Carl that Orizaga would be susceptible to negotiation.

The pilot banked the helicopter in a wide, westerly loop around the house. On Carl's instructions, he made no attempt to conceal their approach. This time, Carl wanted to land in Orizaga's front yard, which consisted of acres of grassland between the huge plantation house and the unpaved road almost a quarter mile away.

A wide dirt path served as the driveway connecting the road to the house, and Carl knew that setback was designed to maintain a separation between the homestead and curious lookers who really had no business there. The guards in the house would be able to see and identify visitors from the road long before they were close enough to the house to cause trouble.

"Okay," Carl said as he unbuckled his three-point safety harness. "This will go one of two ways. Either he'll want his money back, or he won't give a damn about the money, and he'll shoot me on the spot."

"Or, he could have his men haul your ass into the basement and beat the crap out of you for killing his wife and the old lady."

"Yeah, there's that." Carl shrugged. "But if he really wants his money back, then our next stop will be to retrieve the antidote."

"Good luck."

Carl hopped out and ducked as he moved away from the helicopter, then walked toward the distant mansion. He heard the chopper's engine rev behind him and felt the rush of air from the rotor as the aircraft took to the air. Blick would hover a mile out and wait for his signal, which they both hoped would be soon.

He was unarmed, and he was hoping that would at least delay a violent response from the house. Though still dressed in his black combat pants and boots, he'd removed his armored vest and his shirt. The temperature hovered in the mid-seventies, so he wore only a short-sleeve, black T-shirt, no hat on his hairless dome, and no combat goggles.

Three men walked out the grand front entrance of the house to greet him. Two walked behind the front man. Those two were army soldiers, dressed in olive green uniforms and holding automatic rifles pointed somewhat in Carl's general direction.

Behind the approaching men, Carl could see that the entire right wing of the house—where the office and a host of bedrooms had been—was totally destroyed. The missile that the army unit had fired, no doubt at Carl's lookout on the roof, had collapsed the roof and both floors into a pile of rubble.

Carl was certain the front man of the group that approached him was Vicente Orizaga. He was tall and slender with neatly trimmed gray hair. Maybe sixty years old, the man was clean-shaven, and he looked like the kind of man who jogged a few miles every morning to stay fit. He looked exactly like the kind of wealthy power broker who would hang with a mid-thirties gorgeous wife.

Orizaga wore loose cotton slacks of a beige color and a white, raw silk shirt unbuttoned to the middle of his hairless chest. His skin was a rich brown color that contrasted with the light clothing. He wore expensive leather sandals and stood with his hands in his pockets while he waited for Carl to complete his approach.

Carl strolled up and stopped within arm's reach, then stuck his hands in his pockets to match Orizaga's stance.

The man gazed at Carl through hazel eyes, then said, "I'd heard you resemble Alfonso Reyes, but up until this moment, I didn't realize how perfect that resemblance is."

"*Was*," Carl corrected. "Let's not forget the part where he's dead, and I have all his money." He exaggerated about the *dead* part.

"Ah, yes." Orizaga nodded. "So, you've come to return *my* money."

"We can discuss the *Triad's* money, if you like."

Orizaga didn't even flinch at the mention of the Triad, so Carl took that as positive proof that the Triad was in league with Walter Breen in the assault on Melissa Mallory and the infection of the president.

"You blow up half my house and killed my wife and her aunt, who, by the way, were the daughter and sister of one of my Triad investors—he's the Chihuahua connection—and you think there's something *else* we should discuss?" Orizaga gave a silent chuckle and kicked at a tuft of wild grass with his expensive sandal. "That investor is very angry with you, by the way. You have a fifty-million-dollar bounty on your head, so give me one good reason why I shouldn't have one of these soldiers kill you where you stand?"

"I can give you five hundred million reasons, but for the record, I didn't blow up your house. One of *your* soldiers did that."

"Well," Orizaga said with a shrug. "I can't say your visit here yesterday was all bad. What is it you Americans say? The wife was spending me out of house and home." He shook his head and chuckled again. "Actually, no one who lives here is related to me by blood. My wife was a package deal, which included her family members. An arranged marriage in exchange for the investor's participation in various financial activities over the years. Except, I couldn't get rid of them because that would terminate my contract with the Triad." Orizaga shrugged again. "So I suppose I should thank you for liberating me."

He stuck his hand out, and Carl shook it.

Carl smiled, knowing he now had a second bargaining chip. "You're a cold-hearted scoundrel, Mr. Orizaga."

"I consider that a compliment, coming from a man who shot a helpless old woman in the head."

They stared at each other for a few seconds, neither able to intimidate the other.

Orizaga said, "So, if we're through posturing, Mr. Johnson, shall we discuss the money?"

Carl said, "Let's talk about something else first, something that is now much more important to you, in fact."

Orizaga held the grin on his face that made his eyes sparkle mischievously. He seemed to be amused by Carl, like he was toying with him right before deciding to have his men kill him. "And what would that be?"

"You, sir, have twenty-eight hours to live."

"Excuse me?"

"I came here to negotiate a trade—the money for the antidote. But now, I'm thinking you might just give it to me for free." Carl paused for effect. "I'm infected, and now, so are you."

"We know you were in physical contact with Miss Mallory at the time she became active, but if you were infected, Mr. Johnson, you would be dead or comatose by now. Granted, her activation didn't go as planned since she wasn't supposed to succumb to a seizure so quickly. Nevertheless, the president became infected and spread the virus the way it was intended." He spread his hands wide. "So forgive me if I don't fall for your empty threat. You clearly didn't review, in sufficient detail, all the material you stole from my computer."

Carl ignored the taunt. "All this so the vice president can exercise some kind of power fantasy and take over the country? And then what?"

Orizaga laughed again. "Mr. Johnson, Vice President Breen is merely a pawn of the Triad. Last year, we were going to approach your CIA with the possibility of funding our newly discovered *super-virus*—that's what our virologists call it—but apparently, Mr. Breen interceded and decided it was a tool he could use to advance his own agenda against the president. We didn't mind that because his agenda advances our own. You see, we—and by *we*, I mean the Triad—control the virus *and* the antidote."

"But you must have given him the antidote already. He'd be a fool to use a viral weapon like this without having a stockpile of the antidote. How can you control what he already has?"

Orizaga spread his arms wide and smiled. "I apologize, Mr. Johnson. I meant *viruses* and *antidotes*. Quite by accident, we created an airborne version of the virus. The antidote formula we provided to Mr. Breen was designed to cure the version that is transmitted by touch. It also cures the airborne version, of course, but only if administered within the first ten hours of exposure. After ten hours, the airborne version of the virus mutates within the body and becomes immune to the antidote. At that point, there is no cure but death for the infected, and there is yet no anti-dote. Mr. Breen knows this. However, the clinical trials showed that 85 percent of those infected with the airborne virus exhibit symptoms well within ten hours. Unfortunately, it is that other 15 percent that can destroy a country. Mr. Breen was given the physically transmitted version of the virus to make his power play. He was also told that should he fail to heed the wishes of the Triad, we would have no problem releasing the airborne virus on the American population. That virus is especially virulent."

Carl shrugged. "Okay, so the US government funds the development of enough vaccines to inoculate everyone in the country. In a year, your threat will have no teeth."

Orizaga shook his head. "I apologize once again, Mr. Johnson, because I don't think I was clear about the antidote. It isn't a vaccine. It is only a cure. In fact, if someone who is uninfected takes the antidote, they would be subject to a very fast and very painful death. I'm talking about *seconds*."

Carl recalled reading that bit of information in Agent Palmer's summary report.

"If the airborne virus was released in the US, the computer model predicts 95 percent of your population would be decimated." The man paused and glared at Carl. "The United States would cease to exist in about thirteen days."

Carl felt an incredible disbelief at what he was hearing. "Have you forgotten about all the nukes they can rain down on your country? You know, mutually assured destruction?"

"Mr. Johnson, the airborne version of the virus is our nuke. You may have many missiles, but this virus can devastate your country just as thoroughly. It can be released at any time, in any place, and no one would ever know. Look how easily and quickly Mr. Breen killed your entire government. We can infect any number of volunteers who merely have to fly into the US and shake someone's hand or breathe on someone. Then they return home and receive the cure. By the time anyone in your new government realizes the catastrophe is upon them, there won't be enough people still alive to try to prove whether it was an attack or an accident.

"But that outcome is not in our best interests. Mr. Breen wants to reshape the American government, and we want to reshape the western hemisphere. That's a lot easier to do with a friendly leader in the White

House. Mr. Breen's decapitation of the current government advances both our agendas."

"Which is what? Control? You want to subjugate only *half* the world?"

"It's about power, Mr. Johnson. Territorial, economic, and military power. By controlling soon-to-be President Breen, the Triad effectively controls the United States. Next, we will control Mexico, then Canada, and then all the countries of South America. With the military might of the US, the economic power of the entire western hemisphere, and the natural resources of the entire continent of South America, the Triad will become the first and only geographic mega-power on the planet."

Orizaga nodded as Carl's eyebrows tinted.

"Think about it, Mr. Johnson," Orizaga continued. "South America has enough oil that, if shared, would end the western hemisphere's dependence on Middle Eastern oil almost overnight. All the regional conflicts the US is involved with in that part of the world would become irrelevant in mere days. The oil-rich nations would no longer have the power to create strangleholds on our economies. In fact, the oil countries' severely weakened economies would make them dependent on the new Western Alliance. The cheap labor of South American countries will replace that of China in an instant. And the shared South American natural resources—and I'm specifically referring to everything from lumber to all the rare elements so crucial to the high-tech manufacturing industry—would end our dependence on Europe and Asia forever."

Carl nodded. "Forever is a long time, and no empire will last that long." He studied Orizaga and decided the man believed the hype he'd been fed. He sounded more like a cheerleader than an accountant.

"Imagine the strategic value of having powerful US military installations or warships scattered up and down both coasts of the western hemisphere," Orizaga said. "There'd be nowhere on the planet where we couldn't project near-instant military superiority. Imagine maintaining a strategic base only a few miles from Antarctica, where we'd have unchallenged access to the untapped natural resources of that continent."

Carl thought the plan was sound except for the unspoken part, where some nuclear-capable country might start World War III to counter the US's territorial expansion. Or when the existence of Contagion became known to the intel network. History was filled with empires run by power-hungry madmen who got too big for their britches.

"Well," Carl said. "It's a great pipe dream, but what's in it for you?"

Orizaga smiled again. "Power, of course, and money. And a place in the new regime."

"That's assuming you live beyond the next twenty-eight hours."

"We're back to that again?"

"You said it yourself. The president's daughter was supposed to be the carrier, but she wasn't supposed to succumb to the virus. I was right there with her before, during, and after she went active. It's true she took a lot of sedative that activated the viral agent, but I had some of that sedative juice too." He told Orizaga how he'd tested the sedative juice to prove to Melissa it wasn't poison. "After she had her seizure, everyone who touched her wore latex gloves except me. Your plan to create a carrier for this virus was successful, except it wasn't Melissa Mallory. I had some initial headaches and nausea, but beyond that, the virus didn't affect me. Instead, I unintentionally started all those virus outbreaks throughout Albuquerque, and now, here in Mexico."

Orizaga's eyes narrowed.

Carl nodded. "No doubt you've heard that the CDC deployed a containment team to Albuquerque, but none of the president's staff went anywhere near there. You'll start to hear about outbreaks here soon too. The virus is spreading throughout this part of the country, but my guess is no one recognizes it for what it is yet. I've infected my entire team. Some are already in a coma. And now, you have it too. You'll get sick and die unless you do what I tell you to do."

"You overlook the simple fact that all I need to do is kill you to end the Contagion, then just go get a dose of the antidote. I'm due at the lab within the hour to raise the security threat level anyway."

"Well, perhaps if you told them you're infected, they'll give you a dose because they're all nice people over there, right?" Carl shrugged. "On the other hand, maybe they'll call one of the Triad bosses for in-structions. Maybe they'll tell them to lock you in isolation. Maybe your father-in-law is still upset with you because you lost their half-billion-dollar investment, or because your security staff let me waltz into your home and kill his daughter and sister. Or maybe he'll realize you killed me before I gave back the money. So maybe he'll keep you in that isolation cell and study the progression of symptoms," Carl said with a shrug. "Or maybe they'll just leave you in there for four days, and no one will ever come to visit."

He could tell Orizaga believed him.

"I'm not lying, am I?" Carl asked. "You've already heard about symptoms in the area, haven't you?"

"What is your proposal, Mr. Johnson? How can you obtain the antidote for…us?"

"I can't, but Alfonso Reyes can."

CHAPTER 44

CARL'S ASSUMPTION WAS THAT ALFONSO Reyes had been in the secret lab. There's no way they'd inject Melissa Mallory outside of a lab. Emergency containment and medical treatment had to be available. Carl outlined his plan and let Orizaga process the scenario without saying anything more. He could see the wheels of deception turning behind the man's eyes.

"Very well. Call your helicopter. We will go to the office building where the lab is located. Reyes's death was not widely reported, and I have not yet informed the lab personnel."

Carl nodded and pulled a laser marker from a cargo pocket of his pants. It looked like a five-inch black ink pen, and he pressed the little switch on the end with his thumb. Then he waved the business end at the hovering helicopter. Even from a mile away, the laser marker beam would be a bright flash of red light that was easy to spot.

Within seconds, the front of the hovering helicopter dipped as the aircraft sped in his direction. The chopper settled several yards away, and both men ducked as they passed the outer threshold of the spinning rotors.

It was an instinctive reaction for Carl. He'd wanted to prove he was tougher than the accountant and simply strut up to the helicopter. After all, his brain told him the rotors were spinning eight feet off the ground, while he topped out at three inches under the six-foot mark. Logically, he had absolutely nothing to worry about. His instinct for survival had a different perspective. The mere thought of metal spinning near his head faster than lawn mower blades made him somehow feel more helpless than a blade of grass. Should the chopper engine suddenly have a burp, the spinning metal might wobble. At least, that's what his imagination told him. The rotors could separate his head at the shoulders, and manhood be damned, he wouldn't even have time to scream in pain or surprise. So he ducked.

He got the sliding door behind the pilot open and launched himself into the craft, followed by Orizaga, who then slid the door closed. They sat side by side in the two first-row passenger chairs.

"Don't worry about contaminating the pilot," Carl said nonchalantly. "He's already infected too." They were well into the hour-long westward journey to the city of Chihuahua when Carl broke the silence again. "Why would the Triad trust a new president that had murdered his predecessor and his entire government?"

Orizaga looked over, and Carl could see that the man's cocky attitude had sobered somewhat. It was interesting to Carl to watch the man transform before his eyes from being an instigator of trouble to becoming a victim of the very trouble he helped to create.

"I mentioned the real threat before—an infected assassin sent to the US, who would shake the hand of a person who would shake the hand of another, who would shake your hand. Then, the assassin goes home and gets the antidote."

Carl understood the terror potential of the plan. After all, he was doing pretty much the same thing by intentionally infecting Orizaga. Breen had better toe the line. He would never know the identity of his assassin, or when that man or woman—a diplomat or even a child—would come for him.

The accountant continued, "But that is only part of the strategic alliance. The Triad knows that in the new regime, the issue of trust or treason will be overcome by events. Mr. Breen and the Triad will be in bed together, so to speak. It will do neither any good to rock the boat at that time. There will be plenty of power and profit to satisfy everyone involved."

"Sooner or later, the US will reverse engineer a vaccine," Carl said. "If the Triad hasn't already figured that out, they're not as smart as they think they are."

"They know this," Orizaga said soberly. "They're already working on developing new strains that would be immune to the current antidote. They're conducting the research and tests at a secure location even I don't know."

Somehow, that response didn't surprise Carl. It was the way of war. "A bigger, better weapon," he muttered.

"A *more efficient* weapon."

"Your Triad and the vice president are playing a dangerous game. They thought they were smart enough to control every aspect of the weapon, but no one anticipated someone other than Melissa Mallory would be a carrier. The bug has already slipped containment."

"Perhaps," Orizaga said. "But things are far from out of control."

The city of Chihuahua was a modern place. From a thousand feet up, Carl saw many of the same international name-brand stores and food chain restaurants he'd seen in Hermosillo. For some reason, Carl had thought Mexico was a third-world nation. He had no particular basis for that conclusion because he'd never been there before two days ago. From what he'd seen in that two days, though, the cities of Mexico were no less modern than any American city of the same size.

There was road construction everywhere. Many streets below had long lines of orange barrels squeezing two or three lanes of traffic down to two or one. Maybe they borrowed the damn things from Albuquerque—the orange-barrel capital of the world.

As they approached the tallest building in Chihuahua City, Carl spied a huge bus depot off to the right. The squat building covered several acres by itself, and it was surrounded by many more acres of paved concrete serving as parking lots for the buses and a complicated set of bus lanes for arrivals and departures. Out to the left of the helicopter, Carl saw a large park that reminded him of Central Park in New York City. It was surrounded by what he guessed were hotels and apartment buildings of medium height, maybe five to seven stories.

The city below reminded Carl somewhat of Albuquerque or even maybe a city like Phoenix without all the tall buildings. The city was spread out with lots of wide streets and shrub-filled medians, and there was an extensive system of drainage arroyos for channeling rainwater to prevent flooding.

Overall, the earth-tone buildings blended in well with the landscape and scrub, as there was very little grass except in city parks and very few wildly colored buildings. Most of the homes were single story, and most of the commercial and retail buildings were two or three stories with few over five stories. In fact, all the buildings over five stories were clustered around the target building that housed the clandestine viral lab.

Blick brought the helicopter to a hover over the painted bull's-eye in the exact center of the landing pad. As he settled the aircraft onto the pad, Orizaga explained that the roof structure of the ten-year-old building was reinforced during the remodel that installed the secret lab in the building.

That made sense to Carl. If one wanted to secretly import or export equipment or secret material—or the daughter of a US president—things went a lot smoother when you could do so from the roof. There was an oversized freight elevator beside a personnel elevator on the east end of the roof. Next to the elevators was the stairs enclosure.

Carl started counting down from six hundred as soon as he and Orizaga stepped into the elevator. As he and Orizaga rode the elevator in complete silence from the top floor—the seventeenth floor—down to the fifth floor, where the labs were located, Carl took time to evaluate his life again. Up to a month ago, he'd been a good soul, a caring friend to many, and a loving father. In the past month, after losing his son to a horrible mistake of identity, he had transitioned into a bad man. He'd done terrible things to good people and to bad people, and he knew he rightly deserved the title of American Terrorist that the media reported. The fact that he'd rescued the president's daughter and saved FBI Special Agent Cummings, her daughter, and the Chapman family did little to exonerate him or ease his conscience. His previous crimes and his earned reputation as a terrorist were very real, sickening even to himself.

On his rampage of revenge, he had threatened innocent civilians. He'd murdered a federal agent in the most gruesome way imaginable and lured dozens of other agents into deadly ambushes. He'd used children as hostages to achieve his objectives. He'd beaten an innocent woman almost to death just to punish her father, the man he held personally responsible for his son's death. And he did it all in the name of justice and revenge. Worse, he felt at the time perfectly justified in doing those things. But everything he had done paled in comparison to what he was about to do. Carl recalled Agent Palmer's advice.

Be the American Terrorist. Be. Carl. Johnson.

Carl was not so naive as to believe the vice president's plan could contain the virus to the shores of the US. Too much time had passed since Carl's infection—almost fifty-five hours—and he'd unwittingly touched a lot of people in those hours. Those people had touched many others. Some of the second or third generation infected would have traveled on airplanes over the last two days before they exhibited symptoms. Each would become a new Patient Zero in a multitude of states and countries, starting fresh micro-epidemics around the globe.

Vice President Breen's plan centered on containing the person his team and the Triad believed to be the original Patient Zero—Melissa Mallory—and he had probably succeeded in doing that. Melissa Mallory was supposed to be unaffected long enough to accomplish the Triad's goal of infecting the government before Breen's people pretended to discover her illness and isolate her.

It wouldn't take long for the international health monitoring community to recognize the similarity of symptoms in all the micro-epidemics, and they would mobilize and quarantine affected hospitals, cities, or even countries. With infected people not showing immediate symptoms, though, Carl doubted that governments could set up quarantines fast enough to contain the spread of the virus.

Carl had no doubt the international cooperation between agencies equivalent to the CDC would contain *major* outbreaks. Yet, in small communities—such as the one where the municipal airport, Nuevo Casas Grandes, was located—the medical response would be delayed. The small-town hospitals might not report the symptoms immediately. They might not even recognize the relevance of the symptoms, or they might initially misdiagnose patients and actually send the infected back home to spread the virus even further.

Breen and his people expected the virus to be contained to specific parts of the US as detailed in their plan, but Carl, the true carrier, had been trying hard *not* to be found, and he'd been very successful. Many people—maybe tens of thousands of successive generations of infected around the world—would continue to get sick and die before the antidote could be distributed outside of the two initial hot zones of DC and New Mexico, if Breen waited for President Mallory to die.

Now, Carl was using the virus he carried as his own personal weapon. Vicente Orizaga was merely his first victim. He had to force the vice president to use the antidote *before* the president died, and there was only one way to do that. He was going to hit the Triad in their own backyard.

The elevator made the short trip from the roof to the top lab office swiftly.

As it slowed to a halt, Carl steeled himself for action. "Let's get this done quickly," he said. "We don't want anybody getting nervous or suspicious. If they detain us inside the building, neither of us get our dose."

He followed Vicente Orizaga out of the elevator. Suddenly, the accountant was all smiles, and Carl was surprised at the instant change in the man. He was like an actor in front of a camera. He greeted the security personnel and the receptionist cheerfully as he signed a register and engaged them with lively banter in Spanish.

A gray-haired woman approached in a business suit and white smock. She looked like a lead scientist, a senior project manager, and Carl instantly knew he was facing the woman most responsible for developing the virus and the protocols for infecting Melissa Mallory. Maybe she was the one who invented the bug. He suddenly felt an overwhelming hatred for the woman and an intense desire to kill her.

As he gazed at the woman, he realized she was speaking to him…in Spanish. Yet, she had a look of fear in her eyes. She knew him as Alfonso Reyes, and she knew his reputation for charity and violence. He played on her fear. He gave her his best steely-eyed gaze and shook her hand. Then, he motioned Orizaga to proceed down the hall. He followed the pair down the short corridor toward a steel vault door with a numeric keypad. The project manager punched in a long series of digits—too long for Carl to even attempt to memorize—and led them into the section of the lab where the bug work was done. She gave Orizaga a lecture in Spanish, likely a status update, but Carl tuned out their voices and studied his surroundings, looking for egress points.

He'd only seen two security guards so far—one at the reception desk just inside the private elevator, and the other just down the hall at the vault door. They were dressed in black tactical gear. They wore sidearms and carried Uzis strapped over their shoulders, but Carl figured the rest of the security force was probably sequestered on another floor or even down on the first floor, where any serious threat might come from.

When the heavy vault door swung open, Carl found himself entering a small, twenty-foot-square anteroom. The guard entered with them and pressed the heavy door closed. The room held a desk with a keyboard and monitor, but it had no other apparent function, in Carl's opinion, other than for them to wait while the project manager entered her code again to open a transparent glass door in the wall opposite the vault door. This time, the guard remained in the anteroom. When Carl followed Orizaga and his project manager into the first lab chamber, the countdown in Carl's head hit four hundred seconds remaining.

The lab room was about sixty feet wide—the full depth of the building—and had thick acrylic walls. The entry door was sealed into the wall with a clear gasket that reminded Carl of the solid silicone gel commonly used on aquariums. The air pressure of the room was slightly negative so that when the door opened, Carl felt the air flow past him from the anteroom into the lab. He knew the air was sucked from all the hazard rooms and filtered through specially designed filters to make sure no particles escaped. Maybe the air was burned in a high-temperature furnace filter and then sent through coolers for recirculation. He'd heard of that kind of thing before.

The walls of the anteroom were lined with dozens of shoulder-high, stainless steel specimen refrigerators with glass windows in the doors. They were all stacked with identical trays containing small metal canisters. There were a couple of glass-top tables in the center of the room, but he saw no real medical equipment—no Petri dishes, electron microscopes, centrifuges, or anything else Carl thought would be necessary to do real virus development work. There was only a single monitor and keyboard, no doubt tied into a central computer network somewhere.

Carl decided the room was for storage of doses of the antivirus ready for local deployment. The back wall of the room was a shiny, stainless steel bulkhead with a massive steel oval hatch that Carl thought belonged in a high-tech submarine from the future. The shiny surface of the door had an electronic keypad and had hydraulic hinges on the top and bottom of the right side. Carl approached the two-foot-square acrylic viewing window dead center of the door and at eye level, through which he could see into the large lab room.

Centered right below the window was an orange placard with the three black sickles on its surface—the universal biological hazard sign. Carl grunted. That was where the real work was done. Contagion—Melissa's virus and the airborne version—were beyond that bulkhead.

Orizaga issued more instructions to the manager and her technician, who had been in the storage room before they arrived, and opened one of the refrigerators. Carl turned and watched the young man pull out a single metal case and set it reverently on the glass-top table in front of them.

Three hundred seconds remaining.

While the tech maneuvered the case open, Carl studied the scene on the other side of the bulkhead door. There was a small, clear acrylic airlock five feet beyond the steel hatch. That decontamination room held wall-mounted shower nozzles, red coiled hoses, and other items he didn't recognize. Several orange spacesuits hung on specialized hanger assemblies against the left wall.

The entire far wall of the decontamination and changing room was floor-to-ceiling acrylic, through which Carl could see three workers in orange spacesuits going about their business of studying or perfecting virus samples. The hatred for these individuals because of what they'd done to Melissa Mallory boiled up inside Carl again, but he quieted his feelings by reminding himself these people all had less than five minutes to live.

Carl turned away from the window and focused his attention on the glass table in the center of the room. The shiny metal case the tech had laid out was about the size of a laptop computer, but it was about six inches thick. It had rounded edges and corners, with rubber feet on the bottom and sides, along with a handle for carrying the case like a briefcase. Carl got the impression the sturdy case didn't need to be handled as gingerly as the technician was handling it, but the young man's care lent importance to the contents.

The top of the metal box featured a small biohazard placard exactly in the center of its lid. The only other anomaly on the top surface of the case was a two-inch-wide electronic display screen on the top. The tiny screen held a temperature readout with a mechanical gauge. The low end of the scale was forty-five, and the high end was fifty-five. No doubt the box was designed to keep its contents in that temperature range. The black line indicator read forty-nine degrees.

The tech had popped two clasps on the metal case and pivoted the top open. Inside was a foam liner with four rows of five items that looked like the tips of tiny test tubes. Carl reached over, pulled one of the tubes, and examined it. It was a small acrylic vial and was stoppered at one end with a rubbery synthetic material, and it had a thin hard plastic ring around the stoppered end. Two tiny metal pins extended a quarter inch from the center of the rubber stopper. The vial was filled with a light blue liquid.

The project manager continued her dialogue in Spanish with Orizaga. No one paid Carl any attention at all. He replaced the tube in its slot and pulled out a small metal object that had its own preformed depression in the middle of the foam liner.

It sort of resembled a Star Trek hypo-spray device, except it had a handle with a trigger that fit comfortably in his palm. On the back end of the device was a circular receiver into which each acrylic vial could fit. There was a tiny LED counter just below the circular receiver, so he figured there was a tiny gas module in the injector handle that provided pressure to inject the contents of the vials. The LED read twenty, so Carl figured it was a counter for how many doses remained in the injector's charge.

He replaced the injector into its space. He'd seen these kinds of devices on TV, but when he'd gotten his immunizations back in his Air Force days, they still used needles and syringes. But that was thirty-odd years ago.

One hundred eighty seconds.

It was time to move. He closed the lid, snapped the latches closed, and handed it to Orizaga. "It's time to go meet our client."

Orizaga took his cue and spoke in Spanish to the project manager. She nodded curtly and reversed the procedures to take them out of the lab room and the anteroom vault door. The door was big, heavy, and slow. By the time they were back in the reception area, the countdown in Carl's head was at 120.

Carl and Orizaga emerged from the rooftop elevator at the twenty-second mark, and Carl could see David Blick tapping at an imaginary wristwatch. Carl wanted to burst into a sprint for the last fifty feet, but one of the security guards had accompanied them to the roof, so he merely tapped Orizaga on the arm, and the two of them did a slight jog to the helicopter like they really weren't in a hurry.

Blick had the rotors buzzing at lift-off speed, so when they approached the helicopter, the rotor wash threatened to sweep them off their feet. Orizaga, who didn't know the urgency of Carl's countdown, faltered until Carl tackled the man and heaved him into the cabin. Carl leaped in almost on top of him.

Ten seconds.

"Go!" Carl hollered.

His shout was wasted because Blick had the chopper in the air before Carl finished uttering that single-syllable command. He knew Blick was a veteran of dozens of dust-off missions for TER teams, and he'd proved his skill once again.

"Hold on to something!" Blick had seen the full supply of TER-provided C-4 Carl stashed in the duffel bag—a dozen bricks. "We're dead if we don't get below the blast wave!"

Orizaga got himself into a seat and looked at Carl, bewildered. "Blast wave?"

For a moment, Carl thought they were going to escape. He saw the security guard glance at the black bag remaining on the roof and spoke hurriedly into a radio. Then, the security guard pointed his Uzi at the fleeing helicopter, and Carl heard bullets pinging against the metal skin of the aircraft.

Blick flipped the helicopter almost belly-up as he cleared the edge of the building, then dove nose-down toward the street. Carl had not yet gained a seat, so he was pinned against the starboard cabin door. He looked up into the fiery blast as the top two floors of the building simply disintegrated. Huge chunks of concrete and metal blasted hundreds of feet outward above them, riding on liquid plumes of red and orange flames.

The pilot pulled out of the dive only a few feet above the street, just as Carl pushed away from the starboard door. He tumbled to the back of the cabin, bouncing off the two rows of leather chairs. He clamored to his feet as Blick coaxed the aircraft higher into the air. It was then that Carl noticed a deep rumble in the engine that hadn't been present a few seconds ago. He faced front and glanced up at the ceiling. He cursed as he noticed half a dozen holes with daylight shining through them. The guard had shot them through the belly and out the roof.

Carl nodded at Orizaga and moved forward, pointing at the open door. "Secure that door, please," Carl shouted over the air noise blasting into the cabin.

Carl pivoted as Orizaga looked over at the door, then he throat-chopped the man. Hard. Right in his Adam's apple. When the man reached reflexively to his injured throat, Carl snatched the antidote case from him and tossed it onto his own seat. He heaved the man out of his seat and held him by the front of his shirt.

"This is for Melissa," he said. "And for my son."

Vicente Orizaga's eyes widened and he opened his mouth, but he couldn't scream because of his damaged throat. Carl shoved him backward out the door. Holding the vertical safety bar next to the doorway, he watched the man fall five hundred feet to the ground, arms and legs flailing the whole way. The man bounced and tumbled a bit on impact. Carl slid the door closed and went to the copilot's seat.

Blick said, "You sure cut it real close back there. I figure we had maybe a two-second margin."

Carl nodded. "Thanks for not leaving me."

Blick looked over at him through light blue eyes, and Carl had the feeling the pilot was reappraising him. Carl knew the man initially blamed him for the deaths of TER operators who may have been his friends or associates. Now he saw grudging respect in the man's eyes.

"Without the antidote," Blick said, "I'm dead anyway. Figured I might as well stay for the fireworks show."

Carl nodded and looked over his shoulder. The top two or three floors of the seventeen-story glass and steel building were missing, creating a ragged scar that billowed a dark plume of smoke into the sky. What remained of the stricken tower seemed to sink, slowly at first, as the structure collapsed and crumbled to the ground. A huge cloud of gray smoke, dust, and debris exploded outward through the streets like a volcanic pyroclastic flow, and in seconds, all the surrounding buildings were hidden from view by thick gray dust.

Carl turned forward in his seat and put on his seat harness.

"I get that you wanted to steal the antidote," Blick said. "But I don't see the value of taking out the building."

"That's because you don't know what they were playing with inside that lab." Carl paused for a moment. "Pretty soon, the vice president will have something new to think about."

CHAPTER 45

1530 MST, SATURDAY
NORTHERN MEXICO

CARL HELD HIS BREATH AS the helicopter thumped down hard on the tarmac outside the hangar, where he'd left the Gulfstream and his other team members. The mild rumbling he'd felt leaving the rooftop had become an ear-wrenching, continuous squeal of metallic death as the pilot struggled to keep the aircraft airborne. Carl clutched the case of antidotes in his lap. Whatever else happened, he didn't want to lose the case. When it became clear the chopper wasn't going to explode or fall over sideways and grind its rotors into shrapnel, he let out his breath and unbuckled his seat harness.

"Mr. Blick," he said, opening the case, "your job here is done. Get as far away from here as you can and don't look back. If they find you, you're in for a tough time."

"Right. E-and-E 101." When Carl tented his eyebrows in confusion, Blick added, "Escape and evasion."

Carl nodded and stuck a vial into the receiver on the back of the injector handle. He pushed up Blick's short-sleeve shirt and pressed the device against his bicep, near the shoulder. He squeezed the trigger, and the device hissed for a couple of seconds as pressurized gas forced the blue serum out of the injector vial and into Blick's arm.

"I sure hope that antidote doesn't knock you out."

"If it does, I won't feel the pain of the crash."

Carl closed the case and bumped fists with Blick, then jumped out of the helicopter. He closed the door behind him and ran, ducking out from under the rotors as the whine of the wounded engine got even louder. The helicopter lifted off and flew away to the south, a trail of thick black smoke streaming from the portside engine outlet.

Carl turned and looked to the northeast, where a line of emergency vehicles approached the gate barrier of the municipal airport property. They'd flown over the small convoy, and Carl had seen two boxy paramedic trucks escorted by three police cars and two army Jeeps. The police cars normally wouldn't have concerned him. Back in the States, he'd never seen the medical first responders at an emergency scene without police involvement. Often, the police arrived first.

The presence of the army, though, told Carl his time had run out. The Mexican military was undoubtedly mobilizing all over the country. People across northern Mexico were no doubt starting to show viral symptoms, and the vast resources of the government would be needed for quarantining those affected to limit the Contagion.

Carl figured airport employees had already succumbed; hence, the army was here to close down the airport. Hopefully, the first responders would first head toward the tiny passenger terminal or maybe the control tower where someone, perhaps the superintendent, might have collapsed.

The good news was that his team was in the hangar near the south side of the airport complex, and the passenger terminal was on the northeast side, close to the main entrance where the first responders were entering. The control tower was even farther from his hangar, all the way on the northwest side of the airport and on the other side of the main north-south runway.

Carl raced through the personnel door that was integrated into one side of the huge hangar door assembly. He entered immediately in front of the Gulfstream and saw Colonel Reichert sitting in the cockpit with his headset on. There was a concerned look on his face, and Carl figured he was coming to the same conclusions as he absorbed military chatter, air traffic control chatter, or maybe even broadcast radio news.

Reichert saw him as soon as he ran in, so Carl thrust his hand in the air, waving it in a circle and giving what he hoped was the universal whirly-bird symbol to start the engines. Reichert nodded, but as Carl ran down the side of the plane on his way to the office where his team was, he saw the pilot descending the stairs with his electronic tablet in his hand.

"Forget about the safety check, Colonel. If we're not in the air in four minutes, we're dead!"

Carl ran into the office and tended to Agent Palmer. She lay on her side, next to her chair, curled up in a fetal position. She had somehow managed to get out of her tactical vest and black turtleneck. Her black sports bra was all she wore up top, and it was soaked with perspiration. She was unconscious, breathing in ragged shallow breaths.

He straightened her legs and rolled her onto her back. He opened the case and pulled the injector from within. He locked one of the tiny vials of antidote into the injector, placed the business end against her bare shoulder, and squeezed the trigger. He heard the hiss and watched the blue liquid in the vial disappear. Carl wrote Palmer a note on the back of her one-page synopsis and folded it up as small as he could. Then, he hid the note where only she would find it.

If she woke up to find it.

Carl quickly checked the others. Mercs Three and Four were sprawled somewhat arm-in-arm on the couch and had been able to spend their last moments of consciousness together. Merc Three still had a pulse, so he got a dose, but his wife, Merc Four, was dead. Two of the remaining mercs were still alive, so Carl injected them. Luisa and Julia Reyes both registered a faint pulse, so Carl injected them as well.

The LED counter read enough charge for thirteen more doses. His first thought after injecting Palmer was to simply discard the empty vial, but then he realized what an extremely dangerous biohazard that would present. If someone uninfected accidentally broke an empty vial and got the tiniest bit of residue on their skin, they'd die instantly, according to Orizaga and Palmer's report. Instead, Carl replaced the expended vials upside down in their foam depressions so he'd know which vials still held serum. He closed the case and carried it out into the cavernous room of the main part of the hangar.

The colonel had already spooled up the engines. In the closed hangar, the sound was deafening, even though the engines were merely at idle. Carl started to run around the front of the jet, but a quick glance up into the cockpit showed the pilot jabbing his finger with an animated gesture at the red knob near the massive hangar doors.

Carl changed directions and closed the personnel door in the center of the big door he'd entered moments before so its safety interlock wouldn't prevent the main hangar doors from opening. He slammed his palm against the button. A horn blared briefly, and yellow warning lights rotated near the door to warn people to stay away from the tracks of the moving doors. He ran up the starboard-side bulkhead stairs, then closed and locked the cabin door.

By habit of years of programming, Carl headed toward his left to the passenger cabin, then he reversed course and stepped through the open cockpit door. He took the front, right seat, set the case of antidotes on his lap, and opened the case. He removed two vials and pushed one onto the injector. He leaned over to inject Reichert's arm, but the man leaned away.

"What's that going to do to me?"

"Dude, it's going to save your life!"

"No, I mean, is it going to knock me out or make me groggy or disrupt my vision or something? I can't fly in any of those conditions."

Carl nodded in understanding. That was the very reason he had withheld his own injection until his other team members were injected.

"I don't know," he said.

He had no idea what the recovery process was going to be like for a normal infected person who was not already comatose. He pressed the business end of the injector against his own shoulder and squeezed the trigger. The blue liquid hissed into him, and he immediately felt a momentary heat spread through his arm. Then the heat faded.

He waited for something to happen, but nothing did. There was no fainting, nausea, pain, or any other disorientation, but then he was a carrier. He didn't know if the antidote would affect the colonel differently, and he hadn't thought to check and see if David Blick had remained airborne. Hell, he didn't even know if the antidote would actually cure a carrier.

"If I exhibit severe symptoms, then inject me. Otherwise, hit me after we land," he said. "If we live that long."

Carl nodded, closed the case, and stowed it in a small floor locker meant for pilot's gear behind the copilot's seat. He checked the temperature readout. It still read under fifty degrees. Had to be some kind of coolant mechanism built into the case, he figured.

Carl nodded to himself, then secured the locker and strapped himself in beside the pilot. The pitch of the engines increased to a thunderous roar inside the hangar, and the jet leaped through the hangar doors like a racecar and careened to the left.

Colonel Reichert turned the jet around the last hangar, glanced to his right, and cursed. Carl followed his gaze and saw two police cars, an airport security van, and the two army Jeeps racing toward them from the north end of the main north-south runway. He also saw that their best path to the southwest runway included a short jog to the right—north, toward the approaching police—and then left onto the wide runway. It was clear that the approaching cars would reach the intersection first, and they'd be trapped.

"I thought you said I had four minutes!"

"Plus or minus," Carl said.

The colonel plunged the throttles all the way to the stops, and the jet bucked forward, straight across the narrow taxiway and into the grass. There was a tremendous clanging sound as the jet bounced across the uneven grassy strip and up onto the concrete slab of the southwest runway. In Carl's imagination, the front landing gear was slammed to its hydraulic stops when the front tire hit the edge of the concrete runway. Except the lead chase car got there first. It pulled in front of the jet, and the driver slammed on his breaks. The patrol car slid sideways and stopped at the end of two pairs of black skid marks.

Right in the path of the Gulfstream.

Carl knew there was no way Reichert could stop the plane in time.

CHAPTER 46

FOR A SPLIT SECOND, CARL thought they were actually going to slam right over the top of the car and race out into the grass on the other side of the runway. At the last instant before impact, the colonel worked his magic, and the jet swerved to the left.

With his right shoulder pinned against the bulkhead, Carl actually looked down into the police car. He saw the panicked look on the cop's face as the man stared at the behemoth getting ready to plow into his car. The front of the plane missed the patrol car by mere inches, then the jet straightened and sped down the middle of the runway.

"Damn, Colonel!" Carl said. "Where'd you learn how to fly? In the Navy?"

"Air Force all the way, brah!"

"*Shee-yit!*"

At full power, the business-class jet wobbled down the runway for a few seconds as the colonel fought to aim the aircraft true center of the concrete ribbon. At some point, Carl knew they'd be moving too fast for the man to adjust the plane's course, and they'd either stay on the concrete until takeoff, or they'd angle off to the side and crash.

Within seconds, Carl knew the colonel's magic was good stuff. They quickly left the pursuing police and army vehicles behind and raced away into the sky.

Reichert glanced over at him and smiled. "That, my friend, is what we call a combat takeoff. We fly or we die."

"Go, Air Force!" Carl said.

When he went to Officer Training School way back thirty-some years ago, he'd known some of the trainees that were selected for pilot training. Out of a hundred officer trainees, only four were selected. They were young, and they were cocky bastards…and one cocky *bastardette*. Out of a hundred of those elite pilot selectees, only a handful were good enough to get the Air Force to spend millions of dollars training them to fly the world's most advanced combat aircraft. Half of the rest were assigned as navigators or cargo pilots. The remainder were recycled back into non-flying officer billets.

Like professional athletes, the shelf life of an advanced fighter pilot is finite because that career required the fastest reaction times and the highest combination of physical skills, stamina, and mental toughness. He glanced at the colonel beside him and judged him to be in his mid-forties. For him to have been selected at that age to command the president's fighter squadron—the elite of fighter pilots—Carl figured him to be one of the military's most decorated combat pilots. After that takeoff performance, he had no doubt the colonel was the best of the best.

The colonel leveled the plane at an altitude of less than two hundred feet, according to a digital altimeter on the high-tech instrument panel. He assumed that was the colonel's attempt to avoid radar detection. They changed course several times and looped back around far south of the municipal airport. Reichert explained this was to avoid the inevitable Mexican air force patrols that would have been notified by the airport tower or the ground troops.

At the end of the colonel's evasive maneuvers, the Gulfstream was a couple hundred miles east of the municipal airport. To Carl's best guess, they crossed the US border somewhere over western Texas, still flying in the trees. The engines screamed, and Carl felt the turbulence near the ground buffeting the plane.

Soon, it was too dark to continue flying so low, and the colonel took the plane to a higher altitude. Carl looked over at him as the man wiped sweat from his brow. He'd been working extremely hard for two hours, manually flying the airplane, constantly battling with the aircraft's controls, and watching the ground and the instruments.

"That was a nice piece of flying," Carl said.

The colonel just grunted. "We're about an hour from Albuquerque."

Carl had wanted to land farther south, perhaps in El Paso, so he'd be close enough to get doses of the antidote to the president and her daughter. But he knew he couldn't just land the airplane and take a cab to the hospital that was locked down tight by the army or the National Guard.

Or the Unit.

He needed leverage. He needed a plan that didn't rely on trying to convince someone—*anyone*—to listen to him. He needed something Breen and his people wouldn't see coming. Something they couldn't react to.

"So Blick didn't make it?" the colonel said.

"I gave him a dose of the antidote and turned him loose."

"I was listening to an English language news station just before you got back. They say you destroyed five buildings."

"I don't know how many buildings went down around the main lab building."

Fiery debris and chunks of concrete and steel had plowed into every building within a couple hundred yards of the seventeen-story office. As the helicopter flew away, the initial billowing smoke had cleared a bit, and he'd seen gaping holes and gashes in the neighboring buildings as falling debris rained into them. Two buildings had caught fire immediately. Then, the lab building had fallen, and the roiling cloud of dissipating smoke and dust had covered a couple square miles.

"They say dozens of people died. Maybe hundreds."

"Millions," Carl said. "They just don't know it yet."

Reichert looked over at him. Muted yellow and green light from the instrument panel illuminated his face. "Johnson, what did you do?"

Carl took a deep breath and gazed out the front into the darkness. "I saved the president's life. Or…I just killed every human on the planet."

He thought about his former nemesis, Aaron McGrath, again. He didn't envy the man his mission to keep America safe. He understood how the man made difficult decisions and appreciated the inner strength

McGrath possessed to live with the consequences of his actions. Carl was silent for a while as various scenarios slowly threaded through his mind.

"Colonel, we're all that's left. If we fall, the country falls."

"The country has already fallen, Johnson. America is now a dictatorship, and the population doesn't even know it. Breen directly controls the most technologically advanced intelligence infrastructure and the most powerful military force on the planet, and he has no Congress to answer to."

"Yeah," Carl said. "He only answers to a trio of Mexican power brokers."

"This war is over. We need to think about a strategic evasion."

"Colonel, strategic evasion means conceding defeat. It means we haven't done everything possible to save the president."

"There's nothing more we can do. You say the word, and I'll turn this plane around. I know places that will take us in. There's nothing more we can give to the cause."

"It's not over until President Mallory is dead, and we still have about forty-four hours to prevent that." He looked the pilot in the eyes. "Besides, we haven't given everything, Colonel."

The man smiled. Carl got the feeling Reichert was taking measure of his commitment.

"We haven't given our lives," Carl said.

"All right, Johnson. Let's go be heroes."

CHAPTER 47

1605 MST, SATURDAY

UNDISCLOSED SECURITY BUNKER

"**M**R. VICE PRESIDENT, YOU'RE NEEDED in the conference room ASAP."

Walter Breen acknowledged the civilian aide's voice through the closed door. "Tell them I'll be there in one minute."

"Yes, sir."

Breen launched himself from his cot in the small subterranean room and stretched. He'd taken his nap in his suit pants and T-shirt, ready to throw on his pressed white shirt and suit jacket at a moment's notice, in case he had to make a statement by video to the press or to the American people. Soon enough, though, he'd be back in the White House. No more cowering in an underground bunker. He'd be occupying the Oval Office, not an office down the hall. In less than twelve hours, far sooner than he'd originally planned, thanks to Carl Johnson, he'd be the *real* president, not the acting president.

Breen refreshed himself and was quickly ready for business. As he emerged from his small concrete chamber, his stomach began growling, and he remembered the last time he'd taken food was over six hours ago. He walked down the short hall and entered the conference room. He grabbed a stale bagel from a tray on the small conference table.

Dr. Thomas Murphy arrived just after him from an adjoining hallway. He was a tall, slender man with a full shock of curly red hair, and he regarded Breen with dark, scared eyes behind his bifocal glasses. The mid-forties triple-PhD was a specialist in the business of pathogens and the deputy director of the CDC.

Breen hadn't figured a man as experienced as Dr. Murphy was in the business of viral death would be the one to fall victim to fear. Breen had faced a huge variety of stressful situations in his career, but this was a new kind of stress for most of his staff. What Breen and his team were doing was not something one could practice for. They were taking over the country and a good chunk of the world. The dice were cast, and they couldn't turn back now even if they wanted to.

"This is getting out of control, Mr. Vice President," Dr. Murphy said. "We should think about exit contingencies."

He understood the virus expert was feeling trapped, physically and emotionally. Their underground bunker had been scheduled to remain sealed for at least the next two days until President Mallory was dead and the virus was completely eradicated. Only now, the vice president would risk exiting early to publicly take the oath of the presidency.

The secure bunker appeared on no map. Its construction had been managed in secret by a close personal friend of Breen, and it sat on private land owned by a dummy corporation not remotely connected to anyone in the government.

Unfortunately, not everyone on his staff understood that plans were fluid scenarios that evolved as goals were approached. Dr. Murphy was a prime example. Breen's takeover, though planned down to the smallest detail over many months, was happening very fast—too fast for some on his staff. Some didn't understand that mission objectives often had to be modified as external influences made their presence felt.

External influences like Carl Johnson.

"Dr. Murphy, there is no exit contingency for what we're doing." He waved a hand before him in a gesture indicating inclusion of everyone in the conference room. "The risks are high, but we must see this through. We certainly cannot back down now out of fear simply because things are more difficult than we thought they would be." Breen paused, then spoke to all of his staff. "Tomorrow morning, I'll be sworn in as president. Then there will be nothing anyone can do."

Walter Breen stopped at the head of the conference table and studied his co-conspirators as Dr. Murphy took his seat. White House Chief of

Staff Martine Scallow sat to his immediate left. Seated around the large table in the conference room of the windowless, underground bunker were other powerful government officials, including the chairman of the joint chiefs of the military services, the directors of CIA and NSA, the deputy director of CDC, and the civilian director of USAMRIID, the US Army Medical Research Institute of Infectious Diseases. The commander of the Army National Guard was also present.

His team all shared one common trait. They were all men. President Mallory had appointed a diverse mix of ethnicities and gender to her cabinet, and over the months, Walter Breen had discovered which leaders shared his view of Mallory's shortcomings. It was a men-only club. Women could not be trusted to move against the first woman president, as their loyalty would always be suspect.

The majority of Breen's cabal were Anglo. General John Vickers, the chairman of the joint chiefs of staff, was African American. In fact, Walter Breen had begun his career of government service under Vickers's command over forty years ago as an army officer. There was no one Breen trusted more to run his military affairs of the new government.

The CIA director, Whitney Drummond, was also brown-skinned, though he publicly disapproved of the label African American because, as he put it, he wasn't African. He was American. He was very light-skinned because he was a mix of many ethnic backgrounds, but he identified with none of those ethnic origins either. He was an American man, plain and simple. Only American.

The third and last minority on Breen's team was Dr. Ernesto Salazar, USAMRIID's civilian director.

"General Vickers," Walter Breen called across the table. "The military transition plan is in place?"

"It is, sir. The chiefs of staff of each branch of the military services will be replaced with senior officers I have selected who are loyal to you. The civilian leadership of the executive branch will be replaced with your appointees, the judicial branch will be dissolved during this ongoing crisis, and the legislative branch is effectively dead. As we agreed, I've also selected senior military officers to replace the civilian directors of the FBI, NSA, DHS, and other intelligence, security, and law enforcement agencies. Director Drummond here"—the general head-nodded toward the CIA director seated beside him—"will be reinstated to his former military rank and promoted to head of the Department of Homeland Security, effectively putting direct control of all of the intelligence agencies and their nationwide and worldwide assets under military management and, therefore, under your direct control." Vickers took a deep breath and looked around the table. "But that's not why we summoned you, sir."

An aide aimed a remote at the big wall-mounted TV screen and increased the volume. CNN was reporting breaking news from a new terrorist attack in Chihuahua, Mexico. The screen showed a long-distance aerial view of the destroyed buildings from a hovering helicopter.

There were literally hundreds of emergency vehicles in and around the area, their flashing red and white strobe lights reflecting off dusty windows and broken cars, diffusing through airborne debris and dust, creating an eerie scene in the hazy darkness. Carl Johnson's photo was superimposed in the bottom left of the screen.

"What the hell has he done now?"

"He took out the Triad's lab, Mr. Vice President."

Breen narrowed his eyes. "Why would he do this?"

No one spoke.

"I'm growing tired of unsolved mysteries, gentlemen. What strategic advantage does he gain?" Breen banged a palm on the conference table. "And how the fuck did he find out about the lab in the first place?"

CIA Director Whitney Drummond spoke hesitantly, "The army detachment commander at Vicente Orizaga's house reported Orizaga and a man fitting Alfonso Reyes's description left in Reyes's helicopter. In fact, the troops didn't intervene because they thought Johnson was Reyes. Somehow, Johnson convinced Orizaga to escort him into the facility. My guess is he found out about the antidote. We have reports about outbreaks in north-central Mexico. Perhaps he or members of his team are infected."

"Since Mr. Orizaga is our conduit to the Triad leaders, he funneled classified documentation to them for us. He also provided us with ongoing viral program status," General Vickers said. "If Johnson's team confiscated his computer, that would also explain how he or his agent found out about, and rescued, our kill list targets. Agent Palmer is fully trained on intel retrieval techniques."

Breen palmed the table again. "Costas Drake's orders were to destroy the office."

"Which his men did, sir."

"After Johnson escaped with the intel!" Breen took a deep breath to steady himself. "Okay, so Johnson got out of the lab, presumably with the antidote." Breen stood and paced around the room. Then he stopped in mid-stride. "Why destroy the building? What are we missing?"

Drummond said, "He's angry. Perhaps he thinks he can hurt you by destroying the lab."

Breen shook his head. "I wouldn't make that assumption. As far as he knows, we could have another lab, or a dozen or a hundred more. There must be another reason."

General Vickers added, "My thought is that he used the explosion as a distraction to cover his escape. Local authorities would be rushing to the explosion instead of following him away from the site."

Walter Breen said, "Maybe." He began pacing again. "What if he finds a way to make the stolen virus intel, or the fact that an antidote exists, public?"

Drummond shook his head, and his double-jowl wiggled back and forth with the effort. "It won't matter. My people have leaked his name, so he's being blamed for the worst international terror attack since Nine-Eleven."

Breen stopped pacing. "Okay, so he has the antidote. What's his next step? What if he does somehow tell the world he has the antidote?"

"I may have the answer to that," General Vickers said. He looked up from his laptop. "Our AWACS border patrol is tracking a low-flying plane that crossed the border a few minutes ago over western Texas. It fits the radar signature of a small business-class jet, like a Gulfstream or Citation. It's not emitting any transponder signals, so it could be the TER covert ops plane that took Johnson and Agent Palmer down there. There was some chatter about a business jet evading authorities at a municipal airport called Nuevo Casas Grandes a couple hours after the explosion at the lab building. That airport is certainly within helicopter range of Chihuahua, Reyes's estate, and Orizaga's homestead near Hermosillo. The army reports the plane made a reckless takeoff after ignoring orders to stand down. After takeoff, it remained under the radar, so they weren't able to track it."

Dr. Murphy timidly spoke. "What if he's trying to save the president?"

Breen looked around the room for a moment, then settled his gaze on Dr. Murphy. "Then we better save her first. Is her specially prepared antidote ready?"

Murphy nodded.

Breen took a tiny comm unit from his pants pocket and inserted it into his ear. After a few seconds, he said, "Mr. Spoke, this is Rainman. Drop whatever you're doing. I have a special task for you, and it must be completed *right fucking now*."

CHAPTER 48

A FEW MINUTES AFTER COLONEL REICHERT put the plane into a climb, a light blinked on the high-tech control panel. The colonel put on his headset and pointed to a similar headset hanging from the control panel by Carl's right knee. Carl put the cushioned cups over his ears and immediately heard threats of dire consequences if the *unidentified aircraft* didn't turn to a new heading immediately.

The colonel identified himself by his Air Force rank and name. "I am currently attached to the Terror Event Response agency on a classified mission to retrieve the antidote for the virus that has afflicted the president and the government. I have the antidote on board at this time."

That announcement must have gone straight in one ear of the speaker and out the other because her harsh voice said, "I repeat, you must alter course immediately, or you will be fired upon."

Carl and the colonel had already discussed how to present their opening arguments to authorities. As a delay tactic, they would pretend not to know Vice President Breen had the antidote stockpiled for distribution. They would carefully parse information to authorities, knowing that the unencrypted comm channel was being monitored not only by the military but likely also by Breen's people.

Reichert said, "You'll want to clarify that up the chain of command first. We have the only antidote in existence for the virus. If you shoot down this plane, you will be killing President Mallory. I repeat, if you destroy this plane, you'll destroy the only antidote in existence, and the president and the rest of the government will die. Copy?"

There was a long silence, then the voice said, "Standby."

The colonel added, "Also, I have Carl Johnson in custody aboard this aircraft. I'm sure your superiors will want him alive."

"Standby," the pilot said again.

The radio silence lasted nearly fifteen minutes, and shortly before it ended, Carl noticed movement in his peripheral vision. He glanced to his right and saw a dark shadow floating a few hundred feet away. The shadow was just darker than the night sky. There were no lights flashing on the aircraft. The jet out there was ready for war.

"We have company over here."

"This side too," Reichert said. "Good news is that now that we've laid down the gauntlet on an open comm channel, Breen can't give the order to shoot us down."

"If he does, and the world finds out he destroyed what is believed to be the only cure to the virus, that will undermine his plan and his credibility. He has to be very careful."

"Agreed." The colonel paused. "So, what's our next move?"

A new voice came on the channel and identified himself as Albuquerque International Sunport Approach Control. He gave the colonel permission to land. The Gulfstream was approaching Albuquerque from the east, so the air traffic controller gave the colonel a vectored approach around the north end of the Sandia Mountains so he could land on the proper runway.

The colonel said, "Please advise my escorts of my intention to comply."

The no-nonsense female fighter pilot answered. "I acknowledge your intent to comply," she said. "Do not deviate from your landing instructions, or you will be fired upon."

"Copy that."

As the plane cleared the north end of the chain of ten-thousand-foot ragged peaks known as the Sandia Mountains, Carl saw one of the most beautiful sights of his life. He loved flying into Albuquerque from the east because the twinkling lights of the city sprang into view all at once. The city stretched out to the west for miles, and the lights twinkled like stars as the ground heat shimmered the air.

Once clear of the mountains, Colonel Reichert banked south and flew over the city along the western slope of the mountains. Carl heard a lot of pilot talk about approach vectors, speed, wind direction, and altitudes, but Carl tuned all that noise out. He figured they'd be landing on the east-west runway. He'd seen planes make that approach many times from the balcony of his home in the foothills. Sometimes, the planes flew right over his house.

Carl contemplated the reception they'd receive. As soon as they landed, they'd be swarmed by police, both civilian and military, since the airport shared flight operations with Kirtland Air Force Base. No doubt the FBI would show up too. Either way, Carl and the colonel soon would be in custody. Then the real chess match would begin. Or maybe the Unit would get there first. In that case, he and Reichert would be killed.

Carl removed his headphones and reminisced on his new life as a terrorist and the lives he had touched over the last month. A part of him wanted to place all the blame for his son's death on the federal agents who mistook Carl for Alfonso Reyes. Over the following weeks, though, Carl had reviewed in his mind all the known facts, assumptions, and resulting decisions made throughout the various government operations against him. He acknowledged there was no way anyone up the chain could have made any other judgment. If he were one of the feds' decision-makers, he would have done the same things they had done, made the same assumptions and decisions they had made. His son had died because of that mistake, and Carl knew he was as much to blame as any of the feds.

He could have accepted his devastating loss and simply gone home like anyone else would have. He could have cried and lived with the pain—tried to get on with his life. He didn't have to strike out in revenge against the government. He'd thought the feds would capture or kill him early in his quest for vengeance. That would have been his easiest escape from the pain, but he stayed ahead of them. Instead of quieting his pain, each agent who died at his hands, each life he dispatched, merely stoked the fire of hatred in his soul. Soon, he was so deep in the abyss, and his moral compass was so royally screwed up, he didn't know how to do anything other than kill. His path of revenge led him to Aaron McGrath, the director of the TER and who also happened to be the president's fiancé. It was President Mallory who had authorized the operation against Carl, thinking that decision would save her kidnapped daughter.

A part of Carl understood her pain—a parent's pain. At the time, he and everyone else had agreed, again mistakenly, that Melissa Mallory was going to die whether or not the required ransom was paid. Though President Mallory was the most powerful woman on the planet, Carl knew when her daughter died, she'd be reduced to the same level of helplessness that he was experiencing. He knew firsthand how devastating her loss would be and couldn't bring himself to let her go through that kind of pain. So he went to rescue the girl. At least, he *thought* he was rescuing the girl. Now, it was crystal clear that Vice President Breen's plan all along, in collusion with a shadowy Mexican political cartel called the Triad, was to use the girl to set the stage for their plans of global economic and military domination.

Their shared goal to consolidate the economies of the western hemisphere rested squarely on the death of the president and the decapitation of the US government. So, Breen had orchestrated the kidnapping, infection, and release of the First Daughter and used her to attempt to assassinate her mother. When the American government fell, the Mexican government would follow quickly.

He figured the United States wouldn't become a complete police state overnight, though many had argued the country had been on that path, and the rights of individuals had been eroding in the name of national security since Nine-Eleven. Only corporations and banks too big to fail would find a way to exist in the new America. The population would eventually learn how to live with a new reality. They would no longer be able to vote for their president, and their concept of freedom would have changed radically. Everyone would learn to accept that one man made the country's decisions on behalf of the millions, rather than a couple hundred senators and representatives.

Who was to say Breen's way wouldn't be any better or more efficient than the current constitutional way? Many people would argue that America would be stronger with one war hawk at the helm instead of hundreds of professional debaters. For a very long time, Americans had been disappointed over how they took months to make a decision about anything and only after being heavily influenced by big-money corporate lobbyists.

Carl voiced his thoughts aloud. "You know, for most people, this change from the current government to the new one will hardly impact anyone's life. It's going to be pretty much business as usual for millions of Americans. Probably won't affect the majority whose lives revolve around working every day to earn their living, trying to survive in a terribly unbalanced economy." He stared out at city lights representing thousands of those Americans for a long moment, and Reichert said nothing. "But my son is dead because of this new government."

He turned away from the city lights out the right window and found the colonel watching him.

"I get it, Johnson. You have to do this for your son. So what's your play?"

Carl shook his head. "This is no longer about my son. It can't be." He gazed out the front windshield. "This is about who's right and who's wrong. It's about President Mallory. She's the good guy, and Breen can't win. Not this way."

"Johnson," Reichert said quietly. "We can't win this war. We don't have assets, weapons, or personnel for this type of fight. We took this mission to discover the identities of the shadowy figures of the Triad who kidnapped Melissa Mallory. We failed. We know Breen is behind everything, but we have no proof, and we don't know who his associates are." Reichert paused. "We failed, Johnson. We can't stop Breen."

"That's where you're wrong, Colonel." Carl waited until the pilot looked over at him again. "I've already stopped him. Problem is, he doesn't know it yet." He smiled, but it was without humor. "You said back at that airport, Breen was rushing his path to become president because of me. Even though Mallory is incapacitated, I can't see how Breen can become president so quickly. He'd have to convince the nation there's no hope for her recovery."

The colonel nodded. "Only way to do that is if she dies sooner than Monday."

Carl nodded. "He's going to have someone kill her."

CHAPTER 49

AGENT NANCY PALMER'S SLOW JOURNEY back to consciousness felt like a torturous crawl up a steep slope of razor-sharp volcanic glass with no shoes and no clothes. She was aware of a full-body pain. It was a living, breathing entity enflaming every cell of her body, and it intensified with even the tiniest movement. The pain was accompanied by a ravenous hunger and a parching thirst. The pain, hunger, and thirst were so intense, she wanted to scream. In all her deployments in harsh training environments and in actual field operations, she'd never felt such hunger, thirst, or pain.

As she drifted back into consciousness, though, she didn't move or scream. She bore her body's pain and cravings because there was one more consideration that trumped those—safety. She kept her eyes closed and listened to the silence of the room around her.

She was aware of the labored breathing of other people. She heard the swishing sound of material—nylon, perhaps. She heard the clunky shuffling of footsteps moving around the room, as if the person wore oversized rubber boots. She smelled the pungent aroma of antiseptic and instantly knew where she was. She was in a quarantine room along with other infected patients. The typical hospital sounds were lacking—the medical banter between doctors and nurses, and the beeping of medical equipment—so she figured she was in a hastily set up isolation or treatment facility, maybe a school gym or a warehouse building.

Johnson and Reichert had touched the airport superintendent, who had touched others, creating second-generation infected. The second-gen victims had spread the virus to many others—family members, associates, coworkers, friends, schoolmates, and maybe even first responders and hospital staff who had treated them. Palmer figured the total number of local people infected could easily be in the hundreds or thousands, depending on how long she'd been out. Judging by the many people she heard struggling to breathe, the Contagion had clearly spread beyond the TER covert operation at the municipal airport.

A fear crept into her gut as she considered infected people who may have flown from local airports into and then out of Mexico City's international airport before the nature of the Contagion was understood. Palmer was familiar with the characteristics of viral spread. In the first few days of an outbreak, when symptoms didn't manifest for half a day, the number of infected could multiply almost beyond imagination. The CDC and the US military had classified contingencies ranging from containment to treatment to sterilization—the eradication of infected populations that could not be saved.

Even with a relatively small number of first-gen victims, say one thousand, and with each victim contaminating only a dozen people in the course of their daily lives, the total number of infected after only a few days could number in the millions. If only a tiny fraction of those people traveled internationally before quarantines were implemented, a catastrophe of global proportions would erupt wherever new hotspots flared.

First-world countries would adapt quickly once they were given the formula to manufacture the antidote. Second- and third-world countries without adequate viral containment procedures could lose up to 90 percent of their populations. The world could literally lose two-thirds or more of the human race.

There was a point of no return in any Contagion where the spread of the virus would outpace the ability of technology to manufacture and distribute a cure. At that point, civilization would be lost. Under such a scenario, countries would be forced to close their borders, and economies would collapse while the surviving nations waited for the epidemic to run its course.

For such a persistent Contagion, the viral point of no return would be measured in days, not weeks. It was well-known that while the first-world nations would survive the viral outbreak, none would survive the financial devastation that would occur when global economies collapsed like dominoes. Natural resources would become scarce or even unavailable, trade would stop, and limited stockpiles would be consumed quickly as the few remaining countries fought over much-needed supplies.

There was no such thing as a truly independent nation—not in the twenty-first century. Strategic war initiated ultimately by a failing country would become a very real possibility.

Palmer had seen on the news that Vice President Breen's call for martial law came early, so that action undoubtedly curtailed the spread of the virus in the US. The infected government officials had been isolated as soon as the first members fell to the virus. The presidential flight crew that had carried President Mallory back east had been quarantined as soon as the outbreak was publicly known, but by then, the president was back aboard *Air Force One* with a new flight crew, flying back to Las Cruces to be with her daughter. As soon as Mallory began to show symptoms, the entire town and the hospital were quarantined, as was the base where *Air Force One* was parked.

That, Palmer now knew, was part of Breen's plan from the beginning. He wanted to eliminate the government, not the general population, so he had containment protocols in place even before the president was infected. Unfortunately, Breen and his team couldn't control every possible variable of his scenario, which is something that any good chaos theoretician would have told him if asked.

Maybe they did tell him. Maybe he just ignored them.

All these thoughts raced through Palmer's mind as she took stock of her body. Her discomfort began to fade as she began her mental exercises to control the pain, hunger, and thirst. Without moving, she inventoried her muscles and joints, tensing and flexing each limb, finger, and toe. She found everything fully functional.

Palmer heard a sound like the swish of coarse nylon rubbing against coarse nylon nearby and felt a presence hovering over her. When the observer moved on, Palmer opened her eyes and realized she was in the same huge hangar where the colonel had parked the Gulfstream. Without moving her head, she studied the gray corrugated metal wall to her left.

She recognized the Spanish-language red-and-white aircraft safety poster on the wall next to the door to the inner office, where she and Carl's team had taken refuge. The door was open, but the lights and the TV were off.

A bank of industrial floodlights was distantly spaced around the floor of the hangar and cast the collection of beds near her in dim pools of light. She heard the distant hum of the generator powering the lights. She gazed into the darkness above her, but the pools of light near the floor cast the roof of the structure in deep shadows, and she could not make out the metal rafters supporting the hangar roof far above.

Palmer turned her head slightly to her left, then to her right. There were easily two or three hundred beds in the hangar, and they were all occupied. Since her hangar was completely filled, she knew hers wasn't the only quarantine room. No doubt the other hangars were being used also.

The beds were aligned in an orderly matrix, and her bed was fourth from the wall and third from the massive door that could be powered open to admit planes for maintenance. The big aircraft door was closed. A quick study revealed only two attendants clad in red biological space-suits. That surprised her. She expected more. The hangar was a maintenance building that could accommodate corporate-size jets and measured maybe sixty feet by one hundred. She counted nine rows of cots arranged lengthwise, and perhaps thirty or more columns marched off toward the opposite side of the hangar.

Two attendants were not nearly adequate to treat three hundred patients, but then she realized she was not in a treatment center. Since the cure to the virus was not yet available, she knew she was in a "keep-them-comfortable-until-they-die" center. In fact, there was a forest of clear liquid IV bags on posts by the beds, each attached to the head of a cot, and drip lines were taped to the arm of each patient.

She noticed a commotion at the other end of the room, and for a moment, Palmer thought she'd been seen moving. Three figures clad in white bio-suits entered through the personnel access door in the hangar door and converged on one of the attendants in red. One of the newcomers disconnected the IV from the arm of Red's patient, and the other two picked up the lifeless person by the arms and legs and hauled him or her out.

The attendants were there only to make sure everyone was still alive. That's why there were only two of them. The remaining attendant quickly stripped the sheet from the bed and produced a neatly folded sheet wrapped in plastic from beneath the bed. The attendant ripped the plastic open, spread the new sheet, and tucked it in, all in the space of sixty seconds. Red then pulled the existing needle from the plastic tubing hanging from the IV bag and installed a new one. The other two attendants in white reentered the hangar hauling another patient, who they dumped unceremoniously onto the bed. The guys in white left, and Red arranged the new patient on the bed and hooked him or her up to the IV line.

When she was certain no one was watching her, Palmer rolled off the bed, careful not to pull the IV bag and its post down and make noise. She peeled the tape from her arm and pulled out the needle. Then she froze. She felt something out of the ordinary. When she glanced down, she saw the waistline of her black fatigues was unbuttoned, and her fly was partially unzipped. She zipped, buttoned up, and checked her inventory. She'd removed her shirt and tactical vest, so she wore only a black tactical sports bra. Her pants pockets were all empty, so she had no weapons.

When the emergency response team had been called in to contain the outbreak, they'd found Palmer and the others armed for combat and carrying no identification. No doubt the first responders would report the presence of weapons to their authorities. Since they were infected and comatose, there was no need for them to be arrested or separated from the other patients, or even placed under special guard.

Palmer thought about searching for her other mercs or for Luisa and Julia Reyes, but she quickly dismissed that idea. She had no guarantee they'd be bedded near her or even in the same hangar, and she likely had only a few minutes before the attendants made their next round and discovered her bed empty.

She remained low to the floor. A quick glance revealed both attendants at the far end of the hangar, checking on patients with their backs to her. So she made a dash into the dark office. She stood in the darkness beside the doorway and tried to figure out her next move, but she had several options. Escape and evasion topped the list. She needed to find Carl and coordinate with him. Get a mission update. Compare objectives.

She looked around the room. Even in the darkness, she could see that the room had been completely searched top to bottom. All the chairs and couches were overturned, and every drawer and cabinet had been emptied. Junk from those storage appliances littered the floor, but their laptop and all the notes and the reports they'd stolen from Orizaga's residence were gone.

There was nowhere Carl could have left a message or clue for her that would not have been discovered, except one. She smiled in the darkness as she recalled her unbuttoned pants. He must have known the Unit would not strip-search her. She was safe because she was contagious. Reaching inside her panties, she found a folded piece of paper. Palmer held the unfolded letter so the glare from the hospital room allowed her to read it.

Check the OJ. If I fail, get to the president any way possible. -Carl

It was completely Carl Johnson's style to have a contingency plan in case he was captured or killed. Agent Palmer quickly crossed the small office, careful to avoid the debris littering the floor, and opened the refrigerator door just a tiny fraction of an inch to guard against the flood of light attracting attention from the attendants in the hangar. But Carl had foreseen that obstacle also. The light did not come on, and when Palmer pulled the door wide open, she saw the light bulb had been unscrewed but left in place, leaving the illusion of possibly a burned-out bulb.

There were only three items inside on the topmost of two steel wire shelves. There was an old apple that was fading to brown. It looked like it would burst open and ooze gooey slime at the slightest touch. There was half of a foot-long sandwich in a wrapper from Subway, and it looked to be in pretty much the same condition as the apple. And there was a half-pint carton of orange juice turned on its side with the pour spout open.

She carefully poured the remaining juice into the sink. Then she shook out two tiny vials of blue liquid—one antidote for the president and one for her daughter. There was a sliver of paper wrapped around the vials, and when she pulled them out of the carton, the paper fell off. On its soaked surface was smeared ink.

<55F!!!

She put the vials back in the OJ carton and put it back in the fridge until she was ready to make her move.

What is it about that man? Talk about hiding something in plain sight.

He had amazing instincts identifying problems and inventing unpredictable solutions. Anyone searching the fridge would see the rotten food and the nearly overturned juice carton and assume there was nothing in the fridge of interest.

As Palmer scanned the dark room for resources, she realized Carl Johnson reminded her a lot of Aaron McGrath. While McGrath was a great leader and mentor, he kept tight control of his emotions. In the year she had served with McGrath, the only time she'd seen him display any emotional reaction at all was four days ago when he thought his daughter was in the building Carl blew up.

Carl, on the other hand, was equal parts love and hatred, and he had no qualms about showing his heart or his fury. He had recently turned into a stone-cold killer, and she recalled how he had beheaded Agent Klipser with a tree saw. He said he did it to prove he could. He said he was training himself to be ruthless. The very next day, he rushed to rescue the president's sixteen-year-old daughter, but he could only save her by forming an instant empathic connection to her. And he'd succeeded in reaching the wounded girl.

Palmer had also personally seen how Julia Reyes, a girl Carl had known only two days, had responded to his loving embrace. He was flawed, and he knew it, yet he knew when to ask for help and when to show emotion. Palmer found his raw emotions attractive and a little bit exciting.

And that kiss!

He'd ignited a fire in her she hadn't felt in years. He had her by twenty-six years, but he possessed qualities and traits that made him seem much younger than fifty-three. The momentary fantasy ended abruptly as she physically shook herself back to the task at hand. There was no way she could act on her feelings. Neither of them could, and they both understood that.

She turned her attention to escape. She assumed the Unit would have discovered her and the mercs' identities when the first responders reported their weapons. First, she needed weapons because she knew the Unit would be dispatched to take her into custody, or kill her, when they found her empty cot. Second, she needed an escape route off the airport. Third, she needed transportation to the president's hospital. Fourth, she needed a way into the hospital, hopefully without killing American servicemen or women.

Palmer crossed the dark room to the office's exterior entry door. She unlatched the deadbolt and eased the door open, intending to scout military security, when a piercing scream erupted from inside the hangar where she'd just awoken.

CHAPTER 50

1710 MST, SATURDAY

ALBUQUERQUE, NM

CARL CHUCKLED.

The colonel glanced over at him. "What's funny?"

"This is the TER's covert ops plane, and Palmer has plenty of guns back there. She gave me a tour. If this were a movie, I'd open up the door and spray those jets with some automatic rifle fire. They're close enough that I could get all Rambo and shoot 'em both down."

Colonel joined him in a brief laugh. "If you opened a door at this altitude and speed, you'd get sucked right out the plane. Besides, those are F-22 Raptors. They aren't armored, but it'll take a lot more than a rifle to put a dent in their skins."

The humorous moment faded quickly, and Carl found himself wondering what Aaron McGrath would do in his place. *What ruthless gambit would the man employ to save his president and his country? What would Agent Palmer do?* He wished she were on the plane with him. He needed her tactical knowledge because he didn't know what to do.

Carl glanced out his window again at the jet. The US Air Force was not the Unit. Breen could not order the officers to open fire, destroy the Gulfstream, and risk killing hundreds of civilians on the ground with flaming wreckage. But even if Carl managed to get on the ground and avoid capture, what could he do with the antidote? Who could he contact that the Unit couldn't kill or intimidate? What hospital could he get the antidote to that Breen's people did not control? How could he get the cure into the hands of the president's doctors?

No answers came to Carl as the plane sped south over the western foothills of the Sandia Mountains. Out the left window, he saw the red warning lights atop Sandia Peak from the antenna farm that broadcasted television and radio signals across the land. Out the right window, he saw the shimmering lights of Albuquerque's Northeast Heights. Something was missing, though, and the city looked eerily still from four thousand feet up. He quickly realized the anomaly.

There is no auto traffic on any of the streets or highways!

On a Saturday night, just an hour after sunset, he should have seen a constant stream of red taillights and white headlights on every major artery in the city. Instead, the streets were completely vacant, except for the occasional emergency vehicle with its strobe lights flashing. It was a military curfew because of the infections he had spread throughout the city. It had to be.

As the plane began a gentle descent, Carl wondered what city Garcia and the kill list survivors were hiding in. Special Agent Cummings no doubt hid them all somewhere so they wouldn't be found. Yet, when they started getting sick, she probably would have tried to care for them herself rather than letting them go to a hospital where they would risk being found by the Unit.

"Can I make a phone call on this thing?" Carl indicated the radio transmitter by pointing at his headphones.

"The flight phone is on the wall right behind your seat. It's an open channel, though."

He figured out how to operate the phone and dialed the number he had memorized for Garcia's cell phone. It rang for a long time because he and Garcia had switched off voice mail, but Carl refused to hang up even after a dozen rings. He simply held the handset to his ear, hoping someone was still alive to answer it.

As he waited, sadness filled his heart. Garcia, Cummings, and the others had plenty of food and water, but they wouldn't have any way of consuming either after the first twenty-eight hours. They might survive a day in a coma, maybe a day and a half. But without medical attention, they wouldn't last longer than that. When the plane landed, even if the

FBI or the Unit didn't shoot him on sight, there was no way Carl would be allowed to give his friends any doses of the antidote.

Friends? Carl almost chuckled at the thought. Earlier the same week, all those people were his enemies, except Garcia. They all wanted him dead.

What a difference a week has made. What a crazy world I live in now.

The ringing hit twenty, and he finally accepted that no one would answer. For them, it had only been twenty hours, but Carl knew the onset of symptoms was debilitating. He replaced the handset in its wall slot.

Almost.

Right before he shoved the handset into its cradle, he heard a click, so he snatched the handset back to his ear. "Hello? Hello?"

Silence greeted him, but it was not a complete silence. He heard someone. There was a rasping sound like someone was breathing, listening, and maybe trying to talk. Then he heard a croaking voice.

CHAPTER 51

1711 MST, SATURDAY
ALBUQUERQUE FBI FIELD OFFICE

G UILLERMO FIGUEROA, THE SPECIAL AGENT in charge of the FBI's Albuquerque field office, sat behind his desk in his office, listening intently to the live conversation emanating from his speakerphone. His executive assistant, Marshall Stewart, sat in front of the desk, along with the tactical commander, Ed Murray, and the vice president's personal envoy, Costas Drake. They had all just listened intently to the terse exchange between the pilot of the Gulfstream, the control tower, and the Air Force escort pilots.

None could fathom why a highly decorated Air Force officer, the commander of the elite presidential fighter escort squadron, would voluntarily enlist with the world's most wanted terrorist. Add to that team the traitor Nancy Palmer, a highly trained agent of the secretive TER agency, and the mystery was all the more baffling.

"This just doesn't make any sense," Figueroa muttered. "What are we missing?"

Drake said, "It doesn't take sense to figure the man blackmailed the president." Figueroa eyed him unconvinced, so he added, "Look, on Monday, Carl Johnson launched a spree of violence that killed or wounded nearly three dozen federal agents and local police officers. A few days later, an executive order came down through the TER, making Johnson untouchable." The man shrugged. "It's not rocket science."

Maybe not, Figueroa thought, *but it is a mystery.*

The terrorist had gone on yet another killing spree, claiming the families of Aaron McGrath and Special Agent Lenore Cummings. Except there were no bodies, according to the first responders who were now mysteriously sequestered by the TER agency.

"Mr. Drake, I'm not clear why the investigations of both homes were classified."

"National security, Agent."

Figueroa nodded, no stranger to that trump card. He accepted that higher authorities were calling the shots in the case now. His orders were to provide investigative support and local human and technology resources to the vice president's liaison. Costas Drake had been appointed the provisional rank of senior special agent for the duration of the operation against the terrorist. Figueroa's standing orders were to use his assets to follow up on specific leads and then turn that information over to the TER, specifically to Drake's people, for analysis and processing.

Drake's people...whoever they are.

"And Johnson's bombing of the five buildings in Chihuahua City? What was his motive? What's the connection between those office buildings and the death of his son? Did he have operatives in that city who informed on him or his operation? Was it about house cleaning, or was he simply demonstrating his ruthlessness again? Perhaps he was merely trying to establish his credibility more firmly in the global pecking order of terrorists."

Drake shrugged. "I can't give you any more information."

Figueroa neither liked nor disliked Costas Drake. He simply understood the rules of the game. Drake was in command. The man unnerved him, though. He was a tall, thick-set man of about forty, and he seemed imposing even when sitting. His blue eyes were emotionless orbs.

"I can't believe he's going to surrender," Marshall Stewart said. "It's got to be a deception of some kind."

"I agree," Ed Murray, the tactical commander, said. "He could have been anywhere in the world right now. Instead, he's flying back to the US and into certain custody. Why would he do that?"

Drake didn't answer the question. Instead, he said. "I want complete containment of his aircraft when he lands. Our latest intel suggests he has the virus with him, instead of an antidote. We think his people have developed some kind of wide-scale delivery method. There may be some kind of booby trap or airborne release mechanism aboard."

Murray shook his head. "This is Albuquerque. We don't have even a million people here. If tactical release was his goal, he could have been over the Dallas metropolis by now, where he could tally a real body count."

The voice of the tactical communications officer, down in the basement operations center, came through the telephone speaker on the SAC's desk.

"Agent Figueroa," she said, "I'm monitoring an inflight call from Johnson's plane to a local cell phone. We're tracing it now. It rang for two minutes before there was a pickup, but…"

"What is it, Agent?"

"I think it's— Um, you should hear this, sir."

"Put it through."

"Yes, sir. I'll play it from the beginning."

There was a click, and then voices emanated from the speakerphone.

"Hello? Hello?" The men in the room recognized Carl Johnson's voice.

"Carl, is that you?" The woman's voice was raspy, like it came from someone parched with thirst. The voice was well-known to the FBI men in the room.

Figueroa jumped out of his chair. "Christ! Is that Cummings?"

Carl's voice continued, "Is everyone sick?"

"I…I think Garcia's baby is dead. Maybe his wife too."

"What about Lisette?"

There was a long pause and some noises, like Cummings was fumbling with the cell phone and checking on her daughter.

"She's still alive." She was silent, and Figueroa got the impression she was looking around a room, maybe checking others. "The Chapmans are still breathing. The teenager, Tony, was taking care of them for a while. Then he also got sick."

Johnson's voice sounded like he was choked up. "Lenore, I'm sorry I did this to you. I didn't know I was infected. I was trying to save you, and I messed it up. I made things worse."

"How long do we have?"

"Maybe eight more hours until you're all in a coma. Then three days max."

"Okay." Cummings's voice grated. "What is our prognosis? Can I save my daughter?"

"No, I'm sorry," Johnson said. "I've seen their research. It's 100 percent lethal."

Cummings coughed. "If you infected us, why aren't you sick?"

"I was the carrier. I got it from Melissa. I gave it to the president. Then she gave it to the government. And I spread it all over Albuquerque and northern Mexico. Everybody's dying because of me." Johnson paused. "I didn't *save* Melissa. They were going to release her anyway."

Cummings said, "It was Vice President Breen, wasn't it? He was the highest-ranking cabinet member not at the president's speech."

"I can't prove it," Carl said. "But he certainly didn't do it by himself. He had high-level help, and a lot of it. He paid a Mexican political group called the Triad to develop the virus and kidnap Melissa Mallory so they could infect her." Cummings coughed again, and Johnson said, "Tell me where you are. There are people listening who can get you to a hospital."

"They'll kill us."

"The FBI can get to you first. Besides, the Unit will have *me* in a few minutes, so they don't need you anymore. I'm landing at the Sunport, and I have the antidote with me. I'm going to surrender and try to reach someone who can get the antidote to the president. Everyone can't be blinded by Breen's bullshit. Somebody has to listen."

"You can't surrender. They'll kill you." Cummings took several deep, ragged breaths. "You have to stop Breen."

Carl Johnson's voice was silent for a long time. "I already have, Lenore. He just doesn't know it yet."

"What? What do you mean?"

"The Triad double-crossed Breen and his people. They developed a much more virulent airborne version of the virus. That's why I bombed their lab in Chihuahua." Johnson's voice paused. "I released it, Lenore. I let it loose three hours ago, and now, it's spreading unchecked all over Mexico. It's probably in Europe and Asia by now. By this time tomorrow, there'll be too many people around the world infected. No one will be able to stop the Contagion."

"Oh my God, Carl! Why would you do such a thing?"

"Breen started this. I simply raised the stakes." Carl paused for a moment. "I destroyed the Triad's supply of the antidote when I bombed that building. Now Breen's stockpile is all that's left. If he waits until the president dies, then there'll be too many people all over the world infected with the airborne virus, and no one will be able to stop it."

"But millions could die, Carl. Maybe billions."

Carl Johnson's voice grated from the speakerphone, and Agent Figueroa felt a dark dread creep into his soul. "They made me into a terrorist, Lenore. McGrath did. The government did. The Triad did. This airborne Contagion is the only weapon I have against Walter Breen. He has to give up his supply of the antidote before the airborne Contagion is out of control and unstoppable. That means the president will be the first to get an antidote."

Cummings coughed again. "But what if he doesn't?"

"When we land, the Unit is going to try to kill me, but your friends at the FBI better make sure I stay alive. Because I know where Breen's antidote stockpile is located. If Shirley Mallory dies, I won't try to stop it. If she dies, everyone on the planet dies with her. It's up to Breen now."

Johnson paused for a moment. Then he said, "Tell me where you are so the FBI can find you and get you to a hospital."

"Okay." She coughed some more. "We're at the East Central Motor Lodge. Room 129."

"What city?"

Cummings's voice sounded tired and groggy, like she had just come out of a very deep sleep. "We doubled back," she said. "I figured the Unit would set up roadblocks, searching all the highways to the major cities. That's what I'd do. I'd assume fugitives would try to hide in a city of millions, but this is the last place they'd look." She took a deep rasping breath. "Yours is the first plane I've heard all day. You're flying right over us."

"What? You're in Albuquerque?" There was a slight pause on the line, then Johnson's voice said, "I'm coming for you, Lenore. I'm coming for you right now!"

Then the line went dead.

CHAPTER 52

Walter Breen nodded at the aide, who took his cue to disconnect the secure video link. Each of Breen's senior advisors processed Costas Drake's report in his own way, but Breen stood up and paced behind the conference table of the concrete bunker's control center. He was aware every set of eyes was following his movements. He was aware everyone was waiting for his trademark explosion of anger. He didn't care. Instead, he stopped pacing and just shook his head. He had no more anger inside him—only admiration.

"Brilliant. Absolutely, positively *fucking* brilliant." Breen paused. "With all the money, assets, and personnel we have dedicated to this program, this *one man* has managed to derail us at every turn. Somebody try to convince me *now* that Carl Johnson is *just* a grieving father." He stopped pacing and spread his hands wide. "Anybody?"

No one spoke. They all heard the communication intercept from Johnson's Gulfstream jet.

Director Drummond said, "If he's telling the truth, it's a good thing we didn't shoot his plane down before he told us what he has done. We would have found out far too late to stop the epidemic."

Breen said, "Dr. Murphy, is he telling the truth? I would have thought the explosion would vaporize the viral samples. Could the airborne version have been released?"

The CDC scientist cleared his throat. "The lab has countermeasures employed to prevent the release of any viral pathogens." He fell silent for a moment as he consulted his laptop, then looked around the table. "*Had* countermeasures. The final fail-safe was a gas that burns at 3,000 degrees Fahrenheit. That temperature can incinerate any living substance—viral or organic. The gas should have been released into the containment room and ignited by computer at the first sign that any viral pathogens escaped containment.

"Part of our agreement with the Triad is that I personally monitor the lab's computer control system data on a continual basis, so I've seen the data from the final few seconds. Johnson used so much C4 on the roof, the collapse of the building damaged the gas delivery pipes and ignition system almost half a second *before* the containment vessels were breached."

General Vickers cleared his throat. "How much pathogen was stored at the facility? Was it enough to do what Johnson suggests?"

Dr. Murphy nodded slowly. "We were never told the exact amount, but our intel suggests they had several gallons of the pathogen. A significant portion of the released liquid would have been aerosolized. It likely spread over several square miles with the initial dust cloud from the blast.

"When the first responders arrived to begin rescue efforts and triage, they instantly were infected, as were the doctors and nurses who worked at the hospitals the victims in the immediate area were taken to. The hospitals were overloaded with minor wounded, so they triaged those folks and sent them home with bandages to make room for the seriously wounded.

"And don't forget, the particulates would have been carried into the local wind patterns, and we've been told the pathogen can survive outside of containment for up to three hours. By now, thousands are infected outside the blast zone, and they don't even know it."

General Vickers said, "How can it be stopped?"

Dr. Salazar looked at Walter Breen and said, "Like Johnson said, we have to release the antidote. We have to push for complete martial law in every country on the planet and quarantine every outbreak with military troops as fast as possible. We have to shut down all international air traffic. We have to detect the virus, contain the virus, and cure the virus."

Breen nodded and began pacing again. "Director Drummond, how close is August Spoke to the hospital?"

"About two hours, give or take."

"General, I want Johnson's plane shot out of the sky as soon as he passes over military property at the east end of that airport. I've had just about enough of this man." Breen focused on Chief of Staff Martine Scallow. "As soon as Johnson is dead, announce that we've located an existing supply of antiviral medication that is effective against the virus, and we're rounding up supplies for distribution to the affected areas. Of course, we'll send immediate supplies to our neighbors to the south first."

"Do it within three hours, Mr. Vice President," Murphy said.

Breen looked at the slender scientist and tented his eyebrows. "You issuing orders around here now, Doctor?"

"Sir, we only have eight million doses of the antidote. If the airborne virus gets loose in a major population center, like Mexico City with its ten million people, humanity is lost. People will start dying in five hours, but computer projections show that a significant outbreak will consume all of our doses in as little as three hours."

Breen nodded. "General Vickers, make sure your guy in command at the hospital— What's his name?"

"Angus Caruthers is in command of the National Guard forces there, sir."

"Yes. Make sure General Caruthers allows August Spoke access to the hospital. One way or another, I want Shirley Mallory dead inside two hours. If the antidote is going to become available, it's because *I* make it so." Breen stood silently for a moment, then said, "General, a word please."

General Vickers stood and walked around the big conference table so the two men could talk privately.

"John, it's time to consider our secondary strategy."

CHAPTER 53

CARL CRADLED THE HANDSET AND ran to the back of the plane. He used the ten-digit code Agent Palmer had given him for the weapons lockers and rummaged through the drawers and cabinets. He lifted an item from a drawer, pulled it out, and examined it. It looked almost like an ordinary backpack made of black rip-stop nylon. Instead of normal shoulder straps, Carl saw a complicated harness assembly that looked like it might have been borrowed from the seat of a jet fighter cockpit, not that he'd ever seen one of those.

He grabbed a boxy black handgun, which looked sort of like his 9-millimeter Glock. It was a little heavier, a little wider in girth, and the barrel was a tad longer. He pocketed an extra magazine from the drawer beneath the shelf of guns, checked to make sure it fit, and grabbed a sound suppressor, checking its fit also. He was not content to assume all the items were universal or interchangeable.

He put the suppressor in his left tactical thigh pocket before slipping the gun and a spare mag in his right pocket. From another drawer, he pulled two dark gray grenades. They were rectangular and had dark pins that could be pulled out with one finger. He pocketed those and pulled a small black bungee cord from the drawer, closed everything up, and raced back to the front of the plane.

He slung the parachute pack over his shoulders and shrugged his way into the harness on his way back to the cockpit, fastening black metal connectors that seemed like they logically should fit together. The pack was loose, so he looked for and found Velcro pull-straps, which he yanked to tighten the harness.

Carl opened the small locker below the flight phone and pulled out the metal case with the antidotes inside. He wrapped the six-inch rubber bungee cord through the handle of the case and his hip belt loop, then snapped the connector ends in place.

"Johnson, what the hell are you doing?"

"I'm going to save some people."

"Have you ever jumped out of an airplane before?"

Carl shrugged. "Jump out, pull the cord, hit the ground, do a tuck and roll, and don't break a leg. What's so hard about that?"

Opening the metal case, he pulled out a vial and the injector. He snapped the vial into place, placed the business end of the device against bare skin on the colonel's neck, and pressed the trigger. The man didn't argue. He closed the case.

"It's been an honor serving with you, Colonel."

"Likewise."

Carl took two steps out of the cockpit and faced the portside door. Unlike the starboard door, the port door did not have a bulky stairway built into it.

"Wait a minute while I slow the plane to just above stall speed."

"No time."

Carl took a deep breath and yanked the latch a quarter turn clockwise. In the next instant, he realized he shouldn't have done that. Since the Gulfstream was traveling nearly two hundred miles an hour, a hurricane-force wind sheared over the skin of the airplane. As soon as Carl unlatched the locking mechanism, the door popped open an inch. In an instant of time too brief for Carl to even flinch, the wind grabbed onto the leading edge of the door's open seal and ripped the entire door right off its hinge mechanism. Carl, his left hand still locked around the latch release, felt an indescribable pain in his arm and shoulder socket.

The door was ripped from his grasp, and his upper body was pulled halfway out of the plane and into the slipstream. The two-hundred-mile-an-hour wind slammed into the right side of his body like a brick wall and rammed the left side of his body into the edge of the doorway. The wind, a sudden and painful physical force, did as much damage to his unprotected head and face as the doorway did to his left hip.

Carl screamed in pain, but the sound was sucked right from his chest by the icy blast of rushing air. Then he tumbled away into the darkness. He reached for the ripcord at his left shoulder, but in his violent tumbling, he couldn't find the handle. His fingers were numbed instantly in the frigid air.

A memory flashed into his mind of his last trip to the Sandia Peak ski resort in the dead of winter. Even fully decked out in ski bibs with mittens and a thermal cap, it had been frigidly cold with a cutting wind. On that day, at an altitude of ten thousand feet, even the radio towers of the antenna farm had been coated with a thick frosting of ice in the subzero temperature.

Now, he tumbled in the mind-numbing cold wearing only a T-shirt and cargo pants. He had no hat or head glove, and he screamed in agony as the icy wind at eight thousand feet—three thousand feet above the ground—burned his head, face, and arms. His muscles contracted into an involuntary fit of shivers. Carl curled up into a ball and prayed for a fast end to the agony. He felt a heavy drowsiness come over him, and the icy pain thankfully faded as his entire body went numb in about ten seconds.

When he realized he was holding his breath, he sucked in a lungful of frigid air. Suddenly, he was alert again, watching the darkness around him alternate with the bright city lights as he tumbled. For an instant, he faced the ground and realized he could actually see the lights—*the individual lights*—on the streets and buildings.

In a panic, Carl clawed at the ripcord with both hands. He felt nothing with his numb fingers, but he must have found and pulled the cord because he was rewarded with a sudden jerk on his harness that crushed the wind from his chest. The parachute filled with air, and he swung through an arc toward the ground that was only twenty feet below him.

Pull the cord, tuck and roll, and don't break a leg. Don't hit a fucking building!

He bounced against the side of a two-story, corrugated metal industrial building with a loud clang, though he felt no pain on his numb body. Then the chute, still filled with air and drifting in the breeze, yanked him up onto the roof and dragged him across its ribbed surface. He bounced off a satellite dish and an air conditioner unit before he found the fast-release button on his harness.

Suddenly free of the parachute, Carl tumbled down the slanted metal roof and fell over the edge. He plunged headfirst, twenty feet to the ground.

CHAPTER 54

1713 MST, SATURDAY

ALBUQUERQUE FBI FIELD OFFICE

WHEN COSTAS DRAKE REENTERED THE room after a brief conference with his boss on an encrypted cell phone, Guillermo Figueroa observed that the vice president's special FBI liaison held a facial expression that was completely unreadable. This was especially troubling, considering the exchange they'd just heard between the most wanted terrorist in the world and one of the best field agents the Bureau possessed. Lenore Cummings had been rated at or near the top of all her peers for the last dozen years and was a top contender for selection into the Secret Service.

Costas Drake said, "I've been authorized to tell you that what he's calling the *Unit* is Vice President Breen's special TER task force established to deal with this terrorist. They're my quick-response team, assigned to locate and apprehend Carl Johnson at all costs before he can do any more damage or kill anyone else."

Ed Murray said casually, "It looks like you're having as much success as we had last week."

Marshall Stewart said, "Did your team have a firefight with Johnson's mercs at Special Agent Cummings's house?"

"We had intel that suggested his people might show up there and attempt to kill the civilians."

"Intel that you decided to withhold from us?" Murray added.

"My orders were to take the Cummings family into protective

custody. My men were ambushed by Johnson's mercenaries, and now, your field agent is working with him. That makes her a suspect in this investigation. This man is an extremely dangerous and mentally unstable man. You heard him. He knows we're listening, and he knows he can't win. He's trying to deflect our investigation with disinformation. You should know that. He blatantly admitted to bombing an office building in a foreign country. Stating that an ally intends a biological attack on the US and that the vice president is withholding the cure is simply ludicrous. Imagine the worldwide uproar if that lie was ever made public."

Drake took a deep breath, and the SAC had a gut feeling it wasn't a pause for effect. Rather, he thought Drake intended the act as a delaying tactic while he continued weaving his cover story.

The liaison said, "Acting President Breen is working with several companies that have antiviral stockpiles. The CDC has been testing all of these potential antidotes, and several have shown promising results. Some seem to be helpful in at least slowing down the progression of neural damage caused by the virus. They don't want to spread false hope, but I've been assured they're on the cusp of adapting one of these antiviral medicines to successfully fight this disease." Drake paused again, then said to Ed Murray, "And let me remind you that, by acting-presidential decree, *I* decide what intel to disseminate. Not you."

Figueroa raised his right palm in an appeasing gesture. "No need to explain your jurisdiction, Agent Drake. Your mission and your authority have been clearly explained to this office."

He'd been with government service and—in particular—the FBI, long enough to understand the nuances of *involvement* from high-level political individuals with special interests in the outcome of certain investigative cases. The fact that Drake had been granted a rank equivalent to senior special agent by the director of the FBI was a testimony to the VP's interest in the terrorist.

Still, he recognized the appointment as Breen's political maneuver to install his own man at the top of the local decision chain. While Drake didn't *technically* outrank Figueroa, Acting President Walter Breen was calling the operational shots in the terrorist case.

"Then you understand the sensitivity and the importance of my mission."

"Of course."

"Good, because I don't believe for one minute there is an epidemic arising from any outbreaks in Mexico. I think this terrorist is trying to manipulate us into wasting assets that ought to be solely focused on locating the terrorist."

There was logic to Drake's argument. Misinformation and psychological warfare were often more powerful tools of war than guns and bullets. There was no doubt in anyone's mind that Carl Johnson was at war with the US government.

The possibility of the vice president sitting on a cure that could save the president and thousands of other civilians was, indeed, preposterous. It was as insane as a highly decorated Air Force officer, a covert agent, and an FBI agent being recruited by a terrorist. Figueroa didn't personally know the pilot or the TER agent, but Cummings had the better part of her career ahead of her. There was no amount of money in the world that could make her go to the dark side with Carl Johnson.

Unless she believed him.

An agent like Cummings would never do such a thing without iron-clad proof.

Figueroa refocused on the men in his office. "If Johnson does, in fact, have in his possession the antidote that can cure the president, then his plane is our top priority." He looked at his tactical commander. "Prep your SWAT team—"

Drake interrupted, "My team is already en route to the airport, and I will command the operation to arrest them and secure whatever viral substances he has in his possession, if any."

The SAC looked at Costas Drake, and after a brief hesitation, he nodded. Drake was in command of all ops related to the American Terrorist.

SAC said, "You have the full cooperation of this field office in your mission." To his tactical commander, he said, "Have your team on standby as needed for support in case this thing goes south."

Murray nodded. "You mean *further* south." He glanced at the other men in the room. "Perhaps I should send a couple of field agents to the hotel to debrief Special Agent Cummings and to accompany her and her people to the hospital."

Drake said, "I want those people isolated in situ. No one is to talk to them unless it's one of my men."

Figueroa said, "Special Agent Cummings is one of ours."

"She's in collusion with a known terrorist. You heard the conversation." The man pointed at the speaker on the desk. "She faked her own death to help Johnson commit acts of terror, and she was undoubtedly complicit in the murder of my officers this morning."

"We don't know that, and neither do you."

"She's a bad apple, and your people are too close to her. No one talks to her and the others. Am I clear?"

The tone of the phone conversation they'd heard did suggest that Special Agent Cummings was involved in some way with Johnson, but to state collusion and what amounted to treason as facts was a stretch. Only a few days ago, the terrorist had kidnapped her and threatened to torture her daughter. Cummings would never willingly cooperate with him. No mother would. Unless the game had changed, and she knew something no one else knew, something also known by the Air Force pilot and the TER agent.

Figueroa nodded and said, "Your instructions are clear, Mr. Drake."

"Good."

Costas Drake stood and left the room. Guillermo Figueroa watched him go. Ed Murray leaned forward in his seat.

"You want me to go get her?"

Figueroa nodded. "Take a heavily armed team over to that motel and get Cummings and anyone who is with her into protective custody. Take the tactical chopper and get there first. I don't believe for an instant that Carl Johnson is on our side in this, but we can't take the risk that he's lying about releasing an airborne virus. Cummings knows something, and I want to know what it is."

Murray stood. "Carl Johnson is real smart. I got the feeling he was giving us a message when he said the Unit would leave her alone if he surrendered. I think his message was the opposite, but that implies that Drake's men were at her house to kill her instead of take her into protective custody."

Figueroa nodded. "If that is true, I don't see how Johnson's surrender bears any relevance on Cummings's safety."

Murray nodded. "I agree, and I'm sure Johnson would know that. Unless Drake is correct and Johnson is luring us into another ambush."

"Go in heavy this time," Figueroa said.

Murphy nodded and turned for the door.

"Bring our agent back, Ed, but be careful. Anything can happen with this guy, and Johnson tends to shoot first if it suits him."

CHAPTER 55

1713 MST, SATURDAY
ALBUQUERQUE, NM

CARL HIT THE SPEAR-TIPPED CANOPY of an evergreen tree halfway to the ground and grabbed the foliage with a grip of panic. The tree bent over and arrested his fall. He hung with his boots four feet off the ground for a second, then simply let go of the tree and landed on his feet. He stumbled on shaky legs and leaned over with his numb hands braced on his knees.

Fuck me!

His whole body ached, but he had no time to massage his pain away. He shivered violently in the twenty-degree temperature and tried to get his bearings. He struggled out of the empty parachute backpack—a tough chore with numb hands—and tried to rub some warmth back into his arms. Carl took off jogging to the northeast, mostly stumbling until his legs were functional enough for a fast jog.

The plane had been flying southwest on its approach to the airport. He figured the plane was moving perhaps a little less than two hundred miles an hour. Maybe thirty seconds had passed from when Lenore said she heard his plane fly overhead and when he jumped, so he guessed he was a little less than two miles southwest of her motel room, a ten-minute run in his youth, maybe twenty at fifty-three.

As his body thawed, he picked up his speed, but he also began to feel the pain of his new bruises. His boots pounding the cement sent vibrations thundering through his body. The right side of his neck felt like he'd been put in a WWE chokehold from the high-altitude wind slamming into him when he'd jumped from the plane. It was his left hip that concerned him. The more he ran, the more intense the pain became. He hoped it was only a bruise and not something broken or dislocated.

Regardless, he refused to stop. Had Cummings and the group been in another city, they would have been safe. The police or the feds could easily have gotten to them before the Unit could even move a detachment there. The Unit already had a presence in Albuquerque, though, and he knew it was a toss-up whether the feds or the Unit would get to her first.

He caught his second wind and increased his pace even more. He found himself thankful for his fitness regimen. He'd been eating healthy for over twenty years. He'd played competitive volleyball even longer. He still played at a high recreational level—before he became a terrorist—even though his competitive years were far behind him. Until knee surgery changed his life, he'd done a lot of trail-running all the way up to the peaks of the Sandia Mountains. When he turned fifty, his workouts changed. He'd bought one of those late-night infomercial fitness products—an in-home extreme fitness program—solely because the dude who was teaching the course was an old guy also.

If he can do it, I can do it too.

He always used to tell Mark, "Keep your fitness up, son. You never know when you'll find yourself in some kind of emergency. When life throws a test at you, you want to be able to perform."

Carl knew he was taking his life test. If he failed, innocent people would die. Children would die. So he continued to run through the pain.

He got to the motel before the Unit or the FBI and found room 129. He pulled his Glock and screwed the suppressor on, then tested the door. It was locked, so he kicked it in and followed his weapon inside. The room was empty.

As Carl stood in the doorway, he noticed a couple of things. The room looked lived in. The bed had been slept in, and there were fast food packages on the tiny table and in the trashcan. Whoever had last occupied the room had been gone at least two days, he guessed from the smell, and there had been no maid service.

The second thing he noticed was the sound of a TV, but it wasn't coming from his room. The sound was coming from a couple doors to

Carl's left. Curious, he turned to leave, then paused as a particularly nasty thought occurred to him. He crept toward the sound of the loud TV. He scanned the parking lot but saw no activity. There were maybe a dozen cars in the whole lot that looked like it could hold ten times that many.

He approached the door where the sound came from. There were no other sounds from the building, not on the first floor, nor on the second. He tried the doorknob. It was unlocked. He eased the door open partway, and it was just like entering the office at the municipal airport. The room stank of urine, excrement, and vomit.

Garcia and his wife and baby were cuddled in the near corner against the wall near the front window. The heater unit was set to low, and the room was marginally warmer than outside. The young man leaned up against the wall, and his wife lay across his lap holding the baby. They were all silent and unmoving.

All of the Chapman family except Tony lay sprawled across the tiny bed. The teen sat on the floor at the foot of the bed with his upper body parked against the mattress. Anita Chapman's legs hung over the side of the bed, and Tony had wrapped his arms around her legs so he wouldn't fall over. Though unconscious, he still held the MP5 in his grasp. The rest of his family was unconscious also.

Lenore Cummings and her daughter were huddled together in a corner on the far side of the bed. There were half a dozen empty wrappers from MREs and candy bars piled around them, along with empty sixteen-ounce water bottles. A small number of unopened water bottles and meals sat beside Lenore, who had propped herself in the corner against both walls so she wouldn't fall over. Lenore must have seen the progression of symptoms the others had suffered and tried to prepare her space so that she'd have supplies at hand for when she was too sick to move around. Her daughter lay sprawled across her lap.

Lenore's eyes were open, and she was watching the door. When she saw him, she brightened for just a moment, but that seemed to be all the energy she could muster. She had the TV remote at her side, and he guessed she had turned up the TV so he'd hear it. Her service gun was at her side also, but he suspected she was too weak to use it.

Carl slipped inside and closed the door behind him, then turned off the heater and TV and went over to Lenore. It looked like the virus had taken everyone down quickly. It was pretty clear they hadn't moved for many hours, unable to eat or drink.

He opened the case and withdrew two vials. He injected Lenore and Lisette, then patiently tried to feed Lenore water. Most of the water dribbled out of her mouth and down the front of her shirt, but she managed to swallow some. When he pulled Lisette into his lap, he was surprised to see her eyes were open. He cradled the girl against his chest, and she watched him as he held the water bottle to her lips. The girl choked and coughed for a moment before he gave her some more. She continued to watch him, and suddenly, his own eyes rimmed with tears, and he was overcome by a wave of shame.

Carl felt the hot water running down his cheeks as the events of the week flashed through his mind.

"Baby girl, I'm so sorry for what I did to you." He took a deep breath and bit down on his lower lip to keep it from trembling. His words came out as a hoarse whisper. "Please forgive me."

Lisette was too weak to say anything, so he kept feeding her water.

Lenore found the strength to reach out and lay her hand on his forearm. "Thank you," she said.

Carl injected each member of the other families, but he found one of the Chapman twin girls had died. Garcia's wife and his child had also died. A cloud of sadness gripped his heart, and he stepped over to the window to gaze out at the silent parking lot. Central Avenue was completely devoid of traffic, but Carl still looked around, waiting for something to happen.

He got drowsy and felt his eyelids drifting downward. He swayed on his feet and thought about sitting down, but he was afraid he would go to sleep. He was running on adrenaline after all the activity of the last two days, and he hadn't been able to steal any naps. He was also hungry, but suddenly felt too tired to walk over and claim one of Cummings's MRE packets. His reverie was suddenly interrupted by the sound of a powerful engine racing up Central Avenue, and he was instantly awake again. The sound stood out in an otherwise silent night, completely devoid of traffic sounds.

CHAPTER 56

T HE ALBUQUERQUE FIELD OFFICE OF the FBI had exactly one tactical combat assault chopper in its inventory. In fact, it was a new addition on loan from the Denver office after last week's substantial losses at the hands of the terrorist. Ed Murray himself had requisitioned the chopper because of its military-grade surveillance system. It carried low-light and infrared imaging systems.

The chopper was heavily armed, though that weaponry was limited in its use by federal anti-terrorist rules of engagement that specified deployment in a domestic combat environment. The chopper had a laser designator for its minigun, and it possessed small armor-piercing missiles. It also had flack dispensers in case the terrorist's mercenaries had black-market ground-to-air rockets at their disposal. The chopper was also armored against small-arms fire.

The jet-black aircraft, a civilian police variant of the army's Black Hawk helicopter, flew over the empty ribbon of I-40, just high enough to avoid scraping its underbelly against the overpasses. The aircraft was in complete blackout mode. There were no navigation lights or anti-collision beacons anywhere on its surface. That would make it difficult to spot unless an observer was very close, but that was the purpose. Even the reflected radiance from the bright city lights was absorbed by the dull black surface of the aircraft.

Murray scanned the city below him as the chopper raced toward its destination. He'd never seen the streets of Albuquerque completely empty of all traffic, and the sight seemed surreal. That was due to the nationwide curfew ordered by the vice president to contain the sporadic outbreaks of the virus, which Murray now knew were caused by the terrorist. The curfew seemed to stop the local spread of the Contagion, though it was still unclear how many infected had traveled beyond New Mexico's borders. Every now and again, Murray saw emergency vehicles with their flashing strobes, but those were the only vehicles allowed on the streets.

"Thirty seconds," the pilot called.

A flush of trepidation swept through Murray's body. He and the four SWAT officers accompanying him had trained back east with FBI special tactics teams, which included helicopter drop-offs into hot zones. None had actually done it in real combat. That was why he was caught completely off guard at the sudden appearance of two RPG exhaust trails streaking straight for him as the chopper banked over Cummings's motel parking lot. The flare dispensers fired automatically, but the RPGs were moving fast and were too close when they exploded.

Murray heard clanging sounds that threatened to rupture his eardrums as weapons, ammunition cans, and the very seats themselves were ripped from the bulkheads by the dual explosions. Then the chopper fell from the sky.

CHAPTER 57

1728 MST, SATURDAY

ALBUQUERQUE, NM

CARL WATCHED THE SPECTACLE UNFOLD and felt a twinge of sympathy for the federal agents. Just two minutes earlier, he'd heard the big SUV drive past the motel and knew instantly it was the Unit. If it had been an FBI truck, it would have come straight to the motel.

When the chopper finally showed, he saw the multi-spectral surveillance pod hanging down from the nose of the chopper—he used to design military versions of those optical systems back in his Air Force days—and also saw a multi-barrel minigun protruding from its belly.

At least they're trying to do it right this time.

The Unit assassins waited smartly until the chopper flared to land so that it wouldn't be able to evade the missiles, but Carl was surprised when decoy flares exploded from the front and back of the chopper. They performed their function well, causing the missiles to veer away and explode in the clouds of aluminum strips, sparing the crew from instant death. But the double explosions expended tremendous energy against the rear of the helicopter. The first explosion literally knocked the chopper ninety degrees in midair until the cockpit was facing Carl's room head-on. The second explosion flipped the tail up into the air until the top of the rotor assembly was facing Carl's room.

The chopper dropped straight down the remaining thirty feet and hit the asphalt of the parking lot. It didn't explode into flames, but the huge rotor assembly broke off and flashed away to Carl's left with a clanging of metal as the blades ripped through a couple of parked cars. The fuselage simply fell over sideways.

Because the crash was so horrendously loud and violent, Carl at first thought no one could have survived. Even as he was about to close the door to his motel room, he saw a man in combat gear trying to crawl out of the wreckage. Carl ran out and grabbed the cop by his armored vest as the man tumbled to the ground and half-dragged him into the room.

He was about to go back again to see if anyone else had survived, but he stopped suddenly at the chirping of tires on pavement and the roar of an overpowered engine. He quickly closed the room door. When he turned to face the cop he'd just dragged in, he saw the man was pointing a wicked black handgun at him.

Carl just looked at the man. "If you fire that thing, they'll find us."

"They're coming here anyway!" he whispered harshly.

"No," Carl said with a shake of his head. "They're going to room 129."

He nodded his head behind the cop, and the man turned his head and saw a very tired-looking Agent Cummings gazing back at him. He lowered his gun.

"This was her idea," Carl said. "She didn't believe the Unit would let these people live even if they had me, and neither did I. And apparently, you got my message."

Outside, World War III erupted as Unit men poured automatic rifle fire into the wrecked windows and doors of the chopper's fuselage. The gunfire ceased, and after a few seconds, someone yelled, "Fire in the hole!" A muffled explosion rattled the hotel room.

Carl stepped over to the window and peeked around the ratty old curtain. He realized then that the curtain was made of the same material as the bedspread. It was a thick, red flowery fabric. It was tattered and old, and it smelled of years of fast food.

The Unit sent five men this time. After nuking the chopper wreckage, they crept toward room 129. At the leader's hand signal, they rushed in. They literally exploded back out on the leading edge of the blast from one of Agent Palmer's high-tech square grenades. He'd pulled the pin and propped it under the nightstand, which he'd maneuvered as close to the door as he could.

If the Unit men had gone in slowly, they would have easily seen the booby trap. They would have seen the doorjamb had already been kicked in. Carl had plenty of experience with cops and soldiers, and the Unit guys were no different. They went in fast and hard, with plenty of shock and awe.

Carl yanked his door open and followed the suppressor-clad barrel of his Glock like it was a part of his outstretched arms. All five of the Unit guys were sprawled on the asphalt. The three men closest to the door had literally been ripped apart by the blast. A fourth man lay upside down on the hood of an old car. His neck was slashed open, and blood dripped from the hood of the car to the ground.

The fifth man was still alive. He writhed in pain on his back and looked like he was trying to turn over onto his belly, maybe so he could crawl away or something. Carl walked over to him and knelt beside him. He watched the man for a moment, and he lay on his back watching Carl.

"You know who I am?"

"Johnson," the man said. "You're Carl Johnson."

"They've briefed you on what I've done? What I'm capable of doing?"

"Yes." The man grimaced in pain.

Carl was surprised at how young the man was. He looked barely even twenty. He was a big kid with unruly, sandy hair. He wore no combat paint.

Carl placed the suppressor of his Glock against the man's groin. "You realize I will have no problem blowing away your family jewels and leaving you like this, right?"

The young Unit man said nothing.

"Who is your boss?"

The young man grunted painfully. "Costas Drake."

"Thank you." Carl stood.

There were many more questions he could have asked the man, but he knew the merc wouldn't have the answers to strategic questions, and it wouldn't get Carl closer to the vice president.

"Women and children?" Carl said to the wounded man. "Not cool."

He shot the man in the face, then went back to Cummings's room and the group of barely alive people. He cast his gaze upon the wounded tactical officer. At that moment, he knew how he was going to get the FBI to listen to him and save the president.

"Let's go for a ride, Mister."

CHAPTER 58

IT TOOK CARL NEARLY AN hour to reach his destination. The FBI tactical officer, who gave his name as Ed Murray, was in bad shape, but Carl could tell he was a tough and seasoned combat veteran. He had multiple broken bones and shrapnel wounds, one of which was still bleeding profusely. It was too high on the man's thigh for a proper tourniquet, so Murray kept pressure on the wound and bore his not-insignificant pain in silence.

The irony of his latest escape was not lost on Carl. He was driving the Unit's SUV, which was, in fact, an FBI motor pool vehicle. He found the switch for the blue and red emergency strobe lights and turned it on as he departed the motel. He saw faint reflections of blue and red light on darker sections of the street as the grill-mounted strobe pulsed in the night.

He stayed off the interstate highway and the main boulevards for fear the Unit would locate them and launch another assault. He was reasonably certain he was safe from air attack. The Unit was not a government outfit, but through the vice president's authority, they could commandeer virtually any government assets. The good news was that Murray had assured him the FBI had only one combat chopper, and to his knowledge, there were no military units at Kirtland Air Force Base with combat-ready helicopters for the Unit to use.

There were several police helicopters available, but the Unit had deployed them in their operation to secure the Gulfstream at the airport. As Carl pulled up to the main gate of the FBI field office, he glanced over Agent Murray. The agent was on the verge of losing consciousness. His hand had fallen off the pressure bandage, and he had a glazed look in his eyes.

"Are you certain this Figueroa fellow isn't with the Unit?"

Murray nodded and grimaced immediately. "Known him twenty years."

That will have to do, Carl thought.

He had no doubt that Vice President Breen had recruited many high-level government employees to his cabal. His government takeover plan had been in development for a long time, but until last month, when the FBI had confused Johnson for Alfonso Reyes, there was no tactical connection between Breen's plan and Albuquerque. Carl was taking a chance that Breen's sphere of influence did not extend as far down as an FBI field office commander in Albuquerque, New Mexico.

What are the odds, right?

He pulled the big SUV up to the gate and squinted into the bright lights shining through the front windshield. The fence surrounding the property looked very sturdy. The thick vertical posts were painted a neutral color that blended with the landscape. The entry barrier, on the other hand, was a stark black, steel structure that jutted forward near the ground. The front of any vehicle that tried to force its way through the barrier would be lifted off the ground on impact. Carl knew nothing short of a tank could get through.

The guard that had started to approach from the guard shack stopped right outside his window. He recognized Carl, brought up his automatic rifle, and shouted, "Get out of the vehicle! Let me see your hands!"

Ten seconds later, the SUV was completely surrounded by armed guards in full tactical gear. A track-wheeled vehicle rumbled up to the gate and faced Carl's SUV on the other side of the barrier. Armed men poured out the back of the vehicle and spread out, weapons pointed at his head. He didn't know much about armored personnel carriers, but he could easily see this particular APC was armed with a big-ass machine gun, and the barrel of that big gun was pointed right at his face. His SUV wasn't armored, but Carl knew armor wouldn't have made a bit of difference with a gun that big.

Carl sat calmly. He had expected this kind of reception, so he showed them his hands. He raised them slowly with both palms facing forward so the guards in front of the SUV could see the grenade he held. With his right index finger and thumb, he slowly and deliberately pulled the square black pin out of the grenade and waited.

CHAPTER 59

SPECIAL AGENT IN CHARGE GUILLERMO Figueroa stood by the window of his third-floor office and watched the scene below. The alarm had gone off throughout the facility even before the unidentified SUV pulled to a stop in front of the gate. He tapped his Bluetooth earpiece and monitored the chatter on the security channel.

He recognized the American Terrorist in the harsh glare of the security lights before the gate guard did. Then he saw Ed Murray sitting in the front passenger seat. The agent's face was drawn and pale. Johnson held up his hands, and suddenly, all the guards backed off a dozen feet. Over the net, Figueroa heard, "He's got a grenade!"

The SAC said, "All personnel, fall back forty feet. I'll be right down." He stood up to leave his office, then added, "Tactical, I want two snipers on the roof, locked and loaded."

"Already done, sir."

"Hold for my order."

Figueroa pulled off his suit jacket and tossed it over the back of his chair. Then he pulled his black flak jacket on and tightened all the Velcro straps. He checked his service gun as he left his office. He'd been trying to get answers as to why the op to retrieve Agent Cummings had suddenly gone silent. Now he was sure the answer had driven up to his main gate.

In his earpiece, he heard, "Agent Figueroa, he's asking for you by name."

"Tell him I'm on my way down."

The voice on the channel added, "And he says to make sure you don't bring any Unit men with you."

Figueroa stepped into the elevator and said, "Ask him how he knows who is in the Unit."

"He says they'll be the ones trying to kill him."

Figueroa just grunted. Right now, pretty much the whole government wanted that man dead, and yet, here he was at the main gate of an FBI office. Not something your run-of-the-mill terrorist would do.

CHAPTER 60

CARL STUDIED THE FBI MAN as he approached the barrier. He couldn't see much in the way of details about Guillermo Figueroa because of the harsh glare of the security lights, but he certainly carried himself with confidence. He might be a desk jockey now, but Carl could see he hadn't always been. He walked like he'd been around the block a few times. This man had been through a lot of missions and raids. He had confident-cop swag. Figueroa was short and stocky with rounded shoulders and a little extra in the paunch. He figured the guy could probably bench press three hundred pounds, but he didn't do much cardio.

There was an electronic buzz as Agent Figueroa was allowed through the personnel gate beside the guard shack. He approached the SUV with his gun in his hand, though it remained pointed at the ground.

Figueroa stopped at the driver's side window and peered past Carl. "Agent Murray, what's your status?"

Murray leaned against the passenger window but raised his left arm weakly. "Had better days, my friend."

To Carl, he said, "The rest of his team?"

Carl noted the agent didn't ask where they were or if they were even alive. He seemed to already know the answer, but he seemed to need confirmation.

"They flew right into an ambush. The Unit took up position a couple minutes before your men got there. They waited until the chopper was about to land. They brought RPGs to the party this time."

Figueroa grimaced. "And where are these Unit men now?"

"I sent them to hell." Carl paused. "It was no coincidence they showed up just in time to set an ambush. I figure they had inside information." Carl could see the man fuming.

"Indeed, they did."

"I saw them drive past from the east, but there are only a couple of cheap hotels to the east of where Lenore was holed up. If I had to hide some mercenaries, that's where I'd put them."

Figueroa grunted and cast his glance over Carl's shoulder, into the back seats of the SUV. "Christ!" he said. "These people need to be in a hospital!"

Carl shook his head. "The Unit can get to them in a hospital."

"So you brought them here?"

"Agent Murray said you have an infirmary. He's bleeding out. I injected the others with the antidote, but they'll need help recovering. He said I can trust you with their safety," Carl said. "Can I?"

Figueroa seemed to recognize the opening salvo of a negotiation, and he said, "And in exchange…"

"If you guarantee their safety, I'll let you debrief me as we fly down south with the virus antidote." Carl raised up the medical case for a moment. "I'll tell you everything I know about Breen, his assassination plot, and the people he's working with south of the border."

Figueroa glanced around at all the guns like he was trying to make a point. "If I refuse?"

Carl wagged the grenade. "Then we all join those Unit men in hell."

"You have evidence of the vice president's involvement?"

Carl shrugged. "Evidence is your department. I can give you a man who knows where the antidote is stockpiled." He sensed Figueroa wasn't convinced. "Look, Agent. No sane leader would use a bioweapon as an assassination tool unless they had the cure. Too many ways for it to get loose…as it has." He looked over at Murray, then added, "Shirley Mallory trusted me to save her girl. Help me finish the job. Help me save the president and her daughter."

Agent Figueroa started to say something, but one of the guards stepped up beside him.

"Sir, Agent Drake reports that his Unit is returning from the airport. They had to shoot the plane down because the pilot refused to make the last turn on his approach."

Figueroa looked at Carl, who shook his head. "They murdered him. Shot him out of the sky. He was a hero. He gave everything for his president—his career and his life. He had twin daughters about Melissa Mallory's age."

The agent nodded and holstered his weapon, then reached in and closed his hand around Carl's hand that held the grenade. "All right, Mr. Johnson, we'll do this your way for now." He motioned to Carl's other hand for the black metal safety tab and inserted it into the device, then handed it to the guard. To the guard, he said, "When Costas Drake and his Unit personnel return, use all means to disarm and detain them. Deadly force is authorized."

"Yes, sir." The guard returned to his post.

"Open the gate. We're going in." Figueroa climbed up on the runner as Carl shifted the SUV into gear. The agent activated his Bluetooth earpiece. "Comm, vector in the nearest police helicopter to the landing pad, then have the airport tower ground all civilian and military aircraft and establish a no-fly zone over the city for the next four hours. I don't want any more surprises. And have the infirmary send a medical team out front." He leaned down and asked Carl how many casualties he had.

"Eleven plus Murray." Carl had also brought the dead along. He didn't have the heart to leave them behind in the motel. "But make sure no one touches them. I don't know how long it takes for the antidotes to work. They might still be contagious. Good thing you're wearing gloves. I think I'm cured, but I can't be sure."

Figueroa passed along the instructions to prep for biohazard containment, then said, "Have all available field agents prepare to canvass the hotels on Central Avenue east of Agent Cummings's motel. Coordinate with the local police and sheriff's offices, and have all available officers cordon off the area, but wait until Mr. Drake and his men are in custody here. They're no doubt monitoring police and FBI frequencies, so I don't want to spook them. Then assign all local SWAT units to supplement ours. Tell them our suspects are heavily armed, paramilitary personnel wanted in connection with the murder of federal agents. Expect heavy resistance."

Carl drove slowly up to the front of the FBI building, and Agent Figueroa jumped down from the running board.

"Let's go save the president, Mr. Johnson."

CHAPTER 61

THE GIRL, JULIA, BEGAN SCREAMING a few seconds after Nancy Palmer opened the exterior office door just an inch. She'd been scanning the brightly lit tarmac around the hangar building, at least the southwest section that she could see. Ten-foot flood-lamp posts on tripods were positioned every thirty feet or so, forming a perimeter line a hundred feet away from the hangar. Fifty feet beyond that security perimeter was the chain-link fence topped with razor wire marking the outer edge of the airport property.

In the darkness of the night, a ring of light protected the airport buildings from intrusion. No way she'd get through that ring without being spotted. She had to find a way to kill the generator she heard humming somewhere in the night. To get to that generator, she'd have to navigate outside in the light. She'd already sized up the opposing force and decided they were a non-threat. The Mexican army, or perhaps the in-country equivalent of a national guard—weekend warriors—wore basic green fatigues and patrolled somewhat casually holding their old M-16s pointed to the ground. The five soldiers she could see were all facing outward into the darkness while they patrolled, and the lights did more to illuminate the patrols than anything they might be looking for. It seemed clear the expected threat was from outsiders trying to breach the perimeter.

From the posture of the soldiers, she could tell none had true combat experience and didn't expect any incursions deep inside their own country. After all, who would want to break into a bio-zone and rescue a contagious person in a coma?

These young Mexican soldiers were not her enemy, so she wanted to avoid engaging them if possible. It was the Unit personnel she was concerned about. She couldn't see any of them, but she knew they were out there somewhere.

The night was relatively quiet outside, so the sudden screams pierced the night like a siren. A few of the patrolling soldiers turned and gazed toward the southern side of the hangar. Palmer couldn't see what the soldiers saw, but she guessed they were watching a flurry of activity as Unit soldiers jumped into their bio-spacesuits to investigate. Palmer knew she had mere seconds to act.

She closed the door. Through the doorway separating her office from the huge hangar, she saw Julia Reyes sitting upright on her bed, terror-struck. Then the girl suddenly stopped screaming. She clutched the bed sheet under her chin.

For a brief moment, Nancy Palmer considered using the confusion and mayhem to escape, but she had no weapons, and the logistics of escape were uncertain. She was sure she could reach one of the patrolling soldiers, disable him, and take his weapon. Someone would see her, though, and she wasn't sure she could then escape without using lethal force. Before she even considered that option, she had to grab the vials of the antidote and find a thermos or a cooler and some ice. Only then could she attempt her escape.

She had no doubt the Unit would discretely kill Julia when they realized she had recovered from the virus. Palmer felt no emotional attachment to the girl, but Carl did, and his feelings were inexplicably important. He might never forgive her if she let something preventable happen to Julia. She was more concerned with how the girl's death would damage him after the loss of his son. It might push him beyond recovery.

It wouldn't take the Unit long to figure out Carl had injected the girl's mother and the other mercenaries also. They'd kill them too. When the doctors and other attendants objected, they'd die as well. Then the Unit would turn on the Mexican weekend warriors. It would be a bloodbath, all because the Unit needed to protect Walter Breen's secret—the antidote was real, it worked, and President Mallory didn't have to die.

Palmer crept back to the inner door and peeked into the hangar. Julia had started crying and was trying to pull the IV needle tape from her arm. In a weak voice filled with fear, she was calling for her mother in Spanish. When she looked around at all the comatose bodies, Julia saw the two attendants in red biohazard suits running toward her. She started screaming again.

The scene unfolded in virtual slow motion for Palmer as her brain automatically began considering options, attack vectors, and blind spots. The three white spacesuits hurried behind the Reds. All five waddled awkwardly in the bulbous suits, and the sounds of clunky rubber boots and swishing nylon echoed through the cavernous room. One white suit had his hand pressed against the side of his head covering, and his mouth was moving behind his acrylic faceplate like he was shouting into a radio microphone. The white suits were armed with holstered handguns.

Palmer scanned the dark office around her for weapons but found little of use. Among the debris on the floor near her, she saw a couple of ink pens and a tiny flat-head screwdriver used for adjusting small electrical gadgets. While she was fully trained in turning virtually any object into a deadly weapon, she needed weapons she could take into battle against five men, three of which were armed and likely trained combat soldiers. As she looked back into the hangar, she saw that the cavernous room was full of weapons. There was a metal IV post hooked onto the frame of each bed. There were literally hundreds of weapons she could use.

Palmer rushed into the hangar, skipped left, then charged down the center aisle between the rows of beds. The attendants and the soldiers saw her coming. The soldiers in white fumbled for their guns in their bulky gloves, but the attendants froze in her path, blocking the soldiers from getting a clear shot.

By the time they could see Palmer clearly, she was already in their midst. Palmer grabbed the metal IV rack from Julia's bed and ripped it from its plastic fastener. She discarded the hanging bag of fluid, then became a ninja, swinging the four-foot-long metal post like a staff. She spun, stabbed, slashed, and pummeled all five of the suits. She broke their faceplates, ripped open their bio-suits, cracked their skulls, and impaled their faces. In the space of less than ten seconds, she had disabled all five men.

Julia immediately stopped screaming at the sight of her. Palmer laid a gentle palm on her cheek for a brief second, then bent down and relieved the three white spacesuits of their guns. She tucked the weapons in Velcro pockets and helped Julia off the bed. She pulled the IV needle from the girl's arm.

The girl looked around. "Where's my mom?"

"I don't know, Sweetie, but we have to go. Okay?"

Palmer grabbed her hand and started toward the entrance the space-suits used—the open personnel door in the center of the huge hangar door. She could see there was a ribbed, clear plastic quarantine tube secured to the outside of that door. Julia surprised her by twisting the other way. The girl broke free and ran around, aimlessly calling for her mother. Finally, Palmer caught the girl and forced her into a squat beside a bed.

"Julia, look. I'll be honest with you. I don't know where your mother is, nor my other team members, but—"

"Where's Carl," Julia said, looking around again. Her bottom lip trembled. "I want Carl."

"You remember that girl he came here for day before yesterday? Melissa?"

Julia nodded.

"Well, she's in trouble again, and he had to go help her and her mother. But he asked me to look after you, okay?"

"No, he didn't." She looked ready to cry again.

Palmer was silent for a moment, then said, "You're right, he didn't. I just said that because I need you to trust me and help me get out of here." She smiled, and Julia gave her a shy smile in return. "My name's Nancy, and I'm sorry for talking to you like a little kid."

"I'm hungry, Nancy."

"Me too. Okay, first thing, let's get out of here because there are some bad men that want to kill us because we woke up. Second thing is, we find some food and water. Third thing is, we try to find your mom. Okay, so far?"

The girl looked like she was starting to nod, but then her eyes went wide, and she pointed over Palmer's left shoulder. Palmer grabbed a gun and spun in a crouch. She looked under the nearest bed, through a forest of metal bed frames, and found herself aiming a gun at nothing. Trent

Englebaum, the man Carl called Merc Three, rolled off his cot onto the floor and pulled his IV line from his arm. He caught Palmer's gaze and gave her a head-nod. She slid her gun along the floor toward him.

"Watch Julia. I'm going to create a diversion." To Julia, she said, "Stay right here. I'll be right back."

She ran back into the office, swung open the exterior door, and snapped off seven quick shots to take out the six nearest floodlights. The last tripod fell over sideways, but the light remained on because her sixth bullet hit the metal housing and missed the bulb. The seventh shot fixed that problem. She knew the gunshots and the sudden pool of darkness would draw attention. It was the obvious play for someone making a desperate attempt to escape through the perimeter fence. There was nothing but open land surrounding the airport. That's why she and the others were going the opposite way. The Unit or the weekend warriors had to have transportation somewhere near the hangars.

She ran back into the hangar and made the personnel door with the attached quarantine tube her destination, but when she looked for Merc Three and Julia, they were not where she'd left them. Instead, they were several rows away. Julia had conscripted Merc Three into her mission to find her mother, and the man was hefting an unconscious body onto his shoulder. He and Julia moved quickly toward Palmer.

"Mission accomplished," Three said with a wink.

Palmer raised an eyebrow at Julia. "You told him I said to find your mother?" The girl looked like she was going to apologize, so Palmer said, "Nice move, young lady. We'll make an agent out of you yet." She banged her palm against the big red button on the wall and said, "Let's move!"

The yellow warning light and the klaxon activated immediately. The two center sections of the six-section aircraft door began to separate with a loud rumble, then caught the second two sections, then the third. The quarantine tube was torn from its fasteners, and Palmer and Three burst into the open.

Ten feet in front of them, at the other end of the now-torn quarantine tube, was a long, steel RV trailer that looked like it could be towed by a heavy-duty pickup truck. Its shiny surface gleamed under the distant floodlights. There were no windows in the RV, and its two doors, one of which was encompassed inside the quarantine tube, looked like pressure doors. Biohazard labels decorated both doors.

Three said, "There's another containment trailer over here."

Palmer glanced to her right and saw another vehicle connected to a second hangar a hundred yards away, and a third to her left. Beyond the left trailer, two large olive green tents were set up on the concrete tarmac. Towering over the tents, she saw the huge twin helicopter-like propellers of a VC-22 Osprey parked beyond the tents.

Palmer pointed with one of her guns. "Three, that's our destination."

"Roger that."

Between them and their escape transportation were the military-grade biohazard containment trailer in front of them, the two army tents, a hundred yards of tarmac, and an unknown number of Unit soldiers searching for them. With a gun in each hand, Agent Palmer led the way toward the gleaming stainless steel containment trailer. Merc Three followed, guiding Julia by the hand and carrying the unconscious Luisa over his right shoulder. As they approached the trailer, Palmer could see that the vehicle was designed for biohazard duty in a combat arena. Its outer skin was reinforced with sturdy metal straps that ribbed its surface, and thick heavy-duty rivets held the thing together. Rather than go inside, Palmer decided to use the trailer as a shield in case they were discovered.

"Get to the right-most tent," she said. "I'll cover you."

The tent was surprisingly empty, but there were only five cots and a couple desks with open laptops. Out the other side of the tent, Palmer saw the prize fifty yards away in the semidarkness. The Osprey's huge wing nacelles were angled upward so the plane could take off and land like a helicopter. The paint scheme on the plane was desert camouflage, and when she saw the belly and tail guns, she knew instantly the bird was a combat troop and cargo carrier—a special ops aircraft.

The tail cargo ramp was open, and three men in black tactical gear conversed, gesturing hurriedly toward the inside of the plane. They were unaware of Palmer's approach until she was ten feet away. One of the men—a big guy with thick arms and legs—seemed to sense her presence and turned slightly. When he saw her, he went for his gun, not that it mattered one bit to Palmer. Her two handguns were pointed at the men, and she had already decided to shoot the big man. She knew he was not a pilot.

The man wore no helmet, and Palmer's first shot literally destroyed his head. The other two men froze.

"Which of you is a pilot?" She thought she already knew the answer.

The young guy was the pilot. The older guy might also be a pilot, but he struck her as more of a commander type. He was about forty and had severe crow's feet at the corners of his sky blue eyes. His skin was leathery, and Palmer guessed he was an ex-Special Forces killer. He wouldn't yield. She pointed a gun at his head.

"Fuck you," he said.

She pulled the trigger a second time.

Merc Three said, "We've got company on our six. Whatever you're going to do, you better do it now."

Palmer pointed her gun at the young man's head. "If you're not a pilot, then you're of no use to me."

He nodded at her. "I can fly."

"Inside." Grabbing the back of his collar, Palmer led the young man up the ramp toward the cockpit.

The troop cabin of the plane was about the size of a school bus. There were twelve inward-facing jump seats along each wall of the cargo bay, and metal crates of combat gear were secured to the center of the floor by quick-release fasteners. A half-door separated the cargo area from the high-tech cockpit, but that door had been left open after the pilot's exit. They settled into the flight seats.

"Enable weapons," Palmer said. "The minigun." She parked the business end of her gun against the man's groin. "And don't do anything to make me flinch."

"Can't do that while we're on the ground powered down."

"I understand you want to stall," Palmer said. "I'd do the same. But that was your one freebie. They told you who I am, right?"

He nodded. "They told me you're a TER agent."

"And a Navy SEAL, right?"

He nodded.

"So you can assume I know about all kinds of covert combat aircraft."

The young man sighed, and Palmer saw the resistance go out of him like a balloon deflating. He pressed some indicator lights on his high-tech instrument panel, and a display not unlike a video game screen lit up in the center of the digital instrument panel. Left gun still parked against the pilot's groin, Palmer grabbed a joystick and swiveled the belly-mounted gun toward the approaching Unit soldiers. She touched the screen indicator, which enabled auto-target tracking, then touched her finger over each of the seven targets. She touched Auto-Engage. The minigun spooled up with a whine, and less than a second later, it spat out shells at a tremendous rate for precisely three seconds. The green circles that had been following the approaching soldiers changed to red circles representing dead Unit men. The weekend warriors kept their distance.

"Get us into the air, please," Palmer said.

He started the engines one at a time. Palmer heard a whine of an electric motor and glanced behind her to see the cargo ramp rising. Two minutes later, the Osprey lifted from the tarmac.

"Our destination?"

"First, set us down right in front of the center hangar." The pilot did as he was told, and Palmer instructed Merc Three to open one of the metal cargo pods and outfit himself with firepower. She sent him into the office to get the antidote and ice from the freezer.

"Set your course for the hospital in Las Cruces," she told the pilot. "We're going to save the president."

CHAPTER 62

1855 MST, SATURDAY
UNDISCLOSED SECURITY BUNKER

BREEN REFOCUSED ON THE CONFERENCE phone and repeated his question. "One survivor? She killed your entire team? All by herself? You're the only survivor?"

"Yes, sir," the distant voice said. "Well, sir, I'm not counting the pilot she kidnapped."

The vice president slammed his hand down on the star-shaped conference phone to disconnect the call. "Fuck!" He grabbed the bowl of bagels and flung it against the wall.

Director Drummond added, "She has a CV-22 Osprey outfitted for special ops missions with extra fuel tanks for the long haul. She can fly well over two thousand miles before refueling."

General Vickers said, "She's not flying two thousand miles, Director. She's flying two *hundred* miles to Las Cruces."

"She's a SEAL training dropout, for crying out loud!" Martine Scallow shook his head."

Drummond said, "Before she dropped out of training, she was recommended for DevGru in Virginia. That's the Navy Warfare Development Group, commonly referred to as SEAL Team Six. She's that good."

"Great," Breen said. He stood and paced around the room for a moment, then grabbed an empty chair and flung it against the nearest concrete wall. The plastic armrests of the chair shattered, and the metal legs gouged a chunk out of the wall that ricocheted across the room.

"That's just fucking great! We've got a female SEAL trying to rescue a female president, along with a previously unknown deep-cover operator who's been masquerading as a domestic terrorist."

Vickers shrugged. "Johnson's operator pedigree is still a matter for debate, but if Agent Palmer gets anywhere near Las Cruces with her hijacked CV-22, it's game over. We need to intercept that plane ASAP. It's got vertical takeoff and landing capability, and it's got the full covert weapons package. It's armed with an M240 machine gun in the back and a belly-mounted minigun slaved to a nose-mounted, digital auto-tracking target acquisition system."

Drummond said, "Can the AWACS find it so the Air Force can shoot it down?"

Vickers shook his head. "Unlikely. It's equipped with the latest terrain-following radar system, so it can fly on the deck, even in valleys and canyons. It also has state-of-the-art RF countermeasures, active electronic countermeasures, and defensive signal jamming. She'll be hard to find and harder to put down."

Drummond added, "If Johnson and Palmer get on the ground at the hospital—"

"Agreed," Vickers said. "They're cured, but our troops at the hospital will be fighting in full MOPP-4 gear."

"Excuse me?" Scallow said. "What is that?"

The general explained, "It's an acronym for Mission Oriented Protective Posture Level Four. It's full readiness to deploy and operate in a CBRN environment. That's military parlance for an operational battlefield with chemical, biological, radiation, or nuclear elements present. Our people went in with full-body combat hazard suits, gloves, and masks."

Drummond said, "That's an extremely challenging combat scenario for fully trained Spec Ops boys, but for Army National Guardsmen? Against two highly trained combatants who are not restricted to MOPP-4? We'll take heavy losses."

"Shit!" Breen was silent for a moment, then looked at the general. "Have General Caruthers go weapons free. Tell him to expect an imminent air assault."

Breen looked around the conference table at each member of his cabinet. Several wore haggard expressions of frustration. Dr. Murphy kept mopping his hands through his hair, like he was trying to figure out a way to escape the fiasco.

"People, let me put it to you this way," Breen said. "We all agreed that our woman president was not strong enough to lead this country forward. She's too conservative with the rest of the world, and she's eroding our nation's respect and prominence on the world stage. Our enemies think America is a joke, and even our allies are plotting against us economically and with covert intel operations.

"Mallory was elected by a landslide, and she's virtually guaranteed to be reelected in two years. We can do something about that here today, but if we allow Johnson and Palmer to get the antidote to the president, we"—he waved his hand around the table—"are all dead."

"Walter," General Vickers said. "Have you considered my fallback recommendation?"

"My man will come through for us."

"And if he doesn't? We can't afford to take that chance."

Breen eyed his general and nodded. "Very well. Launch the cruise missile. Bomb the hospital and blame it on the terrorist."

CHAPTER 63

2100 MST, SATURDAY
LAS CRUCES, NM

THERE WERE FOUR SEATS IN the police helicopter. Three were occupied. Carl sat in the rear left seat in silence after concluding his two-hour debrief. He'd detailed all the facts and suppositions regarding the kidnapping and rescue of the First Daughter, along with the source and spread of the virus.

Two minutes earlier, the police helicopter crossed the ten-mile line marking the no-fly zone the military unit had drawn around the Mountain View Regional Medical Center. An emotionless voice with an all-business tone announced the imminent destruction of the helicopter if they did not alter course. Carl listened to the exchange between Special Agent in Charge Guillermo Figueroa and the owner of the harsh voice who gave his name as Brigadier General Angus Caruthers. Figueroa, who seemed accustomed to people yielding to his federal authority, was gaining absolutely no ground with the stubborn officer. Unfortunately, Carl knew they had no time for a pissing contest.

In the darkness below, Carl saw a long procession of headlights and blue and white strobes as they approached the Las Cruces hospital. Figueroa had called in every cop and federal agent within a hundred miles, and they were all converging on the quarantined hospital that was protected by American military men and women. If it came to a shoot-out, the National Guard had bigger guns and more of them. Carl knew

General Caruthers would give the order to fire on federal officers because he was in league with the vice president. He had to be.

A shootout would not save the president. Carl grabbed a set of headphones mounted on the ceiling of the cabin and put them on. There was no sound. He leaned forward, tapped Figueroa on the shoulder, and gestured to the cups of his headset. The agent pushed a button on his overhead console, and Carl heard the ongoing conversation.

He interrupted, saying, "General Caruthers, you seem set on killing the president. I'd like to know why."

"Who is this?"

"I'm the person who can save the president. I have the antidote *in my hands*. Why do you want her to die, General?"

"Alter your course, or I will fire on you."

Carl didn't expect any other response. "General, are you really going to kill dozens of police officers for trying to save the president?" There was no response. "If you kill us, you kill President Mallory. I was infected, and I took the antidote. I am alive and cured. In ten minutes, President Mallory and her daughter can be cured."

The gruff voice came back on the channel. It was old and wise. It sounded like a man who had spent decades both participating in and commanding combat operations. Carl pictured a six-foot-tall, barrel-chested man with white hair in a military buzz cut.

"My orders come directly from the acting president. No one approaches the hospital. If you do not leave my airspace in thirty-five seconds, I will shoot you down. If you attempt to land, I will shoot you down. You now have thirty seconds to comply."

"General, the vice president ordered you not to let anyone into the hospital because he knows we have the antidote. He knows we can save her. If she dies, he gets sworn in as president and takes power. If she lives, he loses. End of story."

"Turn your aircraft in fifteen seconds, or I will shoot you down."

"General, I can prove what I'm saying is true."

There was only silence as the seconds ticked away. Carl looked out the window at his left shoulder. The ground was invisible a hundred feet below, but every now and then, he saw native shrubbery flashing by in the reflected light of the anti-collision lights mounted on the belly of the helicopter.

"General, do you want my proof, or do you want President Mallory to die?"

There was no response.

"General!"

The countdown clock in Carl's head hit zero, and Carl had his answer. A flash of fire erupted from the hospital roof and rushed toward the police helicopter.

Carl actually *saw* the missile as it streaked toward him. In the darkness, it appeared as a shadow quickly increasing in size in the center of the fiery exhaust blowing out the back end. The missile covered the two miles in a matter of seconds.

"Well, fuck me sideways," Carl said. He didn't think the general would actually order the murder of FBI agents.

Even as Carl contemplated his death, a huge shadow darker than the night blocked out both the approaching missile and the light from the stream of police vehicles lining up at the security fence in front of the hospital. Multiple blasts of intense light burst away from both sides of the shadow, and the approaching missile came back into view, chasing the decoy flares away to the right. It exploded harmlessly a thousand feet away, but the helicopter still rocked in the wake of the blast.

Brief flashes of tracer gunfire slashed through the darkness from the bottom of the aircraft that had just saved them. Carl saw three separate targets on the ground explode—a fuel tank and two trucks. In the two seconds of reflected light from the minigun tracer fire, Carl saw the distinctive outline of a V-22 Osprey, its two massive rotor nacelles tilted upward like helicopter rotors.

He heard Agent Palmer's cool voice in his headset. "General Caruthers, those three vehicles were unmanned. My next targets will include your exact location. You and your entire command staff will die in my next salvo."

"Identify yourself!"

"This is Agent Nancy Palmer of the Terror Event Response agency. Make no further aggressive acts against government personnel."

The general's voice hesitated. "This hospital is under full quarantine by order of the acting president. I'm ordering you to stand down."

"General, I work directly for President Mallory. My mission is to save her life and her daughter's life, and Johnson and I each have the antidote for them. Stand down your forces and allow the FBI to take control of the hospital."

"Agent Palmer, you have been designated a Tier-One threat to national security, and I have eight surface-to-air missiles locked onto your position. You cannot win this fight. For the last time, I'm ordering you to stand down."

"General, this is a special ops V-22, fully equipped for covert insertion and evac. Your missiles will not touch this aircraft. You should also know I have two nineteen-count pods of Hydra-70 rockets, and I'm also carrying AGM-114 Hellfire laser-guided air-to-surface, anti-armor missiles. I have an M240 machine gun mounted on the back end and a video- and laser-aimed GAU-17 minigun on the belly." Palmer paused, and Carl felt the chill of fear tickle his spine. "I have more than enough firepower to annihilate your entire ground force. We can try to kill each other, or we can save the president. Your choice."

"I'm under orders, Agent. If you—"

Carl heard a brief scuffle and a grunt, followed by a long silence on the channel. A new voice came on the line. The man sounded younger, his voice higher-pitched and not as rumbling as the general.

"This is Colonel Simms. I have relieved the general. Stand down your attack, and I will do the same. Confirm."

Palmer said, "Confirmed…for the moment."

"Very well. Mr. Johnson, you said you had proof. I'll hear it now."

Still on the channel, Carl said, "Agent Figueroa, Vicente Orizaga told me his wife was the daughter of one of the Triad's investors. Can your people find him and put him on this channel?"

"If he has a phone, we'll find him."

It took twelve interminably long minutes. Carl could almost feel the tension and anxiety building in his helicopter and in the dead silence of the comm channel. The police helicopter and the Osprey hovered at two miles. On the ground, the law enforcement vehicles waited at the military gate under the intense glare of the security lights. Finally, a dapper voice spoke on the comm channel in Spanish. Carl heard the name Federico Gonzales.

"Mr. Gonzales, this is Special Agent Guillermo Figueroa of the Federal Bureau—"

Carl interrupted, "Let's cut the crap, folks. Mr. Gonzales, Vicente Orizaga told me you and your family live near him. Are you in Chihuahua now?"

"Who is this? Why are you asking me this question?"

"This is Carl Johnson. When I blew up your office building, the airborne virus was released into the air. Everyone who was at ground zero is infected, and it's spreading all over your city. You know I'm not lying."

The man growled. "You killed my daughter and my sister, and now, you tell me you have released the virus in a heavily populated city?"

"Not just *a* city. It's *your* city."

"What manner of monster are you?"

Carl grunted. "I'm a man who desperately wants to save his president. If you and your family are in Chihuahua City, you are among the tens of thousands now infected. You have, at most, three or four hours remaining in which the antidote will be effective. All of *your* antidote was destroyed when I blew up your lab. The only way you and your family live through this is if you receive your antidote from Walter Breen's supply."

Gonzales remained silent. Carl could hear the man breathing.

"Breen paid you months ago to provide the formula so they could manufacture the antidote. Tell me what company it was and then pray the FBI can trace Breen's distribution network in time. The US government will immediately begin rescue operations for your population…and you."

For a while, Gonzales said nothing. "Do you speak for your government, Mr. Johnson?"

Simms interrupted, "This is Colonel Brighton Simms of the US Army National Guard. I speak for my government and am fully prepared to commit to rescue operations."

"And this is Special Agent Guillermo Figueroa of the FBI. Tell us where the antidote is, and we'll begin immediate recovery and distribution operations."

Gonzales said, "What guarantee do I have—"

"Listen, shithead," Carl interrupted harshly. "Let's go back to the part where we have the antidote and you don't, and the part where you're infected, and your family is going to die."

"Mr. Johnson, I will hunt you and your family to the ends of the earth."

"Mm-hmm," Carl said. "Your daughter said that, and it didn't turn out too well for her. But I tell you what, if you live long enough, I'll be coming for you first. Tell us the name of the company manufacturing the antidote."

The Triad leader was silent for a moment, then he said, "The company we contracted to develop the antidote is irrelevant. Valiant Pharmaceutical was given the storage contract. You will find the antidote there."

The man gave up the location of the company's warehouse. Carl looked at Agent Figueroa, but the agent was busy on his cell phone. He had the device parked on his left ear and was talking fast and animatedly. He had pulled the left cup of his headphones higher on his head, but he was still listening to the comm channel through the right cup of the headphones. His boom mike was folded out of the way.

Carl tapped the helicopter pilot and said, "Terminate that phone call." After the pilot did so, Carl said, "Colonel, may we land?"

"Agent Palmer, hold your position. You will not be fired upon. Agent Figueroa, land your chopper at the main gate. I will personally escort you in."

"Copy that. Please have your troops inside the hospital fall back. This is now an FBI operation."

"Roger that."

Carl heard Figueroa's side of his cell phone conversation, indicating the agent was coordinating with his director in DC to initiate a massive FBI and police raid on Valiant Pharmaceuticals in El Paso, Texas. As the helicopter approached the front gate, the exterior lights of the entire medical complex were turned on, and Carl was surprised by its massive size.

There were two main buildings surrounded by huge parking lots. Green army tents filled a good portion of the parking lots instead of cars. There was a cluster of Humvees around a small building sandwiched in between the two large buildings, so Carl assumed that was where the command staff was headquartered. The burning trucks were located at the east end of the hospital parking lot and posed no danger to life or property. Palmer had chosen her demonstration targets smartly.

The bright flare of exterior light illuminated the rainwater drainage ditch just north of the medical buildings and the empty parking lot just west of the main building. There was coiled wire security fencing around the entire medical center, and dozens of National Guard troops patrolled the perimeter with automatic weapons and truck-mounted machine guns. The parking lot almost directly beneath the helicopter held dozens of army vehicles, and the four-lane road sweeping east to west just south of the complex was empty of traffic.

As the police helicopter slowly drifted toward the main entrance in the Guard's perimeter fence, Colonel Simms's voice came back on the channel. There was a hint of confusion in his tone.

"Mr. Johnson, apparently, your antidote won't be needed after all."

"Excuse me?"

"I was not told before, but the CDC had dispatched a courier with a serum they tested that eradicates the virus."

"Colonel, it's an assassin! When that courier gets here, don't let that person anywhere near the president!"

"The courier has already arrived and was admitted through security over a minute ago."

Carl heard brief shouting in the background. "Colonel, what's going on?"

For a moment, there was no reply. Finally, the man said, "There has been a report of gunfire in the president's wing."

Palmer's Osprey suddenly banked to the right and headed *away* from the hospital.

"Carl," she said, "we've got an inbound missile thirty seconds out!"

CHAPTER 64

CARL COULDN'T CONCERN HIMSELF WITH the inbound missile, but its presence didn't surprise him. Breen had hit them with a cruise missile before, so Carl should have figured he'd do it again. The double move—an assassin and a missile—underscored Breen's desperation. Palmer would have to deal with the missile. Even as the thought tumbled through his brain, the Osprey loosed a steady stream of missiles from its wing pods.

Carl ripped the headphones from his head and shouted at the pilot. "Put me down on the roof! Hurry! On the east end. Then get the hell out of here in case that missile gets through."

The roof lights had come on with the rest of the facility lights when the Guard began to pull back. The helipad was a large white circular slab of concrete with a thick red cross painted in the center. The colonel had turned the communication over to a lesser officer who told Carl he had to go through the roof emergency entrance, down four flights of stairs, down the hallway past the emergency room, make two rights, and then he'd be in the president's wing.

Carl didn't even wait until the helicopter was fully over the roof. The pilot was flying too slow, too careful. Carl threw open his door and leaped when the skids were still two feet shy of the roof parapet and six feet above the membrane material of the roof. The aircraft wasn't even close to the concrete landing pad.

With the metal antidote case tucked in his arms, Carl hit the membrane roof in a tuck and roll. In the next instant, he was up and running. He hauled the emergency door open and flew down the stairs three at a time. His fifty-three-year-old knee joints protested with each step. Other parts of his body joined the protest. His back, where he'd been shot in his tactical vest twice, and his head and his hips, battered by his jump from the Gulfstream, flared with pain with each pounding step.

He hauled open the hallway door right outside the emergency room and saw the dead bodies right away. Two were army soldiers in desert camo and biohazard gas masks. Both had been shot in the head. A nurse and an orderly also lay nearby. Both were dressed in white lightweight medical coveralls, and they wore head shrouds attached to black biochemical breathing masks.

His boot steps squished on the blood-soaked carpet as he ran. Two turns later, he saw more bodies. The men were desert camo-clad Secret Service commandos—the same men Carl had seen almost three days ago when he brought the president's daughter back across the border. Carl felt a pang of primal fear that almost stopped him in his tracks. He'd been disarmed before boarding the police helicopter, and now, he had to face an assassin who had already shot two combat-ready soldiers and four more elite commandos.

As he rounded the last corner toward the president's private treatment room, he saw the door was still closing. He still had a chance, he realized, because the assassin couldn't just shoot the president. He had to make the murder look like an accident. So he hit the door with his shoulder at nearly full speed, and the door slammed open against the inside wall. He saw a man standing beside the president's bed, doing something to her IV bag.

Carl pivoted and threw the only weapon he had available—the metal antidote case—at the man. It struck the intruder squarely in the back of his head and knocked him off-balance, but he didn't fall. In that brief split second, Carl saw a tiny syringe sticking out of the clear IV bag. Blue liquid was spreading lazily into the clear IV fluid.

The man recovered quickly and reached to finish injecting the IV bag, but Carl vaulted over the president's bed and mule kicked the man away.

The assassin bounced against a cabinet, but he immediately spun and charged just as Carl ripped the IV line from Shirley Mallory's arm.

He had a fleeting glimpse of his attacker. The man was tall and slender, dressed in what Carl figured a Secret Service man typically wore—black suit, white shirt, and narrow black tie. He had a white, coiled wire stretching from his collar to the earpiece in his left ear. The man had emotionless black eyes and hard facial features.

"Nice moves, old man."

Carl was scared. He wanted to turn and run away, but he couldn't. He had to stay between the assassin and the president. He had to delay the man and stay alive until the FBI or more Secret Service commandos arrived. If they arrived. A tremendous explosion rocked the building, but it was too distant to do any real damage.

Carl said, "That would be the cruise missile your boss sent to kill you and everyone else here."

The assassin smiled and launched his assault, and Carl did the only thing he could. He charged right into the man's attack. He dusted off a couple of self-defense moves he'd learned some thirty years past. The killer steeled the fingers of his right hand into a rigid blade and slammed that blade straight into Carl's right eye, but Carl had launched a foot maneuver he'd picked up in a basic Savate class way back. When the agent charged, Carl thrust his hips forward and kicked the heel of his foot into the agent's thigh. The impact locked the man's knee and completely arrested his forward momentum. The blade of fingers that would have rammed right through Carl's eye and into his brain merely scraped his eyebrow in a glancing blow.

Without recovering his balance, Carl leaped forward with an elbow strike that connected with the agent's face. He aimed for the temple, a crippling blow, but the agent was too fast. He jerked his head slightly, and Carl's elbow bounced against the man's cheek, doing no damage at all.

In the same fluid motion, Carl did a drop-spin kick that swept the agent's legs out from under him. The man hit the floor on his back, but before Carl regained his feet, he saw the killer launch himself back to his feet like Jackie Chan would. He charged again, and Carl launched a vicious sidekick that hit nothing but air. That was the end of the fight.

Somehow, the agent slid under his leg kick, stepped in next to him, and hit him so hard, so many times, all Carl could do was scream in pain and cover his head and neck with his arms. He tried to drop to the floor, hoping somehow his assailant would end his assault. Before he could, the man rammed a knee against his butt, and Carl found himself slammed headfirst against the IV post and the wall. He heard the vertebrae in his neck crack as his head and right shoulder took the full impact.

The agent stepped in behind Carl and got him in a chokehold. He pulled him backward, and they fell to the floor with Carl belly-up on top of him. The man was incredibly strong, and Carl found himself with absolutely no leverage at all. He lay facing the ceiling with his head hanging off the man's shoulder. He heard the man gasping in his right ear, putting every ounce of his strength into his grip. Carl knew he was a dead man. He had no leverage to force the man to let go, and his own strength was fading fast.

Carl saw speckles of light around the fringes of his vision, and the darkness closed in quickly. He couldn't breathe and felt a tremendous pressure against his neck. He flailed with his arms and legs. He punched and scratched but could do no damage. Finally, he simply pulled in vain at the man's arm until he didn't even have the strength to do that. There were no guns, knives, or pieces of broken glass lying around he could use for a weapon. There was only the IV bag still connected to the post lying on the floor next to his shoulder. The assassin's syringe was still protruding from the bag, but the man had only pushed the plunger halfway down before Carl stopped him.

He'd figured the assassin would give the president the antidote, but he also knew the cure would be tainted with something else to cause her death. Whatever else was in the syringe didn't matter to Carl because, in a flash of desperation, he recalled the warning from Orizaga and from the videos on the virus development. The doctors had tested the antidote as an inoculation on uninfected subjects, and the result was instant, violent death.

He grabbed at the syringe, yanked it from the IV bag, and rammed it into any part of the agent's body he could reach. The man grunted as the needle punctured his leg, then Carl withdrew his hand and slammed his open palm against the plunger. He knew the heart needed thirty-odd seconds to pump blood and any other substance carried by the blood from the outlet side of the heart throughout the body and back to the inlet side of the heart. According to the virus doctors' research, the mechanism employed by the antidote was a nerve agent, and it took effect in a fraction of the time needed by circulation.

Within two seconds, the man's left leg began convulsing, then the rest of his body began seizing, and he instantly lost all control of his muscles. Carl rolled away, gasping and sucking deep breaths. His whole body throbbed in pain, but he watched the assassin's death. The man's eyes bulged, and his entire body froze.

"Yeah," Carl said, using President Mallory's bed to pull himself to his feet. "Not bad for an old man, huh?"

The assassin screamed like a banshee. At about the ten-second mark, his entire body convulsed wildly, and Carl heard the snap of bones in his body as his muscles contracted violently. He repeatedly banged different parts of his body into pulp against the floor. He screamed continuously until a gush of blood and vomit erupted from his mouth and sprayed the wall halfway up to the ceiling. Then he lay still. Fifteen seconds start to finish was all it took for the agent to die a horribly gruesome death.

Carl leaned against the president's bed, and his knees became wobbly. He trembled as an adrenaline rush swept through his body. He took a few deep breaths to collect his wits because his mission wasn't complete yet. He retrieved the metal case and opened it. Miraculously, none of the remaining vials were broken, despite the impact the case had taken against the man's head and the wall. He'd put all his strength behind his toss too.

He injected Mallory in the upper arm, then closed the case. He felt dizzy again and leaned his palms on the bed for support. His entire body protested against every movement. He hardly registered the sudden entrance of Agent Palmer. He simply saw motion in his side vision, looked over, and saw her standing there with a wicked machine pistol in her hand. She surveyed the room and regarded the destroyed form of the assassin, who now more resembled a life-sized hunk of play dough than a man.

"That's August Spoke," she said. "He's Secret Service. Before that, he was a highly decorated Delta commando. One of the best." She lowered her weapon and helped him into the hallway as FBI and Secret Service secured the wing. Medical staff went in to check on President Mallory, and a nurse carried the case of antidote into the next room, which Carl assumed was where Melissa Mallory was.

Carl grimaced as Palmer lowered him to the floor. He caught the agent's gaze as she squatted in front of him. A slight smile curled up her lips, and he offered a discrete smile in return.

He said, "Next time, I'll take the cruise missile, and you fight the Delta dude."

Palmer stared at him wordlessly for a brief moment, then looked away. He knew she was thinking about that kiss. Carl found her shyness very attractive. He was just about to say so when an alarm echoed through the hallway.

Carl gasped. "Aw, c'mon, what now?"

CHAPTER 65

2125 MST, SATURDAY
LAS CRUCES, NM

THE SPEAKER IN THE CEILING announced something about a Code Blue, and a couple more doctors and nurses raced from the president's room to Melissa's. Carl had only been seated against the wall for a couple minutes, but he struggled to his feet with Palmer's help at the flurry of activity. He didn't know what the code was, but he sensed something critical had happened. They stood waiting in the hall, looking at Melissa's closed door, their shoulders almost touching. He savored the moment of peace and enjoyed her presence in his personal space. It seemed like it had been forever since he'd experienced either peace or closeness. He was just going to mention that to her when the door to Melissa's room opened, and one of the doctors came out to update them. The doctor's nametag on her white bio-suit said, "Stirling." She pulled a cloth facemask down from her nose and mouth until it rested below her chin.

"She's had another severe seizure. I don't pretend to understand the full pathology of this virus, but her body is shutting down. We tried administering the antidote you brought, but it doesn't seem to be having any effect. Unfortunately, we don't know the exact protocol for the antidote, and since she is Patient Zero…"

The doctor paused, and Carl had the feeling she had worse news. By her expression, Carl sensed she just then decided to come right out with the bad news. "The prognosis is not good, I'm afraid. She needs a blood transfusion."

Carl glanced at Palmer, confused. "Doctor, this is a goddamned hospital! Are you telling me you don't have blood here?"

"We tried that hours ago, but the virus is so virulent, it compromised the new blood almost instantly. She is so weak, her body cannot withstand that kind of shock. We nearly killed her." The doctor took a deep breath. "She needs blood from someone who has been cured."

Carl said, "I've been cured, Doctor, and so has Agent Palmer."

"Her blood type is B-positive, so we need a B or O donor."

"I'm B-positive," Carl said.

The doctor looked at Palmer, who shook her head. "I'm A-negative."

Dr. Stirling said, "I'd need a minimum of four more people to provide enough blood for her transfusion, and there just aren't any other survivors we can get blood from. At least, not within the hour or so she has remaining."

"Four people? How much does she need?"

"Sir, she needs a total transfusion."

"*How much?*"

"Five quarts. You don't have enough."

"How can I possibly not have enough? I'm almost twice her size. There's no way she has more blood in her body than I do!"

"Sir, you only have five quarts in your body, and she needs five quarts, maybe more. If I take 40 percent of your blood, you'll go into a coma from which you may never wake up. If I take 50 percent of your blood, you will die."

"Doctor, my life isn't worth shit now anyway. At least my death can save her life. No one will hold you responsible."

"I'm sorry. I cannot. I took an oath—"

Carl held up his hand. "Doctor, this girl cannot die. *Am. I. Clear?*"

Dr. Stirling nodded, glanced at Agent Palmer, then nodded again. "Come with me."

Five minutes later, Carl lay on a second bed that had been wheeled into Melissa's room. He gazed to his left as the doctors and techs stuck him with needles and affixed tubes to the needles. The tubes led into a high-tech machine, which he assumed was the pump meant to drain him. More tubes led from the machine into Melissa's arm. Bags of clear fluid and red plasma hung on racks beside Carl's bed, though the doctor said there was no way they could replenish his evacuated blood fast enough. He would die.

A wash of emotions flooded through him at the pitiful sight of the dying girl. He felt his heart tearing. Her skin held a dreadful gray tint, and her skin sagged on her face. She had numerous IV tubes in her arms, and a clear oxygen mask covered her nose and mouth. He could hear her labored breath rasping in and out of her chest.

Dr. Stirling leaned over his bed. "The amount of blood we need to stabilize her will kill you, Mr. Johnson." She hesitated. "Do you understand what you are volunteering for?"

"I understand."

Stirling regarded him for a moment before she nodded at the tech. The young man turned on the machine, and it began a low hum. Carl didn't feel anything, but he imagined he could sense his life draining away.

"Carl," said a distant voice. It sounded like Agent Palmer, but he couldn't be sure. "Can you hear me?"

He found it extremely hard to concentrate on the voice. He managed to open his eyes, but his lids were very heavy. He smiled at the voice.

"Nancy," he said with a heavy, slurred voice. "Promise me you'll bury me with my son."

"I promise."

A shadow leaned over him and eclipsed the ceiling lights, and he felt her warm lips against his—or maybe he just imagined that she was kissing him—but he couldn't find the strength to kiss her back. He just purred contentedly and drifted away. At first, he saw darkness consuming him. Then he saw a light.

He saw his son's face smiling at him. Mark visited him one final time. The young man was proud of him, proud of his sacrifice.

CHAPTER 66

FIVE DAYS LATER
LAS CRUCES, NM

I N SPITE OF ALL THE bad things he'd done, he ended up in heaven. It had to be that place because Mark was there, and the young man wasn't dying as he had been all the other times Carl saw him in his recurring nightmare. Carl hugged his son for a long time, then held onto Mark's hand.

"I love you so much, Mark, and I've missed you terribly."

"I've missed you too, Pops. See you soon. Love you!" he said cheerfully.

Then he turned away, leaving Carl stunned with surprise. He watched his son leave, but he wasn't just walking away. He was *fading* away, slowly losing substance until Carl could see *through* his body.

"Wait, Mark. Where are you going? I just found you again."

Mark just waved.

"No, Mark. Don't go."

Carl opened his eyes and saw his outstretched left hand reaching for the ceiling. The lights were bright, but that's not what made his eyes water. His son had slipped away again. He brought his hand down and covered his face.

He moaned. "Oh, God. What have I done?"

He tried to bring his right hand to his face also, but he discovered that a real person was holding it. He lay on his back on a hospital bed and rolled his head to the right. It was Shirley Mallory.

"You saved me, Carl. You saved my daughter. You saved the *country*."

Carl took a deep breath. The country didn't matter. He closed his eyes and tried to hold onto the remnant of his waking vision. "He was right here, Shirley. I saw him. I saw Mark. This time, he was smiling at me. He was happy, not dying."

The president held his hand between both of hers, and they shared a quiet moment together. He gently freed his hand, threw back the white sheet, and rolled upright, ending with his legs hanging off the side of the bed. He took several deep breaths to collect himself, then looked at President Mallory, who sat on a chair beside his bed.

"He's really gone."

"I know, Carl," she said. "I'm so sorry."

He nodded and looked up as Doctor Stirling entered the room. The president stood. She wore a cream-colored skirt suit over a dark blue blouse. A modest string of pearls adorned her neck.

"Good morning, Madam President," Dr. Stirling said. "Mr. Johnson, how do you feel?"

"I'm alive," he said. "That tells me Melissa Mallory still lives and that you didn't have to drain me dry to make that happen."

The doctor nodded. "You're going to be fine."

"Sista, I'm never going to be *fine*."

The doctor regarded him quietly for a moment, then said, "Miss Mallory is alive and recovering nicely. Over the past five days, we kept you sedated and fed intravenously while we harvested just enough of your blood—two quarts to begin with and then a quart every few hours—to keep her out of critical condition until we could find enough compatible cured donors to supply the quantity of blood needed for her transfusion. Now that you're awake, I'd like to have my people run some blood tests on you. I'd like to keep you here for observation and rest for a few days."

"Negative on the extended stay. Where are my clothes?"

The doctor pointed toward the cabinet by the door, then nodded respectfully to President Mallory and left. Carl retrieved his tactical clothes and slid the pants on under his hospital gown, then finished dressing.

"How many people did we lose, Shirley?"

"A fourth of my cabinet, the Senate, and the House died from the initial phase one culling of the Contagion. About the same percentage of my security detail died, along with the flight crews of *Marine One* and *Air Force One*. The outbreak was fairly well contained back east. Walter Breen's plan there was successful. Out here, we lost a lot more."

President Mallory paused for a moment, and Carl knew she'd been briefed on his use—his *release*—of the airborne virus.

"Just over eight hundred have died throughout New Mexico. Another nine hundred perished in Mexico, not including the Triad's laboratory staff. Slightly less than six hundred have died in small outbreaks throughout South America and Europe from travelers that departed the airport from Mexico City."

He nodded. "What about our people?"

"We took some hits at home, Carl. Special Agent Cummings and her daughter are fine. Mr. Garcia lost his wife and child. Then he took his own life. Anita Chapman lost one of her twin girls. Aaron…" Her voice broke a bit. "They killed him. They burned the operations house down with him in it."

"How long were you two together?"

"A long time." She looked away, and her voice wavered. "A very long time."

An awkward silence filled the room. "I killed a lot of people with the Contagion," Carl said as he tucked in his black T-shirt.

"Yes, you did. We were within an hour of losing control of an epidemic that would have killed billions. It would have destroyed entire nations and crippled our own. You took an enormous gamble, Carl."

"It was no gamble, Shirley." He turned to face her. "When I released the airborne virus, I didn't think Breen would back down. I thought I'd be dead." He took a deep breath. "Walter Breen wanted to rule the world, but I fully intended to leave him with nothing to rule."

The president narrowed her eyes. "But why would you do that, knowing your actions would have destroyed the world?"

"Because those fuckers got my son killed, Shirley. Because they used *a sixteen-year-old child*, your daughter, as a weapon of war." Carl paused. "Because you are the good guy, and Walter Breen is the bad guy." He glared at her. "In my world, the good guys win…or nobody does. End of story."

She nodded. "You sacrificed your life for my daughter. *Twice.* I won't forget that."

"It's what we do for our kids. We give everything we have if we're able. We die if we need to."

"I have a press conference in a few minutes. I'm going to announce my resignation." She looked at him for a moment, then glanced away. "As I promised, I'm going to apologize to you publicly for my part in Mark's death. I'm going to clear your name."

Carl shook his head. "No, Madam President, that doesn't fit into my plans. I require you to remain president. We have work to do."

Mallory seemed genuinely surprised. Her eyebrows lifted, and she said, "Excuse me? You *require?*"

"You owe me, Shirley. As you said, I saved your daughter twice. You can feel sorry for yourself later."

"Be careful, Carl."

"Maybe I have to remind you of the part where you're the good guy, Shirley. The bad guys still live, and they have to pay for what they've done. I need your help with that."

Carl was silent as he and President Mallory regarded each other. She held his gaze, but then she faltered and looked away.

"I know what you're trying to do, Carl." With a shake of her head, she said, "But I can't." She turned and reached for the door lever.

"Shirley," he called.

She stopped but did not turn around.

"I had Mr. Garcia send a small team of mercs to Virginia to get Aaron when he indicated his facility had been compromised. He's safe, and he's probably cured by now, but the bad guys don't know that."

She glanced over her shoulder, and he saw a spectrum of emotion wash over her countenance. She turned and stepped close to him. She pulled a folded piece of paper from her right pocket and handed it to him. "Agent Palmer said you would take this path." President Mallory paused a moment, and Carl saw both sadness and determination in her eyes. "The media is blaming this whole virus attack on the American Terrorist, and the public needs a target to hate. They won't believe a splinter element of their own government was to blame. If I don't fix this for you now, I won't be able to intervene in the future."

"Madam President, the American Terrorist needs no apology." He paused for a moment, then added, "But your country needs you, Shirley. As president. These people did what they did to you, me, and the country because they thought there would be no consequences."

Shirley Mallory nodded. "Walter Breen and his people are missing. Do what you do, Mr. Johnson. Find them and make them pay."

TO BE CONTINUED...

If you enjoyed this adventure, check out Jeffrey Poston's other action adventure thrillers at JeffreyPostonBooks.com or wherever you buy books. Please let other readers know what you thought of the book by leaving a brief review at your favorite retailer. It only takes a moment and reviews are very valuable to authors.

ABOUT THE AUTHOR

Jeffrey Poston is the acclaimed author of the Jason Peares historical western series, as well as the fast-paced adventure thriller series *American Terrorist* and *Call Sign: Raven*. Blending traditional and revisionist historical research, his historical westerns have been praised as "fast-moving" (Kelton) and "exciting, page-turning" (Zollinger) and "among the best writers of westerns" (Biblio.com). His thriller books are lauded as "so realistic," "powerfully intense," and "action-packed page turners." He is a self-described *Rambling Man* and writes his novels wherever he happens to be in his travels.

Find Jeffrey at http://www.jeffreypostonbooks.com/

Facebook: http://www.facebook.com/JeffreyPostonBooks

Twitter: http://www.twitter.com/BooksByJPoston

ACKNOWLEDGMENTS

As writers, we often go into our creative caves to compose a book, but when we come out, there are often dozens of people who help refine a story and turn it into a really good book. No writer can succeed without this special group of people—critical readers, cover artists, professional editors, marketing and PR specialists, and publishers.

I especially want to thank my critical reader and sounding board, Dr. Stephanie McIver. She's helped me through many of my books, offering insight and analysis that added depth and breadth to my characters and my plot.

Special thanks to Debra L. Hartmann, The Pro Book Editor, and her team for copyediting and proofreading. I also want to give a shout-out to the cover art designers of my books: Deanna Dionne.

I'm also thankful for the active imaginations (and the suspension of disbelief) of all the readers who enjoyed my Western and Thriller adventures. I'm especially grateful to the dozens of beta-readers who previewed the book and sent back invaluable advice. Your help means the world to this author!